CITY OF THE DEAD

A SEVEN WONDERS NOVEL

CITY OF THE DEAD

A SEVEN WONDERS NOVEL

T.L. HIGLEY

PUBLISHING GROUP
Nashville, Tennessee

978-0-8054-4731-6

Published by B&H Publishing Group,
Nashville, Tennessee

Dewey Decimal Classification: F
Subject Heading: MYSTERY FICTION \
EGYPT—FICTION \ GREAT PYRAMID
(EGYPT)—FICTION

Publisher's Note: This novel is a work of fiction. Names, places, and incidents are either products of the author's imagination or used fictitiously. All characters are fictional, and any similarity to people living or dead is purely coincidental.

1 2 3 4 5 6 7 8 • 12 11 10 09

To John Cashman

Your years of dedication in the classroom
have endeared you to thousands of students,
of whom I am one.
When our lives intersected, you challenged me to work
harder, to reach further and to think for myself.
On behalf of every student whose life you have touched.
Thank you.

Acknowledgments

D iving into the culture and history of Ancient Egypt proved to be a delightful task for me. I was aided in no small part by the excellent writings of many, and wish to specifically thank Zahi Hawass, secretary general of Egypt's Supreme Council of Antiquities, Craig B. Smith, whose fascinating book *How the Great Pyramid was Built* provided much insight from the perspective of an engineer, and Bob Brier, Ph.D., whose DVD lectures held me spellbound for many hours. I have attempted to stay as close as possible to what these Egyptologists have taught us. Throughout the book, I have chosen to use the Greek words for many terms, simply because these are the more familiar terms for most people.

Besides these scholars, I want to thank those who helped in a more personal way. Our research trip to Egypt benefited from the generosity of many. Don and Sue Eenigenburg, thank you for your guidance before our great adventure! Michael and Marsha Bowen, thank you for your hospitality in your home outside Cairo, and for teaching us to haggle in the bazaar with the best of them! Kristen and Garrett Clemmer, thank you for watching over our children. Also thank you to our parents, Earl and Marjorie Higley and

Joe and Iris Strauss for helping with the children while we were off exploring Egypt.

Thank you to my agent, Steve Laube, for your encouragement and guidance through another project. David Webb, your excellent editing once again improved the manuscript greatly. Julie Gwinn, your enthusiasm for B&H fiction is always a joy.

And thank you, once again, to my very special family. Ron, Rachel, Sarah, Jake, and Noah—you are patient, loving, encouraging, and so tolerant of my craziness. I love you.

GLOSSARY OF ANCIENT EGYPT

akhet—the Season of the Inundation, or the flooding of the Nile, which marked the beginning of the Egyptian year; roughly mid-July to mid-November

ankh—the symbol of life, it resembles the Christian cross, with a loop above the transverse bar

Anubis—god of the underworld who determined the worthiness of the deceased to enter the realm of the dead; usually depicted as a jackal-headed man carrying a a flail, or scourge

Atum—deity and personification of the setting sun

canopic jars—funerary vases used to store one's internal organs alongside the body in a tomb

cartouche—hieroglyph that represents a royal name

deben—a unit of measurement equal to about 13.6 grams

double crown—also known as the Pschent (sh-yĕn), it combined the Red Crown of Lower Egypt and the White Crown of Upper Egypt, thus representing Pharaoh's power over all of Egypt; a rearing cobra and a vulture were fastened to the front of the crown, representing goddesses of Lower and Upper Egypt

Hathor—cow deity originally created by Ra as a destroyer of those men who disobeyed him; later worshiped as a goddess of love and joy

Horus—falcon-headed deity who was the face of heaven, with one eye the sun and the other the moon; Pharaoh was supposed to be his earthly embodiment

Inundation—an annual flooding of the Nile (due to heavy summer rains in the Ethiopian highlands) seen by the Egyptians as the yearly coming of the god Hapi, bringing fertility to the land; crops were planted in the rich, black silt left behind by the receding waters—if the inundation was too low, it would be a year of famine

ka—the spirit and conscience of the individual; the ka was believed to live within the body of the individual and therefore needed that body after death, which is why the Egyptians mummified their dead

ma'at—the condition of order and truth in the universe; the opposite of chaos; named for Ma'at, goddess of the physical and moral law of Egypt

mastaba—a flat-roofed, rectangular building with outward sloping sides that marked the burial site of Egyptian nobility

natron—a salt mixture harvested from dry lake beds, the mineral was used in Egyptian mummification because it absorbs water and behaves as a drying agent; thought to enhance spiritual safety for both the living and the dead, it was also used as a cleaning product for both the home and body

nemes—the striped headcloth worn by pharaohs, it covered the crown and back of the head and nape of the neck and had two large flaps which hung down behind the ears and in front of the shoulders; sometimes worn with the double crown.

Nubian—a native of the Nile kingdom of Nubia to the south of Egypt; depicted in Egyptian art as having very dark skin, often shown with hooped earrings and braided or extended hair

Ra—sun god and creator in Egyptian mythology

relief—sculptured artwork in which a modeled form projects out from a flat background

sistrum—a musical instrument with a frame and small metal disks that rattled when the instrument was shaken by hand, producing a soft jangling sound that resembled a breeze blowing through papyrus reeds

wadjet eye—also known as the Eye of Horus, it was depicted as a human eye and eyebrow as they would be seen looking at a person full-faced; as an amulet, it was placed in the wrappings of the mummy for protection

PROLOGUE

In my dreams, it is often I who kills Amunet. Other nights it is Khufu, in one of his mad rages. And at other times it is a great mystery, destined to remain unknown long after the *ka* of each of us has crossed to the west.

Tonight, as I lay abed, my dreams reveal all the truth that I know.

Merit is there, like a beautiful lotus flower among the papyrus reeds.

"Hemi," she whispers, using the shortened form of my name in the familiar way I long for. "We should join the others."

The tufts of reeds that spring from the marsh's edge wave around us, higher than our heads, our private thicket.

"They are occupied with the hunt," I say.

A cloud of birds rises from the marsh in that moment, squawking their protest at being disturbed. Merit turns her head to the noise and I study the line of her jaw, the long curls that wave across her ear. I pull her close, my arms around her waist.

Her body is stiff at first, then melts against mine.

"Hemi, you must let me go."

Some nights in my dreams I am a better man.

"Merit." I bury my face in her hair, breathe in the spicy scent of her. "I cannot."

I pull her into my kiss.

She resists. She pushes me away and her eyes flash accusation, but something else as well. Sorrow. Longing.

I reach for her again, wrapping my fingers around her wrist. She twists away from my grasp. I do not know what I might have done, but there is fear in her eyes. By the gods, I wish I could forget that fear.

She runs. What else could she do?

She runs along the old river bed, not yet swollen with the year's Inundation, stagnant and marshy. She disappears among the papyrus. The sky is low and gray, an evil portent.

My anger roots me to the ground for several moments, but then the whisper of danger propels me to follow.

"Merit," I call. "Come back. I am sorry!"

I weave slowly among the reeds, searching for the white flash of her dress, the bronze of her skin.

"Merit, it is not safe!"

Anger dissolves into concern. I cannot find her.

In the way of dreams, my feet are unnaturally heavy, as though I fight through alluvial mud to reach her. The first weighted drops fall from an unearthly sky.

And then she is there, at the base of the reeds. White dress dirtied, head turned unnaturally. Face in the water. My heart clutches in my chest. I lurch forward. Drop to my knees in the marsh mud. Push away the reeds. Reach for her.

It is not Merit.

It is Amunet.

"Amunet!" I wipe the mud and water from her face and shake her. Her eyes are open yet unfocused.

I am less of a man because, in that moment, I feel relief.

Relief that it is not Merit.

But what has happened to Amunet? Khufu insisted that our royal hunting party split apart to raise the birds, but we all knew that he wanted to be with Amunet. Now she is alone, and she has crossed to the west.

As I hold her lifeless body in my arms, I feel the great weight of choice fall upon my shoulders. The rain pours through an evil gash in the clouds.

Khufu is my friend. He is my cousin. He will soon wear the Double Crown of the Two Lands of Upper and Lower Egypt. And when Khufu is Pharaoh, I will be his grand vizier.

But it would seem that I hold our future in my hands now, as surely as I hold this girl's body.

I lower Amunet to the mud again and awake, panting and sweating, in my bed. I roll from the mat, scramble for a pot, and retch. It is not the first time.

The sunlight is already burning through the high window in my bedchamber.

The past is gone. There is only the future.

And I have a pyramid to build.

ONE

In the fifth year of Khufu, the Golden Horus, Great in Victories, Chosen of Ra, as the pyramid rose in the desert like a burning torch to the sun god himself, I realized my mistake and knew that I had brought disorder.

"Foolishness!" Khons slapped a stone-roughened hand on the papyri unrolled on the basalt-black slab before us, and turned his back on the well-ordered charts to study the workforce on the plateau.

I refused to follow his gaze. Behind me, I knew, eight thousand men toiled, dragging quarry stones up ramps that snaked around my half-finished pyramid, and levering them into beautiful precision. Below them, intersecting lines of men advanced with the rhythm of drumbeats. They worked quickly but never fast enough.

My voice took on a hard edge. "Perhaps, Khons, if you spent more time listening and less blustering—"

"You speak to me of time?" The overseer of quarries whirled to face me, and the muscles in his jaw twitched like a donkey's flank when a fly irritates. "Do you have any idea what these changes mean?" He waved a hand over my plans. "You were a naked baboon

1

at Neferma'at's knee when he and I were building the pyramids at Saqqara!"

This insult was well-worn, and I was sick of it. I stepped up to him, close enough to map every vein in his forehead. The desert air between us stilled with the tension. "You forget yourself, Khons. I may not be your elder, but I am grand vizier."

"My good men," Ded'e interrupted, his voice dripping honey as he smoothed long fingers over the soft papyrus. "Let us not quarrel like harem women over a simple change of design."

"Simple!" Khons snorted. "Perhaps for you. Your farmers and bakers care not where Pharaoh's burial chamber is located. But I will need to rework all the numbers for the Giza quarry. The time line for the Aswan granite will be in chaos." Khons turned on me. "The plans for the queen's pyramid are later than grain in a drought year. A project of this magnitude must run like marble over the rollers. A change like this—you're hurling a chunk of limestone into the Nile, and there will be ripples. Other deadlines will be missed—"

I held up a hand and waited to respond. I preferred to handle Khons and his fits of metaphor by giving us both time to cool. The sun hammered down on the building site, and I looked away, past the sands of death, toward the life-giving harbor and the fertile plain beyond. This year's Inundation had not yet crested, but already the Nile's green waters had swelled to the border of last year's floodplain. When the waters receded in three months, leaving behind their rich silt deposits, the land would be black and fertile and planting would commence.

"Three months," I said. In three months, most of my workforce would return to their farms to plant and till, leaving my pyramid unfinished, dependent on me to make it whole.

Khons grunted. "Exactly. No time for changes."

Ded'e scanned the plateau, his fingers skimming his forehead to block the glare, though he had applied a careful line of kohl beneath his eyes today. "Where is Mentu? Did you not send a message, Hemiunu?"

I looked toward the workmen's village, too far to make out anyone approaching by the road. Mentu-hotep also served as one of my chief overseers. These three answered directly to me, and under them commanded fifty supervisors, who in turn organized the twelve-thousand-man force. Nothing of this scale had ever been undertaken in the history of the Two Lands. In the history of man. We were building the Great Pyramid, the Horizon of the Pharaoh Khufu. A thousand years, nay, ten thousand years from now, my pyramid would still stand. And though a tomb for Pharaoh, it would also bear my name. A legacy in stone.

"Perhaps he thinks he can do as he wishes," Khons said.

I ignored his petty implication that I played favorites among my staff. "Perhaps he is slow in getting started today." I jabbed a finger at the plans again. "Look, Khons, the burial chamber's relocation will mean that the inner core will require less stone, not more. I've redesigned the plans to show the king's chamber beginning on Course Fifty. Between the corbelled ascending corridor, the burial chamber, five courses high, and the five relieving chambers that will be necessary above it, we will save 8,242 blocks."

"Exactly 8,242? Are you certain?" De'de snorted. "I think you must stay up all night solving equations, eh, Hemi?"

I inclined my head to the pyramid, now one-fourth its finished height. "Look at it, De'de. See the way the sides angle at a setback of exactly 11:14. Look at the platform, level to an error less than the span of your little finger." I turned on him. "Do you think such beauty happens by chance? No, it requires constant attention from one who would rather lose sleep than see it falter."

"It's blasphemy." Khons's voice was low. It was unwise to speak thus of the Favored One.

I exhaled and we hung over the plans, heads together. Khons smelled of sweat and dust, and sand caked the outer rim of his ear.

"It is for the best, Khons. You will see."

If blasphemy were involved, it was my doing and not Khufu's. I had engineered the raising of the burial chamber above ground and, along with it, Khufu's role as the earthly incarnation of the god Ra. It was for the good of Egypt, and now it must be carried forward. Hesitation, indecision—these were for weak men.

"Let the priests argue about religious matters," I said. "I am a builder."

Ded'e laughed. "Yes, you are like the pyramid, Hemi. All sharp angles and unforgiving measurements."

I blinked at the observation, then smiled as though it pleased me.

Khons opened his mouth, no doubt to argue, but a shout from the work site stopped him. We three turned to the pyramid, and I ground my teeth to see the work gangs falter in their measured march up the ramps. Some disorder near the top drew the attention of all. I squinted against the bright blue sky but saw only the brown figures of the workforce covering the stone.

"Cursed Mentu. Where is he?" Khons asked the question this time.

As overseer for operations, Mentu took charge of problems on the line. In his absence, I now stalked toward the site.

The Green Sea Gang had halted on the east-face ramp, their draglines still braced over their bare shoulders. Even from thirty cubits below I could see the ropy muscles stand out on the backs of a hundred men as they strained to hold the thirty-thousand-deben-weight block attached to the line. Their white skirts of this morning had long since tanned with dust, and their skin shone with afternoon sweat.

"Sokkwi! Get your men moving forward!" I shouted to the Green Sea Gang supervisor who should have been at the top.

There was no reply, so I strode up the ramp myself, multiplying in my mind the minutes of delay by the stones not raised. The workday might need extending.

Halfway up the first rubble ramp, a scream like that of an antelope skewered by a hunter's arrow ripped the air. I paused only a moment, the men's eyes on me, then took to the rope-lashed ladder that leaned against the pyramid's side. I felt the acacia wood strain under the pounding of my feet and slowed only enough for safety. The ladder stretched to the next circuit of the ramp, and I scrambled from it, chest heaving, and sprinted through the double line of laborers that snaked around the final ramp. Here the pyramid came to its end. Still so much to build.

Sokkwi, the gang supervisor, had his back to me when I reached the top. Several others clustered around him, bent to something on the stone. Chisels and drills lay scattered about.

"What is it? What's happened?" The dry heat had stolen my breath, and the words panted out.

They broke apart to reveal a laborer, no more than eighteen years, on the ground, one leg pinned by a block half set in place. The boy's eyes locked onto mine, as if to beg for mercy. "Move the stone!" I shouted to Sokkwi.

He scratched his chin. "It's no good. The stone's been dropped. We have nothing to—"

I jumped into the space open for the next stone, gripped the rising joint of the block that pinned the boy and yelled to a worker, larger than most. "You there! Help me slide this stone!"

He bent to thrust a shoulder against the stone. We strained against it like locusts pushing against a mountain. Sokkwi laid a hand upon my shoulder.

I rested a moment, and he inclined his head to the boy's leg. Flesh had been torn down to muscle and bone. I reached for something to steady myself, but there was nothing at this height. The sight of blood, a weakness I had known since my youth, threatened to overcome me. I felt a warmth in my face and neck. I breathed slowly through my nose. *No good for the men to see you swoon.*

I knelt and placed a hand on the boy's head, then spoke to Sokkwi. "How did this happen?"

He shrugged. "First time on the line." He worked at something in his teeth with his tongue. "Doesn't know the angles, I suppose." Another shrug.

"What was he doing at the top then?" I searched the work area and the ramp below me again for Mentu. Anger churned my stomach.

The supervisor sighed and picked at his teeth with a fingernail. "Don't ask me. I make sure the blocks climb those ramps and settle into place. That is all I do."

How had Mentu allowed this disaster? Justice, truth, and divine order—the *ma'at*—made Egypt great and made a man great. I did not like to see ma'at disturbed.

On the ramp a woman pushed past the workers, shoving them aside in her haste to reach the top. She gained the flat area where we stood and paused, her breath huffing out in dry gasps. In her hands she held two jars, brimming with enough barley beer to allow the boy to feel fierce anger rather than beg for his own death. The surgeon came behind, readying his saw. The boy had a chance at life if the leg ended in a stump. Allowed to fester, the injury would surely kill him.

I masked my faintness with my anger and spun away.

"Mentu!" My yell carried past the lines below me, down into the desert below, perhaps to the quarry beyond. He should never have allowed such an inexperienced boy to place stones. Where had he been this morning when the gangs formed teams?

The men nearby were silent, but the work down on the plateau continued, heedless of the boy's pain. The rhythmic ring of chisel on quarry stone punctuated the collective grunts of the quarry men, their chorus drifting across the desert, but Mentu did not answer the call.

Was he still in his bed? Mentu and I had spent last evening pouring wine and reminiscing late into the night about the days of our youth. Some of them anyway. Always one story never retold.

Another scream behind me. *That woman had best get to pouring the barley beer.* I could do nothing more here. I moved through the line of men, noting their nods of approval for the effort I'd made on behalf of one of their own.

When I reached the base and turned back toward the flat-topped basalt-black stone where I conferred with Khons and Ded'e, I saw that another had joined them. My brother.

I slowed my steps to allow that part of my heart to harden like mud bricks in the sun, then pushed forward.

They laughed together as I approached, the easy laugh of men comfortable with one another. My older brother leaned against the stone, his arms crossed in front of him. He stood upright when he saw me.

"Ahmose," I said with a slight nod. "What brings you to the site?"

His smile turned to a smirk. "Just wanted to see how the project proceeds."

"Hmm." I focused my attention once more on the plans. The wind grabbed at the edges of the papyrus, and I used a stone cubit rod, thicker than my thumb, to weight it. "The three of us must recalculate stone transfer rates—"

"Khons seems to believe your changes are going to sink the project," Ahmose said. He smiled, his perfect teeth gleaming against his dark skin.

The gods had favored Ahmose with beauty, charm, and a pleasing manner that made him well loved among the court. But I had been blessed with a strong mind and a stronger will. And I was grand vizier.

I lifted my eyes once more to the pyramid rising in perfect symmetry against the blue sky, and the thousands of men at my command. "The Horizon of Khufu will look down upon your children's grandchildren, Ahmose," I said. I leaned over my charts and braced my fingertips on the stone. "When you have long since sailed to the west, still it will stand."

He bent beside me, his breath in my ear. "You always did believe you could do anything. Get away with anything."

The animosity in his voice stiffened my shoulders.

"Khons, Ded'e, if you will." I gestured to the charts. Khons snorted and clomped to my side. And Ded'e draped his forearms across the papyrus.

"It must be gratifying," Ahmose whispered, "to command men so much more experienced than yourself."

I turned on him, my smile tight. "And it must be disheartening to see your younger brother excel while you languish in a job bestowed only out of pity—"

A boy appeared, sparing me the indignity of exchanging blows with my brother. His sidelock identified him as a young prince, and I recognized him as the youngest of Henutsen, one of Khufu's lesser wives.

"His Majesty Khufu, the king, Horus," the boy said, "the strong bull, beloved by the goddess of truth—"

"Yes, yes. Life, Health, Strength!" I barked. "What does Khufu want?" I was in no mood for the string of titles.

The boy's eyes widened and he dragged a foot through the sand. "My father commands the immediate presence of Grand Vizier Hemiunu before the throne."

"Did he give a reason?"

The prince pulled on his lower lip. "He is very angry today."

"Very well." I waved him off and turned to Khons and Ded'e, rubbing the tension from my forehead. "We will continue later."

The two overseers made their escape before Ahmose and I had a chance to go at it again. I flicked a glance in his direction, then rolled up my charts, keeping my breathing even.

Behind me Ahmose said, "Perhaps Khufu has finally seen his error in appointing you vizier." Like a sharp poke in the kidneys when our mother wasn't watching.

"Excuse me, Ahmose." I pushed past him, my hands full of charts. "I have an important meeting."

TWO

Igrabbed my *cherp*, the staff that had been given by Khufu as a symbol of my position, and tramped to the Great House to appease whatever new concern had overtaken Khufu. I planned to search for Mentu after seeing the king, and fumed at the disruption to the order of my day.

The King of Upper and Lower Egypt, Wearer of the Double Crown, Throne of the Two Countries, is a man who requires careful handling. Many years have passed since we were all princes in the house of Sneferu, Khufu's father. In those days, my noble father was brother and grand vizier to Sneferu, and Khufu and I divided the hours between our lessons and mischief-making. My best friend and overseer of constructions, the missing Mentu, was also one of our circle, as was my brother Ahmose. The years had made men of three of us, and a god of the fourth.

I entered the Great Hall of Pillars and paused at the back, inhaling the calming myrrh and frankincense that perfumed the room. I moved to the small shrine and poured a libation to Atum.

Twelve pillars stood between the king and myself, two rows of six and each thick enough that two men could not encircle them with their arms. Their carved reliefs, brightly painted, reached all the way to the ceiling, far above my head, and ended in fluted capitals reminiscent of lotus flowers. At the room's front, Pharaoh shone forth from his throne under the canopy. I stood and studied Khufu's interaction with the superintendent of the treasury to ascertain his mood. Pharaoh lounged across his throne, one arm draped over the carved sphinx armrest, idly twirling his jewel-handled flail. The superintendent bowed, then kissed the thick carpet at Khufu's feet.

Imperious mood today. Ground-kissing was usually undertaken at one's entrance, not exit.

The treasurer whirled and fled, nearly tripping over the scribe who sat cross-legged near the throne, papyri and ink on his lap.

"Ah, Hemiunu, you arrive at last!" Khufu waved me in.

I took a deep breath, then approached and inclined my head. Pharaoh wore his usual white skirt with the rounded corners, covered with another of fine pleated gold, but today he had added a broad belt with a metal buckle. His royal *cartouche* was delicately engraved in hieroglyphs on the buckle. Across his bare chest lay the heavy pectoral, rows of square gold links with precious inlaid turquoise. He was a beautiful sight, my king, my Egypt. He was Horus on earth. And it was my job to protect him, even from himself.

Khufu sighed dramatically and threw his head back against his throne. The red-and-white-striped *nemes* framing his face slipped a bit, knocking askew the golden snake that reared at his forehead. The Keeper of the Diadem, whom Khufu kept ever ready for such wardrobe emergencies, hurried forward and straightened the headdress, then backed away, eyes downcast.

"The priests are angry," Khufu said. "But the treasurer is happy." He rubbed his eyes. "Why can I not make everyone happy, Hemi?"

I studied the carpet beneath his canopy. "It is your role to keep divine order, my king—"

He fingered the links of the gold pectoral on his chest. "The whole of Egypt is set in motion by my will, Hemi. The taxes are paid to fill my treasury, wars are undertaken to make my name great, buildings are erected in my honor."

I nodded, familiar with his need to rehearse these facts.

"And yet, always there are the old counselors who served my fathers, the generals with their loyal troops, the priesthood with their religious power. I must gratify and placate and watch my back." He slapped a hand on the armrest. "Does this sound like the duties of a god to you?"

"Even the gods—"

"And now this change you have insisted upon. The priests of On are arriving, furious about the dismissal!" Khufu stood and thrust a finger at me. "You could not understand, Hemi. Your men love you. I do not like to anger priests!"

I leaned against my staff. "This great project you have undertaken, Khufu," I began in a soothing tone, "greater than even your father dared build, it requires all that the Two Lands can give. To move the center of worship here to Giza has consolidated your power and your wealth in one place—"

"But to declare myself Ra on earth . . ." He pointed to one of the pillars, with its carved relief of Amun bestowing favor on the king.

"Yes. These are the actions of a true god."

The meat bearer approached, with a meal of gooseflesh and beef on a golden platter. He set the food on the footstool before Khufu, whispered, "Life, Health, Strength!" and disappeared.

Khufu collapsed back to his throne.

It was complicated, our system of worship. Countless gods were assigned to all aspects of Egyptian life, but somehow it brought order to the land. The king would be Ra when he traveled to the west at his death. On earth, he was son of Ra. But to declare himself Ra now, before his death, was to pull support from every corner of Upper and Lower Egypt, brooking no argument. I believed it was necessary for the achievement of our mutual goals.

"And what of the project?" Khufu asked, tearing off a huge piece of meat. "Perhaps it is too much for you."

"If the king would approve plans for the queen's pyramid . . ."

"Is that why people are saying you are behind schedule?"

"Who has said this?"

"You know that everyone expected me to name Ahmose vizier," Khufu said, a slight smile playing at his lips. He popped the meat into his mouth and chewed noisily.

"Perhaps my brother should stick to collecting taxes and leave the building to me."

Khufu laughed. "We are all still little boys, are we not, Hemi?"

Some of us are.

As if on cue, Perni-ankhu, the king's dwarf and cupbearer, scurried into the room with a tall cup of the king's wine.

"Ah, here is Perni, to dance for us." Khufu clapped and took the wine from Perni. "Gladden our hearts, Perni. Hemi here is always much too serious."

From a corner of the Great Hall, waiting there mute until summoned, a lyre struck up a lively tune. The dwarf clamped his hands to his waist, beneath his rounded belly, and did a sidestep away from us, then swayed his hips as he walked an unseen line through the pillars down the hall. The music picked up, Khufu laughed, and the dwarf kicked up his heels.

"He is so amusing, is he not, Hemi?"

"Of course, my king."

"So formal today, Hemi. What is bothering you? Come, sit with me and share my meal."

I am accustomed to these shifting moods of Khufu. I have learned to shift with him, in all things to support him. My very life is linked to his. Not only because of the past we share, but because he is my king. Our ritual with the dwarf was familiar. I ever remain the tight-lipped vizier, and Khufu attempts to make me laugh.

Perni's dance took on a frenzied beat, and I sat at Khufu's footstool and pulled off a stringy section of gooseflesh, though it was not the hour I had established for my midday meal. I wished I could escape and track down Mentu.

Khufu patted my shoulder. "This is better, my friend. Like the old days, when we did not need to think of kingdoms and pyramids, eh?"

I smiled and looked away. "We have many good memories."

"Yes, many stories to be well remembered."

The silence between us spoke of one memory, not as good. I shifted my position on the stool.

Perni's dance ended with a rolling somersault to the foot of the canopied throne, and the little hunchbacked dwarf popped to his feet with a flourish.

Khufu pounded my back with a fist. "By Horus, I am going to send Perni home with you one of these days, Hemi, to lighten you up! You could not be so gloomy with Perni in your house!"

The dwarf bowed and skipped from the room. I followed his exit with my eyes, to the squared-off arch in the center of the east wall. The dwarf disappeared, and someone else took his place.

"Merit." Her name slipped from my lips before I could hold it back. My right hand suddenly grew restless, moving from my knee to the back of my neck, then resting uneasy again on my leg.

She wore a full hairpiece of long curls today, with red-beaded ends, held by a gold headband across her forehead. She needed no adornment. Framed in the arch of the Great Hall, her simple white dress fit narrowly enough to show the curves of her body beneath. The wide straps that reached from her chest to circle her neck were embroidered with red flowers. She had lined her eyes with green malachite and kohl, and they seemed wide enough to peer into a man's soul.

Meritates is a childhood friend, too. Only a childhood friend. It is true we shared many conversations, some laughter. Now she is Khufu's wife, for the good of Egypt.

Khufu saw her too and returned to his meal. Merit's eyes roamed my face for a moment, then she glided into the room like the cool Nile spilling over the barren desert. I wondered if Khufu too soaked up her presence like parched sand. Such thoughts are not good for a man in my position. They bring disorder.

Khufu chewed and swallowed. "Entertain us, Merit. I am feeling restless today."

Her eyelids fluttered. "Restless already? Did I not see Perni leave only a moment ago?"

Khufu tossed back his cup of wine, then wiped his lips with the back of his hand. "Exactly. He has gone and now we are bored."

"You must be feeling better then?" Merit twirled her heavy silver bracelet, encrusted with jeweled butterflies. "Khufu has been alone all afternoon in his private rooms with a headache," she said to me.

The king waved a hand. "Yes, I am well. And bored."

The meat bearer appeared again, took the empty tray and cup, and bowed away. Merit settled in the high-backed chair beside the throne, very near to the footstool where I sat.

I stood and moved away.

"Music," Khufu said. "We need more music!"

The lyre began again, a tune that sounded to me like birds alighting on tree limbs.

"Perhaps someday Hemi will play for us," Merit said softly, her eyes on mine.

"Hemi?" Khufu chuckled. "I should not like to hear the noise that would come from this grumpy vizier. No, he is all about numbers and equations and quarry stones, Merit. I do not believe there is a note of melody in him."

Merit raised an eyebrow at me, and I retrieved my staff, well worn and comfortable, and leaned on it. I hoped that Khufu would not begin again to accuse me of lacking in my duties. Not now.

"Do you think I can learn to dance like the dwarf, Hemi?" Khufu asked. He had gotten to his feet and thrust a toe outward, his hands on his hips. "Step, step, step." He laughed. "Does my talent rival Perni's?"

Merit covered her laugh with her fingers, as though Khufu were one of her boys and not a god. "Sit down, Khufu," she said. "You are being silly."

Khufu yanked the nemes from his head and tossed it onto the footstool. "Faster!" he yelled to the lyre, then danced a circle around me. Despite myself, I felt a smile tug at my lips.

Khufu hopped onto his throne, his head nearly brushing the canopy suspended on four carved wooden pillars. He kicked out one foot, then the other, and I half expected him to try a back-flip off the throne. Instead, his foot caught on the armrest, and he careened off the side.

Without thought, I darted between them and absorbed his weight.

He would have fallen on the queen. Hurt her, perhaps. The metal buckle engraved with his cartouche dug into the skin of my forearm.

Merit was there, hovering over the two of us, her honey-sweetened breath warm at my ear, the elegant line of her jaw close to mine.

"Our Hemi," she said, low and soft. "Like the pyramid he builds. Always solid and dependable, always protecting."

I righted Khufu, who still laughed and clapped with the music. A slave appeared with a wide palm leaf to fan the king.

I turned to Merit and lowered my head.

"My life is yours, my queen."

She smiled and laid a cool hand on my scraped arm, but her touch burned like fire and caused me more pain than the scrape itself.

"So serious, Hemi," she said. "I am only your old friend, Merit."

Yes, only my childhood friend.

The musician faltered at some noise at the entrance to the Great Hall.

The three of us turned our attention there. Khufu's chief servant, Ebo, strode in, his face solemn.

"Your Majesty," he began, "Beloved of—"

"What is it, Ebo?" Khufu leaned forward.

"I have evil news, my king." His eyes strayed to me. "It is Mentu-hotep, Overseer of Constructions."

My hand tightened on my cherp. I stepped forward. "What of him?"

"He has been found dead. Murdered."

Khufu jumped to his feet, and Merit gasped behind me.

"Where?" I asked, fingers digging into the wood. "How?"

Ebo held out his palms. "No one knows who has sent his ka to the west. His body was found in the royal slaughterhouse."

The carved columns of the palace hall seemed to tilt, then right themselves. My breath caught, then surged in my chest. My hands felt slick on my staff.

I looked at Khufu. "I will go," I said.

His eyes told me that he too felt the bond of the day we did not speak of. "We will both go."

THREE

We departed from the Great Hall with haste. Pairs of slaves ran ahead to line the lofty passageway on bent knees with hands outstretched and palms on the floor. We did not wait for the king to be announced, but whispers of "Life, Health, Strength!" followed us through the corridor.

The sun was beginning its descent in the west, and it threw long shadows of the palace over the road. The temple lay two thousand cubits to the north, below the pyramid, and would someday serve as the place of Khufu's mummification. For now, newly appointed priests of Ra served there, and the slaughterhouse stood nearby, between the workers' village and the temple, ready for its double duty of providing meat for the workers and sacrifices for the temple. A sedan chair waited to lift Khufu to the shoulders of more slaves. I chose to walk alongside.

Khufu's head servant, Ebo, accompanied us, as he had done for so many years when we were young. Our destination this day was not so pleasant, however, as the many hunting and fishing trips we had taken together in our youth.

"Who found him?" I asked as we hurried along the road.

Ebo turned to me. A white scar slashed his dark forehead, the cause of which had always been unknown to me. "I received word from another slave, my lord."

Thus far I had refused to let Ebo's announcement penetrate to my heart. It was impossible that Mentu had crossed to the west. Only last night we had been together. Only Mentu understood. About the past, about Merit. About my brother. And my father. I would not believe he was dead until I saw with my own eyes.

We passed the pyramid on our left, still busy with laborers adding to its courses. My eyes strayed there despite our errand. I could never cross the plateau without a loving glance at its perfect lines, as though my own child stood tall to impress me.

We reached the slaughterhouse, a flat-roofed structure with a narrow doorway. An angry bellow tore through the building.

"They are bringing down an ox," I said to Khufu behind me. "There can be no murder here. They would not—"

Ebo pointed through the door. "His body is in the back."

Khufu shoved past me, and I realized that Merit had followed behind us. I lowered my staff to bar her entrance, and her eyes flashed at me.

"Not in here, Merit. Remain outside."

Her nostrils flared. "He was my friend too, Hemi."

"Come!" Khufu called to the two of us from the slaughterhouse entrance.

We crossed under the lintel, into the dusky gloom, to a sight that would have been comical were it not so gruesome. Two slaughterers were bringing down a brown bull, one beefy man attempting to wrap a rope around its forelegs, and one wiry and quick who rose upon the bull's back, twisting at its horns and trying to keep his seat.

The building was filled with the buzzing of flies on carcasses that hung from hooks, their lifeblood draining into a mud-packed floor already stained by the exsanguination of countless others. The place smelled of blood and excrement, and the faintness that swept past my eyes angered me. The ox's tail whipped against its backside, and flicked sweat across my cheek.

I swiped at the wetness and shouted to Khufu over the animal's groans. "Could they not wait until our business here was concluded?"

The larger man heard me, realized who it was that stood before him, and thrust without regard to safety between the bull's legs. Another moment and the bull was on the ground, his hind and forelegs lashed.

The wiry man dismounted and bowed low before Khufu. "A sacrifice for your accession festival, your Majesty, Chosen of Ra." His booming voice mingled with the terrible moan of the ox.

I scanned the slaughterhouse for any sign of Mentu, half-expecting to hear my friend's laughter at the joke he had played.

The beefy man stepped to the ox's head, a flint knife in one hand and a basin in the other. "For his Majesty, Son of Ra!" he shouted, then slit the throat of the ox at the tender place where the vessel carried blood to the head. The bright red fount spurted, then poured into the basin, and the ox gave a last groan and lay still.

I jumped back. I could hear Merit's deep breathing behind me as I fought to remain on my feet.

The slaughterers stood before Khufu now, smeared with the bull's blood, happy smiles upon their faces.

"Well done, men!" Khufu raised a fist.

I stared at him and found there the same expression prompted by Perni's dancing. "We were told that someone—a man—has been killed here," I said. A sweat had broken over my forehead and back, and my neck crawled with it.

The ox-killers nodded, and the muscular one pointed to the back. "We found him back there."

I pushed past Khufu and circled the bloody mess in the center of the room. "And you felt no need to cease your activity?"

The smaller man's glance jumped to his companion then back to me with confusion. "The priests await the sacrifice for the festival."

I waved a hand at their single-mindedness and pushed into the darkness of the back of the slaughterhouse. "Bring a torch," I called to Ebo. He and Khufu were at my side a moment later, the torch illuminating the dark corners. Merit pushed up between us, and we stood in a line, looking down upon the body of my fallen friend.

I could not take it in all at once. Mentu's familiar face stared up at me, his crooked-toothed smile still intact, the large ears that had provoked teasing as a young boy, the deep-set eyes that knew how to show sympathy. He was still the same Mentu, and I thought for a moment that his ka had not fled.

Then I saw the gash. From right ear to left shoulder, his throat had been cut. His hands had been bound. His feet as well. He had been treated no better than the bull. Cut with a flint knife and left to bleed into the dust. I could do nothing but stare, and the blood seemed to drain from my own body.

Khufu whispered beside me, in a voice hollowed by fear, "By the jackal-headed Anubis, what has happened here?" Merit wept softly beside him, fingers pressed to her lips. I wished to comfort her, but she was not my wife.

I knelt to untie Mentu's wrists with trembling fingers, an attempt to restore some dignity to my friend. His bloody hands must have tried to stanch the flow.

"He has been cut," Khufu said.

"Yes. Clearly."

"No," Khufu said and squeezed my shoulder. "His hand has been cut."

I stayed my hand at the bindings. Mentu's wrists had been lashed together, but there was no mistaking the mutilation.

The forefinger of his left hand was missing.

"No!" It was Merit who cried out, but we all felt the impact. A person's body must be whole to travel to the west and join the council of the gods.

This was worse than murder.

This was eternal damnation.

Some men, in the midst of grief, find themselves unable to control their spirit and display a certain chaos of emotion that is unseemly. I have never struggled with this tendency. Instead, now I felt a tightening inside of me, as though the strips of linen wound tightly around a corpse were wrapping themselves about my heart, the black resin hardening. I welcomed this feeling, as it would make me impervious to pain.

I backed away from the body. "Who would have done this? Mentu was not a man with enemies."

Khufu studied Mentu's body, then focused on Merit, who wept violently now. "No. But it seems he had a good friend in my wife."

I searched my king's face, unable to read the emotion there.

Khufu turned the Great Wife away, at last, and circled her with his arms. "We will have the finest physicians attend to him," he said in soothing tones. "They will fashion another finger, attach it well. He will be whole when the seventy days of purification are accomplished. I promise you, his ka will rest with the gods."

A glint on the floor a few cubits away caught my eye, and I directed Ebo to bring the torch closer. I moved toward it on wooden legs. "What is this?"

Ebo answered. "It was found on his body. Those that found him removed it to see if he still breathed."

In the dust at my feet lay a golden mask, the likes of which is rarely seen outside a pharaoh's tomb. I laid my staff on the floor and lifted the mask. It was fashioned as the face of a man, with bright blue inlaid lapis lazuli eyes and red painted lips. The craftsmanship was exquisite, the heavy Nubian gold pounded smooth and the details intricate.

"Found on his face?" I asked.

Ebo nodded. I turned the mask over, looking for the artist's mark but found only a glyph for Anubis, the god of the underworld.

I bent to reposition the mask on Mentu's face, grateful to see that it covered much of the wound on his neck. I touched the forehead with my fingertips and closed my eyes. "I will find the one who did this to you, my friend. I will make him pay."

"Come," Khufu said. "Leave him to the priests and embalmers. You have important work to attend. The project awaits."

I paused to steady my voice, then squared off against the king. "I cannot allow his killer to remain unjudged."

Khufu put his hands to his hips and lifted his head. "Justice will do nothing for Mentu. And I cannot spare you from the building project to chase after a mystery."

Merit's eyes darkened and a crease formed between them, but she said nothing.

"He was my friend," I said.

"And also mine. But as one of your chief overseers, his crossing to the west will endanger the timetable of the project even further."

"Do you care for *nothing* but the pyramid?"

In the dim light I saw Khufu's eyebrows lift in amusement at the accusation I'd heard directed toward myself. He nodded toward Mentu's body. "We never know when the gods might require our presence. And what of Egypt, if I should be called before my tomb is ready?"

Behind us, the slaughterers had begun hacking up the ox's carcass. Death seemed to hover in this place, ready to alight on any of us.

Khufu was right. The House of Eternity I built for him was, in some way, a guarantee of eternity for all of us. As the king went, so went all of Egypt.

Still, Khufu's refusal to pursue justice in this matter troubled me. Mentu's death had brought a disruption to ma'at, that principle of justice and divine order that held all of Egypt together. This also was important.

I raised my chin like a faithful soldier. "I will not fail you," I said.

He gave me a quick smile, as though he knew I would not refuse him, and turned away.

My gaze slipped back to Mentu. Last night had been goodbye, though neither of us knew. *And I will not fail you either, my friend.*

If there were a way to keep crews working through the night on this great project we had undertaken, I would have done so. But the desert at night is as black as the soil after the flood waters have gone, and men fear darkness as much as they love their sleep. As it was, I spent a restless night, tossing in my bed, with images of Mentu's lifeless eyes, oxen blood, and the half-finished pyramid chasing through my meager dreams.

Midway through the night, I finally rose and applied myself to a design I had been drawing in my leisure—a corral of sorts for the masons' tools when they laid them aside on the pyramid. Of late, chisels and drills had been slipping over the edge, injuring laborers on the ramps below. Men of Egypt, even common workers, were not expendable to my mind.

I finished the drawing and rolled the papyrus. The sun god had not yet been reborn in the east, but I undertook my morning rituals and then headed for the workmen's village. It was time to find answers. And to find justice for Mentu, regardless of Khufu's instructions.

The village spread only a few thousand cubits south of my own home on the royal estate and could be reached on foot. We were all connected, the people who had undertaken the Horizon of Khufu. I walked the path with my staff at my side, poking angry holes in the soft sand.

Few people understood the scope of my project. It was left to me to chart the twenty-year course of the work. We were five years in, and only slightly behind schedule. A harbor had been excavated at the edge of the desert, to bring the Nile water and ships from Tura, from Aswan and Nubia, carrying all manner of wood, stone, and gold for the project. The village had been built to house the labor force—forty-five streets intersecting in a lovely grid of sixty symmetrical blocks, like two enormous Senet boards laid side by side. The valley temple at the edge of the harbor was already in place, and the mortuary temple at the base of the pyramid would be finished after the great structure was complete, as would the causeway that would connect the valley and mortuary temples. There were still the queens' pyramids to be built, the boat pits, the many flat-topped *mastaba* tombs for officials and nobles. A true city of the dead.

I passed the wheat and barley fields and the pens of cattle and goats kept outside the wall. The stone wall, about my height, enclosed the village, and I entered through the main gate on the south side. Even from inside the wall, the pyramid overlooked all we did, waiting to be made whole. More than ten thousand men lived in this village which had been called Hotep-Khufu—"Khufu is satisfied."

By Horus, it is I who will be satisfied. But not today. Today, disorder had been brought to my village, and I would root it out.

It took me some time to walk to the top of the village, where the wealthier homes of the project administrators, including Mentu's, lay in the cool shadow of the north wall. The streets filled slowly as the town awoke. Old men took their places on benches outside their homes, and children ran past, with shouts and jeers as their games of tipcats began. A stick fell at my feet, and a child yelled to me to toss it back. I flung it at the boy, still young enough to run naked in the street, and he shouted his thanks and used his own stick to knock it skyward toward his friend.

Serenity had fled from Mentu's house, however. Here, no one sat outside and no children played. Instead, the sounds of a family in mourning washed over the street. I stood outside the door and braced myself for the ordeal, then passed under the lintel.

I had been here many times, just two nights ago when my friend and I had passed the evening in conversation and wine. I took the central passage through the house, until I reached the four-pillared hall where Mentu had entertained guests. Beyond this room lay the open courtyard with its shaded colonnade and squatty palm trees.

My entrance drew attention, and the wailing increased. I bowed my head to Hasina, Mentu's wife, where she sat on the ground. My presence seemed to cause her fresh grief, as though the sight of her husband's friend made his absence more bitter.

Mentu's children huddled around their mother, some too young to understand their loss, some old enough to feel anger at the gods. A brazier burned hotly at the side of the courtyard, incense for gods who did not seem to care.

"Hasina," I said. "I grieve with you in the loss of Mentu."

She squinted at me from where she sat. She was a heavy woman, and her kohl-smeared cheeks quivered, her eyes accusing. "He cared nothing for his own life, only this pyramid you are building together!"

"He cared for you, Hasina. And the children—"

"Then why did he stay out, night after night? Nothing but work! It is not safe out there in the darkness. You should not have allowed—"

"Mentu made his own choices, Hasina."

She shifted her ponderous weight and struggled to her feet. I took a step backward. The children cleared a path as she lurched toward me. "How could you let this happen, Hemiuni?" Her fists pounded my chest, yet I remained still under the blows, feeling they were justified. Her children pulled her away, but she dug her fingers into my arm. "Who did this?" she cried. "Who took him from us?"

"I came to ask you the same, Hasina. Who had reason to harm Mentu? He was not a man to make enemies."

"No." Her sobs echoed against the courtyard walls. "No, everyone loved him. You loved him. He loved you."

I smiled, a narrow-lipped smile that held my emotions in check.

"You should not have insisted he accompany you home, Hemi."

"I did not even know he walked the desert. When I saw him last, he was safe here at home. We said good night, and I returned to the royal estate."

She swiped at her eyes. "No, he came to me in my chamber and said that you requested he walk with you to your home." Her voice sharpened. "You know he could never deny you anything."

I frowned. "I went home alone, Hasina."

"When I did not see him the next morning, I thought he had left early for the work site." She broke out in a fresh round of wailing, and I pried her fingers from my arm.

"I will find answers, Hasina. I promise. Mentu will have justice."

She dropped to the ground again, and her children formed a circle around her, a shield from the truth. But what was the truth? Why had Mentu lied to his wife, and where had he gone after I had left him two nights ago?

I escaped the house and ran to the central streets of the village, to the square where the leisure of old men and children fostered gossip.

As expected, the square teemed with people. There a group of white-haired men huddled around a game board of square blocks, tossing clay pieces and grunting at each other's good fortune. I slid onto a stone bench beside one of them. Their game paused, and one toothless man squinted up at me, wordless. Nonchalance seemed absurd, but I knew better than to begin with questions.

"So whom do the gods favor today?"

A puckered man at the end of the bench wheezed out a laugh. "We will be favored when our bodies are renewed to live again." He coughed. "Here, we merely spend our days waiting."

I nodded as though I could sympathize and joined them in watching those who milled about the square. My presence drew glances from able men who should have been working, which led to furtive dodges into cross streets and alleys. These men could come up with a hundred excuses to be absent from the project, but the scribes kept careful attendance, and one could not escape their duties for long. Still, today there seemed to be an inordinate number of men at leisure.

"You have heard about Mentu?" I finally asked, still watching the square.

Grunts were returned to me.

"I seek justice, but I know of no enemies who would wish him dead." I turned and eyed each of the men. "Do any of you know who would want to send him to the west?"

My question was met with shrugs and averted glances. The talkative one on the end leaned forward. His watery eyes wandered over me, and a spindly finger stirred the hot air before his eyes. "Leave justice—and questions—to the gods," he said in a reedy voice. "There is nothing here that will bring good."

I frowned. "What do you know?"

His shoulders hunched again, and he seemed to retreat.

A hand on my shoulder startled me. The supervisor of designs stood beside me. "Grand Vizier, there is a problem with the new design. Itennu is fuming that your drawings for the upper corridor are off by two seqeds, and the corbelling will be faulty. He asks that you come immediately."

I growled. The old men were too slow to give up their secrets. "I will come soon," I said to the supervisor. "Tell Itenna to push forward."

The men had returned to their game of Senet while I was distracted. "A man discovers divine truth and order by asking questions," I said. "Why do you tell me to stop?"

One looked up, but his eyes moved to something behind me. I turned to find Chuma, one of Khons's supervisors.

"What is it now?" I stood and stared him down.

"The Aswan granite shipment, Grand Vizier."

"Yes? What of it?"

"It has arrived."

I exhaled loudly and closed my eyes. "What concern is that of mine? Can no one do his job without my holding his hand?"

Chuma cleared his throat. "Mentu-hotep usually receives the shipments and instructs the laborers as to where to place the granite."

I tried to roll the tension from my shoulders and looked away. Another man of working age passed through the square, saw me and scurried for cover.

"Why are so many men about?"

Chuma followed my gaze. "The Victorious Gang and the Enduring Gang are not working."

"What? Why?"

Chuma shrugged. "Without Mentu, the supervisors are waiting for instructions. The men have no assigned tasks."

"This is madness! The incompetence and—" I clamped my jaw closed. At a time when we should be increasing our pace, the work had come to a standstill, unable to move forward without Mentu. A fresh pang of grief stabbed at me. I slapped Chuma's shoulder to erase the sting of my accusation. "Tell the ship's captain to begin unloading the granite at the harbor. I will be there immediately." *And I'll have a few things to say to the supervisors who decided to declare a holiday.*

Chuma half-smiled in understanding.

I turned back to the old men and gripped the edge of their table, with a nod to the red-and-white Senet board. "I have no time for games, as you can see. What do you know of Mentu?"

Most of them studied their hands or twirled game pieces in gnarled fingers. My friend on the end of the bench did not fail me.

"You ask questions that will bring harm, not good," he said. "You must leave it alone." His cloudy eyes turned upward to mine and they cleared, focusing on me with the intensity of the desert sun. "For the good of Egypt."

I could have pushed him further, though I suspected I would get nothing more. But there was no time. I glanced over the village wall to the half-finished pyramid in the west. Plans must be revisited, granite shipments directed, lazy men put back to work.

The Horizon of Khufu must be my one and only focus. Without my complete attention, the project would falter.

Perhaps, as the old man said, I must leave questions of justice to the gods.

Surely Mentu would understand.

FOUR

O n the east side of the village lived a man of whom people spoke highly. Senosiris was the construction supervisor under Mentu, but he was about to be promoted. I needed to restore order without delay. I headed to the street where he lived, a rolled papyrus in my hand.

My workforce comprised about two-thirds conscripted labor and one-third specialists—artists, sculptors, and the like. The majority of men were farmers who came to the village for three months of the year while their land lay under water. At the end of *akhet*, the season of Inundation, they would return home to plough and sow. Depending on their rank, some had brought wives and children to the village. Others lived in barracks with dozens of other men.

The houses all looked the same here on the east side of the village—utilitarian mud-brick structures with flat roofs, in straight lines like rows of barley. I intended to ask the location of Senosiris's house of a young man on the street ahead, but when he glanced my way, he darted into an alley and was gone. He was old enough to be a laborer, and I assumed he too was avoiding his work today.

I stopped a running child. "Do you know Senosiris, the construction supervisor?"

A smile like the sun broke over the boy's face. "Ah, Sen-Sen!" He pointed down a narrow street. "The last house. There."

I squeezed his shoulder in thanks and headed down the street. The red-painted lintel confirmed the home was the one I sought. Two large clay pots flanked the doorway, filled with water. A bright white linen hung at the window and billowed outward with the breeze.

A pungent smell greeted me at the door and led me inward. "Greetings," I called. No doorkeeper or resident appeared. To the right, a passage led to the kitchen, and I followed the scent. A soft singing came from the room ahead, an unfamiliar melody, high and sweet. I approached in silence, not wanting the music to stop.

There stood a woman at a brazier, her back to me. She wore no wig that I could tell. Her dark hair hung straight down the back of her bright red dress. Yellow beads were stitched to the bottom hem. She swayed with her tune, and her hair swung in counterpoint.

I exhaled, and she started and turned.

"Oh!" She held a stir-stick, brown gravy dripping from it. She laughed and caught a drip with her hand, placed the stick in a pot on the brazier, then licked her palm and laughed again. "My apologies. I did not hear you." She held out long fingers to the passage behind me. "Please, will you come to the courtyard?"

"Yes." I preceded her down the hall. Behind me, the swish of her red dress embroidered with those fascinating yellow beads blended with the tinkle of the rings she wore on her wrists and ankles, forming its own kind of music.

"I am Hemiunu, Grand Vizier to Pharaoh Khufu, Wearer of the Double Crown." To which she should have replied, "Life, Health, Strength!"

Instead she said, "Yes, I know who you are."

And then we were in the central square of the house, a court-yard not much larger than my bedchamber, yet overflowing with twice the greenery of my courtyard. Terra-cotta pots held plants and shrubs, spilled out flowers, and ringed dwarf trees. A small decorative pool graced the center. She directed me to a stone bench and then floated away to the wall. I placed the papyrus on the floor.

"You are looking for my father?"

"For Senosiris, construction supervisor. This is his home?"

She bent to the floor to retrieve something, and I noticed for the first time the riot of color on the wall. She held a brush in her hand. "Yes. He is my father. He should be home for his noon meal at any moment."

"What are you doing to that wall?"

She laughed. "I am painting it, of course. Do you only know tan quarry stones, Grand Vizier?"

"No, I also know pink Aswan granite." A flush tickled my neck.

She turned and raised her eyebrows, as though surprised by my reply, and smiled. Her eyes were painted with a green that matched the plants around me, and she seemed a natural part of this place.

"I am Neferet," she said, still smiling.

I cleared my throat. "Neferet. Good to meet you."

She turned to the wall. "Would you like to watch me paint?"

"I need to speak to your father."

She dipped her brush into a yellow the color of the sun. I watched as she slowly traced the tip of it across the wall— a feather-light stroke like the kiss of an afternoon breeze.

I flexed my fingers and my knuckles crackled. "How soon until your father arrives?"

She laughed and began her tune again, humming this time.

It does not matter. I could remain here all afternoon.

I shook off the strange thought, then occupied my mind with the tasks yet remaining to me today. I recited them, counting them off as my anxiety built. I shifted positions, drummed my fingers on the bench, cleared my throat. And still she painted. And hummed.

Not surprisingly, it was flowers she painted. On a base of white with a waist-high border of yellow, she painted a riot of lotus flowers, their pink petals bursting open around a yellow center.

"Why are you painting the wall?" I finally asked.

She flung a glance at me over her shoulder, her eyes hidden beneath long lashes. "Why not?"

"Because it produces nothing." I rested an ankle on my knee and jiggled my foot.

She was silent for a moment, her brush outlining a fuchsia petal. "It produces beauty," she said. "And beauty brings forth something from our souls."

I shrugged. "I am a builder."

"Yes," she said. "Yes, you are." There seemed to be a note of sadness in her voice that I did not understand.

"There is beauty in more than flowers," I said. "Even in stone."

She paused, brush in the air, and studied me. "Tell me about your beauty in stone."

I turned my eyes toward the north, as though I could see through the wall, all the way to my pyramid. "It took me an entire year to design it, chart it, choose the site, calculate the artists and laborers needed and the stones and supplies required." I paused for a breath. "Then nearly three years to construct the harbor and canal and the housing, bakeries, and breweries for twenty thousand laborers." I turned back to the girl, whose smile encouraged me to boast further. "And now, at last, we are building, creating a structure so precise, so perfect, the world will wonder at it." I shrugged. "The intricacy of the design, the coordination of thousands of men working toward a single goal, the pyramid itself—is there not beauty in all of that?"

She bowed her head. "My father speaks often of your brilliance. I see you are passionate as well."

A loud laugh echoed from the front of the house. Then, "Neferet!"

Neferet dropped her brush onto a palette and clapped her hands twice with the glee of a little girl. "My father is home. Come, join us for a meal."

I bit back an indignant reply. Her invitation was somewhat inappropriate—a vizier did not typically take his meals with laborers.

Senosiris lumbered into the courtyard and I stood. The man's eyes narrowed as he took me in, standing beside his daughter. "What's this?"

Neferet glided forward and wrapped her arms around her father's thick neck in a quick embrace which he returned. "You have a visitor. Shall I serve the meal here?"

Senosiris looked me up and down. "I do not think it is the grand vizier's practice—"

"I would be honored to taste whatever it is I smelled when I entered," I said and rubbed the back of my neck.

Senosiris held a palm out to Neferet and she smiled and drifted out of the courtyard, jewelry still clinking melodies and hair swinging. When she had disappeared into the passageway, I returned my gaze to her father. I found the older man watching me with an amused smile.

"I have news for you, Senosiris," I began.

He gestured to the bench. "Call me Sen, please. I prefer to leave off the god's name."

Sen dropped beside me, crowding me on the stone bench. But his wide girth matched his wide smile, and I sensed immediately why he was revered.

"What news?" He sat forward slightly, his hands braced against his knees.

"By now you have heard of Mentu's crossing to the west."

Sen sighed and studied Neferet's colorful wall. "He was a good man."

"Yes. Well." I swallowed hard. "His death leaves a gap in management that must be filled. I want you to take over as overseer of construction."

"Me?" Sen bellowed out a laugh and slapped my back. My skin stung under the weight of his hand. "I'm not one of your circle, Vizier."

"I know. But I believe you are the best man for the position."

Neferet returned, hugging a clay pot to her chest and carrying small red bowls with the tips of her fingers. She lowered the pot to a nearby table and a garlic aroma wafted around us.

Sen said, "The grand vizier wants me to be overseer of construction, Neferet."

She smiled and ladled steaming stew into our bowls. "Of course. Who else?"

Sen accepted the bowl she held out. "I am too old. It is for younger men to be ambitious, to advance."

"I need your experience," I said.

Neferet offered me a bowl and I felt her smile alight on me, as quick and ethereal as a butterfly. Her hair swung forward when she leaned toward me.

I dug into my food and found the meat flavored with a peppery sauce that watered my eyes.

Sen chewed and swallowed, then spoke. "I have enough to occupy my time, Hemiunu. My family, my community. I enjoy these simple pursuits. I am a simple man."

I set my bowl on the table. "Exactly why I want to see you in this position, Sen. Your men love and respect you. You are one of them. They will work hard for you."

"If that is true, then I lead by your example, Grand Vizier. You are also much revered." Sen lowered his head, and it surprised me how his admiration warmed me. "You come to me before Mentu's body has even grown cold," he said. "You must be desperate."

My emotions dwelt too near the surface today. I stood and moved to the center of the courtyard, where I stripped a frond of leaves from an acacia tree and rolled the leaves between my fingers. With my back to Sen, I let the choking feeling in my throat subside. "Mentu's death grieves me greatly. I would not have you think me indifferent. But the project must not be allowed to falter. We must bear our grief privately, and the work must go on."

Neferet appeared beside me, and she pried the crushed leaves from my hand, let them flutter to the ground, and wrapped her fingers around my own. I stared down into her eyes and into the sympathy there.

"You were a good friend to him," she whispered.

I did not know why the words of this strange woman would feel like a balm on my scalded soul.

"I will not leave the village," Sen said behind us.

Neferet dropped my hand and I turned. My face felt warm. *Must be the pepper.*

Sen ran a hand over his close-cropped hair. "This is our home, and I won't move up to your royal estate as though I belonged there."

"Fine." I brushed my hands together. "You may remain here among your men, as long as you attend necessary meetings at the palace."

Sen stood, frowning. "I am not certain about any of this."

I reached an arm forward. "Your humility only further convinces me that I have chosen well." He wrapped meaty fingers around my forearm. "Senosiris, Overseer of Constructions," I said.

"Sen. It's just Sen."

I reached for the papyrus I had brought. "I have a task for you already." I unrolled the sheet. Sen looked on, his eyes roaming the drawing. "For the tools on the platform," I said. "To keep them from falling."

Sen lifted his eyes to me. "It is made of wood."

"Yes. I think thirty to forty of them should be sufficient."

"You would spend so much of our rarest resource for this purpose?"

"Wood is rare, it is true. But men are irreplaceable."

Sen studied me a moment more, then took the papyrus. "I will see to it," he said with a trace of emotion.

Father and daughter accompanied me to the door of their home, and I felt some weight of the past day lift. At least this part of Egypt's ma'at, the structure of my management team, had been restored. The project would proceed, and all would be well.

The street had grown oddly still, and we looked both directions to find ourselves alone. And then around a corner came a crowd of mourners, led by a weeping Hasina and the body of Mentu stretched on a pallet. They bore him to the doctor's workshop, where his seventy days would commence and his body be prepared for its journey west.

My satisfaction of a moment before evaporated in a mist of guilt and self-reproach. Mentu's body was marching past me, and there was no divine order.

The pack of mourners pressed through the street like a rodent through the gullet of a snake. One person broke off from the attendant crowd and joined us.

My brother, Ahmose.

"It seemed an inopportune time for tax collecting," he said by way of explanation. I introduced him to Sen and Neferet. Ahmose and Sen were an older and younger version of the same man. That they would like each other, I had no doubt. I did not fear that Ahmose might take an interest in Neferet, as he already had a beautiful wife and three adorable children at home.

And why should I care who takes notice of Neferet?

Ahmose regarded the procession. "I would not have guessed that he would be first."

"First?" I angled my body away from him.

"Of the six of us," Ahmose said, his eyes trained forward. "The first to cross."

I knew of which he spoke. We had gone out, a royal hunting party of seven. We had returned only six.

I said nothing.

"Let us pray to the gods that Mentu will have justice," Ahmose said. I felt his gaze turn to me, and I straightened my shoulders. "Better than she received."

I tightened the linen I wore at my waist. "Sen, I would like you to be my guest at the king's accession festival tomorrow night. We can speak then about your new duties."

With a nod to Neferet and a glance at Ahmose, I fled in the opposite direction of Mentu's procession.

Guilt, uncertainty, and a disturbance of divine order. It was time to visit the temple and do what I must to appease the gods.

Men are often like wayward goats, who need nothing more than a gentle switch across the forelegs to guide them in the right direction. I spent the late afternoon goading reluctant work teams and Aswan granite into place, with thoughts of Mentu crowded behind more immediate crises.

I was forced to climb the pyramid three times, over twenty courses to the entrance, to inspect the changes to the corridor. Without the casing stones yet placed, the pyramid formed natural steps. But with each course nearly as high as my shoulder, the ramps were necessary to reach the entrance, though they circled round the structure and were crowded with gangs hauling blocks upward.

Once each day I continued all the way to the top, one hundred cubits above the bedrock, simply to catch a fresh breeze and survey the plateau. From the ever-rising platform, I could see the valley temple, harbor, and even the Nile to the east, the village and quarry to the south, and the vast western desert. This day, as the sun rested, heavy and orange on the plateau's edge, thoughts of disorder returned, along with my earlier desire to seek the gods' favor in the temple.

I requisitioned a goat from the village, then crossed the desert to the valley temple that lay at the harbor's edge. Eventually this temple would be used for the seventy days of purification of Khufu's body. When completed, a processional up the causeway would escort his body to its hidden chamber in the pyramid where he would begin his journey to the west. But for now, the temple gave those of us laboring on the Horizon a place to honor the gods.

The sun's death was complete by the time I reached the temple, and I cursed those who had delayed me. The darkness was like a heavy, forbidding veil about the temple, warning those who approached of the gravity of encountering the gods.

I climbed the steps to the impressive entrance flanked by two round columns twice the height of a man. Inside, torches and braziers attempted to light the black corners of the temple chambers, but succeeded only in casting ominous shadows upon the walls, each elaborately depicting scenes of the gods from floor to ceiling.

I breathed deeply, then dragged the reluctant goat inside. The gods demanded purity and exacted justice. I had none of the first, and feared the second. Upon my death, Anubis would weigh my heart against the feather of truth. Should my heart prove lighter than the feather, my soul would be judged worthy to pass into the paradise of afterlife. Yet did any among us truly believe his heart would not outweigh a feather?

I crossed through the first chamber, anxious to be finished with this necessary task. In the second chamber, a square recess in the wall held the figure of Ra, the sun god. Above it, carved in relief, was a depiction of Ra as a man, the sun disc balanced on his head, traveling in his sky boat through the day, then stepping into his night boat to sail the underworld by night. Beside the recessed figure, a three-legged brazier burned incense at knee height. Though the ceiling was lost in the shadows high above me, the incense seemed to hang just above my head, weighting the warm room with its heavy perfume.

I shivered, despite the warmth. The goat at my thigh bleated.

A flicker of shadow was all the warning I had before a silky voice spoke at my elbow. "You have come to offer a sacrifice?"

I jumped away from the voice, toward the burning incense, and spun. Firelight played across a face, familiar in spite of the years that had passed.

"Rashidi?"

The little priest bowed low, bringing his head to the level of my belt. His memorable pointed nose still dominated his features. He stood upright again, a full head shorter than I. "Hemiunu," he said, his lips thin.

"It's been a long time."

"I have been serving in the Temple of Ra."

I pushed the rope holding the goat to him, though he had no authority here. "I am sorry about the loss of your position in On."

His small black eyes rose to meet mine and steadied there. "Are you?"

I had been careful that Khufu's dismissal of the priests and moving of the Ra worship would be seen to come from the king and not me. From the disapproval that radiated from Rashidi, I wondered if he suspected otherwise.

A flutter of white nearby sucked our attention toward the entrance.

"Hemi!" Merit drew up short and stood framed in the chamber entrance. She wore no heavy wig tonight, and her hair floated about her face. Her fingers drifted to her throat. "What are you doing here?"

I bowed to my love and the Great Wife. "I brought a sacrifice. I will ask the gods to restore ma'at after the death of Mentu."

Rashidi led the goat into the shadows, and his voice wove its way back to us. "Ma'at cannot be restored when those the gods appoint refuse to obey."

Merit and I watched the darkness where Rashidi had seemed to evaporate. She finally spoke. "He has always been strange, hasn't he?"

I moved back toward the brazier, longing for the heat to penetrate my chilled bones. "Did you also come to offer a sacrifice?"

Merit sighed and studied the statue of Amun, seated on his throne, in the recessed wall. "I came to offer my questions."

I rubbed damp palms together and faced her. "It is not easy to know the will of the gods."

Merit slid beside me, her eyes still on Amun, touched my forearm with her four fingertips, and kept them there.

"Do you ever doubt, Hemi?" she said. "Doubt everything we have been taught about the gods?"

I tried not to move, so as not to disturb her fingers, and hoped that Rashidi was occupied with the goat. The familiar warmth spread from her touch, loosening the ever-present tension between us.

"I have more doubts than certainties, I'm afraid." My mouth felt dry.

Her eyes roamed my face, and her other hand joined the first on my arm. "What doubts? Tell me." She stood so close that the night's chill now fled.

"The afterlife is promised if our hearts are pure," I whispered. "But I know no one whose heart is pure."

"Yes!" Her eyes lit with a conspiratorial glow. "It seems a futile hope, from the womb! How can we go on hoping to reach the afterlife, when in the honesty of our souls, we know we are unworthy?" A desert breeze worked its way into the temple and lifted wisps of her hair from her face. "And they are ever changing, the gods. So many, all competing. Atum for our parents. Ra for us." She stared up at me, eyes bright. "Do you ever wish for one god who does not change, Hemi?"

Looking down at her there, with her fiery eyes and her beautiful lips, I felt myself in grave danger. I stumbled backward and let her hands fall. "I try to focus on a different kind of eternity, Merit. Pharaoh's pyramid will be my immortality."

Her chin dropped to her chest at the mention of Khufu. It is always this way with us, when we encounter each other alone unexpectedly. We pretend for a few moments that it is only the two of us. Then one mentions Khufu, and the spell is broken.

"He thinks of nothing else, either," Merit said, a sadness in her voice. "He is frantic to see it finished as soon as possible. He flies into a fury when he hears of a delay."

"Even Pharaoh fears his mortality."

Rashidi appeared beside us again, as though summoned from the dust by the gods. He held a large alabaster bowl of raw meat and entrails. Merit wrinkled her nose, then turned away. "I must return to the palace. The Beloved of Ra will be asking for me."

I watched her go, wondering if my effort to appease the gods here in the temple had now been negated by the thoughts of Merit that were resurrected each time I saw her face.

Rashidi's nasal voice drew me back to the sacrifice at hand. "I thought you desired to restore ma'at, not create more disorder."

I flexed my shoulders and wished I had brought my staff. "The building project will ensure the afterlife for all of us. My attention there will bring divine order."

He shrugged and moved toward the inmost chamber, through a doorway tall enough to admit a god. I followed. Inside, a larger fire burned on an altar, with hefty joints of oxen smoking at its center.

Rashidi dipped his bare hands into the bowl of gore and lifted dripping fingers. I looked into the flames, letting them burn away the image. The gods demanded my sacrifice, but did they insist that I enjoy the ritual? Rashidi tossed my offering to the flames, then intoned words too dark and deep for me to understand. I felt the weight of omen descend through the temple and settle on my shoulders.

Rashidi stared into the flames and spoke in flattened tones, as if reading my heart there in the embers. "You care only for your own goal, your own name, Hemiunu. You avoid what is necessary, what is important, to further your own ambition."

I shifted and considered that it was time to leave.

"Only when you turn your back on your own ambition," he continued, "and do what you know to be right, will the goddess Ma'at restore her blessing."

Ashes from the charred meat clawed their way upward through the smoke-filled chamber. Some landed on my lips, and I thought I could taste the blackened flesh. Smoke burned my eyes.

"I must concentrate on the pyramid," I said, rubbing the back of my neck.

Rashidi's eyes reflected the firelight as he gazed at me, tiny double flames that seemed lit from within. "You must sacrifice yourself to bring justice." His voice was like the hiss of a serpent in the fiery chamber, but then he lifted it to a surprising volume and delivered his prophecy like a hound baying at a feral scent. "Sacrifice yourself, Hemiunu! Or there will be more suffering, more pain, more disorder!"

I chose to leave the temple now, feeling that I had fulfilled my duties of sacrifice and had done all I could for the gods for one night.

As I crossed under the granite lintel, past the two mighty columns, and stumbled onto the sandy plateau, Rashidi's voice seemed to echo behind me, over me, and out across the valley below. Like an ox-hide drum, calling men to judgment.

FIVE

Sacrifice yourself, Hemiunu! Or there will be more suffering, more pain, more disorder!

Throughout the next day and into the evening I found myself looking over my shoulder in anticipation of the next disaster. I drove the men hard to make up yesterday's slack, but we were forced to quit early, as it was the Day of Accession and the king's yearly festival would begin in late afternoon with a procession from palace to temple.

I stood at attention outside the palace entrance, with thousands of others who thronged the road to the temple. Khufu emerged on his gilded sedan chair, carried on poles by four brawny slaves. He wore the double crown, red and white, and inclined his head gently toward his people, while a fan bearer on either side kept him cool in spite of this tremendous effort. I occupied my mind with calculations and a frustrated reassessment of schedules based on the recent shortened workdays, the tension of the numbers creeping up my back and shoulders.

When Khufu had made his obeisance to the gods and been deposited back at the Great House, I departed to my own more

modest home to get ready for the feast which would begin at
sunset.

My preparations were simple. I shaved my face and head
quickly, then placed my shaving knives in an even line from small-
est to largest as is my habit. I ignored the usual cosmetics and
jewelry, except for a gold armband to circle the midpoint of my
upper arm, and donned a white robe with a gold belt. I would leave
my staff behind. Though I was careful about my routine, I did
not particularly care to spend much time in my house. *An empty
treasury, still waiting to be filled.*

My haste to the Great House did not stem from excitement
over the feast. These evenings of pomp and supposed hilarity never
reached into my heart with their fingers of glee. And there were
far too many of them. Before the Great Hall had grown cold from
tonight's celebration, the Festival of Hapi would be upon us, with
games of skill and more feasting. I usually tried to excuse myself, to
escape from these activities early. Tonight, however, I had a greater
purpose.

I passed through the palace gate, under the mighty arch. The
garden path led me to the palace entry, between two lines of palm
trees and flaming torches. My gaze drifted upward to the palace
walls. A woman watched me from where she sat on the deep ledge
of a window.

The feast had already begun when I stepped into the Great Hall
of Pillars. The room swarmed with nobles, officials, courtiers, and
administrators, all jockeying for the best positions at the low stone
tables that had been placed among the pillars. At the edges of the
room, miniature replicas of the great pillars held alabaster lamps of
burning oil atop their fluted capitals, bathing the painted walls in
gold.

Rashidi's words had struck deep, and although I could not walk away from the project, I also believed that ma'at would not be put right until I had found justice for Mentu. To this end, I planned to use my appearance at tonight's festival to speak to the one man I believed could best handle the search for the killer.

Musicians lined the front of the hall, and I noted that the leading harpist in the kingdom had been engaged for the evening. His twenty-stringed harp was among the finest I had seen, and I felt a flicker of jealousy at the ornate column and neck. Music filled the Great Hall, mingling with the rising conversation and reverberating off the stone walls. The drinking had not yet begun and already the noise grated against my ears.

I searched the hall for the man I'd come to see. He would be easy to locate, the Nubian whom I had engaged to keep a watchful eye and a firm hand on the work site. Axum's basalt-black skin and eyes as white and round as full moons were most intimidating, and even the bravest of the laborers could not stand up to the intensity of his gaze.

Slave girls came to anoint my head and adorn me with a necklace of lotus flowers. I allowed the anointing but could not be bothered by flowers. Across the room, Senosiris lifted a hand in greeting. His daughter stood at his side, watching the festivities with the wide eyes of one new to the pleasures of the privileged.

I spotted the Nubian, Axum, standing apart from the gaiety, at the back of the hall, his back braced against a mighty column.

"Axum!" My voice evaporated in the din. I started toward the Nubian, but a hand around my upper arm held me fast. Behind me, a slender woman pulled up close.

"I've been waiting for a man more exciting than these dull politicians to appear," she said.

I had to bend my head to catch her words, and Tamit interpreted my movement as an invitation. She pecked a kiss on my cheek.

"You give me too much credit, Tamit. I am as dull as any other politician."

She stifled a laugh and encircled my arm with both her own. "Then tell my why every woman in the kingdom without a husband has her eye on Hemiunu."

I lifted my gaze above her head to find Axum again. He still stood against the far column. "I have someone I must speak to, Tamit. You will excuse me?"

She sighed like a woman who is bored with everything life has given her. "You will sit beside me for the feast, Hemi. I'll be certain of it."

"As you wish."

Tamit's flirtations were far from a novelty. Khufu's cousin on his mother's side had been a coy girl when the seven of us were young together, and she had since become a tenacious woman. She'd buried one husband in a grand mastaba in Memphis and was hard at work finding another.

It will not be me.

Axum raised his white orbs as I approached. His shaved head glistened in the torchlight. Though the desert night was cool, the torches, the bodies, and the hot food made the hall stifling as though it were midafternoon.

"Axum, I must speak to you." The Nubian faced me fully, his attention mine. "You have heard about Mentu's murder?" I asked.

A single, slow dip of his head was his only response, and his eyes never left my own. The festival swirled around us like a river rushing around an outcropped stone.

I raised my voice and leaned forward. "I have something for you to—"

The music cut off in mid-note, and the tumult of voices ceased a fraction of a moment later. I let my words hang in the air and turned to the front of the hall.

Khufu entered, trailed by his harem. He wore the double crown again tonight, as appropriate for his accession festival. In the five years since he had taken the throne, he had only solidified the unity of the Two Lands.

A courtier announced his presence. "The god Ra walks among you," he intoned. "The Son of Ra, Horus on Earth, Your Great Pharaoh."

We responded with a shout, "Life, Health, Strength!"

I tried to control the twitch of a smile. Khufu glided through the obsequious crowd, his outstretched arms deigning to touch the hands of a chosen few, his smile falling on others. He was loving every moment of this.

Every woman of the harem was dressed alike, I noted, like stones chiseled to match the others to perfection. They wore only short skirts, low on their hips, with ribbons wrapped about their upper bodies. Each was bejeweled with bracelets, necklets, anklets, and wreaths of flowers. They streamed behind Khufu as though he were the tip of the pyramid and they, the supporting stones.

I stood beside a statue of the cat goddess Bastet and waited in silence for Khufu to pass, though I chafed to speak to Axum before the seating began. The procession finally reached the back of the hall. I met my friend's eyes, and Khufu steered away from me in a pretended insult, his smile turning to a wicked grin for a moment.

Yes, very amusing.

The seating began at once, with courtiers eyeing each other jealously as names were called and people took their places from Pharaoh's seat outward. Two large tables ran along the sides of the hall, with a third at the head. Each hoped to find themselves seated at the head table. I turned to give Axum his charge, but the man had disappeared. I growled. I had hoped to be free to escape this torture whenever an opportune time arose.

Khufu's snub was too soon erased, however. My name was called and I proceeded to the front of the room, where I would sit only a few chairs from the king. True to her word, Tamit was placed beside me. The red carnelians at her throat sparkled as she approached. She winked at me with pursed lips, and we settled into ornate wooden chairs with sloping arms and legs carved into lion's paws.

"I always get what I want," she said, smoothing her dress over her thighs.

I glanced around for Merit, but the Great Wife had chosen to wait to make her entrance.

The seating finished and conversation resumed. People leaned past piles of colorful fruit and great loaves of bread that loaded the tables to call out to friends placed farther down, and the Great Hall soon buzzed. I searched out Axum and found him placed near the end of the table to my left. The man's eyes were on me still, which raised the hair on the back of my neck. Our conversation would have to wait through the formalities.

With a double somersault from the back of the room and a quick front flip, Perni the dwarf appeared at the center of the three tables, his feet splayed wide on the mosaic floor, his chubby arms upraised.

"Perni! Perni!" someone shouted. The crowd picked up the chant, banging hands on the table in rhythm. He bowed as if to acquiesce, then began a slow dance in time with the clapping. This dance was all thrusting legs, leaps and twirls, and the crowd responded by picking up the tempo.

Tamit leaned against me and crooned into my ear, "Only a little longer, Hemi. Then you and I can find someplace quieter." She squeezed my arm and raised her voice over the pounding fists. "You haven't been to see my animals in such a long time."

There are enough preening birds and strutting apes here to amuse me.

The guests' rhythm had reached an impossible pace, and the crowd roared as Perni's feet inevitably tangled and he fell to the floor in a heap. The little man righted himself, bowed to Khufu who clapped louder than the rest of them, and skipped away.

Serving boys and girls poured into the room, offering ointment, wreaths, and perfumes, and ladling wine from alabaster bowls. The drinking began.

I had no desire to engage Tamit in conversation, so I chose the secondary evil, to speak to Oba on my other side. The older man needed only a small encouragement to set off on expounding the deplorable morality of the laborers, leaving me free to think of other things while nodding in agreement.

I caught sight of Axum again, still silent and watching. The man understood that I wanted something of him, and he would not leave before we had spoken.

It was time for the harem women to dance. I sighed and propped my elbows on the table. Already the flickering torchlight and noise had worked their way into my head. I rubbed my temples, hoping to relieve the tension.

I did not intend to watch the women dance, but there was a symmetry to their movements I found pleasing. They began in unity, with slow steps, beating time on short sticks they held aloft. Female singers stood behind them and produced slow, clear tones that carried effortlessly through the heavy air.

Beat, beat, beat. Twenty sticks and twenty feet sounded as one. Their measured steps brought them closer to the head table where Pharaoh was transfixed. Their unity was most satisfactory. I let my eyes roam over each one, appreciating the standards that guided Ra'henem, the superintendent of the harem.

Tamit was at my ear again. "I take it back," she murmured. "It is not only the women without men who have eyes for Hemiunu."

I leaned away but glanced at her. She inclined her head toward one of the dancers, at the edge of the group. I followed her look and found a petite girl, all wrapped with orange ribbons, breaking the symmetry to watch me. My mouth went dry and I looked away.

Tamit laughed. "Have no fear, Hemi. She won't be allowed to do more than look."

I shrugged and reached for a small loaf of bread.

"Besides," Tamit said, running a finger over her lips, "I should claw her eyes out if she did."

Turning away, I chose to scan the faces of those seated at the side tables and mentally recite each of their names. It was a game I played often, pushing myself to know everyone. I found that men felt appreciated when a superior called them by name and would therefore work harder. Most of the men's faces were covered with sloppy grins at the sight of the harem dancers.

I spotted Sen's daughter, Neferet, also watching the dancers as though memorizing their fluid movements. The dance ended with some sort of flourish I missed, and the crowd erupted with shouts and claps. The women twirled out, and musicians took their place, with men singing to the accompaniment of harps and flutes.

Already slave boys were replacing oil in lamps that had been fueled to blaze madly. I exhaled and used the back of my hand to wipe my forehead. Why must the Great Hall be kept so hot? The perfumed wigs and smoking torches were making my eyes swim.

Finally, the servers brought the meat. After Khufu had been served, platters of geese and various game circled the room. The ever-faithful Ebo stood behind Khufu, overseeing the service with a pleasant smile but watchful eyes.

When a boy's ladle sloshed wine onto the table's edge before Khufu, the pharaoh pushed back from the table, taking care not to allow the wine to drip onto his white robe. "Cursed boy! Have you just come from feeding the goats?"

The boy bowed and disappeared, and Ebo stepped in to wipe away the spill. Khufu smacked the servant's arm. "Where do you get these boys, Ebo?"

Ebo's smile never wavered. "I am sorry, Great One. I will attend you myself this evening." The smoothness of his voice testified to many years of soothing Khufu's tempers.

Tamit leaned against me. "Ebo is like a loyal pet, is he not? A faithful greyhound at the foot of his master."

Pharaoh sighed at Ebo but returned to his seat, then raised a smiling face. "It is a night for laughter!" he shouted. He leaned forward, past the few that separated us. "My wife has not yet arrived," he called down the table, too loudly. "Hemi, have you seen Merit?"

Those between us quieted, as if the question held hidden meaning.

I blinked several times, then scanned the room. "I too look forward to the queen's arrival, my king. Perhaps she is taking extra care to beautify herself for you."

There was another moment of silent tension, then Khufu's smile reemerged and he turned away.

I straightened the serving pieces on the table before me, then glanced at Tamit, whose eyes flashed with something more than the wine she had imbibed.

Merit's absence wasn't the only one I had noted. Somewhere at the head table there should have been a seat for Mentu. Already it had been filled by the next one eager for favor.

As if reading my thoughts, Tamit said, "Frightful business about Mentu."

I nodded and studied a torch stuck in the wall.

"But the living must go on living," she said brightly.

And you must go on talking. "Some of us are not so willing to forget."

"Oh? It seems to me that you have not missed a step in your never-ending project."

I turned on her, letting her feel the heat of my stare. "Mentu is not forgotten, and justice for him will be found."

Tamit's smile slipped a bit, and she fingered the gold collar at her throat. Her discomfort fled a moment later, replaced by a wink and smirk. "But not tonight, my Hemi." She lifted a gold cup of wine. "Tonight, we celebrate!"

A storyteller appeared, an ancient little man, with hair that had been allowed to whiten and blind eyes. He lifted his voice, accompanied by a steady beat of sticks from the side of the hall.

"In the beginning there was water, only water." His sing-song cadence brought the room to attention. He told of the eight gods in the primordial waters, then the ninth, Atum, rising from the water on the mound, the predecessor of the pyramid. On through Atum's children, Shu and Tefnut—air and moisture. And their children,

Geb and Nut—earth and sky. As he neared the apex of the story, the room grew silent, save the beating sticks.

"Four children issued forth from Geb and Nut. Isis and Osiris became husband and wife. Their brother Seth was evil, and Nephthys became his wife. Then Isis and Osiris came to earth to establish Egypt. But Seth plotted against them." He told of Seth's trickery, how he had nailed Osiris in a wooden chest and threw him into the Nile to die. Later, when Isis recovered his body, Seth hacked it into thirteen pieces and scattered it. Isis found nearly all the pieces, reassembled Osiris, and fashioned artificial parts so he would be whole. She returned him to life, the first to be resurrected and, now, god of the dead.

"And what of Seth?" the little man asked.

The people hissed.

"It is left to the son of Isis and Osiris to defeat him!"

The crowd knew their part. "Horus! Horus!"

The storyteller bowed deep to Khufu, our Horus on Earth. "Protector of the People!" he shouted, and the crowd cheered.

The festival continued in a blur of food and dance. I chose figs and grapes, beef and goose, jugs of beer and honey-sweet cakes as they passed by on platters. The harem danced again, and the hum of conversation rose in proportion with the wine that flowed, until the ribbons floated on a smoky haze and the music of flute and harp and lyre seemed to clash into one frenzied note.

I needed air. I shoved away from the table, then twisted through the crowded Great Hall. Outside, I welcomed the silent chill of the desert night and moved into the shadows of the palace garden. I inhaled the cool darkness.

The flame-red chaos of the festival seemed a far-off thing amid gnarled fig trunks and the shade of sycamores. I rubbed the sweat from my neck, let the night air cool me, and closed my eyes with relief. Festivals are for people with nothing better to fill their heads. The room had bubbled and frothed like a vegetable stew over a stoked fire, and I had felt like a chunk of basalt sunk to the bottom of the pot.

Footsteps whispered along the garden path.

If that woman followed me out . . .

I was dangerously close to telling Tamit what I thought of her.

But it was Axum's white eyes that faced me on the path, and I held out an arm in grateful welcome. We were men who knew what it was to command, and I admired Axum's strength of silence.

His voice was low and confiding. "A task for me, Grand Vizier?"

I nodded and drew close. Somewhere in the desert a jackal howled. "Mentu's murder has caused a disruption in Egypt."

We moved back to stand under a sycamore.

Axum scowled and his white teeth glowed. "He was a good man."

"Yes. Yes, he was. I want you to find out who killed him."

Axum leaned one shoulder against the tree. "Some things only the gods are meant to know."

I gripped Axum's elbow, below the gold bands that circled his upper arm. "We must find justice. There will be disorder until we do. I—I fear that there will be other . . . problems . . . until ma'at is restored."

Axum looked into the distance, toward the perfect lines of the pyramid against the night. "Should not the grand vizier occupy his mind with his responsibilities?"

I smacked my palm with a fist. "Egypt is my concern! If there is no divine order, no justice, then all that we work for is of no value."

"Perhaps you should find this killer yourself."

I threw my head back to the cold sky above us and tried to let it cool my temper. "The Horizon of Khufu demands my full attention. But I trust you. Will you find justice for Mentu?"

I felt Axum studying me in the dark. "Does the death of one man have the power to change the world?"

The scrape of an approach turned me to the garden entrance. Jackals did not often dare near the light of the palace, but one could never be certain.

A slave boy trotted up the path to the palace entrance. Axum seemed to recognize him and let out a low, curious whistle. The boy stopped and whirled, then ran toward us.

"One of my boys," Axum said to me, with some measure of pride.

The boy was not a Nubian, and I assumed that Axum must employ him in some manner.

"There has been a death, my father!" The boy panted and bowed to Axum.

I raised an eyebrow at this title of honor.

"Another goat pulled from the flock?"

"No." The boy's eyes were wide, and his narrow chest heaved. "No, a peasant woman from the village. She was murdered."

Axum frowned with the look of a parent who's discovered that his children have disobeyed.

"Her husband?" I asked the boy.

The slave boy lifted his bony shoulders and held out his hands. "She was found at the harbor, alone, my lord. No one has yet claimed her."

I crossed my arms and faced Axum squarely. "You see? Ma'at has been disturbed, and now a woman has also crossed to the west."

Axum squeezed the boy's shoulder. "No one knows who she is?"

"No one has seen her face, my father." The boy's eyes sparked with the excitement that youth feels at any sort of intrigue. "When the body was found, her face was hidden. No one has disturbed it."

"Hidden?"

The boy's voice dropped to a whisper. "Covered," he said, "with a beautiful golden mask."

SIX

At the slave's mention of a mask, I stepped between him and the Nubian and grabbed the boy by the shoulders. Anxiety shot through me and my fingers tingled. "Where did you say this woman was found?"

"At the harbor's edge, my lord." His eyes widened and his lower lip trembled. I released him. "Run back to the harbor and be certain no one touches the body. Watch for our approach."

The boy fled and I turned to Axum. The night around us was still. "You have heard about the mask?"

Axum's brow furrowed.

I drew close to the Nubian and bent my head to his. "A mask was also found covering Mentu-hotep's face. I took care that it not be spoken of to anyone. Have you heard people tell of it?"

"I have heard nothing of a mask."

I chewed at my lip and looked north toward where the harbor lay in the distant darkness. "I must see the body."

Axum bowed. "I will call for a chair."

I waved his comment away. "No. I do not have the patience to be borne on the backs of donkeys or men tonight."

Axum stared at me his blank, white-eyed stare.

"The situation dictates the impropriety," I said. "I can get there faster on my own feet."

"As you wish." I heard respect, laced with amusement, in his voice.

I led the way along the garden path, with a glance toward the palace. I should explain my departure to Khufu. It would be an insult to the king to leave his accession festival early, without explanation.

A tall figure appeared at the entrance, a shadow with the blaze of the Great Hall behind her. I recognized Tamit's silhouette. She paused between the twin striding statues of Khufu.

"There you are!" Tamit glided to me and wrapped tight fingers around my upper arm, pressing the gold armband into my flesh. "I knew you wouldn't have left without a good-bye." She pursed her full lips. "You haven't even gotten drunk yet."

The desert and harbor called to me. "I'm afraid I need my wits tonight, Tamit. Will you tell Pharaoh I am needed in an emergency at the harbor?"

She sniffed. "Oh, what emergency? Tell them to wait until after the party to have their foolish emergency."

I pried her fingers from my arm. "This cannot wait. I am sorry. You will speak to the king for me?"

She crossed her arms in a pout. "I will tell him. But you owe me an evening of your time, Hemiunu."

I rubbed at the back of my neck. "Good night, Tamit." Before I turned, I saw the dark flash of her eyes. For all her playfulness, I feared her quest for a husband was fueled by a desperation I did not understand.

But I have other matters to attend.

Axum had remained in the shadows, but he joined me now. He lifted a torch from a post at the edge of the courtyard, and we set out northward toward the harbor.

My half-built pyramid stood outlined against the night sky, a massive, dark angled platform, with only the pale moonlight to set it apart from the desert. It called to me, begging me to spend my attention only on it, without distraction. I averted my eyes and walked with haste, in part to ward off the chill.

Another murder. Another mask. What did this peasant woman have in common with Mentu? Who would have reason to kill both the overseer of constructions and a nameless woman from the workmen's village? Or perhaps there was no connection. Perhaps there was a madman in our midst, choosing his victims at random. The thought chilled me further. A night wind kicked up sand, and I instinctively ducked and turned my head.

"We walk toward a killer, perhaps," Axum said, "with heads down and eyes at our feet?"

I faced the sand and let it punish me. *I should have done more after Mentu's death. Should have focused on finding his murderer.* The priest's words resurfaced. More disorder, because I had been interested in only my own ambition. And now an innocent woman had paid the price for my inattention.

I quickened my pace, anxious that the murder scene may tell me more about Mentu's death as well the woman's.

With the quarry behind us, the pyramid lay only two thousand cubits ahead to the west, and the harbor with its valley temple just in front. The harbor had been built at the beginning of the project, five years ago. Ships docked just below the temple, where supplies and stones were unloaded. From the dock, a stone wall tapered off to mud and reeds. A canal connected the deep harbor to the

Nile. During these months of akhet, when the Nile surged over its banks and swamped the floodplain, the canal all but disappeared, with only a short span separating the flooded farmland from the harbor.

The slave boy I had sent ahead must have seen our torch. He signaled us with a sharp whistle, and we changed course to join him at the water's edge.

The water-logged sand sucked at my sandals, a strange sound in the stillness. The boy stood with the silence of a guardian sphinx beside a tangle of white among the dark reeds. He straightened and threw his shoulders back at Axum's approach.

"You have allowed no one to disturb the body?" Axum asked.

"No, my father. Just as you said." The boy's eyes never left Axum's, and when the older man gave him a quick nod, he lifted his chin and hid a smile.

I inhaled with eyes closed, strengthening myself for the task. I did not want to miss anything as a result of my weakness in the face of blood. I examined the surrounding scene first, from the water to the dry sand. Papyrus had been planted here years ago and had already grown thick, its stalks reaching higher than my head and ending in fluffed plumes. In the darkness, the reeds and water were black and the half-moon a pale slice of reflection in the harbor.

"She is here," the boy whispered. I held up a hand, not wanting to be rushed in my inspection.

The grasses had been crushed in a path leading out from the water. Trampled by the boy's feet? Perhaps. Or perhaps the woman's lifeless body had been brought here. I followed the path to the sand. Scuffled footprints here, as though she had been dragged or had fought with someone along the way, trying to free herself. The trail led in the direction of the quarry and, beyond, the village.

I returned to the water, again sinking into sandy muck to my ankles. The Nubian and the boy watched silently. My mouth felt as dry as sand, and my blood pounded.

She was a tall woman. I could sense this even with her body on the ground and curled against itself. She lay on her side, but her head had been turned to the sky and the golden mask placed over it. Her natural hair streamed from under the mask, and the edges of it floated in the shallow water, mingling with the reeds. Her white coarse linen dress was torn and muddied, with dark streaks across her midsection. I bent to one knee in the grass to examine the streaks.

The memory came unexpectedly, as flashes from the past always do. Though in hindsight the connection was natural. Muddy reeds, tangled hair, a woman at the water's edge. Dead. I remembered the certainty that Merit lay at my feet, the guilt and relief at discovering it was Amunet. Now it was as if I had stepped into one of my frequent dreams, only this time surrounded by darkness.

I shook off the memory. I was not a youth anymore. This woman was not Amunet. And I would not shirk my responsibility. I stilled the uneven beat in my chest and looked again at the streaks on her dress. The dark stains were blood. Carefully, I lifted her left wrist from the ground at her side, fearing what I might find.

The hand was bloody.

"Her finger has been taken," Axum said, shock vibrating in his voice.

I swallowed and lowered the hand back to the grass. I must be methodical about this. *Think of it like an examination of the project plans.* I must work my way through each section, looking for flaws, for the unusual, or something out of place that might point to the killer. There was no need to involve my heart.

I started with her feet—bare. Examined her legs—muddy. Her clothing bore no clues but the blood wiped from her hand. Did that mean she was still alive when the finger was cut from her?

Logic only. No emotion.

I leaned in to inspect her chest and neck and motioned to the Nubian to bring the torch closer. Blackening bruises covered her bare shoulders, crept up her throat and disappeared under the mask. I steadied myself to examine her neck, expecting the gash I had seen on Mentu. But only bruises marked her skin.

Had she been choked to death? And if so, what did it mean that her killer had not used a knife this time? Was it the same man who killed Mentu?

I rocked back on my heels for a moment, pondered the evidence, and found I had only more questions. I looked over my shoulder, feeling the stares of Axum and the slave boy and the weight of the desert solitude pressing in on me.

Whoever she was, she had died far from anyone who cared. The light of the palace was like a distant star on the horizon, and even torches in the workmen's village seemed to belong to the night sky. The desolate harbor, with only the pyramid watching over it, was a lonely place to die.

I ran a finger along the fine details of the mask. It was very similar to Mentu's, with lapis lazuli eyes painted with kohl and a mouth shaped into a peaceful smile that seemed grotesque in such a place. The gold was hammered smooth, and in the gray shadows it seemed to glow with fire.

I could put it off no longer. I curled my fingertips under each side of the mask, just above the poor woman's ears. The gold piece was not attached in any way. It simply lay upon her face, and I noted that it had to have been placed there after death.

I lifted the death mask slowly, like the god Anubis inviting this nameless woman to live again and join the gods. But I knew as I lifted it that I'd find no life underneath.

A distant cloud chased across the face of the moon, darkening the sky.

I set the mask aside. I leaned over the woman's face. Axum brought the torch closer.

And then the memories washed over me again. Only this time the nightmare had become truth, and the desert and harbor and pyramid tilted crazily at the edge of my vision and threatened to topple over.

No, it was not Amunet who lay dead beside me.

It was Merit.

SEVEN

"Grand Vizier?"

The darkness around me shifted.

"My lord?"

I looked up from Merit's body through blurred eyes. "My lord," Axum said, "is that—is she—"

I returned my gaze to her face. "It is the Great Wife. Yes."

Axum placed a heavy hand on my shoulder in silent sympathy. "I will send the boy with a message for Pharaoh."

"No!" I grabbed his wrist. "Not yet. I—I will send word myself. When I am ready."

"As you wish."

Logic only. No emotion. The words mocked me.

"My lord—"

"Leave us!" I turned to the Nubian and the boy beside him. "Leave us," I said again. "I will bring her body to the temple shortly."

The older man frowned but dipped his head and backed away, pulling the boy by the shoulder. And then we were alone.

I reached an arm under her body, lifted her from the mud, and cradled her on my lap. I felt an intense pressure in my head and body, as though my ka was turning to stone. I breathed through the pain, eyes closed and lips parted.

I must look at her. The boy had left the torch speared into the sand nearby, and its light played across her features.

There was something in her mouth.

I leaned over her and nudged her lips open with the tip of my finger. A papyrus plume? I pulled the grass from her mouth, and found that a pink-petaled lotus flower had also been pushed in. I checked my instinct to thrust the offensive plants from me, and instead laid them in the sand at my side.

Merit. *Oh, Merit.*

With one arm I clutched her against my chest, and with the other hand I brushed the wet hair from her face. The moon emerged from behind the wispy clouds, lightening her pale features. I found I was rocking her, a gentle movement to soothe a crying child. I tried to stop the slow movement but could not.

All these years of striving to be an honorable man.

A jackal howled at the newly appeared moon, and I threw back my head and yelled into the night sky as well, a feeble attempt to release the rage. And I realized in that moment that, in some deep part of myself, I had always believed that the gods would reward me for my integrity. That somehow, she would one day be mine.

But it was never to be. Merit would not be mine.

Regret, bitter as bile, rolled over me and threatened to gag me. I had not spoken my heart to her in so many years. Had she known that she still held every part of me in her delicate fingers?

The kohl around her eyes had smeared in the water. I tried to wipe it away, to leave only the fragile lines she would have painted there herself. My hands trembled at her temples.

I would not look at her disfigured hand, would not even acknowledge that such a thing had been done to her. The physicians would make it right. *Do not think of it.*

I cradled her as the night passed, knowing it was for the last time, unwilling to say good-bye.

She was as lovely in death as she had been in life, as she had been when we were all young. I traced the line of her jaw with my finger, then with hesitation and trembling I drew my face close to hers and touched her lips with my own. Gently at first, then with all the agony that ripped at my heart.

Merit. Merit, I love you. I love you.

The words pounded in my chest and kept tempo with the sobbing I could no longer restrain. The moon had risen high above us. The festival was perhaps just ending, and the partygoers would be stumbling back to their estates.

My stomach curdled at the thought of Khufu, giddy with wine, being brought to Merit's side. But there was no avoiding it. I could not keep the knowledge of her death from the king until morning.

With the taste of her still on my lips, I dragged myself to my feet, then lifted Merit's slight frame in my arms, with the gold mask and the reeds and the flower resting on her belly.

The valley temple was not far, but it would be the longest walk of my life. I turned my feet toward it, and chose to fill my mind with thoughts of happier times.

The years have changed us little, I believe. Even then, before Khufu wore the Double Crown, before we were all tainted with the secret of that day, we were much like the selves we were to become . . .

The summer heat at Saqqara often is unbearable, and the royal family has adjourned northward for a month of playful respite. The Nile flows north like the arm of a man, reaching Saqqara at the wrist, then spreading into a many-fingered triangle in its flow to the Great Sea. In the midst of this marshy triangle, there is much good hunting. And at the edge, near the herds of longhorn cattle kept on the plains for royal use, is the summer estate of Khufu's father, Sneferu.

The sun burns hot this day, and the blood in our veins even hotter. We set out from the estate amid the protests of parents.

"You disgrace yourself, my son!" Sneferu calls after Khufu, who mounts the back of a donkey as if he is a peasant slave. Khufu's mother, Hetepheres, stands beside her husband, shaking her head and clucking her disapproval.

The rest of us are also on donkeys, but it is Khufu who draws the attention. "It is not far, Father!" He laughs. "And there is no one but the marsh birds and hippos to see us!"

My own father, Neferma'at, is there, having brought his family to spend the month with his brother, the king. He spreads his hands toward me. "Hemi, speak sense to your cousin. We can rely on you for decorum."

I glance at the others of our party, restless to set out. The pretty and flirtatious sisters, Amunet and Tamit. My brother, Ahmose, and my best friend, Mentu. And Merit, who watches me with a shy but amused smile.

"We are only young for a short time, Father," I call out. "Do not consign us so quickly to the boredom of your generation!"

The rest of our group laughs with me, and I glance at Merit and straighten my shoulders. My father throws his hands into the air, as if to invoke the gods to speak to us.

"At least take a servant with you," my mother says.

I look to Khufu, who shrugs. "Then give us Ebo," he says. "At least he is not a white-haired grouch."

And so we set out for the hunt, but more for the pleasure of being young and doing as we wish. Ebo trails us, driving the donkey that bears our picnic lunch and our bows and spears.

We skirt the marshland, where the sand is firmer, keeping the swamps to our right. Tamit soon gives up on her donkey and, with much laughter and tossing of hair, climbs up on the front of Ahmose's animal and tucks herself against my brother's chest. Ahmose grins at Tamit, at Khufu, at me, and at Tamit's obstinate donkey, now left to be driven behind us by Ebo.

Amunet works to keep her donkey close to Khufu's, and it is not long before the two have taken the lead. We amble along with the leisure of youth. Tamit and Ahmose carry on a private conversation ahead of us, leaving Merit and me to walk quietly side by side, with Mentu our chaperone. The summer-green papyrus seems to wave at us as we pass, and the pale yellow sun rises in the desert-blue sky. It is as if Egypt's master artists have painted us all in blissful harmony upon a temple wall. It is the kind of day, I muse, when a man feels that life will never be better.

In many ways, I am correct.

Khufu chooses the spot where we alight, as we all knew he would. Even now, when he is but a prince of Egypt, we circle around Khufu like moons around the earth.

He has chosen a plain that inclines sharply upward from the marsh, where the ground is dry but the water near. It is only a short walk to the shelter where the boats are kept, should we decide to venture out onto the water for more serious hunting.

Tamit throws herself down onto the grass, pulling Ahmose with her. Khufu and Amunet dismount but talk with heads close together.

Behind us, Ebo will be preparing our midday meal. Merit and Mentu and I find a flat spot on the grass and talk of the weather, of the multitude of geese this year, of anything but our hearts, which are in turmoil over the gap between what is and what must be. We all know that Merit will one day be Khufu's wife. Yet out here, away from the watchful eyes of our parents, Khufu pays no attention to Merit. And I am glad of it.

Mentu pulls a flute from his donkey's pack and begins to play. The rest of us circle around him and clap, until Khufu begins a dance that has us all laughing within moments. Two of the donkeys snort behind us, and we laugh harder.

Ebo is spreading cloths on the grass, and setting out jugs of beer and platters of warm pomegranates. Khufu grabs a cloth, the rest of us still clapping a beat to Mentu's flute, and wraps it around his head in a point.

"Look, I am Pharaoh Khufu!" he calls, twirling, with one hand on his makeshift crown. "Wearer of the White Crown of Upper Egypt!" He stops and points a finger at Ahmose. "You there, bow down!" Ahmose obliges, laughing, and Khufu turns to me. "You, Hemiunu! Fetch me some beer!" Merit smiles at me and shakes her head. I grab a jug of beer from the ground and think for a moment of tossing its contents on my cousin but instead simply hand it to him with a flourish.

"Beloved of Horus," I say, "Drinker of Much Beer!"

Khufu barks a laugh, grabs the jug with one hand, Amunet with the other, and kisses the girl soundly on the mouth. She pulls away, giggling and covering her lips with her hand.

We fall to the ground where our meal is spread and dig into the food as though we have not eaten in weeks. Merit sits beside me, her arm almost touching my own. Sometimes, when she reaches for more meat or a juicy pomegranate, she brushes against me, sending needles of heat scorching through my veins. We both pretend that it has not happened, though the air between us is heavy with the unspoken.

I wear a pouch tied round my waist, and Merit asks me several times what it contains. But I refuse to tell her of the amulet I have brought as a gift to her. Not yet.

The afternoon rolls over us, and we doze and laugh in the sun as those who believe life will always be kind.

Do the gods watch us here, knowing what is to come and scoffing at our foolishness? I do not know. I only know that it is the best day of my life, this afternoon in the sun with Merit, with no inkling that it will soon become the worst.

Merit's body lay in the still dark temple where I had placed her, an alabaster goddess upon a stone table. I had sent word to the high priest, to the physicians, and lastly to Khufu.

The priest had been pulled from his bed only a stone's throw from the interior of the temple, where he resided night and day. Rashidi, the dismissed high priest of On, had come also. I did not know how he knew of the death.

Both priests, with their shaved heads glistening in the lamp-light, now shuffled around the temple, preparing a sacrifice in Merit's honor and intoning prayers to Anubis, who waited on the other side to weigh her heart against the feather of Ma'at. Thoth, the god of writing, would record her virtue from his seat on top of the balance, and the two would advise Osiris as to her worthiness to enter the afterlife.

No one was ever more worthy.

I stood beside Merit, my fingers wrapped around hers, as they had been since I laid her here. Our hands were equally icy.

The temple smelled of oil from the newly-lit lamps. I bent to fill my senses with perfume. I breathed it in and remembered.

The numbness left me and the questions began: Why Merit? Was she connected somehow to Mentu? Why had she been at the harbor? And why dressed as a peasant woman?

I looked at her closed eyes, still unable to think that I could not ask Merit herself for the answers to my questions.

The high priest was at my elbow. "Her seventy days will begin immediately," he said. "But when they are accomplished, where will she be buried? Her tomb has not yet been built."

I did not take my eyes from her face. "It will be finished. I will be sure of it." In my heart, I cursed Khufu for delaying so long in his approval of the plans for his queens' pyramids. It was as if he cared nothing for them, only for his own grand project.

I thought of my own tomb, a flat-topped mastaba that would lay just east of the queens' pyramids. It was not yet complete either, or I would lay Merit there until her tomb was finished. With a pang, I realized that Merit's tomb would stand between Khufu's and my own.

As in life, so in death.

The priests were lighting torches now. I could feel the heat at my back. I tightened my cold hand around Merit's.

The physicians arrived. But still no Khufu.

I called for the high priest. "Where is the Great One, Beloved of Horus?" I asked.

The priest lowered his head. "I have had word that he cannot be roused from his bed. The festival has taken its toll on him. His head servant waits for the wine to run its course."

I turned back to Merit, disgusted at Khufu's absence and yet grateful.

The high priest drew close and stood in silence at my side. "So you will have a bit longer with her," he said eventually.

I glanced sideways. "I stand in place of the king until he arrives."

Rashidi emerged from the shadows. "Yes, you have desired to stand beside her in his place for many years, have you not?"

I lowered my voice, turned on the little man, and spoke through clenched teeth. "Do not be so foolish as to speak in this way again. Not to me, not to anyone. Is that clear?"

Rashidi shrugged. "A priest must be truthful before the gods."

"But he is not required to speak to others of it!"

"Your anger is misplaced, Hemiunu. I warned you there would be more suffering if you did not restore the divine order. You have no one to blame but yourself."

Do you think I do not know that?

"Attend to your sacrifices, priest," I growled. "And leave me to my grief."

The three physicians that had been summoned from their beds moved about the body.

"Tell me what caused her death," I said.

The physicians eyed each other as if unsure whether it was my place to command.

"I am the grand vizier," I said, leaning over her. "Everything that happens in the Two Lands is my concern. And I intend to find out what happened to the Great Wife. Khufu would want no less!"

Ram, the chief physician, nodded. "We will look closely." He glanced at my hand, covering Merit's. "You will need to step away. To let us work."

I tightened my hand one last time. I sensed that this might be my final chance to touch her. Khufu would arrive, and it would not be . . . logical. I opened my hand finally, with regret that felt like a solid thing in my chest. And then I let her go.

The physicians moved in and bent over Merit. I stood close behind one of them, until a glare urged me backward. They examined her legs and arms, noted the bruises on her shoulders and throat with shared murmurs.

One of them took a knife from the table, and I winced. But it was only to cut away her clothing.

I willed my ka to become granite again, to create in me an unmoving piece of statuary. I was unwilling to leave her, even during this examination.

They slit her peasant dress from bottom to top and laid it open. Attention went immediately to something on her leg. I shifted to my right and saw through the physicians' shoulders that a dark cord was tied around Merit's upper thigh.

"What is it? How did it get there?" I had seen nothing like this on Mentu.

One of the men turned to me, the cord in his hand. "It would appear that she tied it there herself. An amulet. For luck, perhaps." He held the cord aloft.

From it dangled an ankh, the symbol of life, in finely-worked Nubian gold with a single violet amethyst in the center.

The strength drained from me, even as I reached for the gold piece. I took it from the physician, who seemed more interested in the body. I stepped away, the jewelry in my palm. With closed eyes, I squeezed my fingers around the ankh and pressed my fist to my mouth. I felt the pain of loss sweep through my body once more, threatening to overwhelm my reserve. Khufu could arrive at any moment. It would not do for the king to see me floundering in grief.

My amulet. She still possessed it, after all these years. Wore it privately, where it would not be seen, as if in silent tribute to secret love.

The knowledge was both a sharp knife and a healing balm.

She knew. She knew I loved her still.

I forced my fingers open and tilted the ankh to catch the firelight. Impulsively I took the ends of the cord in my fingers, lifted them to my own neck, and tied it there around my throat. The symbol lay on my chest, just above my heart.

And that is where it will remain.

I turned back to the physicians and found that they were pulling the fragments of Merit's dress from under her body. Two of them turned her on her side to release the fabric, and two others exclaimed surprise.

I peered around them. "What is it?"

One pointed to Merit's mouth. "She expels water when we turn her."

My heartbeat slowed to a dull thud. "Drowned?"

The physician concurred with a bowed head.

A shouted curse outside the temple turned us all toward the entrance.

Khufu has arrived.

The king rushed into the temple, head bare, stripped of jewelry, and only an undergarment around his waist. I saw in him my childhood friend in that moment, and I wondered at how much everything had changed.

Khufu skidded to a stop and his eyes roamed the firelit temple interior, taking in the priests, the physicians, Merit's body, and finally me.

A scream borne of grief and rage, which I understood, tore from his throat.

And then he rushed at me, hands flexed like claws, with all the madness of a rabid beast.

EIGHT

I watched him come, felt my cousin's fingers tighten around my neck. Khufu's breath stank of alcohol. I swayed on my feet. It required effort to breathe. Self-protection took over, and I dug at Khufu's fingers.

"Stop," I rasped from my clogged throat.

"You killed her!" Khufu's grip weakened. I tore the king's hands away. It was not overly difficult; the man had done no real work in years.

Khufu backed away. He panted with exertion and his eyes blazed, the whites shot with red. "You killed her." The words were breathed out with fierce hostility.

I rubbed at my throat. "How can you even say—"

"You may not have struck the blow," Khufu yelled. "But it is your fault. I relied on you for her protection!"

"Yes." I pulled away from Merit's body, toward the darkened temple entrance. It did not seem fitting to argue so close to her. "Yes," I said again, my voice low and accusatory, "it has always fallen to me to protect her."

Khufu turned on me, his fingers curling to fists at his sides. "Say what you are thinking, then, Hemiunu!"

I lifted my chin.

"Say it!"

Khufu met my silence with two quick steps across the temple and a fist to my jaw. The blow took me down. I lay under the lintel of the temple and stared at the glyphs carved and painted on its underside.

Khufu jumped astride my body. He had grown heavier since we were boys. I did not return the blows that fell on me, each one fanning a flaming torch behind my eyes.

I should have protected her. She was my responsibility. I tasted the salt of my own tears. The temple walls grew dim. Would I soon join Merit? I welcomed the thought.

Blackness fell. And just as quickly, light again.

Khufu no longer straddled me. He struggled in the grasp of Ebo, his head servant, who must have heard the chaos from outside the temple. Khufu jerked his arms from Ebo's grasp, hissed a curse at me, and retreated to Merit's body.

I crawled to my knees, then my feet, and joined my cousin at the physician's table. My jaw throbbed and my legs shook.

The smell of death was somehow there already. Perhaps it followed in the wake of the physicians.

"Forgive me," Khufu whispered, already penitent. "My mind . . . is not clear. I cannot—"

"I know."

Khufu bent over Merit's body and studied her face. His breath came quick and uneven. He lifted her arm, slid his hand down to hers, then cried out when he saw her mutilated hand.

"She is not whole!"

I pulled Merit's hand from his and placed it at her side. "They will attend to her," I said.

Khufu stared at me. "Like Mentu," he whispered. "Like Mentu."

"Yes." I swallowed and rubbed my jaw. "There was also a mask." I pointed to where it lay at her feet.

Khufu's gaze traveled to the mask, then back to me. "Who?"

"I do not know."

The king touched Merit's lips. "There is some mistake, Hemi. She is not dead. Only sleeping." His pleading voice twisted my heart.

"No. She is dead."

Khufu pounded a fist on the table at Merit's head. "It cannot be! I am Son of Ra! Beloved of Horus! I will not allow it!"

I said nothing.

Khufu turned on me. "I will not allow it, Hemi!"

"There are some things that even Ra on earth cannot change."

"No! No, no, no!" Khufu grabbed at Merit's shoulders and shook her as if to wake her.

I pulled the king's hands from her body, pulled him away from the table, across and out of the temple, to the cool silence of the desert night. Khufu went for my throat again, then threw his arms around my neck and sobbed. The sound echoed across the harbor, across the desert.

"I loved her, Hemi. You know that, don't you?"

"Yes." I wrapped an arm around Khufu's well-built shoulder. "I know."

Khufu did not lift his head. "I may not have loved her so well as some, but in my own way, I did love her."

I pulled away, wiped at my own cheeks. We stood there in the darkness, facing each other and for the first time, facing the truth.

"She was a true wife to you, Khufu. Always."

Khufu studied the dark water in the harbor below us. "I sometimes wondered if she would end it. If you both would . . . betray me."

I said nothing, shocked into silence by his brutal honesty.

Khufu walked toward the harbor, as if to escape the horror inside the temple. I followed.

He spoke without taking his eyes from the water. "When the years went by, and still she stayed, I would sometimes tell myself that things had changed." He glanced at me. "But then one look at the two of you, when you thought no one was watching, and I knew that I was a fool."

I felt the weight of his silence, knew I should speak. "I am so sorry, Khufu. We never—"

"I know. I watched. You were both always loyal. To Egypt and to me."

We reached the harbor's edge and Khufu dropped to his knees, as though his strength had finally failed. "Sometimes I think I made you my vizier simply to test you both," he said. "To see if you could remain near to one another, yet still faithful."

I looked down on the king in his sorrow. "I loved her, my friend. You know that. But we both loved you as well." I joined Khufu on my knees.

Pharaoh sobbed again, covering his face with his hands. "I do not know how to rule without her, Hemi. She knew more of what it means to be a god than either of us ever will."

Khufu's grief quieted and we sat in silence for awhile, studying the play of starlight on water.

And then slowly, the king lifted a handful of dirt from beside him and looked at me.

I knew his intent, the age-old ritual of grief.

I repeated Khufu's actions and filled my own hand with dirt. I held my fist closed and bent my head toward Khufu. I waited through his hesitation. Then the king opened his hand over my head and let the dirt tumble over me. My tears fell to the ground at my knees and mixed with the falling dirt. I did the same for Khufu, pouring the soil over his bent head. We then embraced, and in our grief we were joined, as though we buried each other beside the harbor where Merit had died.

I slept with thoughts of Merit biting at me like vicious ants. I roused myself well past daybreak, accomplished each of my morning rituals and knelt before my shrine of the goddess Ma'at to pray and light incense, begging the goddess's favor. Then I left my residence for the Great House, staff in hand.

I had only one thing in mind: to obtain Pharaoh's official sanction on my efforts to bring Merit's killer to justice.

Khufu had sent me home in the early morning hours, borne in the king's own litter by twelve slaves. I was too exhausted to argue, and Khufu wanted to be alone with his wife.

The Great Hall of Pillars had been cleared of last night's celebration already and was empty, save one, when I entered.

Khufu sat on his throne, head in hands. The red-and-white-striped nemes had fallen forward around his face, shrouding him from any who happened by. He still wore a white dressing robe loosely around his shoulders, and I suspected he had neither bathed nor offered sacrifices this morning.

I strode across the hall, letting my footfalls rouse the king.

Khufu looked up briefly, then let his head fall again.

"I've sent them all away, Hemi."

"Who?"

"The treasurer. The superintendent of clothing. The overseer of the storehouses. All the others who want my attention. I have nothing for any of them."

"Pharaoh is grieving. They must understand."

"Do they? How can they understand when I do not?"

I looked to the high-backed chair beside Khufu's throne, often occupied by Merit, and said nothing.

"You must finish her pyramid, Hemi."

"Yes, my king. Your people will devote themselves to making it ready. It will be done in time."

Khufu's eyes found mine. "It cannot delay the building of my own, however."

Of course not.

I ran my fingers over the length of my staff.

"Hemi, you must promise me that the deaths of Mentu and Merit will do nothing to cause the project to falter."

"The work continues," I said, my voice tight. "But I believe that nothing in Egypt will be as it should until these deaths are resolved. I swear to you, Khufu, I will find who did this."

"No!" Khufu stood. His robe fell from one shoulder. "The pyramid must be your only focus."

I frowned. "Surely you want justice to be restored?"

Khufu began a reply, but the sound of a crowd entering the palace cut him off. Behind us, a swarm of men, priests it appeared, tramped into the Great Hall like an army crossing the desert.

They brought with them the smell of burnt offerings, filling the room with the odor of sacrifice.

Khufu scowled. "You approach the Son of Ra without permission?"

An old priest emerged from the crowd. I recognized him as the former high priest of On, recently replaced. He had not shaved his head for some days, sprinkling of white on his dark skin. He still wore the priestly skirt and belt, and a leopard skin over his shoulders, the head hanging down his back. "So you still claim sonship with the god?" he said.

My blood pounded in response to this shocking disrespect. I stepped to the platform where Khufu stood, knowing the king would prefer me at his side.

Khufu sat and lifted the crook and flail, symbols of his Ra-given authority, and crossed them over his chest. "You have come to complain about your recent dismissal," he said. "Take your complaints to the gods."

The priest shrugged. "You have made yourself Ra on earth. Why should we not complain to you?"

I stepped forward. "You dishonor the king by bringing this rabble of malcontents into the Great Hall."

The old priest raised his voice. "And the king has caused the death of a much-loved queen with his heresy!"

I heard Khufu's quick intake of breath and turned to him. He clenched the lion-head arms of his throne. "You blame the Beloved of Horus for the death of the queen?" he said. "You prove yourselves more inept than I had thought!"

The room erupted with outrage, like a herd of angry cows bellowing their disapproval. I moved closer to the king and leaned my staff across him like a shield.

Where are the palace guards?

The High Priest would not be silenced. "You have defied the gods!" he declared, his finger pointed in accusation. "In pride and arrogance you have stolen the worship of Ra from its rightful place in On. You have brought it here to Giza solely to control and manipulate the rites." Spittle flew from his lips. "But the gods will not be controlled!"

Khufu waited for the ensuing buzz to settle, then lifted his voice above the priests. It was smooth and even, the voice of a monarch. Or a god. "You were given land and wealth, each of you. I was not required to act with such kindness. I am Ra on earth, and I do as I please."

The high priest shook a fist at Khufu. "Then why have the gods punished you by taking the Great Wife from you with violence?"

I could remain quiet no longer. I stepped in front of Khufu and raised my staff over their heads. "Get out! All of you! You dishonor yourselves and the gods you serve with your insane accusations! The queen has died at the hands of a human evil. If the gods are truly worthy of our devotion, they do not deal with man as you would have us believe!"

The high priest moved toward the throne, but I met him halfway with my staff held aloft like a club. The priest's eyes were cold with hatred, but he stopped.

"You will not be rid of us so easily," he hissed. His glance went to Khufu. "We will be heard!"

"Not today," I said, with a flourish of my staff. "Get out!"

They backed away in clusters, the high priest the last to turn and stalk out of the Great Hall. When he was gone, I lowered my staff and turned to Khufu, my chest tight with anger.

The king had regained his throne and sat stoop-shouldered, eyes closed. He looked both small, like the young boy I remembered, and old, like his father who had many years ago gone to the west.

"They will calm down in time," I said. "But there is something you must learn from this incident."

Khufu rested his forehead on the heel of his hand. "What must I learn, Hemi?"

"The people will be just as quick to assign reasons for Merit's death. And Mentu's. You must reassure them of ma'at, of justice and order, or they will lose heart. And they will lose respect."

Khufu straightened. "You speak out of your own grief, hoping to neglect your duties to chase the unknown in hopes of revenge."

"Revenge is undertaken by men who would repay in kind the evil done to them."

The king raised his eyebrows. "Exactly."

"But justice is the restoration of divine order," I said. "It requires the guilty to pay because they have transgressed the divine order, not because they have caused hurt to a single person."

Khufu sighed. "I do not want to argue such things with you, Hemi."

Then allow me to do what I must. "I will admit to you, my king, that in my heart, I desire revenge. But revenge for the deaths of those I loved will be accomplished by restoring ma'at. And this is what is best for Egypt."

"But the pyramid—"

"Without ma'at, we have nothing."

Khufu closed his eyes again and stretched the muscles of his neck. "And you believe that you hold the power to restore order and find the truth?"

The question stayed with me after the king had dismissed me with a grudging permission to investigate the two murders. The question followed me to the rooftop of the palace where I escaped to my own thoughts. I stood at the edge of the rooftop and gripped the low wall. Before me, the royal estate was an oasis in the desert.

Revenge. Justice. I had not thought of the difference until I articulated it to Khufu, but now it seemed a truth to me. It was justice I sought, justice I believed in with every part of my being. The goddess Ma'at, in whose name I ordered my life, demanded it.

I looked northward across the desert to the pyramid. It accused me, as though I were a negligent father more interested in children who were not my own. On the distant southern horizon, several other pyramids poked up from the desert, mute reminders of the greatness of Khufu's father, Sneferu, and my father, Grand Vizier Neferma'at, who had built the Saqqara pyramids together. I had vowed to Khufu five years ago that our pyramid would be the greatest the world had seen.

Was I willing to risk that? And for what? To ask questions that may have no answers. I dropped my gaze to study my hands on the wall.

I had carefully structured my world to avoid such questions. In my heart, I feared the unknowable. I much preferred my charts and equations.

From the palace rooftop, one could see clearly in every direction. And I saw my choice clearly in that moment as well. To restore the justice and divine order I believed most sacred, I must face my fear of the unknown and perhaps the unknowable.

The wind carried sand across the desert in the distance and released fragrance from the chamomile in the garden below me. The scent reminded me of Merit, and I knew my decision was made.

No matter the cost, I would find justice for Mentu and for Merit. I would restore the divine order, the ma'at of Egypt. I would find this murderer.

And I would make him pay.

NINE

The embalmer's hall, the Place of Purification, jutted from the valley temple like a broken finger—attached but at odds with the beauty of the temple. I entered and paused inside the entrance to accustom myself to the smell. The task would not be an easy one.

The room was small, with hard lines and sharp angles, only large enough for preparations on one body at a time, though ancillary rooms held vats of *natron* salt for the required days of purification. Paintings of Anubis weighing the heart after death, and tending the body in the presence of Isis, decorated the interior wall.

I pushed inward and greeted the physician-priest with a quick nod. The priest was unknown to me, yet he apparently recognized me. He straightened from his work over a body and set his instruments on the table.

"Grand Vizier," he said, grim faced, "how can I serve you?"

"I have come to examine the body of Mentu-hotep."

"Examine?" The priest's bushy eyebrows drew together.

"I am looking for anything that might point to his murderer."

The priest shook his head. "I do not believe I can help you."

"You are new to Giza?" I asked. "From Memphis?"

"Yes, my lord. I am Urshé. I understand that I owe the honor of my position to you."

"It is Pharaoh who has moved the center of worship from On."

The priest lowered his head. "Yes, of course."

I gestured to the body. "May I?"

Urshé extended a hand. "You are familiar with the process?"

"I have not seen the early work of the priests, only the end product," I said, thinking of the black-resin-wrapped body of my mother, years ago. I drew in a breath and faced the body, reminding myself that the ka of my friend had departed already. The body was simply flesh and organs, waiting to be reawakened.

Mentu's body looked much the same, though in the intervening days it had begun to decompose, as evidenced by the stench. I paused and swallowed.

Urshé handed me a small cloth. "Put it to your nose."

I inhaled the spice-laden cloth with gratitude.

Urshé waved me closer, to stand beside the embalming table which, if not for its gruesome purpose, would have been a beautiful piece. Two white calcite lions stood conjoined, their determined faces looking west, with a smooth top resting on their backs. At the base, surrounded by the lions' tails, a deep bowl had been carved into the table. The tabletop slanted slightly toward the bowl.

Urshé noticed my glance at the bowl. "The body must move into the afterlife completely intact."

I nodded.

He said, "The bowl collects the blood and bodily fluids as we remove the organs."

I breathed through my mouth and brought my gaze back to Mentu's face.

"Today is the fourth day since his ka departed," Urshé said. "So today we begin the extraction." He held up a small bowl and a narrow bronze instrument with a hook at one end. "I have already removed the brain through the nasal cavity. It is of no consequence and so is the only part of the body that can be discarded."

I bent over the body, spiced cloth still at my nose, to more closely examine the throat. I tried to see the wound without noticing the blood, which was impossible. "What can you tell me about the cut here?" I asked.

Urshé scratched his head. "Not much. It was made with a sharp knife, such as is used for slaughtering sacrificial animals. The cut was quick and decisive. There are no superficial wounds around it, only the single death stroke."

"Can you tell me if his attacker was taller than he? Shorter?"

"I am afraid that is beyond my expertise." Urshé left the table and returned with two alabaster canopic jars, one with the carved head of a man and the other a baboon. "For the stomach and intestines," he said. "I will begin extracting the organs now. Please ask any questions you have as I work."

I focused on Mentu's upper body. The blood at his neck had crusted by now and seemed less gruesome than the cavity Urshé opened with his black flint razor.

"Any other markings on him? Bruises?"

"Not that I observed."

"Hmmm."

"This means something to you?" Urshé said.

I took a spice-laden breath. "Perhaps. It would seem he did not struggle with his killer. So either the killer was known to Mentu, or the attack was so unexpected there was no time."

The priest focused on widening the body cavity. A steady dripping sound began at the base of the table as the bowl collected fluid. I regretted the breakfast of garlic and leeks I had eaten before coming. I searched for a safe place to focus my gaze, but my eyes fell on the priest's white skirt, spattered with blood and gore.

I was aware of Urshé lifting things from the body with forceps and placing them into the two jars.

I bent over Mentu's hand. "The finger," I said, swallowing and blinking rapidly.

"Yes?" The priest moved away and returned with two more jars, with heads of a jackal and a falcon. "Liver and lungs," he said, with the delight of a teacher who enjoyed his work.

"Cut with the same knife, do you think?"

"Impossible to say. But some type of knife, yes." He watched me through the narrowed eyes of a physician diagnosing. "The finger will be replaced," he said slowly. "It will not be difficult. He will be whole."

I nodded.

A gold disc, engraved with the wadjet eye, lay on the table near Mentu's head. The wadjet eye and eyebrow were painted in green, with the swoop underneath in black. "What is this?" I asked, grateful for the distraction.

"After the organs are removed, the body cavity will be rinsed with palm wine. Then consecrated oil, pounded myrrh, and other fragrant plants will be packed into it. When it is stitched closed, the wadjet eye will be placed upon it, to declare the body intact."

"And then the seventy days?"

The priest smiled. "Your friend will be well cared for, Grand Vizier. All the incantations will be spoken over the body as it purifies in natron."

"I have no doubt you will be thorough, Urshé. Thank you."

Urshé brought his razor back to Mentu's chest and lengthened the incision across the sternum.

I wrapped my arms around myself and noted the cold dampness of my bare chest. The lightheadedness I had kept at bay thus far would not be put off. I searched for something to count or straighten. Why had I not brought my staff?

When Urshé reached into Mentu's chest and pulled out his heart, a black shroud fell over my eyes, and the Place of Purification turned on its side.

I awoke to the jackal-headed god Anubis leaning over me, peering into my soul.

I have crossed to the west myself.

"Grand Vizier?"

It seemed strange that Anubis would call me by my title. Strange, also, that Anubis's head was crafted of clay.

And then the head lifted from its shoulders, and the face of Urshé the priest appeared. "Did my mask startle you?" he said. "It is worn for the final steps of the preparation, to invoke the god's blessing."

I realized that I lay on the temple floor, and I propped myself up on my elbows. "What happened?"

"The smells often cause a certain faintness," the priest said. "No reason to feel shame."

I had fainted. I clambered to my feet.

"Slowly, my lord. There is no rush."

"I am fine." I brushed imaginary dust from my clothing. "Fine."

Urshé held my arm lightly, as if to steady me. "I am afraid I have not been of much help to you."

"You are a faithful servant of Egypt, Urshé. Thank you." I eyed the clay mask in his hand. "Where is the mask that was found on Mentu's body?"

Urshé pointed to the corner of the hall, where the gold piece lay on a table with other instruments.

I retrieved the mask and studied it. "I will take this," I said.

"As you wish."

The priest pushed the spiced cloth into my hand once more before I left. "Take it with you, " he said. "The smell often lingers."

I nodded my thanks and escaped the embalmer's hall into the windswept air. I was not sure I could perform the same examination on Merit. Not much had been learned anyway.

But this mask. And the other . . .

I inhaled and cleared my lungs.

Somewhere in the Two Lands was a talented artist who had fashioned two beautiful death masks. An artist who was either a killer himself, or had met the killer.

It was a place to begin.

It was unavoidable. I had to address concerns at the pyramid. Senosiris had undertaken his position as Mentu's replacement, but he could not be expected to fill the role without any instruction.

I spent the afternoon at the base of the pyramid, making certain that the hordes of men dragging quarried stone up the ramps were being overseen properly. Their rhythmic chants, keeping time with their feet, tightened my muscles and made me anxious to escape. My usually well-ordered days had become a jumble of questions and fears, further evidence that ma'at had been forsaken.

"Go," Senosiris finally said.

I shielded my eyes from sun and peered up at the project. "Where?"

"Wherever it is that you've been itching to run since you arrived."

I gave the older man a half smile. "I apologize. You have my full attention."

Sen shook his head. "Don't need it. We're on track here. You go."

I gave a last glance at the ramps, then slapped Sen on the arm and left the work site.

I'd hidden Mentu's mask in a small tent I used as my base during the workday. I retrieved it, secured it in a leather pouch over my shoulder, and left for the workmen's village on foot as usual, my staff in hand.

Twice on the way to town, I looked back at the pyramid in progress, as though by the force of my unwavering attention I could maintain order there and force the angles ever upward to meet in the precise center.

At the village entrance I pushed through a noisy line of young boys and women bartering for and offering baskets of breads and fruit and tanned animals skins. Not so many men milled about the village today, I noted with grim satisfaction. Already Sen was proving his worth. I strode toward the southern end of town, where lay my best chance of gaining information.

"Grand Vizier!" A small child hailed me as I moved through the town. The child's mother held a water pot in one arm and pulled the boy back from the street with a shy smile. I lifted a hand in greeting but would not be distracted from my task.

The mask is all I have.

I had brought the best of the Memphis school of artists to work on the pyramid. Sculptors, carpenters, goldsmiths, painters. They were all housed at the southern end of the village and worked in commissioned shops, where they were closely watched by government guards who protected the precious materials from looters and made certain none of the artists helped themselves to government supplies. It was to one of these workshops I now walked, looking for a particular artist.

I stepped out of the sunlight, into the dusty shop, and let my eyes adjust. Sculptures in various stages of completion cluttered the front room, which was empty of people. A small fire burned in a wall shrine to Ptah, god of craftsmen. I could hear conversation from the room in the back. I leaned my staff against the wall.

"Donkor?" I called.

"Donkor is here, for anyone who seeks him," came the reply, in a high, clear voice. I rolled my eyes and joined Donkor in the back room, which was filled with the sounds of tiny tools chiseling fine details out of stone.

"Grand Vizier!" Donkor stepped from behind a large block of limestone and clapped his hands together, releasing a puff of dust. "It is a most propitious day for me!"

Artists were valued for the skill at reproducing the official art of the Two Lands. Creativity was not a requirement. But Donkor seemed to be bursting with it, and his workspace screamed with color and exotic sculptures that would never be purchased by any Egyptian with self-respect.

Two other sculptors worked in the room, both dressed in customary white skirts. Donkor wore red and yellow, with a large belt draped low on his hips and a full wig framing his face.

"Donkor," I said in a low voice, "I've come to speak to you about something."

Donkor sidled forward and brushed limestone dust from his forearms. "If it's about your tomb sculpture, you are just going to have to be patient, I'm afraid. I am simply not ready yet. Not ready at all—"

"It's not about my tomb sculpture." I eyed a piece in the corner, a bust of a woman draped with a piece of yellow-dyed linen.

Donkor followed my gaze. "Oh no, you cannot have that piece! To take it from me would break my very heart!"

I snorted. "I have no interest in that piece. I was only wondering if that is the sort of work I can expect in my sculptures."

Donkor laughed and tapped my arm with his fingertips. "Oh, don't pretend that you are not hoping for something just as creative, Vizier. I knew it the moment I met you. Nothing ordinary for you." He grinned slyly. "And I know that is why you commissioned me as your private tomb sculptor."

I shrugged.

"But we are in no hurry, my lord, are we? You have many years to serve Egypt yet before your journey west. You will see. We will create something grand for you, for the grand vizier!" He laughed at his little joke, another high-pitched sound that scraped across the nerves.

I looked over my shoulder to ensure the two other sculptors were busy at their work, and I pulled the strap of my pouch over my neck. "I have something I'd like you to see."

Donkor clapped his hands together. "A gift?"

"No. I need your help."

"Donkor is always glad to help."

I pulled the mask from the pouch, and Donkor gasped. He wiggled his fingers, eager to take it from me.

"Exquisite! Who crafted it?"

I gritted my teeth. "That is what I've come to ask you."

Donkor's brows furrowed. "You don't know? Where did you get it?"

"Not important. But I need to know who created it."

Donkor turned the piece over and ran his fingers over the smooth gold. He drew it closer to his face and examined the markings on the underside, then frowned up at me. "Anubis?"

I looked again at the god's symbol engraved on the back of the mask. "I don't know what it means."

"There is no other artist's mark."

"I was hoping you'd be able to tell me something from the design."

Donkor tapped his bottom lip with a fingertip. "I can think of several talented gold workers in the village. I suppose one of them could have done it, but I couldn't be certain."

"You haven't heard talk of privately commissioned death masks?"

"Masks? There are more than one?"

The two other sculptors had laid aside their tools now and skulked closer to the conversation. I watched them from the corner of my eye.

"I cannot say more."

Donkor winked. "A mystery, eh?"

One of the other sculptors took a step closer. "The queen's death," he said.

I snatched the mask from Donkor and whirled on the man, tension building in my neck. "What do you know about it?"

He retreated. "I know nothing! I only thought—"

"What?"

Both men reacquired their tools and became suddenly engrossed in their work.

I returned my attention to Donkor, who smiled his amusement. "It would seem that our little community knows some of the gossip, but not the gossip you seek."

I replaced the mask in my pouch, steadying my hands. "Who are these gold workers you spoke of?"

Donkor bit his lip. "I know of only three who do work this fine." He gave me their names, then smiled. "Now I must ask you a question. This sculpture we will create of you for your tomb," he eyed me up and down, "do you want it to be realistic, or shall I make it a bit prettier?"

"What do you mean by that?"

Donkor arched an eyebrow. "Hmm. Nothing. Nothing at all."

I frowned. "Just give me the usual likeness. None of your fanciness."

"Yes, my lord." Donkor gave a little salute. "You will be immortal, Grand Vizier Hemiunu, man of justice and mercy."

I escaped the back room of the shop, limestone dust chalky on my tongue.

Justice and mercy. Donkor spoke of the hands of my sculpted likeness, which would be fashioned with the closed fist of justice and the open palm of mercy. But today I was interested only in justice.

I retrieved my staff and left. Outside the shop, a woman herded several small children past me. Behind me, I heard Donkor squeal, "My children! Come to see your father work!" Despite my bleak errand, I laughed.

It took only a few minutes to cross through several tight alleys and reach the wider street that housed the goldsmithing shops. I called into one of them and asked for the first artist Donkor had named.

A young woman, sweating over a furnace where she worked to refine a small pot of gold, looked up. "Down there." She pointed vaguely east.

I continued down the street, asked a few more questions, until I stood in the shop of a burly goldsmith hammering a sheet flat. His thick fingers would have seemed to render him incapable of fine artwork.

"Badru?"

The man did not look up. "Who's asking?"

"I was told you might be the man I seek."

Badru looked up, recognized me, and straightened sharply before bowing his head. "How can I help you, my lord?"

I pulled out the mask. Badru took it in his hands and flipped it immediately to look for an artist's mark. My hope flagged. He would not look for a mark if he were the artist.

"I am looking for the man who created it."

"Why?"

I gazed around the shop slowly. "It's fine work. I would like him to do something similar for me."

Badru handed the mask back and retrieved his hammer. "I cannot help you."

I moved to stand beside Badru. "Tell me what you know."

Badru pounded his gold again. "It is best you look for someone else to do your work."

"Badru. Please do not forget to whom you speak."

Badru growled, a low angry sound, and tossed his hammer to the worktable. "I know who made your mask," he said. "The eyes give it away. His special feature."

"Who is he? Where can I find him?"

Badru folded his massive arms across his chest and stared down at me.

"He's dead."

TEN

D ead? When?"
Badru rubbed his fingertips along his gold piece, search-
ing for imperfections. "The last new moon, I believe."
"He was murdered?"
He looked up. "Why would you ask that?"
I replaced the mask in my pouch. "How did he die?"
"Fire. The refining furnace in his shop. His brother found
him."
"Where can I find this brother?"
Badru offered me the gold sheet. "His brother will not be able
to make a piece like that. If you're in need of a gold worker, I—"
I held up a hand. "Just the brother."
"Could be anywhere." Badru seemed to lose interest in me.
"Paki. Ask around."
I stared him down for a moment, considered his disrespect,
then turned to the shop doorway. I had more important matters to
attend. "Thank you for the information."
Badru grunted.

The street had filled while I spoke to Badru. A large group swarmed toward me, heading somewhere together. I stepped aside, back against the shop opposite Badru's, to let them pass. And then I realized they were headed for me.

"Grand Vizier!" the shouts came from several places in the group.

"Who sent the Great Wife to the west?"

"Was it one of us?"

"Why do you seek an artist?"

I pulled myself back against the wall and swung the pouch behind me. "I am looking for Paki, brother of a gold worker," I said to anyone who would hear me.

"Is he the killer?" someone called.

"Is he the Scourge of Anubis?" another yelled.

I rubbed the back of my neck. *Gossip blows across the plateau like sand.*

I scanned the mob and spotted Donkor standing at the edge. The sculptor blinked several times, shrugged his narrow shoulders, and raised his palms with a smile that said he loved gossip as much as his coworkers.

The press of sweating bodies grew tighter, until their faces blurred. I took a deep breath and shoved through the crowd. The artist community tugged at me as I passed, still firing questions like tiny arrows that pricked my skin.

"Is it true she was wearing the death mask? Why does Anubis avenge himself upon the royal house? Will Pharaoh protect us?"

One hand reached out from the swarm behind me and dug bony fingers into my bare shoulder, just below my ear. I spun to avoid the touch and faced a dried-up old man. Most of his teeth had gone to the west without him, and those that remained were as blackened as those of an aged mummy. He pushed up close to my face and lisped out a few strange words.

"We knew it was her, even dressed as one of us."

The angry hum continued to swirl around us, but my attention focused on this one old man. I stared down into the filmy eyes. "Whom did you know?"

The man gave me a rotted smile. "The Great Wife. Whenever she came."

"You saw her here, in the village?" My fingers clutched at the pouch I wore.

The old man's attention wandered to the shouting crowd around us. I pinched his arm and he glared at me.

"Here. In the village. She came many times, dressed in peasant garb, as though no one would know her." He shook his head in amusement. "A queen is a queen, no matter the dress." He straightened his shoulders. "She carried herself different, you understand?"

"Why was she here?"

Another man twisted through the crowd to where we stood. "You are asking about my brother, the goldsmith?" Paki was younger than I, with a chest as broad as a grown ox.

I grunted. "Stay here," I said to the old man.

"What do you know about his death?" I asked the brother, turning him away from the crowd.

"A fire. We were surprised. He was always careful. But it was nothing more."

I leaned in to speak into only the brother's ear, though I knew my words would be repeated throughout the village within the hour. "And did he speak of two death masks he had been privately commissioned to create?"

Paki rubbed his chin. "He often worked at night on things he did not let the family see. But I don't know of any masks."

I nodded my thanks, then turned to find the old man. Thankfully, he had not disappeared into the crowd. On the contrary, he stepped up to me eagerly, waiting his turn for fame.

"Why was she here?" I repeated. "Did she ever meet with an artist?"

The man made a few unsuccessful attempts to bite his lip, then wrinkled his nose. "Don't think so. Never saw that."

I gripped the man's shoulder. "What *did* you see, man?"

His eyes wandered again, and I resisted the urge to slap him. But this time, his eyes focused on the edge of the crowd. "If you want to know why the queen came here to the village, you should ask the People of the One."

"What people? What one?"

He raised a withered arm and pointed.

I followed the bony finger through the group of people, to where one woman stood apart, watching, like a goddess too sacred to join the ranks of men.

"Ask her," he said.

Neferet?

I squinted at the man again, to be sure. The old man grinned and slipped away.

I jostled through the herd, clutching the pouch close to my body. The press of people followed me, a jumbled, disorderly horde that rubbed at my senses and tightened my shoulders. Finally I turned to face them.

"I have nothing for you," I shouted. "No answers, no information. If I have need of you, or if there is any reason for you to be concerned, you will be sought out. Until then, go back to your business!" I glared for a few moments, until they began to disperse. Murmurs and sandals crunching over gravel filled the street and finally moved away.

I straightened my belt and turned to Sen's daughter, Neferet. She wore a filmy dress of white today, the fabric thin enough to see through to the skirt underneath. She smiled.

"You knew the Great Wife?" I asked.

Neferet's smile faded. "She was a lovely woman."

"I don't understand. The old man said—who are these People of the One?"

Neferet's gaze left my face and focused on something over my shoulder. I exhaled my impatience and turned on the interruption. "Ahmose. What are you doing here?"

My brother's face was devoid of its customary grin as he strode toward us. "I have been searching for you."

"What is it?" My stomach clenched, sensing more devastating news.

"It is father. He does not have long. He asks for you."

I searched out Neferet's eyes, hesitated a moment, then joined my brother. "I will come." To Neferet, I said, "I will return to see you later. Please do not speak of this to any other."

She grabbed my fingers and squeezed. "I will say a prayer for your father." Her slight smile seemed to flow right into me, and I found myself returning the pressure of her fingers.

"Thank you," I said.

I hurried to join Ahmose, who was already moving down the street. He spoke without turning. "I am sorry to take you away from your business. Thinking of acquiring a concubine, are you?"

"When did Father's condition change?"

Ahmose did not slow. "He has been declining for several weeks, which you could not know, of course, since you have not seen him since before akhet began."

I trudged beside my older brother toward the mouth of the village, where donkeys or slaves would take us to the royal estate and my father's quarters.

Here in Ahmose's shadow I was not grand vizier. I was not the restorer of ma'at. I was only Hemi, a man who was losing everyone in the world who meant anything to him.

ELEVEN

Ahmose had brought two sedan chairs. He must have anticipated that his brother would be on foot. No doubt he thought my habit of walking most places to be beneath the title I bore. We each climbed into a chair, and the dozen slaves lifted us as one onto their shoulders.

"Father has changed much in the past few weeks," Ahmose said, across the sandy path. "You will be surprised."

I settled back into the cushion of the wooden chair. "Is he in pain?"

"Some. He bears it well. At times his mind wanders, and then he usually speaks of Mother. About seeing her again in the west."

"I cannot imagine them both gone." I ran a finger along the gilded edge of the chair. It was an expensive piece. Ahmose had done well, despite his constant innuendos about being cheated out of the position he expected to receive as eldest son.

My brother snorted in derision. "I cannot see that it will make any difference to you. You will go on with your important work, just as always. He is not so much a part of your life that you will miss him."

I tapped my hand on my thigh, in time with the slaves' measured steps toward the royal estate. *Do you not know that everything I build, I build for him, Ahmose?* Aloud, I said, "You have been an attentive son. I am glad Father has had you at his side."

Ahmose looked away. "It matters not. You are the one he—"

"Yes?"

"Nothing."

We moved forward with only the sound of the slaves' feet, until Ahmose spoke again. "He speaks of you more than of anyone. It is always, 'Have you seen the project today, Ahmose? Have they reached the tenth course yet? The twentieth?' He follows your progress as if he were still grand vizier himself."

"His work at Saqqara will outlive him to eternity. He was a great builder."

"Yes. And it is Hemi who has taken the throne of his father."

I sat upright. Ahmose had set his face to the road ahead. "You blame me, I know. But it was not my decision. And I have studied much and worked hard to be worthy of the role Egypt has given me."

"Yes, given you. Despite the man that you are."

I deflated back into the chair again. *Not now, Ahmose. Not when I am facing yet another loss.* My brother's cruelty remained a mystery to me. To everyone else, Ahmose was a loving and pleasant man. Had his jealousy truly poisoned all brotherly feelings?

I leaned my head against the back of the chair and closed my eyes. The almond oil, rubbed into the poles to make them smooth on the shoulder of the slaves, wafted up to me and reminded me of the embalmer's hall. I opened my eyes to break the connection, but the blue jewels inlaid in the gilded sedan chair winked up at me like the eyes of Merit's golden death mask.

Everywhere, death. Always death.

It was beyond bearing. And yet I must bear it.

We reached the royal estate and were carried directly to Neferma'at's home, a large building with steps outside running up to the rooftop garden. A slave waited a few steps inside, and he spoke to Ahmose in low tones, updating him on our father's condition. He led us to our father's chamber, which had been darkened to already resemble a tomb. While Ahmose poured a libation to the figure of Thoth, god of wisdom and patron of architects and builders, I stepped around the square bathing pool set into the floor. In the center of the room, Neferma'at lay on his great bed, a shrunken shadow of the man that he was, with eyes and cheeks so deep set he seemed only a skull.

Despite Ahmose's warning, I cried out.

Neferma'at opened his eyes and turned his head slightly. "Is this my Hemiunu?" he asked in his gravelly voice. "Has he come at last?"

"I am here, Father." I rushed to the bedside, afraid each breath that lifted his bony chest might be the last. "I am here."

I took my father's thin hand in my own and knelt beside the bed. An alabaster half moon propped Neferma'at's head. I touched the older man's forehead with my hand. He still kept his head shaved, disdaining the prominent ridges of his skull.

"How goes the project, my son?"

I swallowed. "We are pushing forward, Father. And the quarries are breaking out stone as fast as we build."

"Yes, you must keep after those quarry workers." Neferma'at took several shallow breaths. "They will hold you back if you let them."

"I will not let that happen, Father."

Neferma'at squeezed my hand with a baby's strength and nodded. "Good boy." He drifted then, into a half-sleep.

I remained at his side but soon grew drowsy. Incense burned to cover the smell of the sickroom, and its pungency weighted my eyelids.

Neferma'at jerked awake some time later. "Ahmose? Where are you?"

My brother stepped from the shadows. "I will not leave you, Father. I am right here."

"Call your brother, Ahmose. Bring Hemi to me."

I could not bear to look at Ahmose. He stepped back again. I touched my father's chest. "I am here, Father. I have come."

"Both my sons." Neferma'at nodded. "Yes, that is good. Come closer, my boys."

Ahmose knelt beside me at our father's bedside.

Neferma'at placed his hand on my head, then onto Ahmose's. "You must love each other, my sons."

I inhaled deeply but could not look at my brother.

"It has been too long," my father continued, his voice low and weary. "Too long since that day. You two were once so close. Nothing has been the same since that day." He grabbed at my arm. "Promise me, son."

"What, Father?"

"Promise me you will put the past behind you. Learn to love again."

I risked a glance at Ahmose, but my brother's face was stony. "I will do all I can, Father," I said.

Neferma'at would not be appeased. "Ahmose, you too. You changed that day. But the past is not important."

"You exhaust yourself, Father," he said. "You should rest."

Neferma'at seemed to take instruction and closed his eyes again.

Ahmose stood and moved away. I rested my forehead on my father's arm.

"He seems chilled," I said. "Is there a blanket?"

Ahmose brought a piece of white linen. "He likes this one," he said and pushed past me. My brother draped the linen over the old man, tucked it around his legs and hips. I watched as a stranger here, and my throat thickened.

"I am sorry I have not been here more, Ahmose."

Voices in the outer passage grew closer. The head servant entered the room, his face pale. "Pharaoh Khufu, Beloved of Horus, Ruler of the Two Lands, Son of Ra . . ." He seemed to run out of titles. "He is here."

I smiled sadly. "Bring him in."

Khufu appeared in the doorway. His usual cheerfulness was absent. "When I heard," he murmured, "I came to—to pay my respects."

I nodded to my cousin and returned my attention to Neferma'at. "He is fading."

Khufu slipped to the bedside, and I considered it a credit to the man that he knelt there, beside his elderly uncle.

Neferma'at opened his eyes and squinted at Khufu.

"Ah, my brother has come," he said. "I have not seen you in years, Sneferu."

Khufu gave me a half smile and took his uncle's hand. His large ring seemed to dwarf the frail hand. "How are you, brother?"

Neferma'at managed a slight shake of his head. "The gods are calling me west, my brother. It is my time."

Khufu patted his hand and Neferma'at grinned, the old spark returning for a brief moment. "But we had some good times, didn't we, Sneferu?"

Khufu laughed. "Yes, indeed."

Neferma'at lowered his voice. "Our boys think this pyramid they're building will be greater than ours, do you know that?"

"Yes. Yes, I've heard that."

"Let them build *three* of them, that's what I say. Then let them speak of greatness."

Khufu smiled at me, a sad smile that spoke of our shared loss.

"Besides," Neferma'at continued, "those boys owe everything they know to us. We taught them what it meant to build a legacy in stone."

"We certainly did, brother. Saqqara will stand for eternity."

Neferma'at gripped Khufu's hand. "But you must bury me in Meidum, remember."

"Yes. Beside Itet. Your tomb is grand."

Neferma'at closed his eyes, energy gone again. Khufu pulled his hand away and placed it on my shoulder. My breath caught, but I focused on my father's face.

"He is a great man, Hemi. He will be greatly honored in Egypt for his seventy days."

Khufu stood, and I with him. We moved away from the bed and lingered in the doorway of the chamber. "What have you learned of this killer in our midst?" he asked.

I thought of the old man with the rotted teeth, whispering of Merit's frequent visits to the workmen's village, disguised.

"Not much yet, I am afraid. I am still asking questions." I hesitated. "What do you know of a group called the People of the One?"

Khufu scowled. "Rebellious sect. Have nothing to do with them."

"There may be a connection to the killer."

"It would not surprise me. They are Egyptians but claim a connection to the Joktanites and have adopted the god of the east."

"Which god?"

Khufu snorted. "He has no name." When I raised my eyebrows in disbelief, Khufu held up a hand. "By Hathor's horns, I speak the truth. They worship only one god, whom they say has no name that man knows, yet is the only god, the creator of everything."

"Hmm. Are they a warring sect?"

Khufu shook his head. "They live among us peaceably. Only contrary to all that holds Egypt together. They meet in secret, all around the Two Lands, from what I hear."

"Why have I never heard of them?"

Ahmose joined us in the doorway. "Perhaps if you two need to speak of official matters, you could move to the palace."

My jaw dropped. That my brother would speak to Pharaoh in such a way shocked me. But then a look into my brother's eyes revealed such grief that I immediately dismissed it. I stepped between Ahmose and Khufu. "I must tend to my father, my king. If you will permit me."

Khufu bowed his head. "Take whatever time you need." He disappeared toward the outer part of the house, where slaves would bear him back to the palace.

I turned to Ahmose. "We were discussing Merit's crossing," I said. "Pharaoh has asked me to investigate her murder, and that of Mentu."

"Of course."

I sighed. Neferma'at called out to me once again, but the old man was already unconscious by the time I reached him. A loneliness, deep and heart-numbing, descended on me. The loss of my father, added to Mentu's and Merit's, and the distance of my brother left me weary. I laid my head on my father's hand and felt the tears flow. My mind carried me back many years, to a day I had cried such, the day my pet monkey had died. My father had comforted me that day. There could be no such comfort at this loss.

I lifted my head sometime later and found Ahmose watching me. I swiped at my face, wishing my older brother had not witnessed yet another weakness. But when I looked at Ahmose, his expression held something other than contempt. Instead, Ahmose looked at me as though I were a stranger.

Ramla, Ahmose's pretty little wife, came with food and with their son Jafari, who had seen only seven Inundations. The boy talked of nothing but being an engineer, a builder like his uncle, the grand vizier. He sat close to me while we ate, peppering me with more questions than there were lentils on my plate.

I answered each with a small glow of pride that was extinguished each time I glanced at my brother's darkening expression. Eventually Ramla shooed the three of us back to our homes, promising to sit with Neferma'at. I grasped my father's hands in what I knew might be our last time together, then walked the short distance home alone and collapsed into my own bed, overwhelmed by the deep well of loss into which I had fallen.

The workmen's village housed ten thousand men, with their wives and children, during the season of akhet, in addition to the artists who resided there year round. But there was also a large contingent of men brought from nearby areas who stayed in the village during the ten-day work week then returned to their homes and families for two days. These men were housed in barracks at the edge of the village, and, when they returned from a day's labor, they were fed in a large hall located adjacent to the bakery and brewery, which hummed with steady work, keeping the men in bread and beer.

I arrived at the dining hall along with my men, as the evening meal was being brought in on steaming platters and circulated among the men on floor mats by women dressed to please them.

I lowered myself to a reed mat near the wall and surveyed the room with tired eyes. It had been a long day on the work site, with a section of stones misdirected to the south side of the pyramid and a small cave-in where we were shoring up the sides of the king's burial chamber. When I had gotten free, I sought out Sen and asked my new overseer of constructions where I might find his daughter.

Sen had raised his eyebrows and the corners of his mouth together.

"I have a few questions about a matter in the village for her," I explained, but the older man only smiled.

"She is usually serving in the dining hall at this time of evening."

"I don't understand. Serving?"

Sen's chest expanded. "She wants to. She knows it is beneath her, and certainly not required. But she cares for the men and enjoys finding ways to help."

She was not here, however, I decided, as I watched the men hoot at the serving women and bang their empty jugs on the floor for refills. The yeasty smell of the hall mingled with the smell of hard-working men, and I wondered that I found the scene pleasant and much preferable to my usual meals alone.

A young woman approached me and held up a jug. I nodded and she filled a cup, then bent to hand it to me. Her fingers brushed mine, and I looked up apologetically. She smiled through lowered lashes, and I realized the touch was intentional.

She doesn't know who I am.

For a moment I was tempted to lose myself in the anonymity. Then common sense prevailed and I studied the contents of my cup until she moved away.

I watched the men, how they talked and laughed together, with a shared experience that paved the way for friendship. I had never really felt that level of comfort with anyone.

A laborer nearby looked at me and I avoided his eyes, not wanting to appear in need of conversation. My own inner silence seemed to echo with hollowness in the midst of the great drone of laughter and conversation.

Finally the man beside me caught my eye and spoke. "You honor us, Grand Vizier, with your presence here. I hope our revelry does not displease you."

I shook my head. "I am waiting for someone."

"Can I be of assistance?"

"Do you know Neferet, daughter of Senosiris, Overseer of Constructions?"

His face opened into a great smile. "Of course. She is a fine lady." He scanned the room, then pointed. "And she has found you."

I raised my eyes and found Neferet crossing through the hall toward me. She stopped several times along the way, speaking to and laughing with men who called to her. I could not hear the words spoken, but it was clear that they did not treat her as the other serving women. One would have thought her twice her years, from the way the men reached for her as though seeking her blessing.

Finally she reached my side. She smiled down at me but said nothing.

I stood and cleared my throat. I forgot why I had come.

Her smile widened at my silence. "My father tells me that you are searching for me."

"Yes."

"Shall we sit?" she said.

"Yes."

I allowed her to find a spot on the floor first, then lowered myself beside her. I offered her my cup, but she shook her head.

The dining hall began to empty, and Neferet shifted so that her full attention was on me. I noted her dress, a different one than last I'd seen, but also sewn with red threads and beads attached.

She followed my look and smiled. "I know. I can never seem to be content with simply white."

"I like it."

She laughed.

"Is that funny?"

Neferet shook her head. "Only the serious way in which you said it, as though you were approving the way a stone was dressed at the quarry."

"I am afraid I have more experience with dressing stones than women." The words spilled out, then I felt myself redden. I turned away.

Neferet laughed again and moved closer to me on the floor. "Why are you here, Grand Vizier?"

Why indeed?

"The old man in the artists' section, he said that the Great Wife came to the village often. He said I should speak to the People of the One. And then he pointed to you."

"And why are you asking about the Great Wife?"

"Because I—I cared about her. And I want to find the man who sent her ka to the west."

The dining hall had grown quiet, and my words echoed farther than I would have liked.

Neferet's eyes never left my face, but she was quiet. I fought the flush that I felt climbing again.

"She was very important to you."

"Yes." I swigged the remainder of my beer.

"For a long time."

"Yes."

"My heart aches for your loss," she said, and I believed her. "How is your father, Hemi?"

"Not well. He is in his last days. But he has lived a good life." Only after I answered did I notice that she had used my little name, not my title or formal name.

"A life well-lived will be missed all the more," she said and reached for my hand.

"You like to touch people, don't you?"

She smiled her wide, happy smile but pulled away. "I am sorry."

I didn't mean you should stop.

I forced the conversation back to Merit. "What do you know about the People of the One? And what connection do they have to the Great Wife? Do you think one of them may have been involved in her death?"

"You ask more questions than I have answers, Hemi. But I do know that the queen came to the village several times."

"Dressed as a common woman?"

Neferet ran a hand over her own clothing. "Dressed as one of us, yes."

I ground my teeth. I could not seem to say the right thing. "I did not mean—"

She held up a hand. "I feel no shame in my status, Hemi. Some women are born to be queens, some are not."

"You would make a beautiful queen." I rubbed the back of my neck and looked away.

"Thank you."

A moment of silence left me wanting to run from the hall like a hunted antelope. No, nothing so graceful. Perhaps a hippo.

"Do you know why she came?" I said. "Did she meet with these rebels?"

"Rebels? Who has called them rebels?"

"What would you call them? They reject the sacred truths of Egypt to worship a foreign god without a name." My voice held a disdain that echoed Khufu's, though I was not so offended as I sounded.

"Have you ever wondered if the sacred truths are really true, Hemi?"

The hall was empty now, save the two of us. I studied the far wall before I answered. "I believe in justice. In divine order. In the existence of ma'at, running through all things."

"Justice. Yes. And what about after death?"

"Justice, still. The weighing of the heart to see if it is pure and can enter eternity."

"What will happen when your heart is weighed, Hemi?" Her words were soft but intensely spoken.

The flutter of a warning echoed through me, like a whispered secret in a cavernous temple. My heart pounded with a desire to confess the truth to her. "I do not know," I admitted. "I have tried—tried to be—I do not know."

"I think perhaps you do. That we all do. But you are afraid to face the truth."

I placed my cup on the floor and twisted my fingers together in my lap. "I am not a pure man. I know that. I do not see how my heart could pass the test."

She leaned toward me. "Nor could any. True justice leaves us all without hope."

"Are you one of them, Neferet?" I lifted my eyes to hers. "The People of the One?"

She smiled, a knowing, patient smile like that of a tutor watching a student slowly learn. "Yes."

"I must know about the Great Wife. Please."

She placed both her hands on mine and whispered one word. "Come."

TWELVE

We twisted through the darkening streets, Neferet leading me like a child. I kept my head down, preferring not to be seen. Lamps flickered to life inside homes we passed as the sun dropped below the wall that hemmed the city. The streets emptied of people, now safe inside their homes, tending to their families. The night seemed under a spell of the gods, silent and warm and full of mystery.

We walked for some time, until Neferet drew up short in front of a modest home flanked by others more prestigious, and faced me. She stepped close, until her head nearly touched my chin, and looked up.

"I feel in my heart that I can trust you," she said. "But I need you to tell me so." I looked over her head at the house. She touched my arm. "No, you must look at me when you speak."

I ran my gaze over her face, her eyes, her lips, unsmiling now.

"I would not betray you, Neferet."

Her slow smile was my reward. She took my hand and led me farther still, to the grand home next door. We passed into the home without being greeted, but once we were in the inner courtyard a servant stepped from the shadows. He was young, perhaps less than twenty Inundations, but his eyes were wary.

Neferet greeted the servant with a kiss to the cheek, but the man's attention was on me.

"I have brought a guest." Neferet held out a hand to me.

"There will be many questions," he said.

Neferet nodded, then pulled me through the courtyard, to a chamber at the back of the house.

I expected to find a small group of the rebellious sect huddled in the shadows and was surprised to find the room empty. Perhaps word of my inquiries had gotten out and no one had come.

Neferet crossed the room purposefully, to the opposite wall. She turned and beckoned to me where I stood by the entrance to the room. And then the far wall became a door, and I realized that it had been cleverly plastered with mud-brick to conceal its purpose. Neferet swung the door open and stepped into the darkness.

With a flicker of doubt at the wisdom of my actions, I crossed the room and passed through the doorway.

I was unprepared.

Three steps down, a chamber larger than the house above yawned before me, lit by dozens of oil lamps and filled with more people than I could count, talking and laughing like beloved family members.

My entrance was like a jug of water poured on a fire. The conversation sputtered and died nearby, and the hush spread outward until the entire room had fallen silent and watchful.

Neferet lifted her chin and smiled at the upturned faces. "He does not come to accuse or control," she said. "He has doubts, as we all once had. He seeks truth. And he may be trusted. Welcome the grand vizier, my friends. Welcome him as you would welcome me."

I smiled my gratitude at Neferet, then breathed deeply and faced the crowd. Their faces did not reflect the welcome she spoke of, however. A mistrust, fear, hung over the room.

Neferet touched my elbow and led me down the steps, into their midst. The people cleared a path and I walked with Neferet to the front of the chamber, where she bade me sit beside her on a stone bench. The others followed her lead and found their seats, most on benches scattered throughout the room. There were not benches to accommodate them all, so some sat on the floor while others stood at the walls.

"Perhaps it would be best," Neferet said, "if you did not stare at them just yet."

I turned and faced the front of the room.

Behind me, a quiet voice hummed softly. The melody was picked up by others, both men and women, then words were added. I stared at my hands. I had never heard men and women sing together.

But the strangeness was soon forgotten as I felt myself woven into the heart of their song, sung smooth and low, with words of their god and his love for them. Of his justice and his mercy. Of his provision and grace. The room swelled with the sweetness of the music, and my throat tightened unexplainably. And then the music ended, and someone spoke from the back of the room. After him, another. And another.

I listened in fascination.

One true god. Only one.

A creator god. One who still watched over the affairs of men.

They spoke of the world destroyed by flood because man refused to be ruled by this god, of a single family preserved by the love of this god. Of man's turning again to self-rule and being dispersed across the earth, their common language splintered into fragments.

And they spoke of one yet to come. Of him, I understood little and wished for clarity.

When it seemed the last of them had spoken, the singing began again. Some of it was familiar now, and I found myself wanting to join them. The last lovely note lifted above our heads and ceased, and it hung there in the air like a low fruit I could pluck and enjoy if I chose.

My eyes were still closed when Neferet touched my arm. I faced her and knew that those eyes were reading every thought in my heart.

She smiled. "Come and ask your questions now. Ask them about the Great Wife."

I stood and approached a cluster of men and women nearby. Neferet introduced them as though I were a new member of their sect. I focused on the names to remember them.

"The grand vizier has questions about the queen," she said and nodded to me.

I lifted my shoulders. "Neferet tells me that she was known here. I am trying to find the one who killed her, to bring him to justice. Do any of you know why she disguised herself and came to the village? Was it to meet you here?"

A thin man, Hanif, whom I believed was a stonemason in the quarry, glanced at his wife, Layla, then answered with uncertain hesitation. "At first she did not come here to meet with us. Some of us saw her a number of times, entering and coming out of the small temple of Horus close by here, always in the early morning hours. We didn't understand why she would come out here to worship." His attention shifted to his wife again, and she picked up the story.

"I finally approached her, with a friend. We asked if we could serve her in some way." She leaned her ample body against her husband, who embraced her with one arm.

I waited for more in silence.

"She seemed surprised that we recognized her." The woman smiled, a wide, toothy smile that crinkled the corners of her bright eyes. "She believed her peasant garb had concealed her identity, but she was so lovely."

Yes, she was. "Did she tell you why she was in the temple?"

"We spoke to her several times after that, and each time we would speak of the gods." The woman broke off and clasped her hands in front of her.

Neferet intervened. "He can be trusted, Layla. I am certain of it. Please tell him what you know."

Layla sighed. "She had many questions and soon realized that our answers were not those of the priests of On or of Memphis. She was curious about our ways. After a while, we invited her to join us here."

Neferet said to me, "It was a dangerous thing to do, but we all agreed. It was too important. We believed that perhaps God had given us this opportunity to make a change in Egypt. If he were calling the Great Wife to himself, there was a chance to have great impact."

"And she came to these . . . meetings?"

"Yes," Layla said. "Over a period of some weeks. She asked many more questions. And then—"

"Yes?"

Layla appeared unwilling to go further. Her husband shrugged, as though unable to determine the wisdom of continuing.

Neferet alone spoke, in the tone of a declaration. "She renounced the false gods of Egypt and claimed the One True God as her own." Neferet's words poured out with the rush of one who has committed to a course of action and won't be turned back. "The Great Wife put her faith in the One to Come to reconcile her to God."

"She became one of you?" I said, circling the group with my eyes. More had joined us as we talked, and we were now the center of the room's attention.

Layla reached out and squeezed my arm. "She became one of God's."

People of the One.

I thanked them all and reassured them that I had no desire to bring trouble upon them. "But none of you know what brought her to the village at first? Or who may have had reason to kill her?"

My question was met with silence and shaking heads.

I offered my thanks again, and the group moved away.

"It grows late," I said to Neferet. "I should be departing."

She smiled. "It is very late. And not safe to travel across the desert. Come," she said. "Come and stay the night with me."

Once more I followed Neferet through the streets, this time certain that I had taken leave of my senses.

I had crossed the desert at night in the past. It was true that there were dangers, but none so far beyond me that a stay in the village was necessary. So why the ridiculous decision to say yes to Neferet's invitation?

At the house we found Sen lounging in the leafy darkness of the courtyard, with one flaming torch throwing dancing shadows. He started, then stood in surprise.

"Look what I have found, lost and wandering the streets, Father." Sen and I both stared at Neferet, and she threw back her head and laughed. "You both look as though you don't know whether to scold me or check me for fever."

Sen bowed. "I am honored to have you in my home again, Grand Vizier."

I did not miss the slight emphasis on the word *again*.

Neferet grew serious. "Will you bring a chair for the vizier, Father? He is going to stay the night."

"Is he?" Sen's eyebrows arched above his dark eyes.

Neferet gave her father a little push. "Yes."

Sen disappeared inside, and Neferet smiled. "I will bring wine and meat," she said, "and prepare a place for you to sleep. Please, rest here until all is ready."

"Thank you, Neferet."

Sen returned, placed a chair near his own, and motioned to it. He returned to his own chair, and Neferet came and kissed the top of his head. "We missed you this evening, Father."

Sen's sharp eyes flicked toward me and then Neferet.

"You didn't—"

"The grand vizier was our guest. You must ask him what he thought of the meeting."

She left the courtyard and I sat on the edge of the chair, then forced myself to lean against the back.

"So Neferet has told you our secret."

"You are part of them too? The People of the One?"

Sen braced his arm across the back of his chair. "Neferet and I trace our bloodline directly back to Shem, who was saved from the Great Flood."

"I have heard of the flood since childhood but always believed it was simply an Inundation greater than any ever seen."

Sen laughed. "That it was. So great it covered the world. The people in the east will tell you that the waters covered all that they know there."

"You have spoken to people east of Sinai?"

"That is where our people come from. And Shem lives there still. You could travel there and hear from his own lips how he lived upon the great boat for one year, until the land appeared again." Sen shifted in his seat. "You must think us all quite blasphemous," he said. "Perhaps you no longer wish me to serve as overseer of—"

I stopped him with an upraised hand. "I have too many questions of my own about the gods to judge you for the answers you claim to have found. I came here for another reason."

The sound of Neferet singing drifted from the kitchen, and I glanced toward the entrance to the courtyard.

Sen's lips narrowed to a thin line. "I suspect you did." He leaned forward, his bulky forearms on his knees. "You may be the grand vizier, but she is still my daughter. Take care, my lord."

I swallowed. "You mistake my intention. I came to the village today to ask questions about the Great Wife. My questions led me to the People of the One, and Neferet allowed me to meet them, to learn more. And then it was late. Too late to cross the desert to the royal estate . . ." My reasons trailed off, as I saw that Sen was smiling, with a knowing sort of dismissal. I sat back in my chair, unwilling to make further excuses, even to myself. "I have great respect for your daughter, Sen."

The older man seemed to relax. "Good. Now let us enjoy the night."

It was a night to enjoy. The torchlight flickered across Neferet's wall murals and seemed to bring the flowers and creatures to life. Beside us, in the center of the courtyard where a small pond had been dug and lotus flowers cultivated, a small frog croaked, as if to join the conversation. The fragrance of night flowers hung in the air, and behind it all, was the sound of Neferet singing.

The tension of the day seemed to drain from me, and I closed my eyes and leaned my head back. A strange feeling of safety enveloped me as the garden embraced my senses. When Neferet returned with bowls of beef and cups of wine, I felt as though this were my own home. Neferet passed food and wine to her father, then patted his shoulder, and a vision flashed before me, of children playing in the courtyard, of Sen as their grandfather.

She disappeared once more to prepare my bed, and the overseer and I ate our meal in companionable silence.

When we had set our cups and bowls aside, I asked, "Are you satisfied with your new position, Sen?"

Sen wiped his mouth with the back of his hand and leaned back in his chair. "The men require constant supervision, but that is unchanged from my earlier role, so I do not mind it. I enjoy seeing the project from a different perspective, seeing the bigger goals."

"You have done well filling Mentu's role. There has been little interruption to the time line."

Sen nodded his thanks. "I only wish that the circumstances were different. He was a good man. The men loved him. He never lorded his position over them. Even used our small temple here to worship."

I cocked my head. "He worshiped here? In the temple of Horus? Near the home where the People of the One meet?"

"Yes, I saw him often in the early mornings, when no one else was about the temple.

My jaw suddenly tensed and I tried to loosen it with my fingertips.

Sen said, "I suppose he liked to spend time there alone, before the priests would come."

Neferet returned. "All is ready."

Sen stood. "The hour is late, and there is much work to do tomorrow, eh, Grand Vizier?"

I stood, my mind elsewhere. "Yes. Thank you."

Sen eyed his daughter. "I think I will show the grand vizier where he can lay his head, Neferet. You may retire to your chamber."

Neferet laughed, a sound like warmed wine on a cold night. "As you wish, Father. God be with you, Hemi."

I lowered my eyes to the floor. When I looked up, she was gone.

"This way, Grand Vizier."

Minutes later I lay upon a bed that smelled of being freshly scrubbed and laid with clean coverings. But I was not thinking of the clean bed, nor of the woman who had prepared it.

Another woman occupied my thoughts. One who visited the village temple in the early mornings, disguised. And Mentu, who was also seen in the temple in the mornings. Both of them now dead.

I thought of Khufu and his jealousy. Of Khufu's reluctance to allow me to investigate the murders.

Like a man who has something to hide.

What began as a foreboding quickly grew to dread, then something else in my chest as I lay in the dark.

Anger. White-hot anger toward the man who had taken Merit from me when we were young. And now he had taken her away again. Simply because he could not have her heart.

THIRTEEN

I awoke, blinked my eyes, and shot upright. The morning was too far gone to still be in bed. *And it's not my bed.* I scanned the chamber, took in the unfinished walls, the mud-brick floor. Sen and Neferet.

I had stayed the night and overslept, my morning rituals lost.

Thoughts of Merit and Mentu meeting secretly, and of Khufu's temper, invaded. I dropped to my back again.

I had come to the village for information and had received far more than I wanted. But with the morning light came doubt.

I have too much work to do to be chasing theories.

Within the hour I was on the plateau, letting the dusty wind blow away the thoughts of last night. I raised my face to the burning sun, then paused to survey the site. The desert stretched as far as I could see to the west, north, and south. From the base of the pyramid, one could see the temple and harbor and royal estate, the village in the distance, and the wide blue sky. In spite of the many thousands of workers buzzing over the plateau and pyramid, there was an isolation here, and I let it work its way inside me.

No time for anything else.

I climbed the ramps slowly, running my hands along the stones. Laborers hailed me as I passed. At the top, I saw that my new design to store unused tools had already been implemented. Masons bowed low, murmuring my titles of honor.

With my ka settled within me, I descended to the stone table that had been set up as my meeting place with my chief overseers. De'de and Khons were already there, and Sen approached from the south.

"Men." I greeted them without a smile. "I need reports."

Khons grunted. "Kind of you to visit, Vizier. We thought perhaps you were occupied with other—"

"Keep your thoughts to yourself, Khons. Report on the progress."

De'de raised his eyebrows and clucked at Khons disapprovingly. "Careful, Khons. You're making Father angry."

Sen leaned his fists on the table. "May I report first, Grand Vizier?"

"What do you have, Sen?"

"In looking at the projections this last day, I fear that we will soon hit a snag on our critical path." He pointed to the stockpile of stones from the quarry, a flock of loosely scattered blocks in a field of sand. "The rate of transfer for courses fifty-six through two hundred eighteen has slowed in recent weeks, while the rate of placement will begin to increase as we attain the higher levels which require fewer stones."

I frowned. "What's causing the slowdown?"

"I don't know, my lord. I haven't had enough time to analyze."

Khons folded his arms. "Shouldn't Mentu have been keeping track of transport rates? Why is this the first we're hearing of it?"

Sen shook his head and held up his palms.

"That's not good enough!" I slapped the basalt table, then grabbed my limestone shard and scratched furious numbers onto the stone. White chips flew across the flat surface. "These men must know that everything depends on the time line. If stone placement on the pyramid catches up with the transport and stockpiling, we will have thousands of stone haulers at a standstill, waiting for stone!" I finished my calculations and pointed. "Look at what a mere twenty-percent reduction in transport rate will do. Here," I pointed, "the number of stones short. And here, masons without blocks to dress."

De'de put his two index fingers to his lips. "I am sure we will be able—"

"You focus on getting beer and bread in their mouths and let us worry about the stones!" I turned my back on the man and ignored his indignant huff.

In truth, De'de's oversight of the commissary, the stores and materials, the workshops and housing were the foundation of all we did here. But I was tired of speculation. I was tired of everything. What had happened to the controlled order of the project that would be my legacy in stone?

As though the chaos I feared had taken human form, Tamit suddenly appeared beside me, all smiles and fluttering eyes.

I sighed. "Tamit, this is a work area—"

"Yes, Grand Vizier." She wrapped fingers around my arm and slithered close. "I want you to give me a tour."

I sighed again and glanced at my supervisors, who looked away with thinly veiled amusement. I knew Tamit would not easily be put off.

"Quickly then," I said and half-dragged her to the ramp. We climbed together, and I purposely pushed the pace faster than

I would have alone. I was rewarded by the sound of her heavy
breathing. Along the way I described building techniques, stone
dressing, and hauling methods, all with tedious detail.

"Inside," she panted. "I want to see inside."

We reached the slotted entrance, and I took a torch from an
exiting laborer and led the way downward until we reached the
juncture where the corridor split to redirect upward.

"What is down there?" Tamit asked.

"An underground chamber. It was to be used for the king's
burial, but the plans have changed."

"What will it hold now?"

I shrugged. "Nothing. It will remain empty."

She smiled and tickled my arm with long fingernails. "Seems
a waste. Perhaps you and I could make use of it. It could be *our*
burial place. A chamber all our own, where we could spend eternity
together."

I pulled away. "Why are you here, Tamit?"

"I told you. I wanted a tour of the pyramid."

I pointed upward. "The corridor ascends four hundred cubits.
Are you ready?"

She squinted up the ascending corridor, then turned to me and
half smiled. "You win, Hemi. I care nothing for your pile of stones.
I wanted to see you, to ask you to join me for a late meal tonight
in my home."

"The work takes all of my time, I am afraid."

She scowled up at me. "And you have nothing to show for your
life except the work!" Her face softened and she leaned close. "Life
is more than building, you know."

I turned from her and headed for freedom. "Not my life."

She followed me in a pout, and I led her down to her waiting litter.

As I reached the meeting table to converse once more with my three overseers, I noticed their attention was drawn to a cloud of sand in the distance. We watched for a moment until a gold sedan chair appeared, carried by twelve slaves.

"Wonderful," I murmured.

The slaves lowered the chair to the ground nearby, and Khufu parted the curtain. He was in full headdress today, with a braided wig hanging down each side and tucked behind his ears. He wore a gold-and-blue-striped nemes over the wig, gathered behind in a knot.

My resolve to forget last night's revelation blew away in a sandstorm of howling anger, and my body tensed.

Khufu climbed out of the chair, and a slave immediately shielded his head with an ostrich plume at the end of a tall rod. Behind him, Ebo announced, "His Majesty Horus, Beloved by the Goddess of Truth, Strong in Truth, Chosen of Ra."

My overseers crossed their chests with fists and responded, "Life, Health, Strength!"

I said nothing.

Khufu sighed. "I am restless today," he said, joining us at the table, slave in tow. "Too much death around me. I felt I should come and see the progress for myself."

I rubbed my eyes and turned away. With eyes closed, I could imagine Sen's cozy, torchlit courtyard as a mirage rising from the burning sand of the plateau.

"Hemi?"

I swiveled.

De'de was grinning. "Pharaoh, Beloved of Horus, was speaking to you."

I bowed. "My mind was on the project, my king. I apologize."

"I was asking why there seem to be more men working on the east side today."

I stared at him. "Are you jesting, my king?"

Khufu frowned.

"They are commencing work on the queen's pyramid."

"Ah." Khufu studied the laborers.

The time line, the slowdown, the unexpected deviation caused by Merit's death, all of it swam before my eyes for a moment, and I thought I might scramble across the table to wrap angry fingers around Khufu's throat.

"Well then, we might fall behind," Khufu said, like a pouting child whose toys do not please him. "Perhaps we could bring in a few more men so we don't lose time."

The other men looked to me for a response.

Cowards. I took a deep breath, then spoke through gritted teeth.

"Your Majesty, we have organized more than four thousand stone masons, eighteen thousand stone haulers, and hundreds of artists to complete this project. The men are divided into crews of two thousand, gangs of one thousand, with five groups of two hundred, each with ten teams of twenty." My voice rose above the work-site noise, and I fought to control the hysteria in my voice. "Together these men will lay more than two million blocks of stone for the internal core and dress one hundred thousand casing stones. Every step they take has been planned and measured, counted and recorded. We cannot simply 'bring in a few more men.'" I bent to brace my shaking hands against the table. "I suggest you leave the building to us and return to your palace. Perhaps your dwarf can entertain you and cure you of your restlessness."

A stunned silence followed.

I straightened but did not break eye contact with the king.

Khufu's eyes went cold. His hands went to his hips and he lifted his chin. "That is a good suggestion, Grand Vizier. Thank you. I would ask that when your work here is finished today, you would come and speak to me in my private chambers."

I bowed my head and watched as Khufu mounted his sedan chair and his slaves carried him off toward the palace.

I had spoken rashly. But there was much more I could have said.

When I turned my attention back to the overseers, they each eyed me with a mixture of fear and pity. It was never a good idea to make an enemy of the Chosen of Ra.

I made my appearance in the palace that evening, my mind a jumble of regret and anger. Conflicting desires to placate and to confront Khufu warred for my loyalty.

Ebo, the head servant, led me to Khufu's private chamber, the House of Adoration, and motioned me through the door. The room blazed with the harsh light of far too many torches, placed in pots around the perimeter. I blinked at the brightness and looked to Ebo. The jagged scar across his forehead shone pink in the torchlight.

Khufu stood on the opposite side of the chamber, his arms extended like falcon's wings and his head thrown back.

Another man, naked but for the excessive jewelry at his neck, arms, and ankles, stood beside the king, shaking a sistrum at him. The naked man paused at my entrance, and Khufu dropped his arms and focused on me. He did not smile.

"Come forward, Grand Vizier. You know Djed-djedi, the magician?"

"No."

Khufu resumed his pose. "He is calling up a prophecy. I have been having dreams."

"I can return later."

"Stay. Perhaps you will discover that your king knows more than you believe."

"As you wish."

The shaking of the sistrum resumed, each wooden bead twirling and beating against the others. The magician picked up a chant, words I did not recognize. I moved to the back of the chamber, alongside Khufu's deep, rectangular bathing pool, and sat in a reed-bottom chair, with my staff across my legs. One of the many torches burned nearby and threw off an uncomfortable heat. The chanting continued.

"It is the ancient language. The first language," Khufu said, his eyes still closed. "Do you know its meaning?"

"No."

"No, of course you do not."

I gripped my staff. "The king is displeased with my comments earlier."

"The king cares nothing for your opinion."

No, of course he does not.

The dozen torches grew unbearable, and I began to sweat. The bathing pool's water looked cool and inviting.

The magician ceased his shaking and produced a small container. He dipped a finger into the package and brought it to Khufu's lips. The king licked the substance from his finger.

"Come, Hemi. Come here."

I leaned my staff against the wall and approached.

The magician focused on me for the first time. He was a little man, with eyes that seemed to cross when he looked at me directly.

"Give him some, Djed-djedi."

Djed-djedi held out the package. Yellow-gold honey pooled in the center.

Khufu licked his lips. "It is sacred honey, from bees hundreds of years old. It imparts wisdom to those who partake."

I held up a hand and stepped back.

"The grand vizier believes he has all the wisdom he needs, Djed-djedi."

Khufu flicked his head toward me, and before I understood the motion, the magician coated his finger again and smeared the honey on my lips.

I sputtered and swiped at it with my fingers, then finally licked the traces from my lips.

Djed-djedi whispered a few words to Khufu, then began packing up his trappings. Khufu went to a small table and bent over a stack of papyrus bound in black hides.

The magician lit incense before he left, and the spicy scent filled the room within moments. He said nothing as he departed, just slipped from the room like the smoke from the incense.

Khufu waved me back to my chair and began to write on the papyrus. Several times he closed his eyes, whether to consult his memory or the gods, I could not be sure.

Finally he closed the book and looked up. "Perhaps someday I will allow you to read the secrets recorded here."

I was familiar with Khufu's secret book, in which he claimed to be recording the history of the world. "Would I discover anything so surprising?"

Khufu's eyes narrowed. "All of Egypt would be surprised."

"Then I should like to read it."

Khufu stood and stretched, and his bronzed and oiled skin gleamed in the torchlight. "Something is troubling you, Hemi. You would not have spoken as you did otherwise."

Troubling me, yes. Though nothing seems to trouble you. Not your dead wife, nor your dead friend. Why is that, Pharaoh?

Aloud, I said, "I regret my words earlier."

Khufu leaned on the table. "I can see it there, just behind your eyes. You have learned something, perhaps? Something that makes you angry?"

"I have asked questions. Received some answers."

"And those answers have led you to believe . . ."

"It would seem that the killer has not chosen his victims randomly. The Overseer of Constructions and the Great Wife shared a common interest."

Khufu went to his chamber window and pushed aside the linen to study the night sky. "And what was this common interest?"

"They met secretly in the early mornings."

Khufu didn't turn. Didn't speak.

"But you already knew that, didn't you, cousin?"

The linen window covering rippled in his hand. I willed him to convince me of his innocence.

"I knew."

I felt like I had been too long held under water and must surface or drown. My fingers squeezed my staff until they throbbed.

"How could you do it?" Even now, I wanted him to deny it.

"I am the king. I had to look to my own interests first."

My rage burst in a torrent. I rushed at Khufu, the staff held over my head. A scream tore from my lips, with all the hatred I felt. Khufu's eyes widened and he threw up an arm to block the staff. A cool wind rushed in through the window, but my anger would not be so easily quenched. I grabbed both ends of my staff and pushed against Khufu's arm, wanting to hear the bones there snap.

With a yell, Khufu lunged forward. The staff spun away from us and dislodged a torch from its perch. I shoved Khufu's shoulders backward against the wall and pressed my own forehead into the king's.

It felt good. Fifteen years of resentment flowed through my chest. Now it bubbled up and spilled out like an acid, sharpening my voice to pointed flint.

"Not this time, cousin," I growled. "I will not be silent again."

The fallen torch blazed up beside us, and the leg of Khufu's writing table joined the flame. Khufu's eyes moved sideways. "My book! The table burns!"

"I care nothing for your book!" Heat poured into my face and I found it difficult to swallow. "Merit's life, Mentu's life, they were worth more than a world of books! And you snuffed them out like used-up torches!"

Khufu's jaw muscles worked and he clawed at my arms, pinning him to the wall.

"I did not kill them, Hemi! I swear by the plucked-out eye of Horus, I did not kill them!"

FOURTEEN

I braced my forearm against Khufu's throat. "Say it again!" I peered into my cousin's eyes, trying to scrape the lies away.

"I am not one of your equations, Hemi! The solution is not so simple."

In my desperation to bring order, had I miscalculated?

"I did not kill them, Hemi."

I released my hold and backed away, blood pounding at my temples.

Khufu dove for his sacred book, snatched it from the table, then grabbed a nearby jug of water and doused the flames.

The torch hissed to a few glowing embers, and the charred table leg smoldered.

Khufu inhaled deeply and turned to me, the jug dangling from slack fingers. "I will admit," he said, "when I learned that Merit and Mentu were meeting secretly, I was incensed. I had always feared that someday she would turn her back on me." He gave me a half smile. "Though I assumed it would be another man who took her away. I was shocked that it could be Mentu. He was not . . . I would not have expected it."

I rubbed at my face, pressed my fingers against the bridge of my nose. Mentu had been a good man but not an attractive one. I had not allowed myself much time to ponder thoughts of him and Merit together.

"I confronted her," Khufu said, "told her that I knew about them." He dropped to the chair beside the table and set the book in front of him.

"Did she deny it?"

"She didn't need to. She told me why she was meeting Mentu. It did not involve her affections."

I waited, arms crossed, heart slowing.

"It was about her pyramid."

"The queen's pyramid?"

Khufu fingered the book. "Yes. She feared that I would never commission the plans, that I was so consumed with my own building and cared nothing for hers."

"She was right."

Khufu acknowledged the accusation with a brief nod. "I know. She was meeting Mentu without my knowledge, to commission him to design plans without me."

I breathed. "Why did she not ask me?"

Khufu lifted his head and laughed, the sad laugh of a defeated man. "Ask *yourself* why Merit did not think it wise to meet with you in secret."

I licked my lips, which still tasted of the magician's honey, and looked away.

"She and Mentu designed the plans together. When I made my accusations, she brought the plans to me, and I could do nothing but approve them immediately."

I thought back to the day when Khufu had finally given me the plans. So much had happened since then, though it had been only a few weeks.

"So if not you, who would kill them both?"

Khufu shoved away from the table and drifted to the window. "I have asked myself that a thousand times. I have no answer."

"Why didn't you tell me all of this days ago, when Merit was killed?"

Khufu turned again, as though he could not remain in one place long. He lowered himself onto his bed, his head supported by an alabaster headrest. "Shame. I did not want you to know what I had forced her to." He closed his eyes. On the headboard above, the golden wings of Isis spread over him. "The strange thing is," he said, "when she brought me the plans, she was not so eager for the pyramid to be built. She said she was unsure that it was necessary."

"She did not expect to cross to the west so soon."

Khufu pulled himself upright. "No. She spoke of doubts about the gods. About the afterlife. I confess I didn't listen well. I thought them the silly notions of an overemotional wife. But now . . ."

"Now?"

He rested his chin on his palm. "Perhaps she had some fore-knowledge of what was to come."

I debated whether to reveal what I knew about the queen's renouncing of the Egyptian gods. "If so, I hope she was at peace."

Khufu sighed, then looked up. "Now that you know about all of this, I am anxious for you to find the one who killed them."

"I am afraid there is little to pursue." I flexed my fingers. "You were the only one I truly suspected." Khufu said nothing, and I regretted my words. I held up my hands apologetically.

"I understand," Khufu said. "We have been here once before, have we not, cousin?"

We do not speak of that day.

Khufu stretched himself on the bed again. "I am tired. Come to me tomorrow with anything you learn."

I left the chamber silently, crossed out of the palace, through the courtyard, and down the path to my own home, refusing to look at my pyramid. My thoughts were muddied with relief, frustration, and anger. While I did not truly wish to know that Khufu had killed the two, I was now without answers or even suspicions.

My home was cold and empty. In my absence, the slaves I kept had no doubt finished their work for the day and gone to their own quarters. Only a single lamp had been lit inside the front door. I carried it with me to the kitchen, where I found a jug of water. I poured the water over my sticky hands and rubbed at my lips. The sweetness of the honey sickened me, and I swigged from the jar to dilute the taste in my mouth. The jug made a hollow clunk when I set it on the table.

My inner courtyard sucked me into its dark silence, bouncing the sound of my steps back at me from its unpainted walls. I dropped onto a bench and studied the plants, several of which had grown brown with neglect.

Why should I pursue these questions any further? The truth would not bring my loved ones back from the west. I hated nothing more than unanswered questions, but if answers could not be found, was it not best to put the questions away and focus attention elsewhere?

I rose and crossed the courtyard to a side room to retrieve my seven-stringed harp. I needed to clear my mind. Back on the bench,

I plucked uncertainly at the first few strings, feeling my way, letting a melody find me.

The harp came out on rare occasions, and only when I was alone. There was a weakness in it somehow, this need I had at times to create music, and I preferred to keep my weaknesses private.

The music was slow in taking over tonight. Discordant notes dropped like hard pebbles at my feet. I closed my eyes, tried to coax the music to flow. Then the beginnings of a melody seeped from my fingers, and I followed its trail. Downward, downward tonight, in melancholy low notes that sang out my defeat. The music swelled inside of me, and I let it flow through my hands. The strings vibrated with all the tension I felt and seemed to take it from me, the notes filling the courtyard and then chasing each other upward into the night sky.

I played on, my senses contained by the music. I did not know how long I played, only that when I stopped it was because I was empty. My face was wet with tears, and I dropped my forehead to the harp's neck.

A noise at the edge of the courtyard startled me. "I have no need of anything tonight," I called, certain that a slave had followed the sound and come to check on me.

A figure in white slipped into the courtyard.

"Neferet!" I swiped at my face, stood, then glanced down at the harp and back to her.

The starlight seemed to glisten on her cheeks, and I realized she was crying.

"What is it?"

Her eyes roamed over my face, and I thought perhaps she was afraid.

"Your music," she whispered.

I set the harp against the bench and stepped in front of it. "It is just a foolish diversion. The music interests me. It is all based on mathematics, you know. I find it interesting to analyze—"

She was shaking her head. "I knew there was more."

"More?"

She crossed the courtyard to stand before me and placed a hand on my chest. "More."

A frightened silence beat between us and lengthened, until I felt like my soul had been stripped bare, and I had to look away.

"Why have you come, Neferet?" I asked and tried to swallow.

She dropped her hand and looked at the ground. "I–I do not know. I wanted to see you. You left quickly this morning."

The pounding in my chest would not abate. I needed to speak of something else. I took a step backward. "You didn't come alone, did you?"

"I came to the royal estate earlier in the day, on some business for my father. I waited for you to come home."

There must be something else we can speak about.

"You should not have stayed so long. Darkness has fallen, you know."

Brilliant, Hemi.

"I know. My father will be angry."

"I will summon my slaves to carry you home. You will be safe."

"Thank you."

I lifted my head to call the slaves, but she grabbed my arm.

"Can we sit awhile?"

No. "Yes."

I shifted the harp and we sat on the stone bench. "I am afraid my courtyard does not have the visual appeal of yours."

She surveyed the plain walls and dying plants, then my face. "With the right touch, it would."

Is there nothing safe to speak about?

She stood and moved to the corner, to my household shrine. It occurred to me that her house lacked such a shrine. The lamp on the offering table was unlit, and no incense burned before the goddess. No libations had been poured. Neferet ran a hand over the goddess's wings and smiled back to me.

"Ma'at," she said. "Not Thoth, the builders' god. But I am not surprised."

"I try to serve her faithfully."

"Have you learned anything new about the Great Wife's death?" Neferet said, turning toward me.

"I do not think there is any way to learn who killed her. She was going to the village to meet with Mentu-hotep, to discuss building plans for her pyramid."

"Why—"

I held up a hand and shook my head, and Neferet seemed to understand my meaning.

"But they have both been killed," she said. "There must be some significance."

"You are probably right, but I do not know how to discover it. And the Horizon of Khufu demands my attention."

She came to me and clutched my fingers. "You cannot give up! What about justice, divine order?"

"You understand me too well."

Neferet looked into my eyes and spoke softly. "I understand that you are in bondage to the past. And I do not believe that you will be able to live your future until you are free of it. Finding the Great Wife's murderer is part of attaining that freedom."

Her fingers were warm on mine. "The future will look much the same for me," I said. "I am a builder. That is who I am."

She squeezed my hand. "More," she said, smiling. "There is more. But first you must reconcile with the past."

"I do not know how."

"Why don't you speak to those who knew them well? Perhaps they had learned something that put them in danger. Find out if they feared anything. Or anyone."

I nodded. It was a good idea.

She pulled away. "I should return home."

"Yes." I jumped up and hurried to call my slaves.

A few minutes later she was situated in my sedan chair, with a blanket tucked around her to ward off the night air. The slaves hoisted the chair to their shoulders, and Neferet reached her hand down to me. I took it in my own.

"Good night, Grand Vizier. Thank you for the music."

I watched her dark eyes, the way they focused on me, as though she saw no one else. The chair moved forward and I heard her soft voice call into the air, like a piece of music unto itself.

"Someday, Hemi, you will play for me again."

FIFTEEN

The princes' school stood very near the palace, but not so near that the king would be troubled with the antics of the boys educated there. The students included his own sons and any others of high birth whom the king allowed.

It was late afternoon when I returned to the royal estate from the work site and passed by the school. The boys were outside, playing at spear throwing, their target close enough to trip over. Their tutor, one of the highest officials in Egypt, watched from nearby.

I slowed to watch them and easily picked out the prince of the blood, heir to the throne of Horus. The boy had Merit's delicate nose. He was naked, as all boys of that age are, and his head shaved bare, save the one side allowed to grow long into the prince's forelock, and banded together to hang below his shoulder. The boy heaved a spear toward the target.

Not bad.

As though he sensed my attention, he turned, then ran over to where I stood. "May the gods bless you today, Grand Vizier," he said.

"And you, Kawab."

"Have you found the one who sent my mother to the west?"

I leaned backward. "Not yet, I am afraid."

The boy looked toward the setting sun. "Will you?"

"I will do my best."

"I miss her, you know."

I smiled. "As do I."

My answer seemed to satisfy the boy, who returned to his classmates.

I continued on, thinking how it seemed only a few years ago that Khufu and I had taken our lessons together, with Ahmose and Mentu always nearby.

A time of innocence.

The estate of Tamit lay within a few hundred cubits east of the school. The front of the house deceived the eye, as it appeared small. Beyond the door a huge enclosure opened to the compound that housed Tamit's menagerie of animals, her curious hobby.

I dreaded this interview.

The doorkeeper ushered me directly through the house and out the back to the sandy compound. To my left, Tamit lay on a chaise under a canopy, propped by an excess of red-and-gold-stitched cushions. She held a gold cup in her fingertips, and a monkey skittered around beneath her chair.

At my approach, she sat upright and adjusted her wig with one hand. "Grand Vizier! I did not expect this pleasure today."

"I was hoping to speak to you."

She smiled and licked her lips like one of her large cats. "I had hoped you would come soon. To see the animals." She gestured behind me, but I did not turn. "Walk with me, Hemi. I will show you my pets."

"As you wish."

The enclosure crawled with loosed animals, gazelle and ibex, porcupine and hare, even a giraffe. A cluster of cultivated palm trees housed a baboon, which hung from a branch and hooted at us. The perimeter of the space held cages of various sizes.

"They have all been taken by lasso or by dogs, in the desert. Some of them as far east as Syria." Tamit paused before a cage where a leopard paced, its golden gaze upon us. "Is he not beautiful?"

I nodded, and we continued on past several hyenas and a caged lion. I paused and studied the kingly beast; he seemed to have lost some of his regal nature.

"Tamit, I came to ask you about Merit."

She sighed and trailed her fingers along the cage, daring her pet to take a bite. "I don't know why she was in the village, dressed as a peasant, if that is what you want to ask."

"No. No, I came to ask if she ever confided in you."

We started back toward the canopy. Tamit stroked her braids, down to their beaded tips. "Confided in me? About you?"

I swallowed. "No! About . . . other things. You seemed to be the only woman of the court with whom she spent any time."

"She was not enamored of the other wives, as you can imagine."

"You and she have been friends since childhood."

Tamit lifted an eyebrow. "Yes, we all go back many years, do we not?"

We reached the canopy, and Tamit poured another cup of red wine from a jug and brought it to me. I reached to take it from her, but she held on, letting me pull her closer until she released the cup only a span from me. She smiled the calculating smile of a woman who knows her power.

"Did she ever mention anyone who frightened her?" I asked. "Threatened her? Was there anything bothering her before she died?"

Tamit closed the tiny gap between us and raised her own cup to her red-painted lips. She sipped at the wine, her eyes raised to mine. Her other hand traced a line up my arm, from wrist to shoulder.

Her nearness brought warmth to my face, and I took a step backward. "Can you think of anything that might have pointed to her being in danger?"

Tamit turned her back on me and paced back and forth a few times, watching her animals. Her restless movement reminded me of the leopard, caged and frustrated.

At the edge of the enclosure, the lion let out a tired sort of roar at the baboon who taunted him from the safety outside his bars.

"We were not close, Merit and I," Tamit said. "We saw each other often, but she never seemed to feel . . . comfortable with me." She turned her wine-red smile on me. "I can't imagine why."

"Was there anyone else she may have confided in?"

Tamit came close again and tipped her head back. I could smell the wine on her breath. "The only one who seemed to bother Merit was you, Hemi. But you already knew that."

I ran a finger around the rim of my cup, then set it down. I ignored her jab. It was part of the past, and she knew better than to speak of it.

The little monkey chose that moment to clamber up its mistress's dress and clutch her around the neck. Tamit made little clucking sounds at the beast, then turned her face to it and puckered her lips. The monkey obliged her with a kiss and then a grin at me.

That is not attractive.

She detached the monkey's arms from her neck, set it down, and tossed it a small onion. The monkey swung under the chaise to pick the onion apart.

"Reminds you of your friend, Mentu, does he not?" she said.

Again, I ignored the familiar insult. I needed her cooperation.

"Merit never had any intimate friends, Hemi. Not since my sister." Tamit smiled. "But then everyone loved Amunet, didn't they? Merit, Khufu, even that little priest, Rashidi. She was that kind of person." Tamit planted herself before me again. "No one ever felt that way about me, Hemi. But I do have my charms, don't you think?" She reached for my hands with her own, but I snatched them away. Her eyes flickered for a moment with what appeared to be sincere pain.

"Tamit, I—"

She turned away. "I can tell you nothing else, Grand Vizier. Perhaps someone else knew her better than I. But I was not her confidant."

I reached a hand toward Tamit's back but thought better of the gesture and let it drop. Instead, I thanked her quickly, escaped the enclosure, and left her to her pets.

I had forgotten about Rashidi's youthful infatuation with Amunet. It is funny how we are all still so connected, even after these many years. Tamit's passing comment took me back to that day once more, to Khufu's teasing and Amunet's coy smile. It was a dangerous, foolish day—the day we do not speak of. We did not know it, but death hung about us like an invisible shroud, anxious to claim one of us for its own.

We lay drowsing in the afternoon sun, our bellies full of the picnic meal, not yet ready to give up our rest for the hunt. Khufu is breaking off blades of grass and tossing them at Amunet. She growls at him as though frustrated, and he laughs.

"Who is your favorite in all of Egypt, Amunet?" Khufu asks.

"Hmmm." Amunet rolls over and props her chin in her hand, watching the rest of us with a grin. "Ahmose is quite fine."

Tamit throws an arm across Ahmose. "Stay away, sister!" She laughs.

Khufu pulls himself to a sitting position. "I know, you are in love with the priest in training, Rashidi, who follows you with his eyes when you pass by."

"Rashidi! That little weasel?" Amunet throws pieces of grass back at Khufu. "I would sooner marry Ebo!" She points up at the young slave, who bows in her direction as if to offer his services if needed.

We all laugh.

"Ah, but you forget," Khufu says, "Ebo will never be Pharaoh. He cannot do whatever he wishes, as I can!"

She shrugs and grins at the rest of the group. "You don't do much that impresses me. At least Ebo can do much heavy lifting."

"Is that so?" Khufu jumps to his feet, and I look at Merit. She rolls her eyes, as though she anticipates Khufu's foolishness.

"But can you do this, Ebo?" Khufu asks. He pulls his donkey forward from where it grazes on the plain, then brings Amunet's donkey alongside it. He leaps onto the back of the first, then brings his feet up and stands in a crouch on its back. The donkey shifts to one side, and Khufu barks at it. Then in one quick movement he pushes himself to stand and braces one foot on the back of each donkey. They hold for him, and he gives a triumphant shout.

"You see? I can do anything! Even the animals submit!"

We all clap, as he expects us to. He holds his position until Amunet cries out, "You'll break your neck!" When one of the donkeys grows restless, Khufu jumps down, arms raised above his head, grinning broadly.

It is always this way. Khufu is the center of all we do. So it is only when Khufu announces that we will begin the hunt, and instructs Ebo to pack the remains of our meal, that we go to the boats.

I hope for bird hunting today, as I am growing quite skilled with the throw stick and welcome the chance to show Merit how I can bring down a bird. But Khufu insists that we hunt the hippopotamus today. Only the biggest beasts for the heir to the throne of Horus.

We pile into two boats and lay our spears in the hull. Mentu is in the back of the boat that also holds Merit and myself. He pushes off, and the prow slices into the green-brown marsh, streaming pale reeds on either side. The brackish water smells of silt and fish, but I trail my fingertips at the side of the boat, enjoying the cool of the water.

Khufu's boat is ahead of ours, and the future pharaoh stands at its prow, one foot on the edge. His profile against the sun gives him the look of a god. I glance at Merit and consider standing in our boat.

She is like the pure white sun here in the marsh, I think. Her eyes widen and she reaches for my arm and pulls my hand from the water. A crocodile lies at the marsh's edge, its eyes half-closed in a deceptive stupor.

I decide it is better to remain close to Merit.

Mentu poles us along from the back of the boat.

Ahead, Khufu shouts. "Hippo!"

I can make out the gray hump of the beast's huge back as it dives below the shallow water.

We scramble for our harpoons, fitting spear points to shafts. The harpoons are crafted so that the shaft frees itself from the point when the animal is hit.

We draw as close as we dare, alongside the other boat, and wait. The hippo cannot stay underwater for many minutes, and it is not long before its cavernous maw breaks the surface, followed by a bulbous head.

Mentu's harpoon flies over my head and hits the water several cubits from the hippo. I release mine, but the head is too small a target. Ahmose has no taste for hunting, so it is left to Khufu to bring the beast down. He waits, with the patience of an expert hunter, until the hippo's body crests the water. His shaft flies true, and the point embeds in the beast's upper back, below his head. The hippo bellows with fury and shakes its head to dislodge the point.

Khufu's shaft is still attached to the point, however; it has not freed itself as it should. He tugs to no avail.

The hippo dives to elude its attackers and takes the harpoon with it.

"Come back, you cursed water demon!" Khufu yells, and I recall his earlier boast about the animals' submission.

Khufu holds fast to the end of the harpoon, unwilling to let it disappear with the hippo. He will need to wound the animal several more times before it will be exhausted enough to be roped and dragged to shore.

"Let it go!" Amunet shouts.

Just as I am certain Khufu will be yanked from the boat, the hippo surfaces again, snorting and rolling. I marvel when my cousin jumps to the prow of the boat and, with a crazed yell, leaps onto the back of the animal and grabs for the spear point.

The women scream, every one of them. I scream myself. We all stand up in our boats, threatening to topple us into the water.

The hippo goes mad with the indignity of being ridden. His head arcs backward, and his body rolls from side to side. Khufu holds the spear like the horn of a saddle and rolls with him.

Then in the blink of an eye, the hippo dives, stealing the future King of the Two Lands.

The Great Wife was a private woman. I searched among the lesser wives, among the servants, even among the concubines, for one with whom she may have shared her fears. None of them knew anything more of her than I, and most of them far less.

As for Mentu, if he had been concerned about any danger to himself or Merit, would he not have told me? Of course, Mentu had kept secret his meetings with the Great Wife. What else had he not told me?

I knew of no one else in whom Mentu might have confided. Not even his wife, as I learned when the woman reacted with anger at my question.

"He didn't talk to me of such things!" she said, with the huff of a neglected woman. "His projects, his work—he kept all that talk for you. Do not come to me with your questions!"

And so once again I had nowhere to turn for answers. Unless . . .

There were others with whom Merit had spent time toward the end. People she seemed to trust.

The People of the One.

I pondered her involvement with the strange sect as I climbed to the plateau to meet with my chief overseers. The winds had calmed today, deadening the sounds above. I climbed in silence.

Perhaps I should go back to the village, to one of their meetings. Afterward, I might find someone to whom Merit expressed fear for her life. Of course, I could not simply walk into their midst. I would need to be escorted by Neferet. *Yes, I should see Neferet again and ask.* Today, if possible.

"Grand Vizier!" The words were shouted in seeming anger, and I turned, surprised to find that I had reached the meeting stone and that my three men were already there. De'de stood with hands on his hips, his lips tightened in annoyance. His eyes were painted dramatically today, swept upward with green malachite. "Did you not hear me?"

"I'm sorry," I said. "I—my mind was occupied."

De'de cocked his head. "While your mind is occupied, this project is falling apart."

"What's falling apart?"

Khons spoke first. "The limestone in Tura has slowed."

"Tura as well? What is going on?"

Khons shrugged. "We received a message from Ako, and his only explanation was that the stonemasons have encountered a design problem."

"How close are we to having—"

"Not close enough. Fifty-six thousand stones either here or still in Tura."

I cursed.

Sen leaned into the conversation. "If the stone haulers here continue at their current pace, the slowdown in Tura won't make any difference. They'll have plenty of time to catch up."

I shielded my eyes from the sun and squinted up at the pyramid. As always, it crawled from its base to its flat top with thousands of laborers. "I don't understand. Why has worked here slowed?"

A dry gust kicked sand toward us, and Sen coughed before speaking. "As best I can tell, it's simply a morale problem. The men are tired. We've been at it for several years, and the project doesn't look even half finished. They're losing their heart for it."

I pounded my staff into the ground like a hammer. "Don't the fools realize that in accomplishing one fourth the height, we've already placed half the stones? From here, it's—"

"Perhaps they do not," Sen said. "But I do not think a lecture on architecture is what they need."

I turned on Sen. "And what *do* you think they need?"

The older man lifted his eyebrows at my tone.

I sighed and scratched my head. "I'm sorry. I have many things on my mind. Do you have a suggestion?"

De'de interrupted. "It is not simply a matter of fatigue," he said. "I hear the murmuring in the village. They are frustrated by all the changes of plans. First, the underground chamber is abandoned, after the best of them spent many months cramped in tiny spaces, chiseling out the bedrock and hauling it up the corridor."

He stroked his chin as though the artificial beard of authority were strapped there. "Now labor is being diverted to the queen's pyramid. On top of that, they do not think it propitious that the Overseer of Constructions and the Great Wife have both crossed to the west within days of each other."

"The Scourge of Anubis," Khons ventured.

I glared at him and he said no more.

"If I may, I have an idea," Sen said, and I waved a hand at him. "What about a competition? Between work gangs. We could establish targets—a certain number of stones laid per day, for example— and any gang that meets its goal will be given extra rations of food and beer. Or it could be a contest between gangs, as to which works most quickly."

I glanced at Khons and De'de to solicit their thoughts.

"Could work," Khons grunted.

De'de shrugged one shoulder. "I suppose it is worth trying. The men do love their rations."

Sen nodded. "I will set it up. But, Grand Vizier, I'll need your help in setting benchmarks. I'm not yet familiar enough with the plans."

I rubbed my eyes, gritty with sand.

It was too much. Supply problems, morale decline, changing plans, and two murders to unravel. How was I supposed to keep it all under control?

When I cleared my eyes and looked up, my brother Ahmose stood at the meeting stone. His head was bare and he wore no makeup. It could mean only one thing.

Our father was dead.

There are things a son must do, regardless of convenience or expediency. Among these is that one must care for his parents, in life and in death. Though Ahmose would prefer to think that he alone attended to our father, the truth is that my position provided ongoing security for him. And I loved our father.

And so I left Sen to deal with the work gangs and promised Khons that I would see to the problem with the Tura quarry. Questions regarding Merit's death, questions for Neferet and the People of the One, would have to wait. There was a tomb well south, in Meidum, that required inspecting by the two sons of the man who would be buried there, beside his wife who had preceded him to the fields of the afterlife.

Ahmose and I trudged aboard the barque of Pharaoh himself the next morning. It was gracious of Khufu to insist we take it, and the boat had been brought to the pyramid harbor for us, manned by Khufu's ten brawny oarsmen.

My brother tossed a parcel into the cabin in the center of the barque and went to stand in the stern, facing east, toward the harbor's entrance. I loaded my own belongings into the cabin but did not approach Ahmose. We had spoken little since he had informed me that our father had crossed.

The boat was long and narrow, only ten cubits across, with room for the small center cabin and a slot on each side for five oarsmen. The front of the boat jutted far in front of me, however, with its long-horned prow ready to cut through the current as we traveled upriver. The pilot hopped across several minutes later with a nod to me. He was a bulky specimen who looked as though he had spent part of his life at the oars. He grabbed the acacia pole that lay in the hull and moved to the port side near Ahmose.

"How long will it take?" my brother asked. "To Meidum."

The pilot studied the water, then the sky. "With a favorable wind, we should make it by this time tomorrow. If the wind leaves us . . ." He shrugged and left his thought unfinished.

We were soon off, through the harbor, down the canal, and out onto the Nile. I had not often traveled the river during the flood season, when the farmers were conscripted to work on the pyramid. The river seemed as wide as the earth today, with palms jutting from the water as though they floated there like overgrown lotus flowers.

Ahmose retreated to the cabin and sat beside me. I did not pretend, even to myself, that the gesture was friendly. There was simply no place else to sit.

I pulled some dried beef from my pouch, tore off a leathery piece, and offered the rest to Ahmose.

"Thank you," he said. It was a beginning.

The oarsmen worked their rhythm, and the sound of the oars plopping into the water in unison was like a lullaby.

"Do you think we will find it still well kept?" I asked.

He chewed the beef slowly. "Since Sneferu abandoned the Meidum pyramid, and had father build him two more at Saqqara, there is no greater tomb at Meidum than that of our parents. I have made certain that it is well cared for."

"*You* have made certain?"

Ahmose snorted and looked at me. "What did you think, Hemi? That we could simply bury our mother there and walk away, with no further thought? It has taken ongoing payments to ensure the preservation of her tomb and chapel. I have seen to it. I know you are busy."

"Ahmose, I—"

He scratched his forehead, eyes closed. "There is nothing to say, Hemi."

"Let me speak."

A heavy sigh was his only response.

"I want to thank you for all you have done for Father. You have been a good son. I am sorry for what I have lacked."

Ahmose lifted an eyebrow and turned slightly toward me but said nothing.

The boat sliced neatly through the water, and the pilot raised the mast that would help the oarsmen propel us upriver. We sat in silence. The sun burned hot, but the breeze cooled my upturned face and carried the smells of wet earth and marshy water.

The pyramid drifted away behind us, until it was a watery illusion on the edge of the desert. I should have felt anxiety at leaving the project, but instead I felt nothing, and the pressing reality of Father's death fell on me.

I had neglected him, perhaps. But everything was for him, really. The harbor, the valley temple, the pyramid, the causeway and mortuary temple yet to come. I directed men and raised stone, all to please my father.

And now he had gone to the west, where none of my achievements could reach him. I was wearing myself out to earn rations that would never be distributed. A hopelessness stole over me, a realization that everything I worked for was meaningless. I shoved the thought away with all the strength of will I could marshal.

The day wore on with nothing to mark the time but the passing of villages, like floating islands in the floodplain, with dykes as their roads. Villagers waved as we passed and ran down the canal banks to get a closer look at the royal barque and its passengers.

We slept in snatches in the cabin and awoke in the morning to the grim face of the pilot.

"Dead calm," he said.

"Now what?"

The pilot moved along the line of men, his hand gripping shoulders as he passed. "We will push on with only the power of the men, but it will be slow going."

With no wind and the prospect of a lengthened trip, Ahmose and I grew restless and irritable. "Perhaps you should take a turn at the oars!" Ahmose said when I complained about the speed. "Perhaps you could do it better, just as you do everything better."

Some time later I tried to engage Ahmose in a remembrance of happier times with our father, when we were young boys. He would not be pulled in.

"I do not think you really want to begin reminiscing," he said in a tone low and threatening.

I retreated to the other side of the boat, and kept to myself. But the gods would not allow us to live in peace on such a tiny piece of wood for two days, and it wasn't long before we were angry again. Ahmose had tried to pass me on the narrow boat, I got in his way, we collided and lost our balance, and suddenly we were shoving at each other.

The pilot yelled. His warning was like spitting on a bonfire.

Ahmose went down first. I would have walked away, but he used a leg to sweep my feet from under me. I fell on him, and he rolled to pin me under. River water pooled beneath my head and soaked into my clothes.

Ahmose straddled my chest, his hands at my throat.

I welcomed the attack. The years of silent hate and subtle innuendo had eaten at me like worms at a carcass.

"Say it, Ahmose! Say whatever it is you have wanted to say these many years!"

But he would not. By Hathor's bloody horns, even now, he would not. Instead he pushed off me, left me there in the hull, crossed into the cabin, and shoved the door panel closed.

I did not move for some time. The pilot came and stood over me, perhaps to ensure that I still lived, then moved away.

I studied the solid blue of the sky and considered that one day, perhaps even today, my brother might kill me.

SIXTEEN

The wind increased, the oarsmen pushed forward, and we reached Meidum in the late afternoon of the second day. The lush plains here extended beyond the floodwater, to the foot of Sneferu's first pyramid.

We disembarked and began the short walk, swigging beer from jugs.

"It must seem small to your eyes," Ahmose said, "now that you build one so grand."

I looked ahead at the first true pyramid and steadied my voice. "Those who built before us taught us all we know. We build on their foundation and would achieve nothing without their accomplishments."

When we were still a slight distance from the pyramid, we reached the twin mastabas, joined at the sides, of Itet and Neferma'at. Together the flat-topped buildings stretched back toward the pyramid, and far to the left and right. A squared doorway opened into each tomb chapel. I had forgotten how large the complex was. In unspoken agreement, we first headed to our father's chapel.

We found all in order, as Ahmose had said. An aged priest led us through the heavy silence of the meandering passageways. The wall paintings had been completed in vivid color. The underground tomb chamber located at the center of the mastaba was blocked by a slab of granite. Ahmose and I worked together to slide it across while the priest disappeared and returned with a torch. We then descended into the tomb chamber and found more stunning decoration and a sarcophagus ready to receive its guest.

"Send word ahead," the priest said, "when the seventy days are completed and you approach. We will be ready with mourners and priests."

"We will bring mourners with us," Ahmose said. "All of Egypt grieves the loss of Neferma'at."

"Of course." The priest bowed his head.

Ahmose gave further instructions about the sacrifices to be made in the tomb chapel, and about the guards to be posted near the mastaba. I let him take the lead, as eldest son and the one who had seen to these details thus far. I moved away, examining the chapel. The smell of river water and sour beer clung to me, and I wished for a bath and perfumes.

When we were satisfied that all would be ready for our father's arrival, we passed out of the tomb chapel into the sunlight again, squinting. We moved along to the second entrance, into our mother's tomb chapel.

I had not been here in years. Carved reliefs, filled in with brightly colored pastes, covered the walls of musty chambers from floor to ceiling. It was still a beauty to behold. Strange as it might seem, my mother had loved this chapel as she oversaw its construction and decoration. She had supervised every painting, every relief. Here was the family receiving offerings. Over there my father holding a fresh-killed duck in one hand, smiling in triumph, his greyhound at his side. Servants performing daily tasks and farming the land. We moved along the walls, a testament to our family's early days. There were reliefs of the gods too. Thoth, my father's god, and Anubis, finding the heart he weighed to be lighter than Ma'at's feather.

But then came the inevitable, and we came to an awkward pause in front of my mother's favorite painted relief. I could still remember her clapping in glee as she showed it to us for the first time. It looked exactly as I remembered.

There on the wall stood two young boys, brothers and best friends, drawing a bird trap shut, a pastime that had occupied much of our youth and brought us unending delight.

We stood apart now, Ahmose and I, separated by years and anger and misunderstandings and resentment, and we gazed upon that painting and remembered.

I reached out and ran my fingers over the reliefs, carved deep into the limestone. I turned to Ahmose, hoping for some sign of the affection he had once felt for me.

He did not take his eyes from the relief.

"I do not think I can remain silent any longer," he said. "I have held my tongue these many years out of respect for Father. But now he is gone. The truth must be spoken, and confessions to priests are not enough."

I held my breath, but he turned away.

"Speak then! Tell me!"

He turned back, his expression confused. "I will not speak to *you* of secrets too long held," he said. "I will speak to the king. And I will let him deal with you as he sees fit."

He departed our mother's chapel, left me staring after him.

With a favorable wind and the current now aiding us, the return passage of the barque was swift. Yet the time stretched taut like a string threatening to snap, and I could induce Ahmose to speak no more.

We arrived back at the harbor the next morning, and Ahmose jumped from the boat, into the arms of his wife. He departed the harbor without a backward glance.

I was not greeted so warmly. Khons had seen the barque approach and was there glaring at me as I climbed out.

"He says you can come and split rock yourself if you want."

"Who?"

"Ako, over at Tura. I sent him your message, and that was his word sent back to you. 'Come and split rock yourself.'"

Hot blood surged in my veins. "I will see to the day's work, then take a boat across and speak to him myself."

"Good," Khons grunted and turned on his heel.

I paused only a moment on the dock, with the water at my back and the pyramid before me. I raised my eyes and took a deep breath. Father was gone, but the work must go on. It was time to think of the future, not the past.

Ahmose's cryptic warnings be cursed. I would leave my own legacy in stone, and I dared him to try to stop me.

I needed to see Neferet again.

I found her outside her home toward the end of the day, surrounded by children. She smiled at me over the tops of their heads.

I had not intended to stay for their evening meal, but she insisted. Sen arrived and only nodded in my direction. On the plateau he was congenial. In his home, he seemed wary of me.

He and I spoke of the project, as Neferet moved in and out with foods that delighted every one of the senses. Red beef and greens with pungent leeks. Juicy pomegranates, fleshy and sweet. Sen relaxed a bit, and I forgot my reason for coming and enjoyed the conversation and laughter around the table.

But when the meal had ended, Sen asked, "Did you come for a reason, Grand Vizier?" He glanced at Neferet. "Other than the pleasure of our company?"

I wiped my mouth and nodded. "I am trying to speak to anyone who had contact with the Great Wife in her last days, to learn whether there was any threat to herself or to Mentu-hotep. I was hoping to meet with some of your friends again, perhaps attend another of your gatherings."

Sen seemed to mask a smile that implied there was something I was not saying. "We would be happy to have you again, my lord. We gather again a few nights from now."

I chewed my lip. "I do not like to wait."

"Is that so?"

Sen's sarcasm was noted, and I smiled. "Perhaps there were a few with whom she spent her time. Would it be possible for me to call on them tonight?"

Sen deferred to Neferet.

"They seemed pleased to speak with the grand vizier the other night," she said. "They would welcome him again."

Neferet offered to guide me to the home of her friends, and soon thereafter we were in their courtyard, the woman Layla guiding me to the best chair and offering food and wine. And behind the kindness, I knew she also was offering me friendship. We sat in a close circle in their courtyard. A fire burned in the center, warding off the night chill and lighting faces with an orange warmth. In the corner, a young boy played a flute softly.

"We will help you in whatever we can, Grand Vizier," the husband, Hanif, said. "But she did not share much of herself with us." He smiled. "Especially at the beginning, when she believed we did not know who she was."

"Did she ever speak of fear?"

Hanif looked to Neferet and she gave a slight nod. "She feared her own heart," he said. "And the changes that were happening there."

"Changes?"

"She wanted to cease her daily offerings to Egypt's gods. She wanted to join us in our sacrifices, which are of a different sort and not in your temples."

I looked around the fire, at the family's glowing faces. "What kind of sacrifices?" I had heard of tribes in distant lands offering their children to the gods. Surely, these people—

"Do you bring offerings to the gods, Grand Vizier?" Hanif asked.

"Of course."

"Why?"

"Because they demand it. Because I wish to appease them, to earn their favor and have them bestow blessings on me."

"The One True God cannot be appeased, and his favor cannot be earned. He sits in judgment of all men who have gone their own way."

I spread my hands on my knees. "Then you are to be pitied, for to fall under the wrath of any god is fearsome."

Hanif seemed to grow bold. "There is only one God. Your gods are stone and wood, no different than the chair upon which you sit or the pyramid you build."

I swallowed and fingered Merit's ankh at my throat, suddenly unsure of the wisdom of speaking with these people. Did the gods care enough to listen to the words of those who did not believe in them?

"What use is there in worshiping a god who has only judgment for you and nothing more?"

Hanif patted Layla's arm, whose face was alight with joy. "I did not say that he has only judgment. Besides, what kind of God would he be if we only worshiped him because we had a *use* for it? He is God. There is no other. He must be worshiped simply for that reason."

I leaned back in the chair and studied his face, then Neferet's. There was a different sort of peace there.

"So if not to appease or earn favor, why do you sacrifice?"

"To atone."

I shrugged. "It is all the same."

"But it is not!" Hanif leaned forward, his fingers pressed together. "His creatures have turned their backs on his holy face, and we can never appease his righteous anger nor do enough to earn his favor. His favor must be imparted to us, and it can only be imparted through the shedding of blood."

A dung block in the fire popped, and the flame surged.

"When you die," Hanif said, "you hope to have done enough good, to have kept yourself pure enough, to be found worthy to enter the afterlife. Am I correct?"

"I hope to, yes."

"But what is 'good enough'? What is 'pure enough'? Either something is pure or it is not." He smiled kindly. "Are you pure, Grand Vizier?"

I shifted in my chair. "If I am not, I do not see that the blood of an ox will make me so."

"No, that is only temporary. But the One Who Comes will change that."

I watched the boy with the flute. His fingers danced over the instrument.

"You said the Great Wife feared her own changing beliefs. Did she feel that her life would be in danger because of this?"

Layla spoke. "She was unhappy about Pharaoh's declaration of himself as Ra on earth. She felt it was wrong, and it bothered her that he had been convinced of it by . . . those closest to him." She looked at her hands. "She planned to speak to him about it. But I do not think she feared him."

I stood. "Thank you for your thoughts, and your hospitality. It is time I left, however."

Hanif stood with me. "Please come again to our gathering, if you like. We do not turn away anyone who sincerely looks for truth."

I bowed. "Then the importance of truth is something we both agree upon."

Layla squeezed my arm, as she had in their hidden chamber the day we met. I looked into her wide smile and wondered why this stranger seemed to care deeply about me.

Neferet led me out in silence. I accompanied her back to her home through the dark village and prepared to leave her at her door.

"Will you stay?" she asked.

"I cannot. I must leave early in the morning for Tura."

"Tura!" Her eyes lit up. "May I come with you?"

I laughed. "Are you thinking of applying your paints to the white cliffs of the limestone quarry?"

She smiled and hit me playfully on the arm. "My brother is a stonemason in Tura. I have not seen him in many months. I would love to visit him, to take him some things!"

I frowned and looked into the night.

"Please, Hemi! I promise I will not cause any problems. I will be as silent as a sleeping cat."

"You must be at the harbor at dawn. I cannot wait."

"Agreed!" She stood on her toes and kissed me lightly on the cheek. "Thank you!" she said and disappeared into her home.

It was not safe to wander home slowly through the desert, but I found my straying thoughts made it difficult for me to maintain a swift pace. The night had given me much to ponder, but I was certain not a bit of it would help me solve the murders of Merit and Mentu, nor help me to restore ma'at in the land I loved.

The harbor at dawn is like a sandstorm in the desert, with man and ship like grains of sand swirling in a frantic rush to get somewhere, anywhere. Supply ships, barges, and ferries clogged the dock, and shouted orders from pilots and crewmen pierced the morning air.

Neferet stood on the quay when I arrived, part of the chaos, in her dress with the red stitching and all those jingling bells sewn to the bottom. At her feet were overflowing baskets of bananas and tomatoes.

Her smile was as big as the blue sky. "I have never been here this early!" she said without greeting as I approached. "Isn't it magnificent?"

I grunted. It seemed to me every craft in the greenish water was in danger of foundering unless someone took control of the disorder, and the baskets and crates of rations stacked on the quay may very well tumble into the water before reaching the village.

A crewman bumped me as he passed, sending me into Neferet. I could smell her perfume, even among the ripening bananas.

She laughed and threw her hands between us. "Grand Vizier!"

I stared at the laborer's back, but he was oblivious.

"Our accommodations will not be luxurious, I'm afraid. The fastest way to get there is the next barge departing for the quarry." I pointed to the black and yellow ship in the water, its prow towering over us.

Neferet grabbed a tomato from the basket beside her, tossed it into the air, and caught it with one hand. "I do not care. It is a glorious morning!" She scooped up a large pouch. "Shall we go?"

She needed some assistance crossing to the barge, as her hands were full with her pouch and her tomato. I wondered briefly what she planned to do with the fruit.

I noticed several overturned empty barrels in the center of the barge, and I righted them as we passed. Neferet stopped to watch me and laughed.

We sailed from the harbor, only narrowly missing two ferries and a supply ship, which Neferet also thought quite funny.

When we were finally on the river, I watched the coast slide by and tried to let the slow passage calm me, like sand blown smooth over crevices in bedrock.

But Neferet had brought the chaos with us.

When she had finally settled enough to allow a moment of silence between observations, and had eaten her tomato, its juice dripping down her arm, she asked about the murders. "Have you learned anything?"

"Nothing." I slapped my palm against the side of the barge where we stood. "No one knew of any danger to Merit or Mentu. They seem to have been meeting to discuss building plans and nothing more. There is nothing else to discover on the bodies or from where they were found. The masks were made by an artist now dead who did not speak of his work. I can find no other connection between Merit and Mentu."

"What will you do now?"

I watched the water ahead. "What I must. I will sail to Tura and speak my mind to a certain overseer of the quarry."

SEVENTEEN

Tura limestone is the best in Egypt. Gleaming white when dressed, fine-grained, and not as porous as that found in Giza, the limestone is soft and easily cut while in the earth, but, after exposure to air for some time, it hardens.

The quarry lay a half day south of Giza, on the opposite side of the Nile, and the barge reached the quarry harbor before noon. We waited while a ferry unloaded its stones onto a departing barge. We passed the time watching the fascinating process of transferring stone from the sledges that brought it from the quarry, to the ferry boats and rafts pulled into the harbor's narrow dock, then out to the barges. The levers that pried and lifted the stone into place had been wrapped in straw to protect the delicate finish of the stone.

From the quay it was a few minutes' walk to the lip of the quarry, where the gaping hole in the earth spread before us in a blinding display. If one squinted, the smooth white cliffs of the gorge could be mistaken for the future wall of the pyramid itself. Everywhere a fine white dust hung in the air.

Ako, the overseer I had come to speak with, hailed me over the ringing of hammer and chisel, as though I were expected. He and

I had been friends many years ago, before the will of the gods had taken us in different directions. He walked toward us, a measuring rod in his hand.

"Grand Vizier," he said, nodding to Neferet, "I did not think you would ever take a wife."

I grasped his outstretched arm in greeting. "This is Neferet, daughter of Senosiris. A friend."

He bowed to Neferet. "I apologize. Now that I see you from a cubit, I realize that a woman as fine as yourself would not be attached to this baboon."

She laughed. "I like him, Hemi."

Ako lifted his eyebrows at her use of my little name and inclined his head toward me. "Hmm," he said.

"Neferet has come to see her brother, a stonecutter here in Tura."

"Yes, I know the son of Senosiris. He works with the Kemet Gang. A good man." Ako pointed down into the quarry, a hundred cubits north of us. "There."

"I think I see him!"

"I will have someone take you down."

"No need. Thank you." Neferet fairly skipped away and quickly found the start of the rubble path that would take her down into the earth.

"Interesting," Ako said, watching her go.

"She is . . . independent."

Ako chuckled. "She needs a husband, perhaps?"

"Tell me about the stone. You must get it to us faster, Ako. You know this."

Ako sliced the air with his measuring rod. "You have no idea what goes on here, Hemi. That is always the way with those who lead. They make demands without knowledge of what the laborers must do."

"Do not subject me once again to your complaints about the laborers' working conditions, Ako. I only want the stone."

The white dust had already begun to settle itself on my body, changing my skin color to that of a foreigner.

"The problem is the cornerstones," he said. "Come, I will show you."

Ako led me to a space cleared above the quarry, where a dozen or so stonemasons worked to cut the casing stones to shape. They would be dressed with more precision on the pyramid site, but here at the quarry while they could still be addressed from all sides, the majority of the cutting was performed. Whenever possible, stones that would lay beside each other on the pyramid were cut from the earth side-by-side, so that they could be fitted together tightly at the line of breakage. Each of the casing stones was rectangular in shape, longer and thicker than a man. Except for the cornerstones.

We passed to the opposite side of the work site, where two men labored over a single massive cornerstone with its complicated angles and proportions. Rather than rectangular, the cornerstone was a squat block, with a notch cut to fit it to the corner.

"The current design is insufficient," Ako said. "Each cornerstone, from base to top, must bear and absorb the tremendous weight sliding down upon it from all the layers above."

"The design is no different than it has always been."

One of the stonemasons looked up from his work. "Exactly," he said. "And Sneferu's pyramid at Meidum already shows signs of eventual collapse. It will not stand for eternity."

"So make it stronger." I glanced over my shoulder at some noise in the quarry behind and below us. The men were shouting at something.

"You know quite well it is not so simple, Hemi," Ako said. "Changing the angles, redistributing the weight—it requires careful design. And until we find the answer, we will not simply churn out our quota to make you happy!"

The disturbance below us had grown, and even Ako seemed concerned now. We walked to the entrance to the path and peered over the edge.

Several work gangs had come to a standstill and were alternating between laughter and hooting calls. I could not make out the shouted words, but the implication was clear. The calls were directed to one petite woman who jingled when she walked.

Ako grunted beside me. "Akhet can be a long season. It has been many weeks since they have seen their wives."

"They would do better to remember their mothers and sisters," I said, starting down the path.

"She will be fine," he called, but I waved him off.

Neferet was not close enough for me to determine her expression. But the hurried way in which she moved—not her usual languid walk that was more like dancing—told me all I needed to know.

She watched her feet as she tread the ledge that snaked up the quarry wall. Several times laborers stopped her and would not move aside to let her pass. I did not take my eyes from her as I descended. *Where is her brother?* Why did he not escort her up the cliff? I felt a spark of anger toward the man I'd never met.

I had almost reached her when I saw her circle around one laughing stonecutter, then lose her footing on the rubble path. With a yelp, she slid down the face of the cliff.

The one who had caused her to fall reached for her, but I shoved him aside and caught her arm myself.

"Hemi!" she cried up at me, fear in her eyes. Dusty gravel floated down around her and she bent her head.

I pulled her up, over the top of the ledge, until she sat beside me. Her leg bled.

I reached for her leg, but there it was again—my infuriating weakness. Something about the way the blood ran red down to the whiteness of the limestone path caused my head to . . .

I became aware of myself again and found my head resting on Neferet's shoulder, her warm hand against my cheek. Cursing, I reached for her leg again.

"I am well, Hemi. Don't look at it. Get me back up this path, and I will wrap it in rags. Do not worry."

It was as close as we had ever been, sitting there together, and I felt the danger of disorder once more.

She would not let me carry her and whispered that she had already drawn more attention than she desired. "Tell me about the problem here," she said as we climbed, my arm bracing her. "Distract me."

"Cornerstones," I said. "They require precision and a structural integrity not required of the rest of the stones. Ako believes our current design is faulty and will not stand."

She slowed and looked to me. "You must call my brother," she said and pointed below us. "He is a mason, not a cutter, you know. He works at the removal site, not at the top yet. But he was just telling me this very thing. That the cornerstones will not hold. He has a better design, he says." She gripped my arm. "Call him, Hemi. Promise me you will bring him up."

"We will bring him up, Neferet. But first we must get you out of this pit."

I had her settled at the top within minutes. The physician who treated the men was summoned and he tended to her leg. Meanwhile, I had Ako send for Neferet's brother.

His anxious face appeared above the edge of the quarry faster than I would have thought possible.

"What has happened?" he said, running for Neferet.

"Just a scratch, brother," she said. "Nothing more."

"I should have brought you up myself," he said, then looked at me. "I should have brought her up. My foreman would not allow it. I should have done it anyway."

I held out an arm. "I am Hemiunu."

He dipped his head. "Grand Vizier. Thank you for seeing to my sister."

Neferet called to us from her place on the ground. "You two must like each other," she said. To her brother she said, "Hemi is a good friend." Her brother's eyes widened a bit, and he brought his attention back to me.

"Neferet tells me you may have a solution to our cornerstone problem."

The man's face brightened like a boy just handed a new spear. "I can see it exactly in my mind," he said and began to explain.

I held up a hand. "Follow me."

We crossed to the masons, and I motioned for Ako to join us. Neferet's brother grabbed a copper chisel and began to scratch in the sand, explaining his new design. I nodded, slowly at first, then with a widening smile. "Yes," I whispered. "Yes."

He pushed the lines of the cornerstone's notched core closer to its edge. "Here," he said, pointing to the bedding joint and digging a new angle, "here we increase by ten seqeds, and then here." His chisel jabbed the notch. "Here we decrease. The weight of the stone above will then shift inward—"

"—increasing its load-bearing ability—"

"—by fifty-fold," the boy finished with a grin.

"Brilliant," one of the masons said behind me.

Neferet laughed. "So I have finally found someone who understands my brother and his numbers!" Her glance shifted between the two of us and she laughed again. "You both look like you've just been crowned king."

By the time the sun set over the western desert, Neferet and I were on an outgoing barge, and her brother had been promoted to master stonemason. Neferet beamed and wrapped her hand about my arm as we stood at the rail.

"Thank you," she whispered.

"It was your brother's design. There is no need to thank me."

She squeezed my arm until I looked down at her. "Thank you," she said again.

The barge floated easily toward the Great Sea, toward the Horizon of Khufu.

It seemed to me that I should focus my attention on these two things alone—the project and Neferet. Perhaps it was time to let go of the past, to let go of my desire for revenge for the deaths of two that I loved. But always in the back of my mind, the priest Rashidi's words tumbled, warning me. *There will be more disorder, more suffering, until ma'at is restored.*

EIGHTEEN

xum, the Nubian who served as the project's guard, met us at the dock when we arrived back at the plateau in the long shadows of early evening, and I knew immediately that something evil had transpired while we were gone.

"What is it?" I asked, helping Neferet from the barge.

"Another murder."

Neferet retained my hand in hers and squeezed. "Who?"

Axum frowned down at her and addressed himself to me. "The Great One, Beloved of Horus, has allowed no one to see the body. He will see only you."

"Someone in the royal estate, then?" I said, too eagerly.

"Apparently. But word has leaked out to the laborers that it was one of their own."

"I don't understand."

"Nor I. But hundreds of workmen have descended upon the royal estate to demand answers."

I pulled Neferet to my side and said to Axum, "Find someone to see her safely home, then meet me at the palace." I turned to her and caught her attention with my eyes. "Directly home," I said. "I do not like the sound of this."

She bit her lip and looked southward to the palace. "But my father—"

"Home, Neferet. No doubt your father is attempting to maintain peace among the workers. I will find him."

She studied me for a moment, as though deciding whether to obey, then gave a quick nod and joined Axum.

I reached the gate of the royal estate quickly on foot, as the sun dipped beneath the line of sand in the west. I pulled up in surprise.

The sycamore grove inside the wall churned with peasants clustered in angry groups, milling about with fiery torches. I passed through the gate and kept my head down, steering my way along the path toward the palace. The tumult grew louder as I passed, until the grove and gardens around the king's lake fairly shook with a hundred voices. Within the high walls the sunset could no longer be seen. Darkness spread.

"The king builds his pyramid on our backs and cares nothing if we are killed while doing it!"

"The Scourge of Anubis takes from all. No one is safe!"

The bodies pressed in around me and blocked my passage. I tried to push through but was shoved back. The crowd of men smelled of sweat and too much beer, and in the growing darkness their brown bodies glistened in the torchlight.

Khufu must have sent out some of his servants. They wrestled through the crowd, torches held aloft, and demanded that the men return to their homes and barracks. Up ahead, more shouting broke out, and a circle widened. I twisted through and found one of the king's servants on the ground, surrounded by laborers who kicked at his ribs.

"Enough!" I shouted and yanked one peasant aside to get closer. He responded with a fist to my face. Stunned, I took a step back and tasted blood.

The man was sober enough to recognize me, and I enjoyed the fear that washed over his features.

"Your name?" I said and wiped at the trickle of blood at my mouth.

"Grand Vizier! I did not realize—"

I wasted no more time on him. The servant on the ground had taken a beating. "What is this?" I yelled. The crowd backed away, and I bent to the man, helped him to his feet and supported him. We walked to the palace.

When we reached the side of the royal lake, I gave him over to the care of his fellow servants and climbed up on a bench to be better seen and heard. Silence rippled across the sea of bodies and dark faces turned to me expectantly, eyes reflecting the torchlight. I waited for their full attention.

One of them yelled from the safety of the crowd. "What will you do to protect us from the Scourge of Anubis?" Then a wave of low murmurs.

I held up a hand. "I have only just arrived, and it would appear that you know more than I. There is no reason to believe that you are in danger."

Another shout. "With a killer among us?"

"I am certain we will identify this killer. And when we do, we will discover that his victims were chosen carefully, not at random. There is no cause for fear!"

"I will still sleep with my hand on my spear!" one called out and more murmurs of agreement spread through the night.

"You have worked hard for me for five years now," I said. "I have treated you fairly and paid you well. Trust me now to take care of you in this. Allow me to investigate this most recent misfortune. I make you a promise that word will be sent down to each of you as soon as anything is known."

The mood of the mob had settled, and I pushed. "Go home now. Back to your women and your bread and beer. Sleep well, assured that you are safe. Your king, the golden Horus, holds your fate in his hands, and he will not let you suffer. Go home!"

This last was delivered with force, and it had its intended effect. The crowd began to disperse and I took advantage of the cleared path to hasten to the palace. Inside, a servant seemed to be expecting me and led me with only a nod to follow him.

I had to admit to myself a certain excitement about this third murder. I had exhausted every avenue of questioning with the previous deaths and could not discover any further connection between Merit and Mentu. But a third killing . . . certainly it would provide a clearer picture, if my assurances to the men held true and these were not random victims.

We crossed through the Great Hall of Pillars, beyond the private hall and into the House of Adoration, the private chambers of Khufu.

The king sat upon a three-legged stool. His back was to me and his head drooped on his chest. My heart skipped for a moment and I wondered if in fact it was the king who had been killed. But then he sensed my presence and lifted his head.

Khufu was much changed. A gray pallor like aged granite had spread over his face. I thought he looked as though years had passed since I saw him last, rather than only a day.

He stood and waved away the servant who had escorted me.

Behind Pharaoh, a man's body lay on the floor. His face bore a mask, now too familiar.

"He has killed again, Hemi."

The trace of tears on Khufu's cheeks surprised me.

"Who? Who is it?"

He stepped aside and I tread forward carefully, scanning the floor for anything the killer may have left behind.

I knelt at the body, which was dressed as a servant. I saw no obvious injuries. I reached for the mask, tried to still my trembling hands, and lifted it from the face.

Ebo.

Khufu's trusted head servant since we were children.

I rocked back on my heels and looked up at the king's face, where fresh tears flowed. I laid aside the mask and went to him, grasped his shoulder.

"I did not realize he had grown so dear to you."

Khufu wiped at his face. "He was a good servant, it is true. Well trained and trustworthy. But in truth, I feel more distress than grief."

"Distress?"

He raised his eyes to mine, with all the intensity he had shown as a youth. "Don't you understand, Hemi? There is only one thing that connects the three of them. Merit, Mentu, and now Ebo. Only one thing."

I looked back to the body and my soul chilled.

Khufu was right. I had found the connection I sought.

"It is all coming back," he whispered. "What was long buried will not stay hidden." Khufu's face had paled to a deeper gray. "And who, Hemi," he asked, "who will be next?"

Justice and truth, the divine order, will always rise above the petty trifling of man, his vain attempts to hide and protect and avoid. On that day long ago, when a hippopotamus dragged Khufu into the marsh water, still gripping the shaft of his spear, we did not realize that events had begun that would change us all, that ma'at would find us regardless of what we tried to conceal . . .

We stare at the water where our future king has vanished. The hippo can stay under far longer than a man. But this hippo roars to the surface again, thrashing and bellowing. Its mouth opens wide, revealing blackened teeth.

A gaggle of geese lifts from the marsh to our right.

In the other boat, Amunet screams. "He'll be drowned!"

Ahmose shouts, "Not if the fool lets go!"

We all know there is little chance of this.

Khufu retains his hold, but he looks barely conscious.

"Let go!" we all scream.

He does not let go by choice, I do not believe. Instead his grip weakens with exhaustion, and his fingers slip from the shaft. He slides from the hippo's back and into the water beside, still as death. The beast seizes its chance to make a victim of his attacker and turns on Khufu.

I have brought our boat as close as I dare. We have only a fraction of time to help. Without thought, I leap across the water to beast and man and grab Khufu around the shoulders. He fights me, barely aware of his situation, but I maintain my hold and kick furiously toward the king's boat. Ahmose reaches an arm down and grasps mine. Together, we haul Khufu over the side and into the hull. His eyes are closed, but he is breathing.

And then a moment later, the unthinkable.

Khufu's eyes pop open. He bolts upright, still dripping marsh water, and begins to howl with laughter.

"Did you see that! Did you see me swim with the hippo? No king of Egypt has ever taken such a ride!"

I shake the water from my head and arms and move away.

There are too many people in this boat now. Mentu poles our boat alongside, and I climb across.

Merit holds out her hand and her smile as I sit. "You were wonderful," she whispers and glides tentative fingers across the bare skin of my shoulder to wipe away some marsh grass that clings there. Her light touch jolts my senses alert as when I wrestled with Khufu in the water. "You saved his life." She looks at Khufu from lowered eyes. "Whether he acknowledges it or not."

By mutual agreement, we return to our grassy field where we had taken food. No more hippo hunting this afternoon. "Birds," Khufu announces with his indefatigable laughter. It is time to hunt for birds.

We tumble out onto the bank and are met by Ebo, who holds a robe out to his wet master with a sour expression.

"You should have been there, Ebo!" Khufu says. "It was a thing to behold."

Ebo wraps Khufu's shoulders in the robe and nods. "I am certain my prince was excellent in the hunt as usual."

Khufu pats himself dry. "Not the hunt, old man." He often calls Ebo "old man" though he is no older than we. "I rode the hippo!"

Ebo's brow puckers.

Khufu slaps him on the back. "The shaft did not fly loose, so I went after it."

Ebo surveys the rest of us with a look of sharp disapproval. "The prince of the blood should not risk his life for the sake of a harpoon," he says, rebuking us for allowing such a thing.

Khufu jabs Ebo in the side. "Now you begin to sound like an old *woman*, Ebo. Don't you want me to have any fun?"

Ebo stares him down. "What I want, my prince, is to see you healthy and happy and on the throne."

Master and servant study one another in a moment of strange silence. For the first time I realize how devoted Ebo has become to Khufu, and I see that he would do anything to protect the heir to the throne of Horus.

Khufu also seems to realize it. He grasps Ebo's upper arm and dips his head in acknowledgment. Then the prince turns to us. "We are too many to stay together for birding. They will hear us coming long before we are in range. We must split up."

Ebo is studying the horizon, where thick clouds cluster, a rare threat in this land. "Evil approaches," he says. "We should return."

We wait, knowing Khufu will direct us. He speaks as though Ebo has said nothing. "Amunet and I will go ahead, raise the birds."

Tamit lunges toward my brother. "I will stay with Ahmose."

There are no surprises in the way we have paired so far, until Mentu glances at me, then at my brother, and announces, "I will stay with Ahmose and Tamit. I want to see this new skill with the throwstick he has been boasting of."

Tamit glares at Mentu as though she could launch a throw stick from her eyes, but he only looks to me and winks. He is a good friend.

Each of the men procures his weapon from the donkey's pack, and I note with interest that as Amunet and Khufu wander away, Ebo follows. Perhaps he is unwilling to let Khufu take further risks today.

I turn to Merit, whose eyes are to the ground. I lift her chin with my fist, and she sighs and looks to me with a sadness that hurts. I had thought she would also be glad for Mentu's kindness.

"Shall we walk?" I say.

We move through the reeds in silence, waiting for Khufu and Amunet and the escort Ebo to frighten birds into the air, where we will attempt to take them down. The marsh is a strange place, with small land bridges crossing stagnant pools and little islands of reeds among the streams that flow northward from the Nile to the Great Sea. I wish that we could lose ourselves, Merit and I, in the marshes. For a while.

A heavy silence reigns between us now that we are alone. I am aware of my wet clothing. I smell of marsh water. "What saddens you?" I ask.

She sighs and breaks off a papyrus reed. "I do not care much for Khufu," she says and begins tearing pieces from the reed. "And yet to see the way he acts with Amunet . . ."

"You feel betrayed?"

"But how can I feel betrayed? Not yet, at least. Nothing has been formalized."

"Still, he disrespects you with his attention to her."

"It feels shameful to me, Hemi." She tosses the rest of the broken reed to the grass and grinds it with her toe. "Sometimes I wish that little priest Rashidi would take Amunet for his wife and we could be done with this!"

I half smile at the uncommon outburst.

"And yet," she says, "I cannot help but like Amunet. And I cannot help but like . . . another."

We slow to a stop and I turn to face her. She focuses on something over my shoulder, however. I turn and see Ebo walking back toward the donkeys.

"Has Khufu given up so soon?" I call.

Ebo's head jerks toward us. I have startled him. "He is still for the hunt," he says. "He wishes to go on alone, however."

Beside me Merit mutters, "Alone with her."

Ebo continues past us, and I pull Merit toward me. "It is unfair," I say into her green-painted eyes. "Unfair the way he treats you, the way he attends to her. And unfair that our paths are chosen for us by those too old to feel passion any longer."

She looks as though she wants to pull away, but she does not.

"I have something for you," I say, touching the pouch tied to my waist. "But first you must tell me the truth."

Her eyes hold fear. "How are we any better, Hemi?"

"Better?"

"Than them. Khufu and Amunet." She leans away, though does not break my grasp on her. "To speak like this, to always try to be together. How is this any different than what they do? Could Khufu not say the same as I? That I have betrayed him?"

"He is senseless to it, Merit. That is the difference. You do not flaunt your fickle affections for the world to take note. You cannot change the way you feel."

She does pull away now. "But I *must* change it."

I will not let her go until I hear the truth. "Tell me, Merit. Tell me how you feel."

Her eyes fill with tears, and I realize that caring for me has brought her pain. But I am young and I would rather have my affection returned than see my beloved happy.

She studies my face, then my shoulders and chest, then all of me. My mouth goes dry.

"I wish that you were the prince of the blood!" she says, then dares me with her eyes to protest.

Our heavy breaths mingle in the damp silence between us, an invisible embrace. But it is not enough. I pull her to me, hold her there until I see surrender in her eyes. I feel the tension flow out of her, and she lifts her face. Her lips graze my jaw, and I know nothing more than Merit, her eyes, her hair, her mouth. She returns my kiss with the quiet passion I have sensed so often in her.

The sky darkens around us, but in a haze of bliss, I pull the amulet from the pouch and circle her neck with it. She turns and lifts her hair, exposing her neck to me. I tie the cord well and kiss the skin beneath the knot.

Then she is in my arms again. But the impossible truths loom over us, and I feel her ka retreat. My hunger rises to call her back. I kiss her again, feeling the desperation.

"Hemi," she whispers, "we should join the others."

"They are occupied with the hunt." My voice is muffled against her hair. The cloud of birds rises.

She resists. "You must let me go."

"Merit." Her name is at once painful and beautiful. "I cannot."

I find her lips again with my own, and she allows me a moment. But then she senses what I know to be true: I am not in control of myself. She backs away, fear clouding her eyes.

And then she runs.

Ebo was correct. Evil approaches.

Khufu and I remained for some time in his chamber with the body of Ebo. I felt it necessary to make a thorough examination of the body, but I began with the surrounding area.

"Who found him?" I asked.

"I did."

"Here?"

"Yes. I returned from meeting with a few noblemen in the Great Hall, and he was there." Khufu pointed. "Just like that."

"Did you remove the mask?"

Khufu rubbed his eyes. "I knew it was him. But I needed to see for myself."

"And then you replaced it?"

"I did not want to see his face longer than I must."

I flexed my shoulders. "I want to examine the body."

"Of course. I will remain here though."

It was a strange way to express his desire to stay, as if he expected me to chase him out or thought I had something to hide.

Or perhaps it is he who is hiding something.

The floor around the body yielded no clues, and I moved on to Ebo's body, beginning with his work-worn feet. Behind me, I heard Khufu sit on the stool again and knew that he watched my every action. I tried to remain detached.

Thankfully, there was no blood on the body. Strangely, there appeared to be no injuries at all. I ran my fingers firmly over Ebo's legs and bare torso. The action felt oddly intimate though I had known this man many years. His body had cooled. I examined the throat, unmarked, and the reposed face, where I saw nothing amiss but the old scar across his forehead.

I thought to check his hand and was surprised to find the finger missing, despite the pattern established by the killer. In the absence of blood I had not though of it at first. I pondered this, but it told me nothing.

The mask was the same as the other two. High-quality gold from Nubia, hammered smooth. Blue lapis lazuli eyes inset and glowing. On the back, the mark of Anubis.

Khufu's stool scraped the floor, and I jumped. The silence in the chamber had numbed my senses.

"Anything?" he asked.

"I do not know how he was killed. There appear to be no injuries. Even strangulation or suffocation would leave bruises on the neck or marks of some sort."

We sat in silence for some minutes, each lost in our own thoughts. I crossed my arms over my bent knees. A weariness fell over me, and I lowered my head beneath the weight of unanswered questions and possibilities. Gradually, a thought surfaced. I lifted my head.

"There is a peculiar smell in here, Khufu. Have you been burning some different sort of incense?"

Khufu shook his head.

"A new type of perfume for your hair?"

"Nothing, Hemi. And I don't smell anything."

I shimmied toward the body and sniffed. "It is stronger here."

Khufu joined me and inhaled. His brow furrowed for a moment. "It makes me think of the temple."

I closed my eyes and focused on the scent. And the temple.

My eyes flew open.

"It is a drug! Such as the priests use on small animals before they lay them out for sacrifice."

Khufu wrinkled his nose in concentration, then nodded. "You may be right."

I leaned over the body once more and this time used my two fingers to open Ebo's mouth slightly. In doing so, I noticed tiny white flecks at the corners of his lips that I had missed. I sniffed his mouth, then sat back. "He has been poisoned."

Khufu stood, then returned to his stool and dropped his face into his hands. "Eight of us went out that day, Hemi. Including Ebo. Now four of us remain." He lifted his head. His eyes were like two points of light in a dark sky. "And one of us is a killer."

I stood. "I will call a priest to remove Ebo's body." I looked toward the window. "Your people are frightened. They have heard that this victim is one of them."

Khufu snorted. "He was hardly a peasant! He was chief servant of the Beloved of Horus!"

"Even so, it would be best if you were seen by them, if you spoke words of comfort."

Khufu sighed. "Tomorrow."

Part of me longed to remain in his chamber. The tomb-like silence had remained unbroken since I entered. Ebo was the only one who would dare enter this sanctuary without permission, and he was already here. This place felt safe, sealed off from the rest of Egypt and from whatever truth lurked out there waiting to be revealed.

But the divine order would not be denied, and I was learning that ma'at will be restored whether we assist her or not. There had been a disorder in Egypt since that day long ago, and it would not be left alone.

I stepped across the threshold finally and made my way out of the palace. As I crossed between the pair of massive statues, a woman bustled toward me out of the dark. She slowed as she saw me. A thin woman, she nevertheless managed to block my way.

"What have you done?" she said. Her lips trembled when she spoke.

It took me a moment to recognize her as Ebo's wife.

"I am very sorry for the loss of your—"

"Sorry! You are sorry! No doubt it was for your secrets that he died!" She clutched at her throat with pale fingers.

"My secrets?"

"Do not pretend with me! I wouldn't care if you were the Great One himself. Ebo told me of your bribes."

"I don't understand."

"The money. A great deal of it. Ebo told me that you gave him money—to thank him for his discretion, for keeping your secret all these years." She shook a fist up at me. "He was loyal. Always loyal! And this is how he is repaid? Ma'at will find you, Hemiunu! Ma'at will find you and deal with you!"

NINETEEN

I had more questions than answers. I believed that perhaps Tamit knew more than she had told me. I sought her out the next day at midday and was told by her head servant that she had taken her son's meal to him at the princes' school. I located her there, in the schoolyard where the boys had just been let out from their lessons and were still whooping for joy at their temporary freedom.

Tamit stood at the side of the yard, watching the celebration. Like animals loosed, the boys ran in all directions, unsure where to go first. Kawab, Merit's son and heir to the throne of Horus, and Tamit's son ran together like brothers, reminding me of Khufu and myself when we were young.

I joined Tamit and she glared at me. "What are you doing here?" she demanded.

Her son ran to take his rolls and small jugs of beer. He stared at me a moment, and Tamit stepped behind him and crossed her arms around his upper body.

"I don't want you here," she said to me.

"We must find answers, Tamit."

She wore a thick collar of gold, with jewels like tiger's eyes. The jewels caught the sun and shot a shaft of light into my eyes.

Tamit leaned down to whisper in her son's ear. "Go and play with your friends." She gave the boy a tiny shove, and I watched him skip across the yard to where four boys drew concentric circles on the ground to begin their games.

Tamit's fingers dug into my arm. "In here," she said, her voice guttural.

I allowed her to pull me into the donkey stall at the edge of the schoolyard. The sharp stench of manure watered my eyes.

"You said something the other day—" I began.

"I said many things!" Tamit's eyes darted to the boys, then back to me. "I do not wish to be part of this."

"Then you have heard about—"

"Everyone from Libya to Sinai has heard of the Scourge of Anubis, Hemi." She rubbed her upper arms as though chilled. "But only a few of us know the truth lies in the past."

I gripped my staff. "And that is where the answers will be found."

Tamit stepped away from me. "We do not speak of that day."

"I *will* speak of it, Tamit!" The words flew from me like shards of limestone, as though the stones that walled off the past had begun to crack apart, and the tide of truth would soon rush in to drown us all.

She stepped back and a shadow seemed to pass over her face.

"When we spoke last, Tamit, you told me that Merit seemed bothered by me. What did you mean?"

Her eyes narrowed, like the tiger-eye jewels at her throat. "She wanted Khufu to get rid of you."

I rubbed at the dampness at the back of my neck. "Why would she—"

"She didn't trust you any longer."

I thought of the amulet around my neck, still tied to her thigh when she died. "I do not believe you."

Tamit laughed, the sound more like the hiss of a snake. "No, of course you would not." She stepped toward me, chin up. "She did not like the influence you had on Khufu. The way you convinced him to declare himself Ra on earth. She thought it blasphemous for a man to call himself a god."

I looked away. This fit with what I knew of her recent preoccupation with all things religious.

Tamit poked a finger into my chest. "Even the grand vizier is subject to the laws of Egypt."

I returned my attention to her beautiful face, now twisted into a snarl.

"She rejected you," she said. "And she turned on you. It seems clear to me that only one man had reason to kill the Great Wife."

I stalked the courtyard of my own estate, unable to sit, though the day had been long. Tamit's accusation still stung. Khufu's fear. Ahmose's strange threats.

The pretense must end. None of them had the courage to speak the truth. To follow the truth, no matter where it led.

And so I would begin it.

I circled the courtyard once again, more focused on my plan than the growing chill of desert darkness. My stomach churned with thoughts of what was to come.

First, Khufu. It had to begin with Khufu, as it had all those years ago.

I pulled up short, determination flooding my veins. I would not wait another day. The truth would be known tonight.

The cool breath of the desert snaked into my courtyard and seemed to coil around my ankles. My eyes shifted to the front of my house, sensing someone's entrance.

"Grand Vizier?" In spite of the respect of the title, the voice was authoritative, demanding.

"Who is there?"

A soldier stepped out of the dark hall. "The Beloved of Horus, the Beautiful Silver Hawk, commands your presence in the Great House immediately."

All the better.

"You may tell him that I will be along shortly." I needed a few moments to compose my thoughts.

"I am to escort you there directly, Grand Vizier."

I studied the soldier's face, his pockmarked cheeks and set chin. "Has something happened?"

"I do not have information, only orders. Pharaoh will not wait."

"Very well."

I grabbed my staff from where it leaned against the wall and was made to follow the soldier, but he stepped aside to place me in front of himself. We stood at odds for a moment, until I acquiesced.

We walked in silence. What did it mean that Pharaoh had sent for me? That he had sent a soldier to bring me on foot rather than a litter to carry me on the backs of slaves?

No matter. Tonight was about truth, not pride.

We crossed through the royal estate, a city unto itself. The moon hung heavy over the pyramid tonight, like a watchful eye, full of portent. I thought of Merit, of Mentu, and of Ebo. Of the secrets we all carried. And I felt the weight of what was to come.

I expected to be taken to Khufu's private chamber. Instead, once inside the palace, my armed escort prodded me toward the king's private audience hall.

I was the last to arrive.

Three others stood among the carved columns, speaking in quiet tones. They turned at my entrance. Khufu did not smile, nor did Tamit or my brother.

My escort faded away behind me.

"What is this?" I asked.

"Tamit has demanded audience," Khufu said. "She is not certain of her safety."

"I am not a fool!" Tamit said. Even as I crossed the hall, I could see her eyes, white and wide.

Ahmose nodded to me, a tiny movement of his head that I might have missed had I not been watching.

"I am glad you are all here," I said, pausing to gain control of the conversation. "It is time for us to speak of it."

Only one brazier had been lit in the hall tonight, and our shadows played across the columns, with their happy painted figures in reds and yellows and greens in gruesome contrast to the four of us eyeing each other in dread.

Tamit crossed her arms in front of her and shivered. "We are all that is left," she said. "Only four."

Khufu looked at the floor, and I could see his throat constrict with an effort at swallowing. "It means nothing," he said. "It could still be that the Scourge of Anubis chooses his victims at random."

I tried to catch his attention, to ascertain what had caused this change since we spoke over Ebo's body.

Tamit snorted. "Foolishness."

My brother remained silent, his lips pressed together and the muscles in his jaw locked tight.

"You think one of us has killed these three?" I said to Tamit.

"Four," she said. "Who else had reason?" Her eyes sparked and her voice pitched slightly higher.

I returned the glare. "And what reason do any of us have?"

She regained her composure and looked away, toward the columns with their pleasant scenes. "To hide the truth."

"Then let us have the truth now." I raised my hands to Ahmose and Khufu, who remained apart. I could read neither of their faces. "If we are to discover who has killed these three whom we loved, we must first know the truth about the death of Amunet." I nodded to Tamit. "Your sister."

Khufu paced away from us, his gaze directed upward to the star-splashed painted ceiling. Tamit concentrated on the floor, and my brother simply closed his eyes.

My blood rose to beat in my ears, and a twitch began in my right eye. "We no longer have the luxury of secrets!" To Tamit and Ahmose, I said, "We must speak what we know, what we suspect, regardless of titles and authority. We must go back, back to the time when we were young and equals, and speak the truth!"

Tamit raised her head. She licked her lips twice, and a flush crawled up her neck. "I believed from that day that Khufu killed my sister."

From his place a few cubits away, Khufu groaned.

"But now," Tamit watched me like a lion about to tear apart its prey, "now I am not certain."

I sensed Khufu's quick turn of the head.

"And what has changed your mind, Tamit?" I asked, trying to resume the role of dispassionate interrogator.

She turned to face me fully and raised a pointed finger. "Because you had reason to kill Merit."

Khufu was beside us now, his attention on me. I took a step back and glanced at Ahmose.

"You think I killed Merit? What possible reason could I have to kill Mentu and Ebo?"

Tamit smiled, as though the prey had been cornered. "So you do not deny you had reason to kill Merit."

"I cared for Merit very much!"

She laughed. "Oh, yes, we all know how much you 'cared for' Merit from the time we were young."

The single brazier seemed to throw off more heat than the room required. A bead of sweat ran down the channel of my back.

Tamit turned to Khufu. "Since we are speaking plainly, did you never notice the attention paid your wife by your grand vizier?"

Khufu's gaze traveled between us. "He loved her. I know that. And he would not have harmed her."

"No? Even if she came to you with doubts about his ability to advise you?"

Khufu blinked and studied me. "Did you know that she came to me with these concerns?"

I took a deep breath and found my voice. "I know now. I did not know it before her death. Even so, I would not—"

"She rejected him," Tamit said. "He tried to force himself on her, and she would not have it."

Khufu's hands turned to fists at his sides. "Is this true?"

"I was young, Khufu. You were not yet king, she was not yet your wife—"

Khufu swiveled back to Tamit. "Do you speak of when we were young? Or of the present?"

She shrugged. "Does it matter?"

I wanted to shake her. "Speak the truth, Tamit! Merit never told you that I acted improperly toward her. You were not even her friend. Your jealousy—"

She turned on me, her upper body leaning toward me. "Jealousy! Why would I be jealous? Do you think I wanted *you*?"

The words were spat at me with disdain, but I wondered. Could that have been true? I pushed the thought away as self-aggrandizing. What would Tamit want with me?

"Stop!" Khufu said, his hands spread between us. "Even if Hemi was hurt by Merit, felt betrayed by her, I do not believe he would have killed her. And why Mentu? Why Ebo?"

"We speak in circles still," I said. "We must discover the truth of what happened to Amunet before we can find answers for the present. Tamit, do you truly believe I killed Amunet?"

She chewed her lip. "How can I know what happened so long ago?"

We were accomplishing nothing. It was time to face the past. I lowered my voice and began. "We returned from the water, where Khufu rode the hippopotamus," I said. I could feel the recoiling of all three as I spoke. "Khufu, you decided we would break apart for birding. You and Amunet went off together, and Ebo followed you. Mentu went with the two of you," I pointed to Ahmose and Tamit. "And Merit and I were alone."

Our little group grew tighter, as though we instinctively huddled to keep the truth from spreading outside our tiny circle. A silence fell over us, no one willing to take the story further, to accuse or to deny.

We remained in silence for some moments, and so it was a fright to us all when a strident voice pierced the audience hall. "No more secrets!" the voice shrilled.

We broke apart as though guilty of some conspiracy.

Ebo's wife flew across the audience hall, arms swinging. "I have spoken to the priests!" Her voice shot to the ceiling and reverberated back to slap us with its accusations. "I must tell what I know, though I am a peasant and you are grand vizier!"

I breathed slowly through my mouth. I had told no one of this woman's revelation to me yesterday.

She eyed Ahmose and Khufu, giving no attention to Tamit. "He was paying my husband," she said. "Paying him to remain silent about what he knew!"

Tamit ran long fingers through her hair and pursed her lips. "Who is this woman, Khufu?"

Ebo's wife shot her a look, surely noting Tamit's use of the king's name. She threw her shoulders back and tilted her chin upwards.

"She is the wife of Ebo," Khufu said. His eyes found mine and I saw confusion painted there.

"Ebo, who is now dead, no doubt because of him!" She pointed at me, and I felt the strength drain out of me. "He kept your secret, but still he is dead."

"What secret?" Khufu's words were for the woman, but his eyes were on me.

"I do not know! How should I? My husband was loyal. He wouldn't tell even his loving wife what he knew that was so terrible. But I do know this," she said. "This secret bothered him terribly. And I believe he thought it was not right to keep it. But he was a man of honor!"

Khufu nodded to the woman. "He was faithful, and you need not be concerned for your future, woman. You will be cared for. And justice will be sought for your husband. You may go."

Her anger seemed to deflate, along with her bravado. She bowed low once, then backed out of the audience hall.

The other three watched me, even Ahmose, who had remained so quiet it was as though he wished to be unseen.

"I do not know what money the woman speaks of," I said. "I never paid Ebo any money."

Tamit huffed. "You had reason to kill Merit, who was attempting to remove you from your position. You had reason to kill Ebo, whom you were paying to keep a secret he was thinking of revealing. Perhaps this secret was that you killed my sister."

I pounded my staff on the floor twice and shot looks at all of them. Khufu drew himself up as though ready for a fight. "This is outrageous!" I said. "I never paid Ebo. I did not know of Merit's concerns. And I would have no reason to kill the only man who ever truly thought of me as a friend!"

I regretted the words as soon as they were spoken. Khufu's eyes clouded and he looked away.

"Ahmose," I pleaded, "say something. Tell them that I am not a killer. Whatever else you may think of me, you must know that!"

Ahmose's eyes seemed to roam my face, as though to pry out the truth. His expression drifted from hope to sadness and finally to resignation. He turned his body from me and faced the king.

"I have known that Hemi killed Amunet since that day in the marsh. I saw him with her."

Khufu's eyes went wide and Tamit gasped.

"And you said nothing?" she shouted.

Ahmose looked to the floor. "He is my brother."

I staggered backward a few steps. My grip loosened and my staff clattered to the floor. The grief of these many years of distance between myself and my brother swept over me, and I saw the truth. It was not jealousy that had torn my brother from me; it was integrity. Ahmose believed me a murderer.

I reached for him, but it was as though I stretched out my hand from the grave and he could not even see me. "Ahmose," I whispered, and my eyes filled with tears. He did not look at me.

But Khufu was looking at me. On the column behind him, his own painted likeness looked out with placid satisfaction, like a distorted mirror that reveals the opposite of a man's emotions. "I thought—" he said. "All of these years, I believed—"

"It is not true, cousin!" I said. "I did not kill her!" I turned to Ahmose. "I found her body, it is true. I found her dead in the marsh, after—after Merit ran from me and I went in search of her. I saw the body. But it was not hers. It was Amunet. Dead. Already. I—I believed that it must have been Khufu. I was afraid." The tears flowed in earnest now, and they made me angry. "I was an ambitious fool, and I believed that an accusation against Khufu would destroy my future too. So I left her there." I covered my face with my hands. "I left her there to be torn apart by crocodiles, until her body was so broken there was no hope of her crossing to the west."

Tamit flew at me. Khufu pulled her from me, but not before she had clawed a scratch across my face.

"Don't you see that none of this makes sense?" I protested. "I had no reason to kill Amunet. I would not kill Merit. Or Mentu or Ebo. The rest of it is fabricated. Someone is trying to shift blame to me." I looked to their faces. Ahmose, a mixture of confusion and hopelessness. Tamit, all angry grief for her dead sister. And Khufu, holding her back as though unsure if he should bother.

"You will see!" I said. "I will find the truth. Somehow I will find the truth!"

But my declaration was met with silence.

I snatched up my staff from the floor and stalked from the audience hall, leaving behind me the fiery sting of false accusation.

TWENTY

The moon still stared down at me with its single unblinking eye. I took to the path outside the palace with vengeance, and with each step my staff pounded a hole into the sandy dirt.

Justice and truth. Justice and truth. The words beat in rhythm with my steps. Ma'at had not yet been put right, but I would not let it go.

They suspect me of killing Amunet? Me? All of these years, that is what my own brother has thought of me?

We were no closer to learning the truth. Still none of us told all that we knew. And somewhere in those secrets was the truth about these new killings.

I passed a servant on the way, the only other person about at this hour. He scurried toward me, head down, then lifted his head as we passed one another. A look crossed his face, of surprise and perhaps fear.

The royal estate was guarded by soldiers at all times and had never given me reason to fear, but tonight it seemed as though the rules had all been broken. I quickened my steps, anxious to be behind my own walls. There was a killer about, after all. Khufu's words came to mind. *Who will be next?*

My stomach grew tight as I replayed the confrontation with my brother, my cousin, and Tamit. When my house finally emerged from the shadows ahead, my fingers had grown weary from their grip on my staff. I passed through my doorway with uncharacteristic relief at arriving home. The house was dark, and I went directly to my private chamber, uninterested in food or leisure.

I was quick about my preparations and soon stretched on my bed, my head on the alabaster headrest given to me by my father years ago. He had carved it himself.

Something about that memory triggered emotion in me once again at all that I had lost over the years. Over the past few weeks. I closed my eyes, trying to turn my mind to the problem that still faced me and to devise a plan.

When the morning comes, I will go to each of them in turn and force the truth from them. Only when I understood exactly what had happened that day would I find answers for the present.

My body slowly relaxed. An involuntary jerk of my muscles started my heart pounding, but I closed my eyes again and focused on my breathing. Sleep was the great healer, and I now sought it in earnest.

My mind drifted and I followed it down the paths of memory, willing to see where memory would lead. I thought of Merit, but then her face dissolved into Neferet's. And then it was Neferet who was drowned.

The scrape of a sandaled foot snatched me from my dream. I sat upright, ears tuned to the sound, palms sweating.

Another noise, outside my chamber.

I swung my legs over the side of the bed and stood, ready for an attack.

The door jumped open.

In the darkness, the figure at my door seemed as black as the jackal Anubis himself.

"What is it?" I said.

A moment of silence met my demand. Then a low voice. "It would seem, Grand Vizier, that the favor of your king has come to an end."

I stepped toward the man, squinting to make him out. The whites of his eyes were all that appeared in the darkness. "Axum?"

The Nubian's face was passionless. "Pharaoh, Lord of Crowns, Beloved of Amun, has commanded that you be brought to the prisoners' chamber. You must come with me."

I grabbed a robe from my bed and covered myself. "This is insane, Axum. You know me. You know I have done nothing worthy of imprisonment."

"I serve at my king's command, Grand Vizier, and cannot act of my own accord."

I turned away and cursed. "Why didn't he throw me in there hours ago," I said, "when I stood before their accusations?"

"It is my understanding that new information has come to the attention of the king," Axum said. "Information that points to you as the Scourge of Anubis."

I sensed Axum's displeasure at his orders.

"What new information?"

"We must go, Grand Vizier." Axum reached for my arm, but I jerked it away.

"I'm not going anywhere, except to Khufu to hear what this is about."

"Those are not the orders of the king. You must come with me."

I stepped up to Axum, my nose to his. "Understand this, Axum. You work for me. And I am going nowhere."

Axum's eyes did not leave mine, and the set of his jaw was unchanged. Still nose to nose, he let out a shrill whistle, surprising me. I pulled back, and in that moment, three other Nubians appeared like a wall of basalt behind Axum. He did not take his eyes from me as he ordered his men.

"Take the Grand Vizier to the prisoners' chamber."

They surrounded me, grabbed at my arms without respect.

I pulled away. "Let go of me!" I demanded. "I will have each of you flogged!"

Two of the beasts gripped my upper arms while the third swooped low from behind me and knocked out my legs. A sliver of a moment later they carried me like a sack of barley out of my own home.

But not without a fight. I kicked and twisted, cursed and threatened. I was no match for four trained guards. When my strength was spent, they set me upon my feet, each arm still bound in their grip, and forced me along the path toward the palace, where they intended to imprison me beneath the palace walls. My legs shook and a sweat broke over my chest. The grip on my arms numbed my fingers.

"Take me to Khufu," I said to Axum just ahead of me. "We will discuss this like friends, like cousins. He is angry right now, but I can calm him. I can always calm him."

Axum's countenance remained stony, and his gaze never turned to me.

Outside the shaft that led to the underground chamber, I dug my heels into the sand. They dragged me on. Axum lifted the pin that unlocked the gate, and the other three forced me through. One of them grabbed a torch from the outer wall, and it spilled only enough light ahead for me to see a step or two.

The shaft plunged downward, only wide enough for one man. I tried to block our passage with my body, but one of the guards prodded me in the back with his sheathed sword and we moved forward.

I have spent many hours in the shafts of Khufu's tomb without any sense of fear, but sliding downward toward this chamber felt like death to me. It smelled of death. Every part of my body tensed now. The shaft opened to a passage of tiny cells. They dragged me to the first.

Axum shoved past me to unpin the lock.

And then I was on the other side, and they were sealing the door behind me. Axum's face flickered with something like regret, but he would not be moved.

From the darkness inside the chamber, the scuttling of barely human feet came toward me, and a hand grabbed at me. "Grand Vizier," a voice rasped, "have mercy! I will repay all that I stole!"

I looked down in the last of the receding torchlight and recognized the now-emaciated face of a laborer I had consigned to prison some weeks ago for stealing rations. His collarbones angled painfully from chest to shoulder, and hair grew in dirty patches from his head and face. He looked wildly up at me, his rotting teeth protruding from thin lips.

"Please, Grand Vizier," he begged, "release me from this place!"

Axum and the guards were well away now, the torchlight gone and the two of us left in darkness. The man still gripped my hand.

And then slowly, his clutching hand released and his feet shuffled backward. There came a sound from him, and it took me a moment to comprehend that it was laughter. The strange sort of quiet huffing that comes from being left too long alone.

"You have not come to visit," he laughed. "You are a prisoner. Like me."

I wrapped my arms around my chest, wondering what else lay in the darkness around us. Were there other prisoners? The terrible laughter faded, and I heard the *tick-tick* of insect feet scurry across the floor.

"You are afraid, Grand Vizier?" he said. "Afraid of what terrors the chamber holds?" His voice had grown close, and I smelled him powerfully now. The smell of a man forced to live in his own filth for many weeks. The laughter began again, and I realized that he held me responsible for his torture. And as surely as the gates, he also held me prisoner.

"What is your name, peasant?" I snapped.

"Wati," he hissed. "You have not given me another thought in all these days, have you?"

"You brought this upon yourself, Wati. Egypt is great because the divine order is well kept. You are the victim of no one but your own poor choices. Justice has been handed down to you, and you have no cause for complaint."

"Justice, eh?" he said, his voice mocking in the darkness. "And what of mercy, Grand Vizier? What of mercy?"

I said nothing.

"Well then, as there is no mercy for the peasants, there shall be no mercy for the royals either." His voice built to a crescendo, and I sensed him coming for me.

I sidestepped, but he caught my shoulder and knocked me into the wall behind. A shower of dirt drifted down, gritty in my eyes and mouth. I shoved my hands out, but he had me pinned against the wall, his hands at my throat.

"I am grand vizier," I choked out. "Surely you will suffer more than prison for harming me!"

His voice was low, his foul breath at my ear. "Do you think I care? Do you? Death would be welcome now. I shall cross into the west and live forever in the ripe fields, instead of crawling in the darkness to find the food they toss to me like a diseased dog."

I brought my hands to his grip and tore him from my throat. His wrists felt like reeds in my hands, as though I could snap them without effort. I pushed him backward and he cried out, a mixture of anger and pain.

But I would not show mercy yet. If we were to live here together for any time, Wati must know who held the power. I pushed him to the floor and placed a foot on his throat. He whimpered, then begged again for his life.

All the anger I felt at the injustice of my entrapment seemed to run in sparks through my arms and legs. "You will not touch me again, do you understand?"

I felt his head bob under my foot.

"We will leave each other alone. I will not kill you for threatening me, and you will not speak to me, come near to me, or touch me."

"Yes, Grand Vizier. Yes."

I released him and gave him a half-hearted kick in the ribs to punctuate my thoughts. He rolled and crawled away to the other side of the chamber.

My eyes had by now adjusted to the darkness sufficiently to see the edges of our prison. The chamber was roughly the size of my bedroom, with no furniture of any kind. I went to the wall closest to me, slid down it and sat upon the dirt. My fellow prisoner was true to his promise and neither approached nor spoke to me again that night.

And so I was left truly alone, as I wished. Alone with my thoughts.

What new information had been given to Khufu that accused me? Already he believed I had reason to kill Merit and Ebo, and Ahmose had accused me of killing Amunet. My mind worked at the problem, trying to come up with a solution that would bring about what I sought more than anything: justice, truth, divine order. Ma'at.

But as the night wore on, and my thoughts swirled around the fetid air of the prisoners' chamber, something gave way inside me. Doubts, at first as small as the dung beetles that tapped in the darkness around me, grew into shadowy beasts that threatened to devour me.

Justice and truth. I had served the goddess Ma'at all my life. And yet, what divine order did I truly see? All was chaos around me. The pyramid project was failing without my oversight. People I loved were dying. I stood accused of horrible crimes. Where was justice? Where was truth?

A rebellious thought began to take root, one I had long denied. I let it grow in the night. I nourished it with my attention and willed it to grow and take over my mind.

There are no gods. There is no ma'at.

Finally, finally I let myself dwell upon the truth that I had been running from for so many years. If there were truly justice in the world—and in death—no man or woman would reach those blessed fields of which Wati spoke. Not one of us could claim purity to curry favor in the afterlife.

And so death could only mean condemnation.

I scratched at the dirt floor with my feet and tried to stay warm with only my own arms to cover me.

Yes, I had known the truth of justice all my life and had run from the admitting of it for just as long. If death were condemnation, then life—this life—is all there is. My mad, driven push to leave a legacy in stone, to achieve and accomplish, all of it was to avoid this ultimate truth.

If the gods awaited me with justice on the other side of life, then justice would surely destroy me. If nothing awaited me on the other side, then I was equally cursed.

Given the events of the past weeks, and the disorder that continued to thrive in spite of my best efforts, I began to believe that the gods were a lie, that ma'at existed only in my imagination, and that nothing awaited me but an endless black void.

In all the years that have passed since the day I found Amunet's body in the marsh, I have never allowed myself to wonder what might have changed had I made a different choice.

But I wonder now. I let myself return to that day, to the moment when I lifted her head from the water, chest beating with the sick certainty that my beloved Merit was dead . . .

Relief floods me, followed hotly by guilt, as I realize that it is Amunet who lies dead in my arms.

Amunet, who was alone with Khufu. Khufu, who will be Pharaoh. And I his grand vizier.

My knees sink further into the mud. The unnatural water falling from the sky beats against my bare skin. I wipe away the reeds from her face. My mind seems to lock, unable to choose.

But I do choose.

I lower her body to the water's edge once more, climb to my feet, walk a few paces away and wash my hands in the river water.

And then I turn my back on Amunet.

And somewhere in the reeds, unknown to me, my brother watches.

Some time later I discover Merit, standing on the grassy bank, her eyes wet, with tears or sky water, I cannot say. "We should return to the donkeys," I say, and she nods. I reach for her, but she ignores my hand.

Ebo is waiting beside the donkeys. Three beasts are already gone, and he tells us that some of the others have fled back to the royal estate. We decide to follow, and I think that I should be glad for more time alone with Merit. But a shadow has passed over us all. Even Ebo is not himself. Merit and I return, with only the startled bird calls in the marsh behind us to break our silence. Halfway home, the clouds roll back and Merit pulls a packet of honey-sweetened cakes from her pouch. She shares one with me. The sticky sweetness sickens.

Merit and I part inside the quiet pillared hall of the estate, each to our own quarters. I try to rest then, but my dreams disturb me.

I am waiting for ma'at.

And then the summons comes. We assemble in the audience hall, like restless greyhounds. All of us except Amunet. Our parents are tight-lipped and stern. The painted scenes on the high walls look down on us.

"Amunet has not yet returned," Pharaoh Sneferu says. "We have sent servants to search the marsh."

Tamit's brow is furrowed and she chews her bottom lip. I take a deep breath and stare at the floor.

"I do not understand," the queen says, "why she was left alone."

Tamit shakes her head. "But she was not! She returned here with Hemi and Merit." She looks to me.

Merit speaks. "We never saw her, Tamit. Not after she and Khufu left to be alone." Merit's voice drops at the last few words. I glance at Sneferu, but his dark eyes are on his son.

Tamit also turns on him. "You said that she had returned with Hemi and Merit."

Khufu lifts his shoulders. "That is what she told me she planned. We—we had a disagreement. And she was tired of the hunt. She said she would return with them." He points to me.

Sneferu looks me over. "And you and Merit were together all this time?"

Except for when she ran from me.

The entrance of three servants ends the questioning. Between them, they carry something wrapped in linen. Even across the hall, I can see that blood soaks the linen. A tremor flickers at the back of my knees. I feel Merit's light touch on my arm, steadying me. It is not simply the sight of the blood, however. It is the realization that when I left her, there was no blood.

Behind me, Tamit shrieks.

She runs for the bundle as they lower it to the ground. "No!" One of the servants steps in front of Tamit, blocking her. "Let me see!" she screams. "I must see her."

The servant lifts his eyes to the rest of us and shakes his head furiously. My mother flies to Tamit's side and wraps arms around her.

"Come, dear. There is nothing you can do. Do not cause yourself more pain—"

"I want to know! I must see for myself!" Tamit jerks from my mother's comfort, lunges for the linen coverings, and rips them away.

The silence of the hall goes on and on as each one of us faces the awful truth.

Only pieces of Amunet remain.

Tamit throws her head back and opens her mouth wide in one long, piercing wail. The sound echoes from the walls and ceiling of the hall and reminds me of the birds in the marsh.

I taste bile in my mouth overpowering the sweetness of the honey cakes that still lingers. And then I am retching, in front of them all.

The servants cover Amunet and carry the body from the room. Tamit is stretched on the floor where her sister's body has just lain. The rest of us stand silent amid the room's stony lifelessness.

Tamit rises slowly and faces Khufu. "What," she growls, "have you done?"

Khufu spreads his hands before him. "I swear to you, Tamit, she was alive when last I saw her. There was evil in the sky. I—I do not know what happened!"

Tamit screams again and throws herself at the future king. It is my father who intervenes this time, pulling her from Khufu and pinning her arms.

In the ensuing silence, we all wait on Sneferu. The burden of decision is heavy on him, we can see. He studies Tamit, studies Khufu. Surveys the rest of us. We are all silent, with eyes averted. Like young children discovered playing at tipcats in a forbidden temple. I find my brother watching me with hard eyes.

Finally, Sneferu speaks. "What is done, is done. We can do nothing for Amunet now. It is clear that a crocodile has been the cause of her death. A grievous accident." His gaze travels the room, until he has the attention of all. "An accident," he repeats. He lets the word hang there in the hall, roll over each of us. Even Tamit, who is still held in Father's grip. Sneferu brings his attention to rest upon Tamit. "We will give Amunet all the honor she deserves—"

"You cannot repair her body!" Tamit shouts, with the foolish disrespect of youth.

"All the honor she deserves," Sneferu continues, watching Tamit. "But we will never speak again of this day." He looks at each of us. "Never again, do you understand? You are the future of Egypt, each of you in your own way. You are Egypt. Nothing can be allowed to disrupt the way of this." His eyes go back to Tamit. "If ever I hear of accusations, of rumors of accusations, of gossip of any kind about this day, there will be repercussions. I will not allow Egypt's future," here he glances at Khufu, "to be harmed."

We all look at Khufu then, but his head is dropped upon his chest.

And so in that moment, we all make a choice, each one of us. The choice to remain silent. To ask no questions. To keep a secret. For the good of Egypt.

Or so we believe.

TWENTY-ONE

B ut it was not for the good of Egypt. And not for my good
either.

When morning came, I stirred from my cramped posi-
tion at the prison wall and tried to stretch the painful knots from
my back and legs. The sun was still low on the horizon and sent its
rays down the shaft into our chamber. The shadow of the gate's bars
lay like stripes of lashes upon my body.

The hopelessness of the night still held me captive, but in the
daylight I decided that even if the world were indeed chaos and
the gods an invention of man, still I wanted to live. And I wanted
to be free.

My cell mate lay unconscious on the other side of the chamber,
and I should have thought him dead if not for his raspy snoring.

Some time later I heard a guard approach and leaped to my
feet to meet him at the gate. He was a large man, heavy about the
jowls and middle, and he carried two puny haunches of meat in one
hand and a jug of beer in the other. He lowered his head in respect
toward me, then pulled himself upright, as if embarrassed by the
force of his habit.

"The captain has ordered extra rations for you, Vizier." He pushed the food through the bar. "It's more than he ever gets." The guard jutted his chin toward Wati, still lying in the brown muck behind me, who chose that moment to moan something about the noise.

"Come and eat, you ungrateful dog!" I'd listened to his death rattle all night. To the guard, I said, "You must send for the king, to come and speak to me. I have things that he must hear."

Beside me, Wati appeared and tore at the gooseflesh. The guard tipped the jug of beer and spilled a few drops into the man's greedy mouth. He motioned for me to do the same, but I had no intention of letting him spill beer all over me. "The king," I said. "It is critical that I speak to him."

"My orders are to guard the cell and bring you food. That's all." He tipped the jug once more and I shook my head. He shrugged. "I will be back tonight."

"The priest then, man! Send me a priest!"

He hesitated, and I sensed he must be devout in his own religion. I reached a hand through the bars, grasped his arm. The sight of my filthy hand on his clean flesh startled me.

He pulled away. "When you are summoned, then you will speak. It is not my place to do the summoning."

"My men! Surely you don't wish the Horizon of Khufu to be delayed because the grand vizier is not present to direct it. Send for my overseers. Khons. Or De'de or Senosiris."

But the guard had disappeared up the shaft without a word.

It was hours before I heard footsteps in the shaft again. I closed my eyes, trying to force the appearance of Khufu with the strength of my will. Yet when I opened my eyes, the face at the gate was even more welcome.

"Neferet!" I staggered to my feet and threw myself to the bars.

She wore a dress of sunny yellow today, with pale blue stitching along the straps, and tiny yellow flowers woven into her hair. She was like the open sky, and I reached for her.

But she stood apart and I saw the creases between her eyes. I dropped my hand, suddenly cold.

"I do not understand any of this, Hemi," she said. "One day you are trying to hunt the murderer, and the next you are accused of his crimes." Her eyes sparkled with unshed tears, and the heart-breaking doubt on her face left me hollow.

"Neferet, look at me. You know me. You know I could not have done this."

She inclined her head and sighed. "Do I know you, Hemiunu? It has only been such a short—"

"You know me." I drew up close to the bars and looked into her eyes. "You know me."

She moved toward me then, reached through an open space just above her waist and intertwined her fingers with mine. "I am dirty," I whispered.

She shook her head. "What can I do, Hemi? How can I get you out of here?"

I smiled. "A moment ago you were accusing me—"

She squeezed my fingers. "I only needed to hear you say it. I already knew the truth." She glanced over her shoulder, up the shaft, and leaned in. "I have a plan," she said. "I will bring food to the guard, something that will make him sick. When he has fallen or run for the weeds, I will unlock—"

"Absolutely not," I said. Her shoulders fell and a pout formed on her lips. "Keep your crazy schemes for the day of my execution."

She gasped. "I did not mean that. But I will not allow you to also become a prisoner. Besides, what good will it do to break me out? Where would I go? I must clear my name."

"Tell me what to do," she said.

"Go to my brother. Find out why the king has put me here and what he plans. Someone has given him false information to accuse me, and I need to know what it is before I can fight it."

Neferet nodded. "Do you need anything? Food? Water?"

"I am fine. But listen," I held both her hands now. "Go quietly to Ahmose. I do not want you involved in this. I trust him, but I do not know who might be watching. Do you understand?"

"I will be careful. I promise." She pulled her hands from mine too soon but then reached one hand through the bars and cupped my cheek. "Do not fear, Grand Vizier," she said. "I still believe in justice. And I will find it for you."

It was midday when she returned. I had slept in pieces in the mud and felt disjointed and grimy. I dragged myself to the gate to hear her news.

"I spoke to Ahmose, Hemi. I tried to convince him of your innocence. It seemed a strange thing to have to say to a brother. He is much confused by all of this."

"We have many years of misunderstanding between us, I'm afraid. I hope to put it right."

"He is a good man."

"Yes. Yes, I believe he is."

"But he knows nothing, Hemi. He says that after you left the king's audience hall last night, he went straight to his own estate and heard nothing more. I was the first to tell him of your imprisonment. I think it was being kept from him."

I frowned. "How did you hear—"

"Gossip travels quickly among the laborers and soldiers. Those who brought you here last night were eager to tell their tale."

"I am sure." I paced in front of the gate, debating my options. "What shall I do now, Hemi? Do you want me to get my father?"

"Your father would do no good now. I must find a way to speak to Khufu."

"I will go to the king."

"No. No, it is not safe for you to be seen as my ally. I cannot risk having you also pulled into this."

Neferet unstrapped a pouch she carried and opened it. She passed me a parcel of food through the bars, then a small skin of water, and lastly a papyrus and ink. "Write a message to the king. I will carry it."

"Neferet, I cannot—"

"Hemi." She held my gaze. "I will not sit by and watch you be falsely accused. Write the note. I will carry it. Trust me to take care of myself."

I smiled. "I think you could take care of yourself better than any woman I've ever met."

Her laugh was like pure water washing over me. I closed my eyes and wished it would continue.

Minutes later, with my scrawled message in hand, she was whispering good-bye and promising to return with more news. Before she turned to go, she reached through the bars once more, curled her fingers around the back of my neck and pulled me toward a space between the bars. She pressed her lips to mine for one gentle moment.

When she was gone, it seemed to me as though the sun had been extinguished.

The day wore on with no word from Neferet. I worried, and my fears spilled over into rage at Wati, who never ceased his moaning.

"By the horns of Hathor, will you shut your rotted mouth!" I yelled as the sun set, then regretted my words. My actions had put the man in this place forsaken by all the gods, a fate I was coming to believe no one deserved.

At last I heard the clump of soldier's feet down the shaft. I raced to the gate, telling myself it might only be another scrap of greasy gooseflesh and watered beer.

But the soldier held no food, and he reached for the gate to unlock it.

"I am being released?" I asked, gripping the bars as he worked at the pin.

"His Majesty Horus, Who Protects Egypt with His Wings, has called for your trial in the Great Hall."

"Trial!" I staggered back and the gate swung inward. "He still insists— But he cannot have summoned the nobles already."

The guard shrugged and jerked his head toward the shaft. "Go."

I climbed the steep slant, my feet like blocks of stone. At the head of the shaft, another guard blocked my exit. He slung a length of rope at the one behind me, who grabbed my arms with his sword-roughened hands and lashed my wrists together behind my back.

"You would tie up the grand vizier like a common thief?"

They said nothing.

Up and out of the prison they shoved me, toward the entrance to the palace. I looked up at the grand arch as they dragged me under it. How many times had I strutted through this entrance as though I were the king himself?

They pushed me through the outer courtyard, with its gardens and pools, and into the Great Hall where trials were conducted. I expected to see the hall filled with nobles of the land, come to see my degradation. Instead the cavernous room with its dozen lofty pillars stood silent and empty, save two figures at the front who turned to watch me stumble into the room. At the corners of the hall and along the walls, atop columns the height of a man, oil lamps blazed in fiery glory.

Somehow the empty hall frightened me even more than facing the land's leaders. Only Khufu and his new high priest stood as my accusers.

It was the prerogative of the king to declare a trial private, if certain matters needed to be kept from the people. In the past, court intrigues such as royal wives plotting to install their own sons on the throne of their fathers had met with private trials. In such cases, the king was judge, witness, and jury. There would be no appeal to the mercy of the court.

The soldiers disappeared behind me, and I stood rooted to the floor in the utter silence of the room. Khufu and the high priest regarded me from under the canopy at the front of the hall. Khufu stood and the pure whiteness of the full robe he wore from shoulder to floor seemed to glow in the firelight. A heavy incense hung in the air, a signal that Khufu was in one of his especially pious moods when he believed himself to be in communion with the gods. After the dank and fetid smell of the prison, I should have been glad for the incense. But like the absence of nobles, the heavy air was a forbidding omen of things to come.

The rope at my wrists bit into my skin, but I welcomed the pain as it kept me alert in the drowsy air.

We stood there in the silence for some moments. I thought of a hundredfold ways to argue my case before the king, but none of them reached my lips.

Finally, Khufu spoke. "Come forward."

I inhaled deeply and trudged toward the canopy. When I was but a few cubits from Khufu, the high priest stepped forward as if to protect his king from the man with wrists bound behind his back.

"Khufu—" I began.

He held up a hand for silence, his face still a mask of stone. "I want to hear nothing from you."

"Not even the truth?"

Something shifted in his eyes, a flame of great pain, and then died. "I have all the truth I need. You placed yourself in a position to identify this—this Scourge of Anubis, so that you yourself could remain undetected as the killer."

"Khufu, think of the years we have spent—"

"Silence!" His roar echoed from the walls, and the lamps seemed to flicker with the force of it. "I have thought of nothing else, Hemi." His eyes rested on me for only a moment. "Nothing else. But I cannot deny the proofs that have been brought against you." His breathing grew rapid, and I saw any doubt had been eclipsed by his anger and pain. "You have taken everything from me that matters. First the love of my wife, then her life. Even the Horizon of Khufu is in jeopardy because of your falseness!"

His face had grown flushed and jewels of sweat glistened on his forehead.

I tried again, in the soothing voice I always used when he was in a rage. "Cousin, you are vexed. Please—"

Two quick steps down from the platform, then he silenced me with a vicious slap. My eyes watered at the fire in my cheek, and I licked the corner of my mouth, tasting blood. Khufu turned back to ascend to his throne. I took a step forward, but the high priest was there in an instant and applied the end of his staff at my shoulder to shove me to my knees before Pharaoh.

The king whirled, his white robe floating out from him like a cloud, and in that moment he did seem a god to me. A god with no mercy in his eyes. His eyes were like hardened flint stones that could no longer set a spark.

"Who accused me, Khufu? What proof do you have that I have done this evil?"

Khufu sat upon his throne and stretched his hands across the lions' head armrests. I had never seen him like this. His usual petulant rages were more like the tantrums of a child. This coldness, this deadness seemed to coil up in my stomach like venom.

"Merit's concerns accuse you," he said. "Ebo's wife accuses you. And Rashidi has told me that you and Mentu argued fiercely just before he was killed. That Mentu was going to come to me with something he knew of you."

"This is madness, Khufu! Mentu was my friend. Rashidi seeks to bring me down because I removed him from his position as High Priest of On. It is nothing more than that! And the rest—it is also madness."

He stood over me. "You would call Ra on earth mad?"

"You are not Ra on earth, Khufu!" I let the arrows in my soul fly at last. "You are nothing more than an arrogant, selfish man. And if anyone deserves judgment, it is you. For it is you who killed Amunet and began all of this!"

Khufu's jaw twitched and his lips tightened until they were no more than a slit in his face. "Leave us," he hissed to the high priest, who bowed his head and backed out of the Great Hall through the square arch at the side of the room.

Khufu never took his eyes from me as the high priest made his exit. When we were alone, he descended one step, until he towered over where I still knelt. I waited for a blow, a kick to the head, anything.

But when he moved again, it was to shake his head, a slow movement that barely moved the tresses of the wig he wore and the striped nemes that framed his face. "You will never, ever speak of that day again, Hemiunu, son of Neferma'at. You have been judged by your king and your god and found guilty. Your name will be chipped away from the carving of Egypt's greatness. It will be blotted from the scrolls that speak of her history. You leave nothing. No family, no son, no legacy. Your sentence is death. In the custom of nobles, I will grant you the favor of death by your own hand. That is as far as my mercy will extend."

With my hands still bound behind me, I could only lean forward to touch my forehead to his leg. "Khufu," I pleaded, my eyes squeezed shut. "Think. It is I, your friend and cousin. It is I."

He stepped away from my touch. "For many years you believed me insensible to you and Merit, Hemi," he whispered. "As though I was too foolish and vain to care. You were wrong. I loved her too, Hemi. From the day I met her, I loved her."

I looked up at him, pondered his whispered confession. "But Amunet," I said. "Your attention was all for Amunet."

His chest rose and fell with each breath he took. "How would it look for the future king to watch from the side while his cousin stole the heart of his future bride, of his only love?"

I licked the dryness from my lips and swallowed. "I didn't know, Khufu. I swear to you, I didn't know."

He turned away. "Then I am a better actor than even I knew." He sat on his throne again. "You took her from me twice, Hemi. I cannot forgive you that. I can never forgive."

He called out a command over my head, and I heard guards trotting into the hall behind me. They grabbed my arms and lifted me to my feet.

"Return the grand vizier to a cell," Khufu said. "And when he is safely locked inside, toss him a knife." Khufu looked into my eyes. "Do the honorable thing, Hemi. For once, do the honorable thing."

And then the guards turned me from my king, my Egypt, and dragged me from the Great Hall.

How long does it take a man to find the courage to end his own life, when it is not his desire to do so? This I wondered as I huddled in the corner of my new cell, empty of any other prisoners.

I would have welcomed the whining of Wati.

The knife was unassuming. Not a sword, nor a battle-worn weapon that had defended Egypt from her enemies. No, it was a simple blade, a mottled green-and-gray flint that had perhaps chopped heads from chickens or scraped the scales from carp.

The silence of the prison pressed around me. Two guards kept watch, I knew, at the entrance. Perhaps one slept while the other remained vigilant. They did not speak. The smell of the Great Hall's incense clung to me still, even here in the rancid underground, and I thought how much it was like me, this blended odor of royal incense and rotting criminal. Or perhaps the incense was only the smell of funerary spices. My skin seemed alive with the touch of insects. I brushed at my arms and legs.

Sometimes, I believe, in the late watches of the night, a man will ponder that even with a wife at his side and children safe in their beds, he is alone. The very nature of man is that he is an individual and thus alone inside himself. But it was not this isolation that I pondered this night. It was a deeper, more pervasive emptiness that reached in to constrict my heart like a vise. The knowledge that my parents had already crossed to the west, that my brother would not mourn my death. I had no one. No one.

Yes, there was Neferet, my conscious mind argued. But my heart told me she would soon forget. Now that Sen had been made overseer of constructions, she would be noticed by a noble in the court and taken as his wife before my body had grown cold.

I touched my thumb to the blade edge of the flint. They had not even done me the courtesy of giving me a sharp knife. Was it dulled by the deaths of other criminals? Was this the knife given to all who must die alone by their own hands? I had seen traitors sentenced this way before and had never given them a thought after they had left the Great Hall.

How was it accomplished? Would I somehow place it under my chest and fall upon it? What if it were not deadly enough to pierce through to my heart, and only wounded me so I would lay here in the dirt to slowly bleed my life away? And what then? Would I learn the true weight of justice, as I feared? Did the gods await me, as I had been taught?

The taste of hopelessness in my mouth was a bitter herb.

I do not know how many hours passed in this manner. I had the sense that dawn would soon arrive, and I wondered if there were a deadline on my sentence. The word made me laugh with the irony. I had lived for deadlines all my life though none had been so . . . terminal.

The guards were now waking to their duties, and I heard the hum of conversation coming down the shaft. Two voices at least, maybe more. My heart reached out for human contact, and I wished one of them would come down here and stay with me.

One of the voices was low but definitely female, I realized. A seductive, flirty voice that made me think of Tamit. Had she come to watch me suffer? The conversation at the top of the shaft continued, as though the woman had come only to visit the guards. I strained to make out their words.

And then the woman laughed, a sound that caused the knife to slip from my fingers and thump to the mud floor.

I knew that laugh.

I stood and went to the bars of my cell, turned my ear to the shaft. She laughed once more, then spoke again in that throaty voice. It was only her voice for a while, and I wondered what she would find to speak so long about to two prison guards.

I heard the shuffling sound of heavy sandals scraping across the stones. Then the slap of smaller feet descending the shaft.

Neferet appeared, torch in hand, and eyes dancing. She rushed to my cell door. "Hold this," she said and thrust the torch at me.

I reached a hand through the bars and held the torch. She worked at the pin with trembling fingers. I could hear the sound of my own breathing.

"Neferet—what—how?"

Her glance flicked up at me for an instant, her brown eyes glittering with honey-colored flecks and a tiny smile on her lips. "You said to save my poisons for the day of your execution," she said. "Today seemed close enough." The pin came free in her hands, and she snatched the torch from my shaking hand and swung the gate open in one motion.

"Come!" she said and grabbed my arm. "There is not much time. They have both run for the weeds, but they will be back."

I pulled from her, retrieved the knife, and tucked it into my belt. "Neferet, no guard would leave his post to vomit!"

She winked at me. "Not vomit. Something even worse to succumb to in front of a woman."

She ran toward the shaft and I followed her up, up and out, and felt like a falcon released from its cage, as though I could fly upward forever. We ran past the guards' empty bench and into the night air. The dawn was tickling the edge of the eastern desert and already lightening the sky.

I now led the way, across the small enclosure outside the prison walls, and rounded the corner to take to the path to the wall of the royal estate.

A massive chest met me at the corner. We impacted and both recoiled. Our guard was back, his face pale and angry. He reached across his body for his sword.

The injustice of the past day boiled inside me. Before he could unsheathe his sword, I fisted my hand and pounded his jaw with all the anger I felt. He staggered back a step or two. Neferet stood between us and brandished the torch as though trying to frighten off a desert jackal. I went at him again, a passing thought of the knife at my belt. But he had not wronged me and was only doing his duty. He threw up an arm to block my blow and shoved me backward with his forearm.

We fought at the entrance to the prison yard. An unlit torch rested in a socket on the wall. Perhaps the guard feared killing the grand vizier, for he had reconsidered and chose the torch as weapon instead of his own sword. The wood was black and greasy with bitumen, and he wielded it with skill in a quick blow to my head. I went down, blinking away the fiery flashes behind my eyes. Self-preservation took over, and I swept at his legs with my own in a fury of retaliation. He hit the ground beside me, with a crack of his shoulder. We both struggled to our feet, then his face contorted in the unmistakable bared teeth and squinted eyes of a severe stomach cramp. He doubled over, and I gave the back of his neck a satisfying chop with the side of my hand. He moaned and fell forward to his knees.

I glanced at Neferet, and she nodded. We ran.

Through the village that made up the royal estate, past my own house, which would surely be searched, and toward the open gates.

For a free man, the desert is a wide and wonderful open space of sky and sun. For a hunted man, there is no place to hide.

TWENTY-TWO

S top, Neferet," I said. "We must have a plan."

She whirled on me with torch held aloft. We stood inside the gates huddled close to a sycamore. A rectangular reflecting pool ran along the path. "We must first get out of the royal estate," she said, catching her breath. "No place to hide here, no one you can trust."

For the first time I noticed how she was dressed, the robe a riot of color, cut wide to expose her chest. She wore an ornate wig and her face was heavily painted.

"For the guards," she said, her face flushing.

I took the torch from her hands and thrust it into the water. The flame disappeared with a hiss and sizzle. An oily film spread across the water.

The darkness along the wall felt safe. I dreaded the open desert.

Neferet carried a pouch and from it drew two dark robes. "Here." She thrust one at me. "These will help us remain unseen." We covered ourselves, then with a mutual nod moved toward the gates and out of the royal estate.

We kept to the wall at first, until it rounded away from the path to the village. "It is the only place to hide until we know what to do," Neferet said. "There are a hundred crevices where a man can get lost in the village."

A wave of dizziness swept me, and I put a hand to my head where the guard's torch had struck me. When I pulled my hand away, it was sticky with blood.

Neferet cried out. "You are hurt!" She was close beside me in a moment, her hands exploring my arms, my face, my neck for other injuries. I let her touch me, let the sparks fly through my blood, and my breathing shallowed with something other than pain. "We will go to my home first," she said, her hand still on my face. "For only a moment. I will take care of your wound there." She let her palm drift down to my chest, and I half expected her to claim she would also care for my heart.

The edge of the desert was a strange and fiery red now, and I lifted my eyes to the evil portent, wondering what it meant.

Neferet saw it too and took my hand. "Come, we must go. Dawn arrives."

We hurried down the path to the workmen's village. Soon the laborers would rouse themselves from their beds and drag themselves along this road for another day at the pyramid.

The pyramid. How long since I had given the Horizon of Khufu any real thought? Was it possible that something so important to me only days ago could now seem like an inconvenient burden? I felt it glowering down upon me now in disapproval, knowing that I only thought of myself.

The silence of the desert was broken only by an occasional howl in the distance or the nearby scuttle of snake or lizard. I felt as if all my senses were heightened, as though they had been rubbed raw until even their slightest stimulation would cause me great pain.

Ahead, a dark huddle of moving forms approached. "These robes will draw attention now," I said. We stripped them off and Neferet shoved them back in her pouch. We continued on, and I prepared to meet either friend or enemy on the path ahead.

When they were still two hundred cubits away, the mysterious jangle of camels come to trade from far-off lands reached our ears. Neferet dropped behind me with a nod.

Within minutes we had intercepted the traders. To not speak to them would have aroused more suspicion than we desired. One of them slid from his camel and stood beside the red-tasseled beast.

"Welcome to Giza," I said, bowing my head at the huge man, who was dirty and bearded, with a robe that would grow hot in this land. He wore a banded head-covering such as the people of the eastern desert wear. Tools and weapons of all sorts hung from the thick belt at his waist, and he wore one large wooden hoop in his ear.

He bowed in response to my greeting and pulled a pouch from the camel's pack. "Does my lord have use for some Nubian gold?" He looked over my shoulder. "For the lady, perhaps?" His words faded off as he took in Neferet's appearance. He gave me a black-toothed grin and a knowing wink. "One must keep these kind of ladies in gold, you know, for them to be of proper service." He barked a laugh and his three companions, still astride their camels, joined in.

I swallowed and the muscles in my arms tightened. "No gold today, my friends. But I wish you well in your trading. You will find those in the royal estate much enamored with Nubian gold."

The trader replaced the pouch into the camel's pack and gave his companions a glance. "I believe," he said, "that I am much enamored with your woman."

The others prodded their camels to their knees, then came to stand beside him. I could feel Neferet draw up close behind me, could hear her rapid breathing. Her small hand found the hollow of my lower back and trembled there.

I drew myself up and glared at the leader. "She is my sister," I said. "And I am a priest, a holy man. Do not tempt me to call down the fury of the gods upon you."

The trader laughed. "Your gods do not know me, Egyptian. What have I to fear from your gods?"

In that moment, for reasons I did not understand, the gods chose to assist me in my lie.

Only twice before in my life had I witnessed the dark sky turn to gold as though the sky goddess Nut had hurled a fiery torch to earth. But in the early morning half light, the sudden flame in the sky blinded us all. A moment later, Nut's torch seemed to strike the far-off mountains with a mighty crack that shook the very earth on which we stood.

I composed myself quickly and turned an icy glare upon the traders. "Do you still claim no fear of my gods? Shall I beseech Nut to slay each of you with her fiery torch?"

But they were already up and on their camels, clucking at the beasts to move along. We watched them only a moment, then continued on toward the village.

"What does it mean?" Neferet asked. "The sky?"

"There will be floods from the heavens. A great evil. We must hurry."

We moved toward the village with haste. A few minutes later, Neferet said, "Your *sister*? Why did you not claim me as your wife? They might have been less inclined to—"

"Because no man with self-respect would allow his wife to dress as you are dressed." My reply silenced her and I feared hurt her. I regretted this but had no idea how to rectify it at this moment.

We drew close to the village, and the pungent odor of manure assailed us. Scattered over the fields outside the village, sheep and cattle grazed while their shepherds dozed against rocks, relying upon their dogs to warn them of approaching danger.

"We cannot risk the dogs," I said and pulled on Neferet's arm to slow her.

"I know. Follow me. We will circle the village to the back. I know a way."

But the dogs sensed us—perhaps smelled us—anyway. As we dropped over the edge of a ridge to a canal a few feet below, the hungry bark of sheepdogs raised the alarm. Shepherds called to one another with shouts of concern. Neferet and I crouched and ran along the canal bank that circled the village.

I had a moment to ponder my situation as we ran, and I marveled at how my once well-ordered life had so quickly turned to chaos.

TWENTY-THREE

The sky changed from its odd shade of red to a brooding gray as we ran. I called to Neferet to halt a moment, and we stood at the canal edge, hands on our knees, panting. Moments later we were running again and were soon on the east side of the village, where the floodplain neared the village wall. We slowed to a walk.

"How will we get in?" I asked.

"You will see." Her voice caught on the words and she coughed. We stopped, and I was helpless to do anything but pat her back. She raised a hand and shook her head. "I am well. Let's walk."

We continued on and Neferet pointed to a tree that grew close to the wall, its roots stretching toward the floodplain. "When I was younger I used to tell father that I was going to see a friend on the other side of the village. But I would really sneak over the wall here and walk along the water, sometimes all the way down to the river."

I frowned at the isolated stretch of canal outside the village wall. "Not safe for a young girl."

She smiled. "Yes, I am much more careful now."

She meant it to be humorous, but her words struck me and I looked down in guilt. How had I allowed her to be put in danger this way?

We reached the tree and Neferet jumped to grab a limb and swing herself to the trunk. On the run under this strangely threatening sky, I should not have had cause to laugh, yet I did. To see her go from limb to limb like one of Tamit's pets gave me great amusement.

"Are you afraid?" she called down to me, laughter also in her voice. "Surely the grand vizier of Egypt can climb a tree."

"Surely he can," I said and followed her up as quickly as my throbbing head would allow.

We reached the middle limbs and Neferet shimmied across a thick one to the village wall. I still did not know how we would make it down the other side, but I trusted the little-girl-turned-woman who had come this way before.

When we gained the village wall, about as wide as my body, I saw that we were behind the Temple of Horus, where Merit and Mentu had met in secret. Its stone walls crept close to the wall, with only a narrow alley between. It was too far to drop to the ground inside the wall. Neferet crawled on hands and knees along the top of the wall. We would not be seen, with the temple wall blocking us from the rest of the city.

Stone chips littered the top of the wall and dug into my palms and knees as we crawled. Jagged cracks in the wall threatened to topple my balance. After a few moments I climbed to my feet and walked with one foot placed carefully in front of the other. Neferet looked over her shoulder at me, then copied my actions.

"I was never brave enough for this as a child," she said.

"How far?"

"Only a few more cubits. There." She pointed ahead, to where the temple ended and the enclosure wall, at about my height, ran parallel with the city wall for a length.

We dropped onto the enclosure wall, then were able to manage the rest of the drop to the ground.

"You did this as a child?" My ankles and knees had protested the jump.

Neferet put her finger to her lips. The temple and the street beyond were not empty. "We can let no one see you are in the village. You are far too easily recognized."

We hurried along the edge of the wall and peered out into the street engorged with people standing and watching the sky. At this time of the morning the laborers should have been heading toward the pyramid, but a holiday seemed to have been declared.

"We will never get through this crowd unseen," I said. I gripped the back of my neck, aware of the tightness building again.

She shrugged. "Their attention is elsewhere. And it is sometimes easier to remain unseen in a crowd than as a lone traveler."

"If anyone sees me . . ."

Neferet bit her lip. "I know."

"I don't think I should be here, Neferet. I've put you in enough danger."

"Where will you go?" she said, hands on her hips. "Back to prison? Will you run across the desert until the jackals take you?" Her nostrils widened as she spoke.

"You are angry with me?"

"I am angry that men do not like to be helped. But you need my help, Hemi. You have no where else to go. And no one else to help you."

"Perhaps I should return to prison and accept my sentence."

"No!" The anger left her then, and she flung herself at me. "No. No, let me take you to my house, to tend to your wound. Then we will figure out what to do."

I pulled her from me. "The guards saw you, Neferet. They will come here very soon looking for you, and for me."

"Then we must hurry," she said and took my hand.

The streets hummed with the crowds, and we plowed through, heads down. I feared to make contact with another's eyes, certain that I would be recognized and hailed.

Another flash and crack from the heavens sent women and children squealing and running in every direction. A young boy rammed me, and his head drove the air from my stomach. I righted him and continued on, trying not to lose Neferet's feet.

It seemed to me that we twisted in circles through the village, winding past the bakery and brewery, then around the barracks and through the sections for families. At last Neferet slowed, reached back and grabbed my arm, and pulled me through a familiar doorway.

The silence inside the house was like a protective shroud. I followed Neferet without speaking, through to the central courtyard of the home.

Sen was there, pacing like a caged animal.

"Neferet! Where have you been?" His eyes strayed to me, and his face went dark. "I thought you were in prison."

"I got him out," Neferet said. She went to her father and embraced him. His arms lifted automatically to encircle her, but he stared at me.

"What have you done, girl?"

"Sen," I said, "the king has sentenced me to die for the murders. I am innocent. Neferet—she helped me to escape before my death."

Sen pulled Neferet away from him and held her by the arms. He scowled at her painted face and revealing dress. "And guaranteed your own death at the same time!"

"I had to do it, Father. I could not allow an innocent man to die and the murderer to go free."

Sen pushed Neferet aside with the gruffness that comes with anger at a loved one. "She is impetuous and foolish, but you—" He paced away from me, then back, his open palm upraised. "You I would have expected to take more care! How could you have endangered my daughter this way? Do you not care for her at all?" Thunder rumbled again, but Sen's voice roared above it.

I hung my head. "You are right. I should never have allowed this, nor put you both in more danger by coming here."

Neferet glared at her father, then at me. "I must get some things to tend to your wound," she said, and marched away.

Sen grew quiet. "Guards hurt you?" he finally asked in the murky light of the approaching storm.

"It is nothing. I should not have come."

A deep crease formed between his eyes. "The young do foolish things."

I half smiled. I had not been called young in some time, and Sen was far younger than my father, but it warmed me somehow to have him treat me so. We were far from grand vizier and overseer today.

"Allow Neferet to tend to my head, Sen. Then I will leave, and you can tell the king's men that you don't know where I am."

"And where will you go?"

I shook my head. Neferet returned with a jug of wine and some clean rags. She poured some of the wine on a rag and gave me the jug. "Drink." She pushed me toward the bench beside the small pool.

I sat and swigged the wine. The cool bite of the spirit revived me, but I could have merely waited for the sharp sting of Neferet's treatment. She cleaned the wound on the side of my head, then dipped the rag in the pool before cleaning the blood from my neck and shoulder.

"You need to shave," she said, running a finger over the stubble on my head and cheek.

"Should have used the knife Khufu gave me."

She swatted my arm. "That is not funny."

"Are you finished? I need to leave."

Sen watched from across the courtyard, his arms folded. "I ask you again, Grand Vizier, where will you go?"

"I have no idea. I could perhaps find a way upriver to Thebes or Aswan. Maybe I could join up with traders and go on to Sinai, or to Nubia."

Neferet's eyes clouded. "And be a fugitive for the rest of your life?"

I exhaled and looked away.

"You must stay and fight, Hemi! Fight for your freedom, and fight for justice. If you run, there will be neither."

Sacrifice yourself, Hemiunu, or there will be more suffering, more pain, more disorder.

I felt tired but knew it was dangerous to linger. I wished I could stay forever, under Neferet's care. But to stay would bring destruction upon this house.

Sen grunted from his place against the wall. "You have brought your trouble here with you, now you must let us help you deal with it." His voice carried anger, but it was like that of a raging bull with no horns. "We will hide you."

"Where? They will surely look for me here."

"There is a place. A place that we have created to be kept secret from those who wish us harm."

The People of the One. I remembered the hidden door, the great chamber that had been made by combining households that adjoined, at the center of the village block.

"And then what?"

"We will make a plan once we have you there. There must be a way to find the true killer. But first, you must be safe."

"Father, the meeting place is on the other side of the village. There are so many about today. How—"

"Leave that to me," Sen said. He pushed away from the wall, gave me a final glare, and disappeared into the front of the house.

Neferet smiled, like a little girl whose father has given her sweets. "I knew he would help you."

I laughed. "I think I knew it too."

We were sitting on the courtyard bench side by side, Neferet and I, when the rain came.

I do not know what rain is like in other lands. I have heard that far from here, where there is no life-giving Nile to pour its moisture over the land every year, the rain falls gently and often. But here in Egypt, we have no need of water from the sky and do not know what to do with it when it comes.

Neferet screamed, and I threw an arm around her shoulder and hurried us both under the cover of the house. We went to the kitchen, where Neferet cut melon and figs for me.

Sen returned, with rainwater running in channels from his head, down his chest, and pooling on the floor beneath his feet. "We leave soon," he said simply and grabbed a fig from the board.

"While the sky still cries?" Neferet found a rag and began patting her father dry.

"All the better." Sen pulled the cloth from her hand and finished the task himself. "Most are indoors. Those that are crazy enough to be about are well occupied."

"But he cannot simply walk down the street. Many will be in their doorways."

Sen smiled, as a father will smile at his child, and patted her cheek. "Trust me, daughter."

Neferet's eyes filled. "I—I am afraid."

Sen pulled her into an embrace, and I watched with not a little jealousy. "I know, child. But I will take care of him."

My own eyes watered, and I turned away. How had this happened? I was grand vizier, second in command of all Egypt. Not long ago Senosiris was practically a nameless laborer to me. And now I stood in his home, my fate in his hands like he was master.

Or father.

From outside the house, I heard a whistle.

"Here they are," Sen said. He pulled Neferet from him and turned to me. "I have called for that cursed litter you arranged for me to travel in when you gave me my new position." He moved toward the front of the house and motioned for me to follow. "We will ride inside together with the curtain drawn. No one will stop us."

From inside the doorway, we surveyed our transport. Four slaves stood in the rain, heads down, awaiting us. I hoped we could rely on their silence, for I was certain they would recognize me.

The litter was not fashioned in as ornate a style as my own, but the cedar poles and box were lovely. Gold rings encircled the four poles near the joints of the box, and a tan curtain with red embroidered palms covered the front. I saw at once, however, that the litter was only large enough to house one man on the bench inside it, and not even a large man such as Sen.

He lifted an eyebrow in my direction. "It would appear that we are soon to know each other even better."

"Father, stay here," Neferet suggested. "Send Hemi in the litter alone."

He patted her shoulder. "It is too risky. If the rain does not deter them, I would expect Pharaoh's guards to be here any moment. They will come looking for me, and it would not do for my litter to be crossing the village without me in it." He leaned down to peck her on the cheek. "Trust me."

I was beginning to glimpse that trust was something that did not come easily to Neferet. I set aside the thought for future pondering.

"Ready?" Sen asked me. I nodded and took a deep breath. He extended a hand, indicating that I should climb in first. I ducked out into the rain, pushed aside the curtain, and scrambled to the back of the box.

Inside was a simple bench, just wide enough for a man and deep enough to recline. I sat all the way back, with my legs stretched in front of me. Sen was in a moment later, and from his hunched position facing me, he snorted. "This will be interesting."

"Sen, I—"

He held up a hand. "Say nothing. It is better to say nothing."

He rotated his bulk in the box, then sat heavily on the front part of the bench, between my knees, with his legs painfully crossed in front of him. Neferet peeked her head through the curtain and looked as though she couldn't choose between laughter or tears.

"Stay indoors, Neferet," Sen said.

She waved a hand at me in farewell and I smiled.

The curtain fell closed, leaving the inside of the box in twilight. I could see nothing but the tan of the cedar and the darker tan of Sen's back.

With much groaning, the slaves heaved the litter poles to their shoulders. The box rocked as they lifted, pushing the two of us against first one side and then the other until we were at last positioned parallel to the ground. We started off with a dip and a lurch that knocked Sen back against my chest. I heard him exhale heavily and knew he was not pleased.

My legs soon grew uncomfortable, spread as they were to accommodate Sen's girth. The woodsy smell of cedar mingled with our sweat and the rainwater, bringing to mind a sarcophagus for some unknown reason.

We moved through the streets, and I could hear the rain pound the top of the litter above and the streets below, a strange unearthly sound.

The hard-packed dirt of the village streets is not capable of absorbing a deluge of water from the sky. Within minutes I could hear the splashing of the slaves' feet, as though we ran through the shallows of a canal. The litter rocked unpredictably as our carriers avoided low spots, knocking us against the sides and each other. It seemed to me that the village had grown twice as wide since last I crossed it.

My legs cramped, and I tried to shift position but only succeeded in causing Sen to glare at me. "Keep still," he said in a whisper like coarse sand.

Once, when we tilted to the left, the curtain parted slightly to reveal the open street beyond our tiny compartment. But the rain poured like a second curtain around us, protecting us from those who roamed the streets imploring the gods to spare them from this evil.

In other circumstances, I would have joined them. If for no other reason than the lost hours of labor on the Horizon of Khufu and the possible damage to ramps and supplies. But all of that had become as a distant memory to me, and I blessed the rain that hid me from prying eyes.

We had thus far moved at a rapid pace, so it came as a surprise when the slaves now slowed to a stop. Sen leaned forward and poked a finger between the split curtains, opening a tiny window. "What is it?" he called.

One of the slaves turned his head to be heard above the rain. "The street is flooded, master. We cannot pass."

"Then take a different route!"

I felt the litter circle around and head back the other direction. I cursed quietly, and Sen grunted his agreement. We traveled in silence for a few more minutes, until the litter stopped again.

Sen pushed the curtain apart. "Is there no way through this village?" he shouted, then pulled the curtain partway shut again, so that only his face extended beyond the inside of the box. "Yes, what is it?" he asked, and his voice had taken on a different tone than a man dealing with his slaves.

"You are Senosiris, Overseer of Constructions?" a voice called up to the litter. The Nubian. Axum. I pressed my head against the wood and fought the nausea that swept over me.

"What brings you to me at such an evil time?" Sen answered, as though annoyed.

"There has been some . . . difficulty at the royal estate," Axum said. "The grand vizier's presence is required. I thought perhaps you could tell me where he is."

Sen waved a hand. "The man does not consult with me on his schedule. And as you can see, we are not working today." There was a long pause, until Sen said, "If you will step aside, I will continue on my way."

"You are visiting someone? Today?" Axum asked. "For as you say, you are not working."

"The holiday is for the peasants," Sen said. "For those of us who hold the project in our hands, our work is never done. I must speak to the artists about the temple statuary."

"And your daughter? Where is she?" Axum's voice had a knife-edge to it.

He knows. He knows Neferet helped me escape. I suddenly regretted that we had left her alone. What had I been thinking?

"She will probably be about the men's barracks, keeping them in beer and bread on this evil day."

Another long pause, and I could picture the Nubian studying Sen with his black eyes, his eyebrows drawn together and lips tight.

"You will send word if you see the grand vizier about," Axum said, his words a command and not a request.

"Of course. I will be certain to tell him you seek him."

I closed my eyes, waiting for Axum to release us. I smelled the sweat and wet wood when I inhaled, and I realized I had been holding my breath.

The litter moved again, and Sen closed the curtain and reclined, his back touching my chest. "I am supposed to tell you the Nubian is looking for you" he said dryly.

"I'll be sure to pay him a visit soon."

The slaves proceeded slowly now, whether because of the flooded streets or because they grew weary of their double load, I could not tell. But the minutes stretched, until at last they slowed and then lowered the litter to the ground with an excessive bump.

Sen wasted no time in exiting from the box, and I had the urge to embrace the man for the sacrifice he was making on my behalf. I waited until his hand poked through the curtain and waved me out.

"Quickly now, quickly," he said.

I jumped out into the rain and dashed before him into the large estate I had visited with Neferet many nights earlier. Inside the door, we were met by Layla as though she expected us. And then from behind her stepped Neferet.

Sen growled. "Child!"

Layla smiled. "She is a woman now, Senosiris. With her own mind. Leave her alone." Layla reached for me and pulled me into the house. "Let's get you hidden, and then we can speak freely."

If Sen had become a father of sorts to me today, it was Layla who was my mother. She clucked and fussed all the way into the back chamber with the hidden door, fretting about my filthy, wet clothes, my injured head, and my unjust imprisonment. I surrendered myself to her care and felt that in this strange place, with people I did not understand, I had somehow finally come home.

TWENTY-FOUR

I stepped through the passageway into the central part of the house, where the People of the One held their meetings. Neferet followed.

From behind me, Sen pushed forward and knocked me into the room. "How did you get here?" he said to Neferet. He looked as though he might shake her. Her dripping clothes and hair made the question unnecessary.

"I couldn't stay home alone, Father. Not until I knew that you were both safe."

He shook his head and crossed the room to speak with Hanif.

"I'm glad you came, Neferet," I said. "We were stopped in the road and your father was questioned. I feared they would next go to your home."

"You weren't seen?"

"No, Sen was brilliant. I'm not sure he'll ever speak to me again, however."

Neferet laughed. "He never holds a grudge."

Layla was back, arms full of clothing and rags. "Come," she said, "you must get out of your wet clothes."

She glanced at Neferet's dress and raised her eyebrows. "And into something decent."

Neferet looked down at the dress she had worn for the guards, now stuck to her skin with rainwater. "A long story, Layla," she said, smiling.

Layla winked. "Later you tell your story. Now you get dry."

Neferet touched her hand to my arm. "And Hemi must rest. He has been through much."

"Yes. A good bed and perhaps some hot food, yes?"

Here, the tightness flowed out of my shoulders. I allowed the women to lead me by the arm through the meeting room, across to the other side. Sen was still engaged in conversation with Layla's husband, but he paused and glanced at our procession. Layla took us into the back of the house opposite the one we had entered. It took me only a few moments to realize that this was her home, which I had been in some days before. I had not realized at the time that it also connected to the meeting room.

Layla deposited me in a small chamber with a wide bed, presumably hers and Hanif's. Neferet she took elsewhere. I stripped off the wet and prison-dirtied skirt I wore. The rain had washed the dirt from me, and I used the rags to rub my skin dry, then dressed again in the clothes Layla had left, a white skirt similar in style to my own, though not as fine a cloth.

When I had finished, I poked my head from the chamber and checked the passageway, but no one was about. Tentatively, I made my way through the house. I reached the central courtyard, but the rain still fell so I remained under the protection of the roof.

Layla's face appeared at the end of the passage. "You are hungry," she said. It was not a question. "Come. Eat."

The kitchen steamed and bubbled with a meaty broth on the fire that looked good enough to swim in. She ladled me a bowlful, then filled another and reached past me to hand it to Neferet, who had entered the room. She now wore a simple white sheath dress. No embroidery, nothing that jangled when she walked. I smiled to think of how she must detest the simplicity.

"You both eat, get warm, and then rest," Layla said. Others will be here later, and then we can talk about what we are going to do for our grand vizier here."

I swallowed a mouthful of broth. "No, Layla. You are not responsible for me. I did not come here to burden you with my problem."

"Problem?" Neferet said. "You were sentenced to death!"

"And I would not have you suffer the same fate for helping me."

"Children," Layla said, with a soft hand on each of our arms. "Things will look differently after you have rested. Besides," she said with a look at me, "you must let us do what we can. It is what the One would have us do."

She pushed us into chairs and brought bread and beer. After the hot and spicy broth, Layla fed us sweet and juicy watermelon, ripe and fragrant. I ate until my fingers were sticky with the juice and my belly full. The fire worked its way into my muscles, and I rested my head back against the chair.

It seemed only a moment later that Layla shook my shoulder, but I guessed that time had passed. "Come, Hemi," she said. I pulled myself to my feet and followed her to the chamber where I'd changed my clothes and, at her insistence, fell into the bed.

I awoke much later, if the light was to be believed. Though it had been a strange day for light, and I could not be certain. Perhaps it was even the next morning. I was loathe to move, to arise and find out. Instead, I rolled to my side, intending to drift back to sleep.

Neferet lay beside me.

By the shimmering wings of Isis, she was beautiful. Had I admitted that to myself before now? I watched her lips, slightly parted in sleep.

What was happening to me? It seemed that the death of my friend Mentu had begun a series of happenings that carried me on a strange current, and I had no knowledge of where I would finish my journey. My life had previously been confined to order and structure, and the only thing that ever upset the careful balance was my occasional interaction with Merit.

But now Merit was gone, the pyramid project lay unattended, and this woman beside me made me forget what order and structure even looked like.

Neferet stirred and opened her eyes. Her smile was slow and sleepy. "How do you feel?" she asked, in the low voice I had heard her use with the prison guards.

"Like I could stay here for another hundred years."

"Hmmm," she nodded and closed her eyes.

The house was quiet. The rainfall must have stopped. I nevertheless still felt a sense of isolation and protection here.

"Hemi?" Neferet whispered, and a wisp of hair fell across her eyes, still closed.

"Yes?"

She sighed. "Wherever you go, I want to go with you."

I reached to brush her hair from her face. Her eyes flew open while my hand still touched her cheek, and we both knew it was the first time I had reached out to touch her. She leaned closer to me, until our bodies touched.

"I have no answers, Neferet. No answers."

"I do not need answers."

A gentle throat clearing at the door pushed us apart. I propped myself up on an elbow. "Is anything wrong, Layla?"

"No, my child. But the others have come and are gathered in the meeting chamber. Will you join us?"

Neferet slid to her feet and I too climbed from the bed. "Of course."

We passed to the back of Layla's house and through her own hidden door into the chamber, now lit again with a dozen lamps and filled with people. Already I felt more comfortable in this place than on my prior visit and nodded to a few familiar faces as we descended.

I expected another meeting such as the first, but tonight's gathering appeared to be more of a celebration. Tables around the perimeter of the room were laden with food, and people sat in small clusters, talking and laughing. I tried to remember if it were a feast day, but then realized that the People of the One perhaps had their own calendar of auspicious and holy days.

"What do they celebrate?" I asked Neferet.

She answered my question with a look of confusion. "It is only a meal," she said. "We often take our meals together, to encourage and enjoy one another's company."

I followed her to the food, then to a bench, now carrying a full bowl. A few heads turned my way in recognition, but I saw only smiles and warmth.

I tasted hot lentils and thought back to the last banquet I had attended, Khufu's festival of accession. I remembered the posturing and jealousy, each person focused on furthering his own position in court, the demand for entertainment, and coarse joking.

By comparison this gathering was that of a large and loving family, and I marveled at the difference. Neferet must have sensed my wonder, for she leaned against me and said, "We are more than the People of the One. We are his children. And that makes us all brothers and sisters."

I tore at a piece of bread and chewed, my thoughts heavy.

Several of the group came to speak to Neferet and nodded their welcome to me. Layla stopped to ensure that I was eating enough. She stood over me and took my head in her hands, rocking it back and forth to examine the gash on my head. "Huh," was all she said, but I assumed she approved of Neferet's doctoring.

Later, when most had eaten and the conversation still hummed, Neferet slipped from my side and went to speak into the ear of a young man near the front. He smiled up at her and nodded. I watched his eyes, trying to gauge his interest in Neferet. But she was back to me in a moment and pulled me to my feet. "Come," she said. So I did. She led me to the front, where the young man appeared again, this time with a seven-stringed harp in his hands.

Neferet smiled at me, eyes sparkling. "Play for us, Hemi."

"Absolutely not." I was embarrassed that she would have even asked. It was a private thing, my music.

She drew up close. "There is no shame in beauty. It is a gift."

The boy with the harp approached. "I have only just begun to play," he said. "Neferet tells me you have great talent. I would so much like to watch you. I am sure you have much to teach me."

I narrowed my eyes at the boy, whose smile betrayed an awareness of his skill at manipulation.

"Please, Hemi," Neferet said, and I found I could not deny her.

I took the harp from the young man, sat upon a bench in the corner, and placed the instrument before me. The room still flowed with conversation, and I hoped that my quiet playing would go unnoticed. I plucked a string or two and noticed little reaction.

I focused on the strings, my fingers ready, waiting for the music to come. My eyes drifted closed, as they often did, and my fingers began to move. I sensed Neferet draw close, and perhaps the young man, but I continued on.

My past several days had been strange and disturbing, and the music told the story. The quiet passages with Neferet, the minor notes of standing over Ebo's body, the discordant clash of Khufu's sentence. I played through the rising crescendo of my escape from prison and subsequent sprint through the desert to the workmen's village, the steady beat of the rainfall on Sen's litter as we traveled the sloshing streets, and then the gentle rhythms of warmth and food and rest in the care of Layla. And when the music ended, sweet and tender and filled with joy and fellowship, I knew that this was here and now.

I opened my eyes, drifting back from the far-off place I had gone. Every eye in the room was fixed upon me, and the last note floated above our heads like the wings of a dove. I saw that somehow, even in my ignorance, I had led them to a deep sense of worship. The knowledge stirred something unknown in me.

Neferet kneeled in front of me and put her forehead on my knee. I covered her head with my hand.

"I—I do not always understand what I play," I said to the young man who had lent me his harp in exchange for a lesson.

He smiled as though he understood and looked over the others in the room. "This beauty, this creativity, this freedom," he said, "they are gifts of the One True God. He gives them to us, for us to lift up to him along with our hearts. It is always our hearts that he wants."

"I do not understand."

Sen appeared out of the shadows and stood before me. He spoke to me but loud enough for the room to hear. "From the beginning it has been thus. God walked with man, in relationship with man. This was his desire, that our hearts be one with his. But man turned his back on the One. And many followed. We made it impossible for the Perfect One to be in relationship with us." Sen turned to face the gathering. "We condemned ourselves, with only the feeble hope of somehow earning back the lost favor with our pitiful efforts. And yet," his voice lifted with a joy I knew he felt from deep within. "And yet, the One True God has not left us hopeless. There will be One Who Comes who will take away the sins of the world."

I had heard them speak before of this one to come. "When?" I dared to ask, and Neferet squeezed my knee and smiled.

"We do not know," Sen answered. "We know only that he is our only hope. He is our Redeemer, who will provide the way for us to be reconciled to the One True God. I have prayed that I will be allowed to see this day."

I pondered this God who desired reconciliation and love, unlike any god I had been taught to fear.

Sen lifted his hands as though in blessing over the group. "And we have faith, do we not, my friends? Faith in the One Who Comes."

I handed the harp back to my new friend with a smile, and our eyes connected. We shared the music, but there was the beginning of something more, I realized. My smile faltered. I feared I was beginning to share more than their food.

It would have been easy to remain there among these people, to pretend that the Scourge of Anubis did not still roam free and that my cousin and king had not sentenced me to die for the killer's crimes.

But this was not to be. For while we still soaked in the final words of Sen's impassioned speech, there came a noise outside the chamber that caused me to instantly regret my presence here and consider the possibility that I had brought doom upon these people.

TWENTY-FIVE

The People of the One immediately fell silent. Outside the chamber there was angry conversation, the snap and growl of determined palace authorities. I listened, trying to distinguish words, but it was difficult to hear over the pounding in my chest.

To whom did they speak? I scanned the room and saw Layla standing like a statue of Mut, the mother goddess, beside a table of food, her fingers twisted together in front of her ample waist.

The stomp of feet and angry voices drew nearer. I wrapped an arm about Neferet's shoulders. Sen noticed my movement and inched closer to us. I tried to read his expression. Not fear, not anger. Just listening, as we all were.

Around the room, several lamps were quietly extinguished.

Then Axum the Nubian's voice worked its way into the chamber, and any doubt that this was about me disappeared. Once again I cursed my own stupidity for putting these people in danger.

Others were with him, though not soldiers from the argumentative whine of their voices as they questioned Layla's husband, Hanif.

Priests.

Was this a religious or criminal investigation?

The voices came closer, as if they searched the house. Inside our underground hiding place, the utter silence of such a group seemed unearthly. Neferet trembled beneath my arm, and I could feel her skin grow damp.

"And where is your wife?" Axum could be heard asking.

"It takes many hours of labor to feed our family, I am afraid. Trips to the trading stalls, fetching our rations. She works hard."

An answer, though not a lie.

"When is the last time you saw him, peasant?"

A pause. "He was here earlier today."

I winced. Hanif had sealed his fate by admitting that I had even been here.

"And his daughter, was she with him?"

Not me. Sen.

"She did not come with him."

"Did he speak of the grand vizier? Tell you anything about the happenings at the palace?"

"It may surprise you to learn we do not concern ourselves with happenings at the palace."

There came the sound of a blow and a crash.

A whimper slipped from Layla, and she covered her mouth with her hand.

"Get up, peasant!" It was not the Nubian's voice this time, and I strained to identify it.

"He knows more than he says," the voice said. "He is part of the rebellious sect that does not worship the great ennead of gods. They refuse to acknowledge that the Great Pharaoh, Beloved of Horus, is Ra on earth."

This religious babble was plenty to tell me that the man was a priest.

"I care not who the man worships!" Axum said. "My only interest is in the grand vizier."

I lifted my eyes to the group huddled around me, expecting to see condemnation and fear. But their faces were a puzzle to me. Sadness and joy mingled.

Another voice now shouted. "If the grand vizier is involved with these people, then they must also be your concern! It is clear that Hemiunu is responsible for the recent upheaval of our system of worship. He is trying to undermine all the beliefs we hold sacred. Perhaps you wish to see the Great Pharaoh bow down before this foreign god who allows no other gods to be worshiped!"

I frowned. A former priest of On, obviously. Like Rashidi. Furious over the changes that had resulted in his dismissal. I remembered Rashidi's anger when he confronted Khufu in the Great Hall.

A child across the room asked a question of his father. We all turned, and the father covered his child's mouth with his hand and lifted an apology with his eyes. And still, I did not see fear in any of them. Did they not realize that they survived only at the whim of a king who did not think them worth his attention? That if I were found here their destruction was guaranteed?

Somehow I could see that they did know it. Facing the door that separated us from capture, each looked more like a parent who knows his child is about to do something foolish yet must let it happen to teach the child. Despite the ponderous complexity of Egypt's religious order, were these simple people the keepers of true wisdom?

Neferet eased away from me and I realized my grip on her shoulders had tightened. She touched my face and I saw concern pass over hers.

"I must leave," I whispered. Her eyes widened.

I stood, and Sen's brow furrowed. "I cannot stay," I said to him. "I cannot involve you any further." I moved toward the hidden door.

Sen's iron grip wrapped around my upper arm. He came behind me and put his mouth to my ear. "Think, Hemi. You leave now and you endanger all of these people."

I took a few breaths, trying to slow my heart.

The voices outside the door moved away. Still we waited, frozen. Minutes later, the door slid aside. Hanif stepped in and closed the door behind him.

"They are gone." His thin face seemed to have aged.

Sen released my arm.

"Why, Hemi?" Neferet asked, jumping up to stand beside me. "Why must you leave?"

"This is something I must do on my own. I must find the truth." I turned to Sen. "I will not jeopardize her further."

Sen nodded but said, "You have involved us all now, and we will not turn our backs on you. What can we do?"

I sighed and studied the closed door. "I am not sure what I can do. But somewhere out there are answers. And I cannot hide myself away."

I thought of Tamit, of Khufu, and of my brother. Which of them, even now, was in mortal danger?

I waited until nightfall to leave. Many of the people stayed to send me off, and as I stood at the door, I found it difficult to say goodbye, to go back out in the night and the unknown.

Layla hugged me tightly, and when she pulled away, her warm brown eyes roamed my face. "Be careful, Hemi," she said. "Do not fall back into the lie." I wasn't sure of her meaning, but I suddenly longed to stay and let her care for me.

I then endured a multitude of hugs and shoulder slaps from well-wishers. I tried to study each face, to remember so that I would know them again if I saw them elsewhere, but my eyes were occupied with blinking away unfamiliar emotion.

Neferet kept her distance, unwilling to say farewell. But then the people parted and looked her way, and she had no choice.

"What will you do?" she said.

"I am not certain. I must find a way to prove to Khufu that I am innocent. But when I last saw the king, his anger toward me was fierce. I dare not go back until I can show him the truth."

"Are you in danger?"

"I am as guilty as any of us were, I am afraid." I thought of Amunet, and of the way I left her body in the marsh. "Maybe more so."

Neferet lowered her eyes, and Sen stepped to my side. "I will go with you as far as my home," he said, "and give you some things that may help you in your journey." He turned to Neferet and kissed the top of her head. "Stay here until morning." A look at Layla confirmed that she would make sure the girl was safe.

Sen pushed ahead of me, through the hidden door and into the back room of the house. Neferet reached for my hand and squeezed it. I returned the grasp, gave her a quick smile, and followed her father.

We slipped from the house carefully, watching the dark streets for late-night revelers. But the earlier rain had been enough to keep people indoors this night. I shivered. Leaving the People of the One felt like being stripped of something vital. I ran behind Sen, along the walls, through the back streets, until we reached his home.

Within minutes, I was back out on the street, a pouch slung over my shoulder. Sen grasped both my arms warmly and looked into my eyes. "Take care, Grand Vizier," he said. "Do not force me to give my daughter bad news."

"Thank you, Sen. For all your kindness. I will send word when I can."

And then we parted. I left him standing in the doorway of his home, and I fled through the back alleys once more, toward the gates of the village.

Twice I passed someone lounging in a door frame. I kept my head down and hoped for the best.

By the time I made my way out of the village and back out onto the desert path, the moon had risen, throwing a paltry light before me. I left the path quickly, moving eastward, closer to the edge of the floodplain, where a canal ran north toward the pyramid and the royal estate.

My feet carried me swiftly toward the unknown. The water in the canal ran high from the day's rain. I could hear it sloshing at its banks as I ran, and the sound kept me oriented. Somewhere to my left, an animal joined my run. It pawed the sand in time with my own feet and crashed through the scrubby bushes at the waterside. Was it better to stop? Was a jackal more likely to attack a running man?

The workmen's village faded away behind me, and the pyramid complex, the harbor, and the royal estate now filled my vision. I focused on the plateau above me. The gray clouds had broken apart, now drifting across the moon in shades of black and purple. The dark outline of the unfinished pyramid sliced through the clouds like a broken blade.

My chest expanded in sharp and shallow breaths. I slowed my run and listened for the animal. I heard nothing but the water. A cool breeze blew on the dampness of my neck.

Ahead, I could make out the small valley temple at the base of the pyramid complex. I tried to absorb the hard edges of temple and pyramid, to let the stone fill my veins and strengthen me for whatever lay ahead.

I approached the royal estate along the wall that surrounded it and stopped before I reached the entrance. It was madness to go back inside after my escape with Neferet yesterday. I pulled Sen's pouch from my shoulder and removed a long, full-braided wig and a robe to conceal my build. I hoped it was enough to keep the casual observer from recognizing me.

Deep breaths.

I slipped along the wall, head down, but then lifted my head and strolled through the estate entrance as though I belonged.

The walls of the royal estate had been erected as protection from animals and from the sand that blew continually across the desert, but Egypt had few enemies that would cross the Red Lands to attack. And so the entrance was not guarded. I rounded the corner and moved quickly to the gardens that led the way from the entrance to the palace. Small reflecting pools, trees, and paths lined with palms and flowers made it easier to remain unseen.

The palace was lit from inside, and as I drew close I could hear the lively twitter of conversation and the melodies of harem singers. Another feast? I tried to remember if today were a festival day.

The Festival of Hapi is tomorrow. I had forgotten. Khufu loved the games and had established a day of competition and entertainment for nobles and laborers alike. And always, a feast was held the night before for those who lived on the royal estate.

I leaned against a large sycamore, one of many that ringed the palace like a secondary wall. Beside me, I heard the croak of a frog and a small splash as it plopped into one of the pools. The evening air was unusually damp and close. Behind me somewhere the People of the One probably still met together in their pleasant hidden chamber. Ahead, the nobility feasted and drank and danced in the firelit Great Hall. I stood alone among the leafy greens and felt I belonged to neither of these two worlds. The sycamore's bark reached out to snag my robe. I pulled away and a dead leaf crunched underfoot.

Thick fingers grabbed my elbows from behind and held me fast.

"Grand Vizier," a deep voice grated against my ear. "We have missed you."

I half turned. "Axum. You are effective as always in hunting down your prey."

The man lowered his head. "Though I would much prefer to work *for* you, my lord, than against you."

I welcomed the tone of respect in his voice, like a man who has gone too long without. "I cannot find the truth from a cell, Axum."

His grip loosened and I faced him.

"The king has set no higher task for me than apprehending you," he said. "Though in truth he seems to have little more appetite for it than I."

I stared into the Nubian's luminous eyes. "Trust your instincts, Axum. I have served at the king's right hand for many years."

Axum crossed his arms and pulled on his lower lip. "I am not certain the king's *new* advisor serves him so faithfully."

I frowned, inviting more.

"Rashidi, the little priest," Axum said. The name seemed distasteful to him. "He is ever present at the king's side. Interpreting dreams, whispering advice."

"Rashidi." I turned him over in my mind, trying to chase an elusive thread of thought.

"It is my duty to drag you before the king now, Grand Vizier."

I returned his look. "Yes. Yes, it is."

Another look passed between us, one of men who have taken the true measure of each other. Then Axum nodded in silent agreement. He closed his eyes, lowered his head, and waited for me to disappear.

I hurried for the temple. The robe Sen had given me was long on my legs, restricting my movements, yet I dared not remove it.

My thoughts tumbled as I drew toward the temple, like a small boat pulled downriver by a current I could not control. The determination I had felt upon leaving the workmen's village now grew into anger. I must have answers tonight.

I approached the temple on silent feet and halted on the stone slab set in front of the door. I pressed my back against one of the massive carved columns that stood on either side. A fire had blazed to life inside the temple, then another. Rashidi was lighting the braziers. The flames threw wavering shadows on the walls and reached out to graze the column behind me.

I heard someone coming from the direction of the harbor, and I pulled back into the darkness. Three men approached in quiet conversation. From their dress they appeared to be young priests, still in training. They crossed under the lintel and entered the temple. Solemn greetings were given and returned by Rashidi. I moved back to my position near the door.

Within moments, a series of intonations drifted from inside the temple, low and unintelligible, that raised the hair on my neck. I crept to the edge of the doorway and set my cheek against the edge, watching with my right eye.

The four men stood before an altar, where something had been sacrificed. Red blood ran from the stone and one of the young priests lit a fire. Smoke puffed in gray billows above their heads and hung there. One of them held two wooden sticks and he tapped them together in a slow rhythm while the others continued to moan. I pressed my cheek against the cold stone, vainly seeking some sort of comfort from its solidity. The moaning, the tapping, the blood and burning continued for some time. I grew dizzy from my careful position.

At last Rashidi raised his voice above the rest, and they ceased their noise. "Tomorrow it shall be revealed that a great evil has been done, my sons," he said.

The others lifted their heads in attention.

"They will understand that they have done wrong, and they will regret their actions. All will be made right at last."

The young men murmured in agreement.

"I must know that you are ready to carry out your part," Rashidi said. "That your hands are strong for your task, that you will not back down from what is asked of you."

Again, agreement was given.

"You must strike quickly and all at once. This is important. You have the knives that I have given you?"

I ground my cheek into the wall now, let it cause me pain in the hope that it would harden me.

"We are ready to do the will of the gods, Rashidi," one of the younger men said.

I felt the fool for not seeing it sooner.

Rashidi, who pushed me to investigate the murders. Ebo's wife and her claim that a priest had told her to reveal that I had been paying off her husband. And I had seen the rage in his protestations before Khufu. Rashidi, who knew how to drug a man like an animal and how to slit the throat of an ox.

Yes, Rashidi. Another piece of our past. The young man who had loved Amunet. The dismissed priest who had cause to hate me for taking away his position.

Three young priests. Three more victims in Tamit, Khufu, and Ahmose. Then there would only be Rashidi and myself.

"Ra will grant our efforts success, I am certain," Rashidi now said. "He will not allow the evil to go unpunished."

He tossed some leaves of fragrant myrrh onto the fire. The flames popped and a shower of sparks lifted above their heads. A pungent aroma now filled the temple and reached out to the portico where I stood, teeth clenched and hands curled into fists at my side.

I sensed that their meeting had drawn to a close and disappeared around the corner of the temple. I had learned all I needed about Rashidi's three young assistants, but I would not let the priest go so easily. Before morning came, I intended to pry from him each of his many secrets.

TWENTY-SIX

Rashidi's apprentices departed soon after. I remained hidden in the darkness and watched them drift away into the night. Rashidi remained inside.

I returned to the entrance of the temple slowly and leaned into the doorway. The fire had burned down to embers now, casting a reddish glow along the walls. I did not see the little priest. I ventured farther into the doorway and inclined my ears.

From deeper in the temple, I heard the sound of soft chanting.

The valley temple served the workmen and royal estate while the pyramid complex was still under construction, but when all was complete this temple would be the location for Pharaoh's mummification, and his body would proceed from here to the pyramid via the stone causeway that had already been partially built. I had not yet commissioned the walls and roof of the causeway to be completed, but the ramp itself led from the back of the temple up to the base of the pyramid, where the mortuary temple would be built for the ongoing worship of the king when he became Ra.

I circled to the back of the temple, scrambled up the rubble ramp upon which the causeway was built, and descended down to the back entrance, where a small chamber currently housed the statue of Ra. It was here that the priests would daily offer libations and sacrifices. I stood just inside the back entrance and listened again for Rashidi's chant.

The temple was silent, and I thought for a moment that perhaps he had left through the front while I was circling around. But then the low chant came again, very near. I stepped backward in surprise but managed to hold my ground, and I braced myself against the temple wall with one hand. In my other hand I held a pebble I'd picked up when climbing the causeway, and I grasped it now between thumb and forefinger. The focus helped me settle my fear.

The wall here was carved with a relief of Anubis. Fitting. It occurred to me that Anubis was never depicted holding the shepherd's crook of leadership, only the whiplike flail of punishment. Small comfort for those who awaited his judgment.

From my vantage point I was not able to see the priest. It served no purpose to listen to his chant and the odd scraping that accompanied it, so I leaned in farther.

I saw Rashidi in profile, working at something over a stone block. He paused a moment and set down an instrument. A long knife. Beside him, an oil lamp flared. He was adding oil. He bent back to his work.

Sharpening. He scraped the blade against the stone again and again, continuing his low, monotone singing all the while. The smell of burnt flesh still filled my nostrils. A moment later he lifted a hunk of charred meat from the table where he worked. He wrapped his hand around the shaft of the knife and stabbed at the flesh. Then again, with more force. Again and again, until the meat hung from the bone in ragged tatters. But he was not satisfied, for he went back to his sharpening.

Why would the priest be sharpening a knife at this hour, the night before he planned to take his revenge? I could think of only one reason.

"Rashidi?"

After the long minutes of silence, the voice that rang from the front of the temple nearly startled me into revealing myself. Fortunately it also surprised Rashidi, and the priest dropped the knife against the stone. He circled to the doorway quickly and moved into the antechamber.

"Ahmose," I heard him say. The name chilled me. I pushed forward into the space Rashidi had just vacated and positioned myself at the doorway to the antechamber, ready to spring to my brother's defense.

The priest's voice was low and silky. "What are you doing out at such an hour?"

"What have you done, priest?"

I knew that tone well.

"Only what the gods require of me, Ahmose. Nothing more."

"You went to Khufu. And now my brother has been sentenced to die!"

There was a long pause, during which I imagined Rashidi attempting to hide his pleasure.

"Sometimes justice is harsh, my old friend. But Ma'at is what sustains us, and we must bow to her wishes."

I crept backward two steps and took the knife from the stone where Rashidi had dropped it.

"I am not certain," Ahmose said, "that we have seen justice at all."

"Ahmose. Of all people, you know that what has transpired was necessary. You told me so yourself."

"I—I did not think—"

"You did not think that truth and divine order applied to your family?"

"I did not think you would use my words against my brother!"

"It is you who desired to hurt your brother, Ahmose. You know that. All these years of holding back the truth. This was not right. It had to be made so."

"Not by you!"

The knife felt heavy in my hand. I now stood at the edge of a doorway and watched the actions of those who did not sense my presence.

"There is guilt enough to go around, Ahmose. Hemiunu is not the only one with blood on his hands. Others also played a part. And they must suffer. They will suffer."

My brother lifted his head to stare at the priest, and for a moment it seemed that he looked past him and directly at me. I saw the fear in his eyes.

"Where is your brother, Ahmose?"

"I do not know."

"Do you expect me, expect Pharaoh to believe that?"

Ahmose huffed. "My words sealed his fate. My words began all of this. Why would he trust me now?"

Rashidi lifted his head, and I could feel the ice in his stare even from behind, could hear it in his voice. "Your words did not begin this, Ahmose. A young girl's death began it. The lies that came after, this is what began it. But it will all come to an end. And the guilty will pay."

The knife hilt dug into my tightened palm, urging me, tempting me. An overwhelming desire left me dizzy—the desire to rush into the antechamber, grab Rashidi from behind, and slit his throat like he had Mentu's. To heave him up onto the altar and set him ablaze as an offering to his gods.

I fought to refuse the call of the knife. To give in to my urge would only heap more guilt upon my head, with no way to prove my innocence. No, I needed more proof than overheard conversations and a sharpened knife.

I heard Ahmose's labored breathing and knew that guilt plagued him as it did me.

"Go home, Ahmose," Rashidi whispered. "Go home and wait for justice to find you."

I back stepped quickly, replaced the knife upon the sharpening stone, and resumed my position outside the causeway door.

Rashidi appeared a moment later, carrying a basin. I pulled my head back as he entered the chamber, waited for a count of five, then dared to lean in again. He had placed the basin upon the stone and disappeared. I heard his returning footsteps from the back of the chamber. He walked past me, near enough that I could have reached a leg out and tripped him. Near enough that I could see what he carried.

Hammered gold winked at me in the lamplight from the face of an ornately sculpted death mask.

The pebble was still in my left hand, and I tightened my thumb and forefinger around it, willing myself to silence. Twice more the priest disappeared and then returned, each time with another mask in his hand, until the three were laid in a row on the sharpening stone. Then from the basin, he scooped water in his palm and sprinkled it over the masks, the low chant beginning again.

He is purifying them. Consecrating them. What kind of evil sickness is this?

Three masks. One each for Tamit, for Khufu, and for Ahmose.

Was this the proof I sought? Could I go to Khufu with what I had seen? I had only my own word against that of the priest. The numbing sense of choice weighted my limbs and left me cold.

I wished for more proof to vindicate myself. But I had seen what a choice made out of ambition and selfishness could do.

Did I dare wait for Rashidi to incriminate himself?

TWENTY-SEVEN

I needed to go home. Needed to bathe, to change my clothes, to eat. To prepare myself for what was to come.

In spite of the risk, in the late watches of the night I stole back into the royal estate, through the gardens and trees, and into my own home.

No guards. And the servants seemed to all be in their beds.

I found my way through the darkened passageways and reached my chamber with relief. With the door closed tightly behind me and a piece of sackcloth thrown over the open window, I dared to light a tiny oil lamp and place it on a table.

The water left in the jug and basin had no doubt been there for days, but it was a relief to wash just the same. I dried, found a clean white skirt and fastened it about my hips with a knot.

In my hike back to the royal estate a plan had begun to form. I propped a bronze mirror on the table and pulled out tiny jars of pigment—kohl, juniper berries, and ochre, rarely used. I pawed through a basket of random items until a tiny applying stick finally surfaced, and I dipped it into the kohl. With a careful, though largely unpracticed hand, I lined the bottom rim of my right eye,

---

from the bridge of my nose all the way to my temple. Then another line along the top eyelid, joining the first in a point, then a swoop along the temple. I repeated the process on my left eye, then filled in the eyelids with yellow ochre. I placed a small amount of red juniper berries on my lips, enough to alter the natural curve of my mouth slightly.

I dumped the pigments back into the basket and went to another box where I kept the equally seldom-used jewelry. There was not much of it, and I put on every piece. Gold armbands now encircled my upper arms, and a heavy pectoral necklace weighted my chest over Merit's ankh. I had several rings and put them on too. When all was complete, I put on the wig Sen had given me, a longer style than my own, and tried to survey my reflection in the blurry image of the bronze.

It would have to be enough.

I extinguished the lamp, removed the window covering, and stretched upon my bed, trying to rest but ready to spring up in an instant if the need arose.

In the quiet moments as I tried to settle my mind, thoughts of Neferet intruded. Would I ever see her again? Or would this be the day I discovered whether the gods were truly just in the afterlife?

I slept only in tiny fragments of time, ever watchful for the lightening of the sky outside my window. Long before dawn had arrived, I was gone from my home and hidden in the one place no one would ever search for me—directly in the center of the royal estate.

A small arena had been built here for the purpose of hosting games and entertainment. Underground, several stalls held bulls for the fight and animals for sacrifice, and a few chambers were hollowed out for entertainers to prepare. Dark passageways concealed these rooms. The arena would be the center of the festival's activities, and I hoped the assembled crowd would not notice one man wearing too much eye paint.

Crouched against the cold mud-brick wall of the underground chamber, I waited and readied my mind. Tucked into the belt at my waist was a knife. Nothing large but decidedly deadly.

I would find my brother and watch him from a distance. Wherever he went, I would follow. Eventually his path would cross with the priest's. I would wait for the moment when Rashidi's apprentices were about to attack, and I would intervene, thus proving my innocence.

Despite the cold at my back, I finally dozed.

I do not know how much time passed, but I became aware of the stirring of life in the air above me, around the arena. The noise grew slowly, like the gradual rise of the river waters, until I knew that the estate had been flooded with nobles and peasants alike, ready to celebrate.

There was a brief hush, then the lifted shout of many voices. The games had begun. My fingers burned with anxiety and rage. It was time.

I crept from my hiding place and twisted through the underground passage, up into the harsh morning light. The enclosed arena was already brimming with celebrants, as was the sandy court around it. Thousands of laborers, overseers, and royals teemed through the streets and gardens of the royal estate. I had my usual passing thought of how much work could be accomplished if all this energy were put toward labor instead of a day of recreation. But my ideas about the overabundance of festivals had never been welcomed by Pharaoh. Khufu did enjoy a celebration.

I worked my way through the crowd that flowed to the arena, wondering for the first time how I would ever find Ahmose in this

mass of people. It would be easier to find Khufu, I knew. He would
be the central figure in today's events. Tamit also tended to stand
out from a crowd. My brother would be more difficult to locate, but
it was my brother I was most determined to keep watch over. In spite
of his betrayal, I believed I could convince him of my innocence and
procure his help in stopping Rashidi.

A couple carrying two small boys created a breach in the crowd.
I pushed through it, heading for the arena, where wrestling matches
had begun. My brother was once a talented wrestler himself, in
younger days, and I guessed that this event would be likely to draw
his attention. I worked my way around the perimeter, trying to
search each face in the crowd while remaining unsearched myself.

The press of brown bodies in white skirts and white dresses
melted into sameness. I despaired of finding Ahmose. What if
Rashidi had arranged to meet them before the games began, to do
his work then? Did they already lie in some unknown place, their
faces covered with golden death masks?

I shoved through the masses of flesh, my eyes scanning every
male face.

There. I saw him only from behind, but the set of his shoulders
was too familiar. I skirted a cluster of young women, cheering for a
wrestler who had just been taken down so violently that the physician had been called to his side. I moved to the edge of the arena's
half wall and turned my head to study my brother's profile.

*Ahmose. At last. Go nowhere now, my brother. Watch the wres-
tling and think only of the days that once were.*

I risked moving closer. There were so many people. I knew
that if he moved quickly, I might not be able to keep him in sight.
A new match had begun and the grunts of the wrestlers mingled
with the shouts of the crowd. Bets had been placed, and the mood

of the people was more intense than jubilant. The wrestlers were evenly matched in size, and soon their sweaty limbs made them difficult to tell them apart in the sand.

I saw Ahmose bend his head as though he had dropped something, and then realized that his son, Jafari, was with him. He said something into the boy's ear, and Jafari grinned up at him and nodded. Ahmose gripped the boy's shoulder in a loving gesture as old as fathers themselves. I felt a familiar pang for that which was missing from my own life and moved closer. I had to speak to my brother, to warn him, but it must be done discreetly, before he had a chance to cry out and alert others to my presence.

A winner was being declared in the center ring, and the crowd hushed to hear. In that moment, I heard my nephew say, "When will he return, Father?"

Ahmose's expression grew stony. "Quiet, Jafari," he said, his voice a harsh whisper. "Do not speak of your uncle. Do not speak of him again, do you understand?" He glared down at his son, and the hand on the boy's shoulder tightened.

It is as if I am dead to him. The thought chilled me.

Another match would begin in a moment, but people were shifting, some toward other games, and some to get closer to the wrestling. I fought to retain my ground in the press and shove. Faces pushed up near mine. Any moment someone would recognize me and sound the alarm.

From behind, a hand reached out and fingers tightened around my arm. I jerked free and whirled, my fist raised to strike.

An old woman reached for me, trying to regain her balance. I lowered my arm and pulled back, away from the arena.

Ahmose. Where had my brother gone? I searched for the top of his head above the glut of bodies. I shoved my way through the

crowd now, insensible to the looks it caused. *I have to find him.*
I could not allow the three to meet with Rashidi with no warning
and no protection.

Ahead the crowd broke into fragments. I thought I saw Ahmose
pushing through, but Jafari was not with him. *It's not him.*

My chest pounded and my mouth grew dry.

The crowd opened to a wide sandy area. I started to sprint
across, in hopes of finding Ahmose on the other side. The *thwack*
of a loosed arrow flying past and sticking in a cow-hide to my left
stopped me cold: I had nearly been struck while running across the
target-shooting field.

Another *thwack* and then a high trill of laughter. I searched
the archers and saw that Tamit was among them, wrapped in
some kind of scarlet cloth I had not seen before. She held the bow
at her side and grinned in triumph to those who stood around her.
I ducked and ran around to the back of the strung-up hides, hoping
Tamit had not seen me.

I was out the other side of the archer's field and into the crush
of the people again. They formed a circle, ten deep at least, around
another game, I could not see what.

I wormed through the people, each of them too focused on the
fight to pay me attention. The rapping of sticks in the center of
the circle told me that two prize fighters tore at each other. Each
would have a short stick and another small piece of wood tied to
their left arm to protect them from their opponent's blows. The
sticks struck each other in a steady *tap, tap, tap* mixed with the slide
of sandaled feet on the ground. Then would come a pause, and the
crowd would yell its approval at a blow that struck flesh.

My anger and frustration built. I could not find Ahmose. Had
he gone to meet with Rashidi?

I looked back at the target range. From this distance and with the blur of faces and bodies, I could not tell if Tamit was still there. I had not seen Khufu since I emerged from under the arena.

Was this it? Had the time come?

I cursed myself for my selfishness. My desire to prove my own innocence had stayed my hand last night, when I should have slit Rashidi's throat in the temple and been done with it. There would have been no danger today had I done what was right last night. But it would seem that my desire for justice and truth was largely focused on finding it for myself first of all.

I tried to scramble through the crowd toward the palace, in hopes that if the three had gone to meet the priest, this is where it would be done. I did not imagine Khufu holding audience anywhere else. And since he had declared himself Ra on earth, he had stopped going to the temple. After all, why should a god go to sacrifice to other gods?

The overwhelming stench of humanity—the perfume, the sweat, the beer—it sickened me until I knew I must get apart, if for only a moment. I stumbled to the granary that bordered the palace and stepped out of the sun into its cool silence. My labored breathing was the only sound that echoed along the granary's walls. I pressed my slick forehead against the brick, braced my fingertips there, and focused on a tiny crack that ran from the base of the wall to disappear under my sandal.

Breathe, breathe, breathe.

When the silence and coolness had fortified me, I moved to the doorway of the granary. From here I could see the entrance to the palace. If I had come earlier, I could have watched for the three to enter, or the priest to go ahead of them. It was possible they were already inside.

I was a fool for thinking I could stop this.

The royal estate was like a pot filled to overflowing, boiling its wretched excess out onto the ground. I yearned for the hardened simplicity of my pyramid and the beautiful lines of my charts.

But today was not a day for building. It was a day for destruction.

I ran for the palace entrance.

TWENTY-EIGHT

The inner courtyard lay desolate. No one would be about when the festival was in full gaiety outdoors. I crossed to the Great Hall, glancing through the forest of columns for signs of four people meeting in secret. Then on to Khufu's private audience hall, which was also empty. I ventured up the stairs at the back of the palace toward Khufu's private bedchamber. In the passageway outside his chamber, I encountered what seemed to be the palace's only inhabitant, a young woman I recognized as one of the harem.

I froze in the passage, then tried to look at the floor and appear casual. But the ruse was ridiculous. I had no business there, and she recognized me at once.

She was foreign and exotic, with hair cut short and a body whose curves belied her youth. I remembered her from the accession festival not long ago, the girl who had watched me as she danced.

She glided close to me, a playful smile on her lips. "It seems I have found the man all of Egypt is searching for." Her voice was smooth and slow.

"I wish no harm on anyone—"

She ran a cool finger up my arm. "Have no fear, Grand Vizier. I do not plan to raise an alarm." She licked her lips. "In fact, you are even more fascinating to me now. Perhaps you need a place to hide?"

I jerked my arm away from her touch. "Do you know where I can find Pharaoh?"

She laughed and even this was a slow sound, like sweet honey, poured cold. "He is not nearby. We are quite alone." She mistook my concern.

"The king is in danger. Tell me where he is!"

She lifted her face and leaned toward me. Her breath smelled of herbs. "Take some time to rest before you begin to run again, Hemiunu."

I stepped back. "Is the king in the palace?"

Her lips formed a pout. "He would not miss the bull fight. Go and find him there if you must hurry to seal your fate."

I backed away. Would she speak of finding me here? I suspected she would not.

The venue that had hosted the wrestling match was the site of the bull fight, a favorite among all Egyptians. The open yard surrounding the walled arena still thronged with onlookers, and the crowds were building. The enclosure was currently empty, though the bullfight was due to begin soon. I melted into the crowd once more, wary of each face that turned my direction, and watched for the king's arrival.

I did not have long to wait. Directly across from me, Khufu appeared, surrounded by attendants. A cheer erupted from the people when their king waved, and I lifted an arm with those around me in effort to blend in. Khufu took his seat on a carved chair that had been placed on a platform, slightly elevated.

I am not close enough.

Dancers tumbled out into the ring to entertain before the fight began. They ran the length of the arena, and I moved in the same direction, slicing quickly through the crowd.

The dancers wore short skirts, so that their movements would not be impeded. The long braids of their wigs were held close by red and gold bands at their foreheads. Several of them carried large balls.

I reached the end of the arena at the same time as the girls, but as I circled around they whirled to begin their feats. I had always been fascinated by the unusual ways these women could contort their bodies with such grace, but I had no time for entertainment today. I needed to get as close to Khufu as I dared. I did not intend to be left guessing again at his whereabouts.

I pressed forward, drawing angry looks from those who believed I was trying to take their place at the wall. I reached an adequate position from which to observe. At the same moment the girls all flipped together and let out a triumphant yell. The crowd cheered, the girls laughed and bowed, then scattered from the arena like sands to the wind.

Khufu stood. He wore the double crown, and the wide-throated golden snake reared at his forehead. The crowd quieted in expectation. Pharaoh waited, extending the moment as he was wont to do. It was as if all of Egypt stilled to hear his words.

When he spoke, his voice carried across the arena, and even from where I stood I could hear the sadness in it.

"The Festival of Hapi is to be a joyous time." He braced his hands on the wall in front of him. "And I wish each of you a day of joy in celebration of the gift of the Nile, and the fortuitous Inundation we have had this year. The ground will be fertile, and Egypt will be strong!"

The people lifted a brief cheer that dropped off suddenly, as though they sensed that the king had more to say.

"But it is also with heavy hearts that we mark the high point of the floodwaters this year. The Great Wife has crossed to the west, and we are more desolate without her presence." Khufu's voice broke for a moment, and he looked to his feet. When he lifted his head, I recognized the hardened determination there. "Do not fear," he said, "the evil that has befallen our great land. The gods will deliver the guilty into our hands, and the divine order will be restored!"

The people responded as Khufu surely knew they would, with loud blessings of "Life, Health, Strength!" called down upon his head.

Khufu raised a hand and silence spread over them. When the last child was stilled, Khufu gave a shout. "Bring the bulls!"

The pen doors were released at opposite ends of the arena, and two brown bulls with dirty horns charged forth to snort and paw the ground.

My attention was on Khufu, who regained his seat and seemed satisfied with himself. The razor-sharp tension in my shoulders eased a bit. It should be a simple matter to watch Khufu from here, with all eyes in the arena on the bulls.

The two beasts hurled themselves at one another, their equally massive heads colliding at the center of the arena. Around me, onlookers screamed out in support of the bull they were backing. A little boy beside me chanted "Broad-Striker, Broad-Striker," and beat his fist against his palm. The bulls' horns became locked, and men ran in from the perimeter with sticks to disengage the animals, then fled back to safety.

I had almost begun to lose myself in the fight, but then a movement near Khufu drew my attention.

Rashidi.

The priest stood behind the king, near enough to slip a knife into his side. I leaned forward, as though my fists could reach him.

Turn, Khufu. See the traitor at your side!

And Khufu did turn. He lifted his chin and acknowledged Rashidi behind him. The priest bent his head down to Khufu's. I pushed aside several people to get closer.

Khufu nodded, as if in agreement, and the priest stood upright again.

I stopped my forward movement. Rashidi lifted his head to the bulls, and as the two animals once again cracked horns, I saw a smile creep across the face of the murderous priest.

Moments later the bull fight ended with a nasty goring by Broad-Striker. Those that had backed the winner lifted a cheer. Around me, the losers complained alternately that their favorite had been half-starved or overfed before the match.

The vanquished bull lay in the arena, a growing pool of blood seeping into the sand. The first blood-letting of the day.

How much more before the day is over?

Slaves came to drag off the dying bull while Broad-Striker was led back to a pen. Then a long-horned bull covered in a red cloth was released into the arena to prance before the crowd, and the previous match was forgotten.

On the king's platform, Khufu arose from his chair and followed Rashidi down the steps. I would have lost him in the crowd had he not commanded a following of attendants. This procession led forth, away from the arena and toward the palace, with Pharaoh shielded from the desert sun by a canopy on a pole, carried by a slave following close behind. I also followed, my fingers gripping the hilt of the knife at my waist.

The sea of people parted at Khufu's approach. He moved through them with head and shoulders thrown back, smiling upon all like a benevolent god. He left a wake as he passed, and I kept to the right so that the parting crowd would not leave me exposed.

As they approached the palace, though Khufu led, it seemed to me that Rashidi directed their steps. Would Tamit and Ahmose already be there? Should I wait until all the players were in place before entering the stage?

Tamit then approached, drawing the attention and the greetings of many, and my decision was made.

I moved alongside of one of the huge granite statues of Khufu that flanked the palace entrance. My eyes came to just above the carved left foot. At the statue's side, on a much smaller scale, a carved representation of Merit looked down on me. I reached out a hand to touch her leg and kept my eyes on Tamit.

She laughed and smiled her way to the palace entrance, acknowledging hails of congratulations on her win with the bow. She stopped to blow a kiss in the direction of a court official. Her scarlet dress was the color of the bull's blood in the sand.

I drew in a gritty breath and watched her disappear into the palace.

Then Ahmose was there, also moving toward his destiny inside the palace. He alone walked as though he had cause for shame, with his eyes to the ground, his steps sluggish.

Be alert, brother!

I leaned my upper body against the coolness of the granite. My feet and legs seemed to twitch with an urgency to move. I felt like a leopard stalking its prey in the marshes, muscles tensed to spring.

Ahmose disappeared beneath the lintel, and I breathed a count of ten, giving them time to assemble before I breached the palace. When the entrance was clear, I filled my lungs and rounded the base of the granite statue.

Twenty steps from the entrance, a small figure slipped from the garden grove and ran for the palace.

Jafari.

I could wait no longer. My nephew was inside.

I ran through the palace entrance and into the first courtyard. No Jafari. I dashed around the pool and ran to the wall, then shuffled along it until I reached the arch leading to the Great Hall. I looped around the doorway to the wall inside the hall and followed it forward. The massive columns running the length of the huge chamber would partially conceal me.

At the front of the Great Hall, I sprinted across to the opposite side and into the passageway that led to Khufu's private audience hall at the southernmost edge of the palace. Still no glimpse of Jafari, but I could hear voices as I approached. I slowed to a walk. Outside the doorway I paused to listen, then moved close enough to observe.

Rashidi stood facing me. I pulled back slightly, but his attention was on the three who stood in a line before him. Tamit stood on his left, Khufu in the center, and my brother on the right. A stray desert wind snaked into the hall, and Tamit's dress snapped around her legs. Rashidi began chanting, a strange staccato sort of sound unlike any I had heard.

In turn, each of the three knelt and lowered their heads. I watched the double crown tumble from Khufu's head. He caught it before it clattered to the floor.

I rubbed the knife hilt between my fingers.

Where were Rashidi's apprentices? Did they wait in the wings, ready to pounce?

Rashidi covered Tamit's bowed head with his hand, as though preparing a lamb for the slaughter.

I could wait no longer.

I pulled the knife from my belt, pushed into the chamber, and hardened my heart.

A flash of white on my left startled me.

"Uncle, you have returned!"

Jafari's youthful voice seemed to fill the chamber. The four at the front of the room rose and turned as one. At the same moment I rushed them, knife raised.

TWENTY-NINE

Tamit screamed, and Ahmose threw himself in front of the king.

Rashidi retreated until his back was against the wall.

"Where are they?" I shouted at the priest.

"Hemi!" My brother's hands were raised in front of his body. "What are you doing?"

"Stand aside, brother!"

"Hemiunu!" Ahmose's command was like the voice of our father. "Stop! I will not allow you to harm the king."

I stood panting before them, my blood hot and surging under my skin. "Harm the king! I have come to protect you all from *him*." I pointed at Rashidi with my knife. "The Scourge of Anubis!"

Khufu carefully pivoted so that he could see the priest, keeping Tamit at his back. "What is this, Rashidi?"

The little priest raised his hands in feigned innocence. "He is deranged."

Khufu spoke over his shoulder to Tamit. "Go, woman. Raise the guards."

"No!" I held out a hand. "Tamit, wait. I can explain."

She hesitated.

"I will give you a moment, Hemi," Khufu said. "Out of respect for our former friendship. But give your brother the knife."

"Thank you, my Pharaoh." I hated to give up the weapon with Rashidi still free, but I trusted Ahmose with it. I reached the knife across the space between us. He closed his hand around the hilt and delayed there a moment, as if to signify his support.

I jutted my chin toward the priest. "I have discovered the true identity of the Scourge of Anubis. It is not me, as I insisted. Rashidi takes his revenge for the killing of Amunet."

"Amunet? I do not understand."

"He loved her, Khufu. You must remember how we used to laugh—"

Rashidi's face darkened.

Khufu bit his lip. "Yes. Yes, I do remember. And then he went off to study in On."

"Yes, after her death. He was devastated. But Sneferu had ruled the matter closed, and there was nothing Rashidi could do. And now he is exacting revenge on those of us who kept the secret of that day." I lowered my hands, aware that I had been waving them as though I were deranged, as Rashidi had accused.

Tamit smoothed her dress at her sides. "No. He is helping us, Hemi. Helping to rid us of the guilt, to appease the gods. That is why we are here. The king has had a dream—"

"Rashidi has used the dream to lure you here. Three of his apprentices are waiting to rush in and kill you all."

They glanced to the shadowy corners of the hall and the passageway beyond.

Behind me, Jafari spoke. "Father, who is this Amunet—"

"Go home, Jafari!" Ahmose's voice was harsh. The boy drew up beside me, and I reached toward him. Ahmose stepped forward, and I stayed my hand. "Do as your father says, son," I said. "All will be explained later."

Jafari raised his large eyes to mine, then nodded and ran from the chamber.

Khufu replaced the double crown on his head. "There is much evidence to suggest that you yourself are the killer, Hemi. Why should I believe this story you weave for us now?"

I clenched my fists at my sides. "Think on it, Khufu! Do you really believe me capable of killing Merit? Mentu? Of murdering anyone? You know I cannot even stand the sight of blood. Last night I saw Rashidi sharpening his blade and instructing three men to move quickly and strike without hesitation. And here you are before him, on your knees."

Khufu looked to Rashidi, who again shrugged and maintained his puzzled frown.

Tamit's eyes flicked back and forth among us.

Khufu sighed. "Hemi, your attempt to shift the blame is transparent. Even I can explain Rashidi's actions. He has made his complaint about the way that we took the priesthood from him, and I have listened and heard. Today, I honor him by allowing him to close the festival with the ritual sacrifice to Hapi. The knife he sharpened was no doubt for the sacrifice. The three young priests are appointed to help him, to move quickly to the sacrificial bull and to strike without hesitation. That is all you heard."

My eyes blinked, too rapidly. The fight was beginning to drain from me. Probably due to the lack of sleep. The faces before me seemed to pale, and I became aware of my own shallow breathing, like the rasp of a dying man.

The room silenced then, and I could hear, as if from a day's journey away, the roar of the crowd outside. "He is the killer, Khufu. I swear to you. And I will tell you how I know this without a doubt."

The others watched me carefully.

"Last night after I heard him instruct his young priests, I saw him preparing something else. Three golden masks." I pointed at Khufu. "One," I said. Then to Tamit, "Two." And finally to Ahmose, "Three."

Behind them, a smile curved the corners of Rashidi's mouth. He did not defend himself.

Khufu looked to Tamit and nodded, and she exited the chamber. To my brother, he said, "I am sorry, Ahmose. I wish that it were not so."

Ahmose studied his feet.

"I do not understand," I said. "Did you not hear me? I *saw* him readying three death masks!"

Khufu breathed deeply and studied my face, with pity, it seemed.

"Those were the original three death masks you saw, Hemi. The masks found on the faces of Merit, Mentu, and Ebo. I gave them to Rashidi to purify before the burial of each."

The room drained of all sound and color before me. I thought at first that Rashidi was laughing at me, but I probably imagined it. He may as well have laughed. "My king," he said softly behind Khufu, "perhaps it would be best if we removed you from the hall before the guards arrive."

Khufu gave me a final glance, then turned and followed Rashidi from the chamber.

I was left alone with Ahmose. We stared at each other for only a moment, then two guards trotted in and each grabbed my arm.

I had been tried and sentenced again. This time, I knew, there would be no escape.

The guards led me away. I turned my head, my eyes still on my brother, whose expression I could not discern. I fought for some final words to say to him but could find none.

We were nearly out of the hall when Ahmose finally uttered a sound—a long, guttural moan like that of a wounded animal that built to a scream behind us, even as it drew closer. The guards instinctively released my arms and turned. Ahmose was upon one of them in an instant, the knife I had given him clenched in his fist.

Without thought, I pulled a knife from the belt of the other guard.

It all happened like lightning. Stunned by my brother's assault, the first guard dropped his drawn sword, and Ahmose snatched it up and felled the guard. The other guard drew blood on my chest, but the wound was not deep. Ahmose sliced the back of his leg, and my opponent fell to his knees. This gave us the moments we needed to race through the palace courtyard and out of the Great House, into the sun. Ahmose threw the sword aside. We both tucked our knives into our belts and plunged into the center of the crowd.

When we had pushed our way into the clog of people, Ahmose reached for my arm and I slowed. He looked into my eyes as though it might be the last time. "Go, brother," he said. "Run."

I didn't know if he would be safe, but I could not keep him so. It was best for us both that I should disappear.

And so with the festival games still churning around me, I twisted and wove through the press of people, with no idea of a destination and even less hope.

THIRTY

I wished for the knife I had given to Ahmose. Though I still had the guard's, I wanted nothing more than to fill my arms with weapons, to strap them to my legs and chest. I would wield another in my teeth if I could.

I could abide the crowds no longer. I kept my head low and shoved my way through the playing fields, through the gardens, past the pools and sycamores, and out of the royal estate.

My furious march took me in the direction of the quarry.

The plateau sloped toward the quarry, and it seemed I was alone in the desert. Was the entire population of the pyramid city inside the walls of the royal estate?

My steps took me down, until I stood on the lip of the quarry. I stared into its jagged depths. Despite the hopelessness of my situation, I did not consider what it would be like to hurl myself over the edge. I thought instead of throwing Rashidi to the rocks below.

A narrow path led down, and I took it. The ledge brought the Tura quarry to mind and with it, Neferet. I tossed the memory aside.

At the bottom of the deep pit, I leaned my back against the rock wall. From above, no one would see me. From across the quarry, I would be too small to recognize. Unless someone descended, I was safe here for now. And I did not expect anyone at work in the quarry on a festival day.

Cursed, cursed Rashidi. By the scattered limbs of Osiris, I hated him and his sickening, smug smile. He had bested me. I had thought to expose him, to prove my innocence and condemn him for the murders. Instead, he had the ear of the king and I was at the bottom of a hole.

And what now? I looked at the dried blood where the guard's sword had cut across my chest. Should I fall on my knife as Khufu had commanded? And allow Rashidi to exact his revenge?

Even with Khufu's explanation of all that I had seen the night before, including the three death masks, I still believed the priest to be the Scourge of Anubis. Somehow he had fooled them all. But he had not fooled me. If nothing else, that look he threw me in the palace hall before he left with Khufu told me what I needed to know.

Smug little weasel.

My throat constricted and I coughed with the dryness that comes of running in the desert. I found a barrel of water near a small pitched overseer's shelter and scooped up a handful. The water was brackish and carried the quarry grit. I swallowed anyway and shuddered. Then I splashed some on my chest. The cut stung like fire.

Two mallets lay nearby, left behind by careless workers, and I hefted them in my hands. The mallets were meant to pound small clefts into the rocks, so that wooden pegs could be inserted and then swelled with water to crack the rocks along a prescribed

line. I had no desire for such precision today. Only to crack rocks.
I lifted one of the mallets above my head and ran at the wall.
I skidded to a stop before it and let the mallet fly over my head.
It slammed the rock with a *ching* that rang through the quarry.
I backed up and used the other mallet against the wall. Then the
first again. And the second. The mallets swung in a haze about my
head, as though wielded by a mad sculptor. The rocks refused to
be dislodged. They bared their disfigured faces at me, mocking me
to strike them again. The mallets scraped at my hands, and still
I pounded at the wall. Stone chips flew into my wig, and I knocked
the stupid thing from my head.

When my strength was spent, I backed away and hurled curses
at the rocks instead until I could think of no more evil to invoke
upon them.

Finally, I fell silent and still, and the last of my fury echoed
across the quarry and died there.

I must stop Rashidi.

Which meant I would have to kill him.

I dropped the mallets and fell to my knees in the sand, then
lay on my back and stared at the cloudless sky. It was right that
I could not see my pyramid from this hole. It was lost to me now.
I knew that there would be nothing for me after this. My dream of
building a legacy for my family, a pyramid to stand for a thousand
generations, would be like the desert sand that drifts away to the
west. If I did not carry out my own sentence, as Khufu had ordered,
I had no doubt it would be done for me. No one could kill an
"innocent" priest of Ra and live. And yet it had to be done. This
was justice, I knew. Rashidi had killed Merit. And Mentu. Even
Ebo deserved to have his death avenged. And Rashidi still planned
to murder Tamit, Ahmose, and Khufu, I had no doubt.

Why he did not seem to have a plan to kill me, I could not understand. But perhaps it was enough to see me blamed and executed for his crimes.

I had done all I could to find justice. There was only one way left—manufacture justice by my own hand.

The sand ground into my bare back. I shoved over to the rock wall and leaned against it.

I must find the priest alone. Could I kill a man in his bed?
Yes. This man.

I searched the sky again. It was well past midday, but it would be many hours before darkness had fully fallen and the royal estate emptied of revelers.

So be it. I would rest first. I would prepare my mind, my body, and my weapons. And one more thing I would do before I restored ma'at.

I would find Neferet.

And I would say good-bye.

A few hours of fitful sleep did nothing to abate the hardening passion in my stomach. When the moon was high and the night cold, I climbed from the quarry and continued south along the plateau to the workmen's village.

I had little thought of being apprehended. My mission had become so fixed in my mind that it seemed impossible anything should keep me from it. I moved confidently through the darkness, my thoughts on Neferet. Would she cling to me, beg me not to do it? She was a strong woman, but I knew that she desired my safety.

The stars above seemed cold tonight, as though they would pour their silvery electrum into my blood and make me strong for the tasks ahead. I studied the constellations as I walked and wondered if the gods really lived among the stars, if the Pharaohs that had gone before had truly ascended to live among the gods and now looked down upon us. Did they care about those of us left behind on this corrupt, sandy plain? Or was everything I had believed about the gods the fabrication of men? Did the People of the One pray to the One True God, as they believed, one who cared enough about our wretched race to reconcile us to himself?

The lights of the village wavered before me, like a mirror image of the sky. I widened my path and circled the wall to the back. Pushing pointless thoughts of the gods aside, I climbed Neferet's tree, walked along the village wall, dropped to the temple wall and then to the ground. This path did not seem so much an adventure this time. Each step took me closer to an encounter I both longed for and dreaded.

The village still swirled with a celebratory mood, even with the lateness of the hour. I moved through the streets, avoiding eye contact but not caring much who saw me. I did not believe I would be apprehended here in the village in time to prevent me from fulfilling my task.

Outside the door of Sen's home, I took a deep breath, then pushed through. In spite of his new position, Sen had yet to engage a doorkeeper.

I was loathe to call out, not knowing who was inside. Instead, I treaded softly through the passageway to the courtyard. A single small lamp flickered amid the foliage, vainly trying to dispel the darkness. A lone figure sat on the central bench. I knew from the shape that it was Sen.

"Neferet?" he said, his voice low but hopeful.

I took hesitant steps toward him. "It is I, Sen. Hemiunu."

He stood. "She is not with you?"

My chest tightened. "What has happened?"

Sen rubbed the top of his head with his hand. "I do not know. Nothing, perhaps. But it is not like her to be out this late, to not tell me where she is. Sometimes she goes to help with a birthing or with a workman's injury. But always she gets word to me." He half smiled. "She knows I worry."

"I am sure she is well."

Sen slumped to the bench again. "I heard about this morning. At the palace. They say you tried to attack the king then escaped. I—I thought perhaps you and she—that you had fled together."

"I would not take her from you in that way, Sen."

He nodded. "You are a good man, Hemi. Somehow, with everything, I know this."

I flexed my hands at my sides and looked away. "How is it that you know this after such a short acquaintance, and yet my cousin and my own brother suspect me of murder? Those who know me best?"

"Are you certain they know you so well?"

The flowers on Neferet's wall drew me with their tranquility. "They have known me all my life."

Sen inclined his head and studied me. "And yet I suspect that they have not seen your heart. That not many have."

"Some of us are better than others at expressing ourselves."

"Yes." Sen looked at Neferet's painting with me. "And often they have a way of seeing into a heart that is closed to others."

"Where do you think she is, Sen?"

Sen's voice tightened. "I am worried, Hemi."

I dropped to the bench beside him. "I came to say good-bye."

"What will you do?"

"Kill Rashidi. After that, I do not know. I will wait to see what the gods will do with me."

"There is but one God, Hemi. And he loves justice also. But be careful that you do his will and not your own."

"How can a man know the will of a god, Sen?"

He reached to the ground, lifted a jug, and handed it to me. "He must listen very carefully."

I took the cold jug in my hands and let the wine soothe the dryness in my throat. With the wine, the anger also flowed back into me, and my resolve hardened. I pushed the jug back at Sen and stood. "I cannot stay."

Sen held out an arm. I grasped it.

"Tell her—tell her—"

"She knows, Hemi. She knows." He stood and embraced me. I should have felt a different emotion at our parting, but all I could see was my anger. Anger that I could not stay here, could not wait for Neferet, could not even say good-bye.

"Senosiris?" a male voice called from the front of the house. Sen glanced at me, then inclined his head to the shadowy side of the courtyard. I retreated, and he crossed into the front passageway. I could hear the voices but not discern the words. I leaned my head against Neferet's painting and focused on the tiny white lilies that grew along the base of the wall. I remembered the chipped quarry wall where I had spent the day with her. I thought that perhaps these flowers were the only pure thing in this evil world.

Sen was back a moment later, a papyrus in his hands, and a strange look upon his face. The look of a man expecting bad news but afraid to hear it. He held the papyrus out to me.

"What is it?" I asked and took it from him.

He did not answer.

I looked at the papyrus, covered with demotic script. The language of the priests. Sen would not be able to read it.

But I could. And it was a message meant for me.

I read it aloud. "Hemiunu," it began. "You spoke once of the goddess Ma'at and the need to serve her above all others. It is time for us both to live according to that injunction. Too many years have passed with the divine order disrupted. All must be put right. But how does one atone for the evil of the past? It must be repaid.

"And so I take what is precious to you, as you once took from me. And in the same place, under the same midday sun, I will offer up this sacrifice to Ma'at, and justice will be restored."

My breath came shallow now, and I forced myself to read on. "I tell you this, Hemiunu, so that you may witness the restoration of the divine order you love. The secrets must end. Ma'at will not be silenced any longer."

It was unsigned. There was no need.

"I do not understand," Sen said. "Why was this brought here? Who sent it?"

I took in Sen's creased brow, his piercing eyes. "I must go, Sen."

"It's Neferet, isn't it? Someone has taken her? Is that the thing that is precious to you?"

I smiled, though it was with the sadness of a truth realized perhaps too late. "Yes, Sen. She is the thing that is precious to me."

He swallowed, and I knew he worked to remain calm. Then he gripped my shoulder. "I trust you, son. I trust you. Bring her home."

I covered his hand with my own. "Pray to your One God, Sen. If there is true justice in this world, I fear only a god can find it for us now."

I left him there in the leafy courtyard and let my feet carry me from the house, from the village, across the plateau. The heat in my veins carried me forward, and it seemed but a moment until I was perched on the edge of the harbor.

The dark water spanned my vision, out to the canal and on to the river. She was out there somewhere, I knew, traveling downriver toward the marshy wilderness at the mouth of the Great Sea. And beside her was a crazed little man who lived only for revenge.

Boats clogged the quay of the pyramid's dark harbor, their noses knocking against the stone wall. I did not see one that would suffice. Each of them required the labor of oarsmen and a pilot to pole-steer them through the canal and down the river. I had no such labor at hand and did not intend to rouse sailors from their beds with an insane request to help a fugitive chase a priest of On into the marsh.

I stalked the quay, scowling at each of the cargo and tow boats, as well as the large boats of nobles who had traveled to the royal estate for the Festival of Hapi. The water smacked against hulls and stone, a lonely sound. At last, at the shadowy end of the dock, I came upon a small skiff, narrow enough for one man to operate both of the small oars fitted into rowlocks. It was made of a light wood, perhaps a foreign pine, and rose up high in the back, with only a third of its length touching the water. This craft would skim the water with speed, I knew. A steering pole lay in the bottom.

I jumped aboard with little thought as to whom the boat belonged to. My thoughts were on Neferet, somewhere out there in the night with Rashidi. With little effort I untied the boat and poled it out of its position at the dock. Once I was clear of the other moored boats, I set to the oars and hurled myself toward the mouth of the harbor. The journey would not be a leisurely one. The rough oars chafed at my hands.

I navigated the small craft through the wide canal toward the river. In the darkness the canal seemed to empty into the night sky at the horizon, and I thought of tomb paintings I had seen depicting the deceased sailing the sky to join the stars.

I kept the boat close to the bank to avoid the stronger current that would make it more difficult to steer. The pole was not long enough to serve me well in deep water. The oars splashed the water in rhythm, occasionally thwacking reeds that jutted out from a sandbank.

The night wore on, and my arms grew weary with the unaccustomed motion. I paddled without thought now, sometimes with my eyes closed, focused on the steady splash of the oars and the wind in my face, pushing into the blackness as though traveling through the underworld.

I was jolted from my reverie by the sudden scrape and halt of the boat.

A sandbank had snagged its bottom.

I left the oars and stood in the bow, pole in hand. I was still ten cubits from the riverbank, but under me the floor of the river had risen to capture the boat. The pole was rough but solid in my hand, like my own staff, and I used it to push the boat from the

sand. The action revived me somewhat, and I returned to the oars
with renewed energy.

To my right, the night was already fading. I had perhaps an
hour until dawn. It was difficult to say how far I had to travel. The
last time I had traveled to the marsh for hunting, it had been in
the cabin of Pharaoh's barque, taking my ease. This journey seemed
to last an eternity by comparison.

At last, when I feared my shoulders and back could bear no
more, I saw streams and tributaries running off from the river on
both sides. The sun crested the eastern horizon, shooting flames of
gold along the surface of the river. I followed the fiery path, casting about in my memory for the best way to reach the place I had
avoided for so many years.

I was soon deep into the marshy reeds and gave up my oars to
stand in the bow and navigate the shallow waters with the pole.

The early morning sounds of the swamp assailed me, a slither-
ing and splashing sound of creatures awakening and finding their
way to food and water. Even the wind seemed to be rising, and a
hint of coolness traced its way across my back. The familiar smell
of wet earth and decay resurrected memories I had thought better
left dead.

With an awareness of time running out, the sun seemed to
climb the sky at double speed now. I poled through streams and
pools, around tangled beds of reeds and over floating gardens of
lotus, growing frantic that I would not be able to find the place
where we had picnicked and hunted the day that Amunet had died.
For it was here, I knew, that Rashidi had taken Neferet. To punish
me as he felt he had been punished.

Would I arrive only to find he had already killed her and left
her body to the marsh? As if to mock me, a large crocodile lifted

its head from the bank and surveyed me with slow, watchful eyes. I passed by the greenish-brown monster and pushed farther into the labyrinth of water and reeds. I yearned once more for the open sky and sand of the pyramid plateau, to be free at last of the twisted years of secrets and lies that had held us all captive.

I passed a strangely gnarled sycamore-fig and cursed. I had seen that tree some minutes earlier. I was traveling in circles.

Hold on, Neferet. Be strong. I am coming.

If only I had not hidden like a beaten dog in the quarry yesterday. Had I gone immediately to say good-bye to Neferet, to find Rashidi and finish this, she would be at home this morning, painting her walls, laughing and singing.

I jammed the pole into the muck once more and thrust myself and the boat further toward the unknown.

THIRTY-ONE

The marsh opened before me into a wide grassy plain, and I knew that I had found the place where we had taken our rest while hunting. How Rashidi would have known this, I did not know. Had he ever traveled and hunted with us? I did not believe so. A chill ran up my spine to think that perhaps he had watched us from the reeds, his presence unknown to us.

I levered my small boat to the side of the stream and jammed the prow into the bank. I returned the pole to its shaft and forced it down into the mud to secure the boat. The sluggish current here was not much of a threat.

I alighted and my feet sank into the marsh, squishing mud between my sandaled toes. I shook each foot in the water and climbed onto the bank.

I crested onto the grass and looked across the familiar plain of my youth.

On the other side, still twenty cubits from me, Rashidi rose to his feet and pulled Neferet up to stand beside him.

We stood there, opposite each other on the grass, without speaking. I looked to Neferet to see if she was hurt.

She was angry. I could see it from here, in the set of her mouth and the stiffness of her posture.

"You received my message," Rashidi called. "And your guilt has led you to the right place."

"Not guilt, Rashidi. Justice."

The priest smiled, and I ventured closer.

"Yes, justice. Even better." He frowned. "Come no closer, Hemiunu. Unless you wish to see your woman thrown to the crocodiles right now."

I saw that he had a knife, perhaps the very one he had been sharpening in the temple, pressed to Neferet's side. I tried to give her strength with my eyes. She held my gaze and gave a slight nod, as if to signify that she was well.

"What do you want from me, Rashidi?"

The priest pursed his lips. "I want you to die for the evil you have committed."

"I have committed no evil."

Even as I said the words, they sounded foolish to me. Leaving Amunet in the marsh. Remaining silent all these years. These acts were evil enough to condemn me when my heart was weighed. And they were only the beginning of a life lived in selfishness and hard-heartedness.

Rashidi laughed and pulled Neferet closer. "Perhaps you deceive her, Grand Vizier. But you do not deceive me."

"I should not have kept silent, Rashidi. I know that now. Amunet deserved better than that. I regret the secrets. But must more people die because of one's death?"

"Secrets? You think that's what this is about, Hemiunu?" Rashidi's voice rose, and I took several slow steps closer.

"Lies and deception must come to light, it is true," he said. "But today I avenge her very death, not the lies that followed. Today you will pay for what you did to Amunet. And you will pay in ways you never expected."

I moved again and Rashidi twisted Neferet away from me.

"Not yet, Hemiunu. Not yet. First, we eat."

Eat? "What are you talking about, Rashidi?"

The priest indicated a parcel that lay on the grass nearby. "Is that not what you did? You and the other royal whelps? Took your meal here, lay about with no cares at all, then into the marsh for the hunt? So that is what we will do."

I looked from the priest to Neferet. I was close enough now to see the way her eyes went dark.

"Open it," Rashidi said.

I went to the parcel and untied it. Inside was a packet of dried fish and some hard bread. Rashidi lowered himself to the ground, taking Neferet with him. He held her against himself as though he loved her, and my stomach twisted.

"Sit down," he said.

I sat on the grass. The sheathed knife at my belt bit into my skin and reassured me.

"Eat."

"You have been misled, Rashidi, if you think that I killed Amunet."

"Eat!" His voice filled the reedy enclosure.

I ripped at the salted fish with my teeth and chewed like an angry jackal.

It was very like that day, sitting here with food and sun with the green smell of the marsh around us. A flock of birds lifted behind Rashidi and Neferet. Their calls took me back.

"This is madness, Rashidi. You must stop now, before another is harmed."

"Another?" He squeezed Neferet to him. "Do you mean your peasant woman?"

I sneered at him. "You speak to me about titles and birth? Is not all of this about your low birth? That you could not have Amunet?"

Rashidi's upper lip twitched. "Do not forget I was educated at the palace just as you were."

"Yes, out of pity. Given a place at the princes' school only because you showed an aptitude with writing that would have been wasted in the fields. But it was not enough to have Amunet."

Neferet watched me without blinking. Did she fear that I would make Rashidi angry enough to harm her? It was a dangerous game, but I had to take the upper hand.

"It was you and your friends who made it impossible," he spat. "All of you who convinced her that I was worthless."

"She had the eye of the prince of the blood. Why would she want a weasel of a priest in training?"

Rashidi jumped to his feet then wrapped his fingers around Neferet's upper arm and dragged her upright.

"All these years," he said. "All these years I believed that the prince—Khufu—was the one who killed her. I insisted back then that Sneferu hold his son responsible. He silenced me, then made me a priest of On to ensure I would remain so. I did my best to serve the gods and to forget."

"You should have stayed in On."

"How could I? There was no life for me there. You made certain of that, with your whisperings in Khufu's ear. When I learned that you were also responsible for the death of Amunet, I could forget no longer."

I threw the fish aside and closed the gap between us. "You are wrong, Rashidi. I did not kill Amunet. Someone has lied to you."

He laughed. "Oh? Your own brother? Would he lie to accuse you?"

"Why would Ahmose say such a thing?"

"Because he could no longer contain his guilt. When I spoke to him about the king's decision to move the center of worship, Ahmose confessed to me that it was in fact you who were responsible. The same man who murdered Amunet."

"And so you decided to take your revenge?" I shifted my position, hoping Rashidi would not notice.

He wrapped an arm around the front of Neferet's shoulders and pulled her against his chest, the knife at her throat now.

"You still have no idea what is happening here, Hemiunu."

"Then tell me."

"Yes, it was time for you to pay. Do you know what I am going to do, Hemi?"

I said nothing.

"I am going to slowly cut this woman open until you confess to me what you did to Amunet. Then I will end her pain quickly." Rashidi recited his plan like it was an incantation, and all the light seemed to have gone out of his eyes. "When she is dead, I will take you out with me to the water's edge, and you will watch me feed her to the crocodiles just as you once did to Amunet. When you have seen that she will not pass to the afterlife, then I shall kill you too."

I ran toward the two of them, but Rashidi held the knife to Neferet's throat and screamed, "Stop!"

I stopped.

"If you move again, Hemiunu, I will cut her throat open right now." He wrapped a hand over her mouth.

I held up two hands, palms out. "Priest of the great god, Ra," I said. "Think of the afterlife. Think of your own heart, weighed against the feather. You do not want to do this evil."

"Tell me what you did to Amunet."

The tip of his knife angled toward Neferet's delicate throat, then traced a path along it. A thin red line chased the tip of the knife. Neferet's eyes went wide as the pain reached her consciousness. I saw the blood drip down her graceful neck to caress the pounding hollow of her throat, then continue down to the edge of her white dress, like a grotesque distortion of the red embroidery she often stitched into her clothes. I waited for the faintness to rush through me. Instead, I felt only a hardening anger.

"Say it, Hemiunu. Say the words." Rashidi's voice had flattened. I wondered how many animals' throats he had cut as priest. If he ever felt pity.

He would kill Neferet. I knew it. This was no idle threat, no trickery to bring me to a confession. He would kill her and I would never know what could have been. She could have saved me, I knew. She and her One God. Why had I not seen it before?

I still held my hands out to him. "What do you want to hear, Rashidi?"

"The truth."

I think not.

"That you lured Amunet out here into the marsh. That you killed her here, then left her body to the water beasts to ensure that she would not join the gods."

This was the truth Rashidi wanted. This was truth for him, but that did not make it true.

Neferet swayed on her feet. I thought of the first time I had seen her, swaying to her own music in her kitchen. Rashidi held her upright, his hand still gripping her mouth. I watched her eyes, the way they danced even now.

I could not rush at him, even with the knife at my belt. He would cut her deeply before I'd moved three steps. Her only chance was to get away from him, to give me more time.

I caught her attention with my own eyes. "I am sorry, Neferet," I said softly, forcing them both to focus on the soothing cadence of my voice. "Sorry that I could not be the man you wanted. I am sorry that I will never dance with you." My eyes bore into hers. "Even now," I said. "I would like to see you dance again."

She understood.

I brought my hand to my waist, slowly. Slowly. Then the slightest of nods to her.

In a movement so fluid, so graceful it seemed borne of the wind and the water, Neferet twisted away from the knife and Rashidi's hand on her mouth, dipped her head through the crook of his arm, spun her body to the left, ducked under his swinging knife hand, and slammed her forearm against his, sending the knife spinning through the air. I admired all of this with part of my conscious mind, even the way her hair swung away as she spun. And I ran at Rashidi with my own knife in my fist and a cry of fury on my lips.

Rashidi reacted with the litheness of a panther. He grabbed Neferet and shoved her toward me.

I had no time to shift direction.

With horror, I felt my knife meet resistance, then slip into flesh.

Neferet fell against me, her breath warm on my neck.

I pulled her away, a desperate prayer seeping from me.

My knife had penetrated the fleshy part of her upper arm. She looked at it as though from a great distance, then slowly wrapped her fingers around the wound and stared up at me.

"Go," she croaked. "Go and get the priest."

With reluctance, I let her go.

The priest had disappeared into the reeds.

I heard the splash of something hitting the water but knew not whether it was man or beast.

Bloody knife still in my hand, I ran into the parted reeds.

The thought of Neferet's eyes, the way the blood ran on her neck, fueled a rage in me like I had never known. I hacked at the reeds with my knife as I ran. Wished that Rashidi would appear so I could hack at him.

Perhaps I am *a murderer at heart,* I thought. But I did not care. He had threatened to take her from me. He *had* taken Merit. And Mentu. *No more.*

I ran on. *No more.*

Rashidi's flight through the marsh was simple to track. Broken reeds, crushed undergrowth, muddy footprints at the water's edge. I pounded on, back the way I had poled through the marsh in my stolen boat.

It felt good to give chase, to have a focus for my hatred after all this time of chasing the wind. A face for the Scourge of Anubis at last.

Ahead more birds squawked and beat their way out of the reeds into the air. I thought the priest must have startled them out. But then a throw stick hurled through the sky and knocked one of the geese from its hurried flight.

Hunters nearby.

A renewed urgency hit me. I could not allow Rashidi to find another victim to use as a shield.

And then I saw him. The slight build, running ahead of me. His head and back glowed with sweat, and mud licked the back of his legs. He must have heard me. His head pivoted over his shoulder, and his eyes found mine.

It was a mistake. His feet faltered in the mud and growth. His frantic flight carried him forward, even as his feet lost purchase.

I was on him in an instant. I rolled him onto his back and straddled him, my knife at his throat.

"Finish it, then," he said, his lips white. "Finish it here in the marsh, where it began. I died that day anyway."

There was raw pain in his voice, even after all these years, and I saw for the first time how he had been a victim too. Egypt would withhold from him the woman he loved, would not give him justice for her death, would not even allow him the peace of the priestly life he had chosen.

My pity was ill-timed. Rashidi was not as resigned to his fate as I imagined. He must have sensed my faltering resolve.

His sinewy body twisted under me. He brought his forearms up hard to break my grip. The impact knocked the knife from my loosened fingers, and its point lodged in the mud at the water's edge, a few cubits away.

Rashidi fought to reverse our positions, a strange laugh gurgling in his throat. "Your brother was right," he said and shoved my shoulder into the mud. "You are far too weak for the role you've been given."

I saw him rise above me, knew he would go for the knife.

The many years of my brother's enmity now hardened to a solid thing in my chest, turned my fists to stone, and ground away any pity I had left.

In a blur of hatred, we went at each other, until I again straddled the smaller man and gave vent to my wrath, pounding my knuckles against his face in one glorious strike after another.

The priest's eyes blinked. Then fluttered. Then closed. Finally, my rage spent, I stopped and breathed.

We were alone in the marsh still. No hunters happened by.

There was no one to witness how this would end.

I pulled myself off the priest's unconscious form, crawled to the edge of the water, and retrieved my knife. My chest heaved and my throat closed, as though I had drunk my fill of marsh water.

I stood and tightened my grasp on the knife hilt. I stood over Rashidi's unconscious form.

Then I went to a clump of papyrus reeds, taller than my head, and sliced a thin one from its root at the base.

I flipped the priest over onto his belly. He moaned but did not resist.

I pinned his legs with my own, then used the reed to lash his wrists together. Back and forth, around, between, under. I twisted the pliable reed around his soft hands and again thought of the lies and secrets that had been buried in this marsh. Finally, they were coming to an end.

Rashidi was fully conscious now and flopped his head around to remove his face from the mud. I pulled him to his feet and spun him back the way we had come.

A stream of curses called down upon my head flowed from him as though he had practiced them for years. His gods did not answer, and I pushed him ahead of me with no small amusement at the frenzy with which he interceded for my destruction. But the insults and curses soon grew hard to ignore, and I stopped and held my knife to his throat, reminding him who held his life now. "It is not so pleasant to feel like an animal marked for sacrifice, is it Rashidi?"

He said nothing. But there came a crashing through the marsh ahead of us. I pointed the knife in that direction, still standing behind Rashidi, with my other arm wrapped round his shoulder.

Two figures burst through the reeds and drew to a stop.

Ahmose? Khufu?

"Hemi!" Ahmose yelled. "What are you doing?"

"He is going to kill me," Rashidi said, his voice the whimper of the innocent. "Help me."

Khufu moved toward me, hand upraised. "Hemi, lower the knife. This man is a priest of the gods. You cannot—"

"You are always ready to think the worst of me, aren't you, Khufu? After all these years." I dropped my arm and stepped to Rashidi's side, retaining my hold on his arm.

Ahmose ran a hand over his head. "Hemi, let the priest go. We can settle this another way."

"There is nothing to settle, Ahmose. If you would but hear the truth." I looked at the two of them. "Why are you here? How did you find us?"

"Sen," Ahmose said. "He showed us Rashidi's message. We knew you would come to the marsh."

"Then you know he took Neferet, that he wanted me to follow so he could kill us both."

Khufu crossed his arms over his muscular chest. "I know only that the two of you have unfinished business." His voice seemed to bounce around the clearing in which we stood.

Rashidi took advantage of this moment of ambiguity. "Your Majesty, Beloved of Horus, you know that I would do nothing to bring disorder to Egypt. I sought justice alone, for the death of Amunet."

Khufu's face passed from stern tyrant to uncertain young man.

I shook Rashidi by the arm. "Justice? You think that the deaths of the others brought justice?"

Rashidi laughed. "You are a fool, Hemiunu. A fool. I—"

A misplaced yet familiar sound buzzed through the marsh. The sound of sliced air, and then the *thwump* of a target well struck. Rashidi turned his eyes to me, a look of surprise on his features. He lowered his head to examine his chest. An arrow had buried itself there, deep and true.

Ahmose and Khufu shouted and turned together. Behind them, Tamit stood, bowstring still vibrating at her shoulder.

She held there only a moment, then reached for another arrow.

"Tamit, hold!" Khufu yelled. "What are you doing?"

"The arrow was meant for Hemi," she called. "I will not miss again." She nocked another and lifted the bow.

Beside me, Rashidi still stared at me. And then the staring eyes clouded with the confusion of death, and his legs failed him. I loosed my grip on his arm. He fell to the ground at my feet.

"No!" It was another voice, from behind Tamit still. She turned, arrow ready.

Neferet held up her hands as a shield. Her left arm was red with blood.

My breath caught in my chest.

"Tamit," Neferet said. "It was Rashidi who forced me here. To kill me. And to kill Hemi. It was Rashidi. Hemi rescued me."

Tamit swung her bow back toward me. "That doesn't matter to me," she said. "For Hemi killed my sister." She closed one eye and stilled her posture.

"No!" It was Khufu's shout this time. "I killed her! I killed Amunet!"

THIRTY-TWO

The marsh quieted at the shout of confession, as though it had waited many years to hear it, and Khufu's chest heaved as though he had run many miles to tell it.

Tamit's bow faltered, then lowered. "You?"

He turned to her, the sorrow of a decade in his eyes. "I—it was an accident, Tamit. I swear upon the life of the gods."

Tamit dropped the bow to her side, and her voice was dry, like desert sand. "How?"

Khufu pressed his fingers into his eyes. When he spoke, it was with the voice of a younger man, one who had not yet ascended the throne of his father.

"She was so lovely. You know that. And Merit." His voice wavered. "Merit loved another."

I looked to Neferet. She wandered closer, her eyes on the king.

"We went together that day, into the marsh to raise the birds. We were laughing, teasing. She—she let me—" He stopped and lifted his head. The agony on his face broke my heart.

"Say it," Tamit whispered. "Say the words." The repetition of Rashidi's demand chilled me.

Khufu was crying now. My mouth had grown dry, and I licked at cracking lips. "She let me kiss her," Khufu said. "Let me—touch her. And I could think of nothing but the way that Merit looked at Hemi, not me. And I wanted to hurt Merit like she had hurt me. To show her that I could love another." His chest jerked in sobs he tried to suppress. "I thought of nothing but my own pain, of nothing but myself. I—I forced her to the ground. She knew, she could see it on my face, what I wanted. And she fought me." Khufu's eyes drifted to the sky at his left as though he had slipped back to that day. "'I am the future king of Egypt,' I told her. 'Nothing can be refused the prince of the blood.' But she spat in my face and told me that I was no king yet and she would not have me. My anger— I was so angry. I struck her. She beat her fists at me, and I struck her again. Harder."

He lowered his eyes to me, as though he must make his confession to me alone. I felt my own sorrow rise, hot and full of regret, to my face and my eyes. Khufu saw my empathy and it seemed to destroy his resolve to remain in control. He sobbed in full now and dropped to his knees in the marsh. "I did not mean to kill her. I am sorry. So sorry." He fell forward, hands in the mud, like a dog waiting to be whipped. "I never meant—I never—" His voice trailed off to an unintelligible whisper.

I swallowed and looked to Ahmose.

He stared at me. The look of a man whose world has been turned on its head. "But I saw you," he said. "I saw you with her. Dead in your arms."

Tamit's head whipped toward me.

"Yes." I wiped at the tears that coursed down my own face and onto my chest. "And I have lived with the shame of it these many years. I found her there, where Khufu had left her. I found her, and

I suspected what had happened." I rubbed my forehead and risked a look at Neferet. Her expression did not condemn me. Not yet. "I knew that Khufu would soon be king. And that I would be grand vizier. I feared that none of that would come to pass if I told what I knew. And so I left her there." I looked to Tamit. The bow had slipped from her fingers and lay at her feet. Her face had whitened, and her red-painted lips looked like a bloody gash across her face. "I left her there, where the animals could reach her. For the sake of my own ambition." The rest remained unspoken. We all knew what my actions had meant.

Ahmose cried out. With hands to his head, he turned a slow circle where he stood. Khufu fell to a sitting position on the ground.

"All of this is my fault," Ahmose said, with such pain I had never heard in his voice.

"Ahmose, you are perhaps the only innocent one among us!" I said.

"No, no, no," he said. "Do you not see? It was I who went to Rashidi. I told him my suspicions. I caused him to take his revenge, to kill the others." He leaned over, hands upon his knees, and heaved. Neferet slipped behind him and put a gentle hand on his back.

"All these years," Ahmose said, wiping at his eyes. "All of these wasted years." He turned grief-stricken eyes to me. "Thinking that you killed Amunet. That you somehow convinced Khufu to name you grand vizier anyway."

I now saw in my brother's eyes the realization that his distrust had kept us apart for so long.

The tension that had held us all apart seemed to break in that moment. I went to my brother, who stood and fell upon me with the regret and sorrow of the years and embraced me for the first time since we were children. "Hemi," he cried. "Hemi, I am so sorry."

I wrapped my arms around him and wept on his shoulder for the lost years. It was good, very good. "It is behind us now, Ahmose. All of it is behind us."

We pulled apart. Khufu climbed to his feet.

Tamit still seemed to be paralyzed with shock. "She never would have harmed anyone," she whispered, her dark eyes trained on Khufu. "It should have been Merit that day, not my sister." Khufu looked away.

I went to Neferet, who tried to smile but who seemed pale herself. "Let me see it," I said and reached for her arm.

"It hurts a bit," she said. And then she fainted.

I carried Neferet through the marsh. Ahmose and Khufu transported Rashidi's body between them. Tamit trailed behind.

We passed the group of hunters, trapping birds by pulling the four corners of a spread net. Without a word, Tamit passed the bow to one of them, and I realized she must have procured it as she came through the marsh with Ahmose and Khufu.

The bleeding had been stanched in Neferet's arm. The wound did not threaten her life with blood loss, but it had weakened her. She barely stirred in my arms. I tried not to remember that it was I who injured her. I wished for water to wash the wound and clean rags to bind it, but the marsh was not the place for such ministrations.

We walked in silence, each of us captured by our own thoughts. After some time, we reached the skiff that the other three had used to reach us from a larger boat left in the wider river.

"Take the women," Ahmose said to me. "Put them on the boat and come back for us."

I did not argue. I placed Neferet carefully on the mat of reeds bundled together with a threefold rope. Tamit sat beside her without speaking. I used the pole to propel us southward.

We reached Pharaoh's sailing barque quickly. I carried Neferet onto the boat with care and laid her on a woven mat in the cabin. "If she wakes, Tamit, tell her I will return very soon."

Tamit turned her eyes to me but said nothing. I realized she had not spoken to me since Khufu's confession in the marsh.

I retrieved Ahmose and Khufu, and we laid Rashidi's body on the skiff. The king and my brother had removed the arrow while I had taken the women and had closed the priest's eyes. He lay reposed, as if in sleep, if not for the open wound on his chest.

Ahmose took the pole from me. I gave it up willingly and sank to the floor of the skiff. The warm smell of blood and marsh floated around my senses.

We left the marsh then. Birds floated overhead, their lazy calls unaware of any danger. I felt myself pulling away from the marsh with more than my body alone. It was as though some part of my heart had remained here all these years and was finally going home.

Back at Pharaoh's boat, I returned to Neferet. She opened her eyes and blinked at me once, then returned to sleep. I washed her arm and neck with water the oarsmen had brought to drink and bound her arm with linen torn from the inner folds of my skirt.

Tamit sat beside us watching my every movement.

Neferet awoke and whispered to me that she was cold. I carried her out of the cabin, into the sunlight. Tamit followed.

I laid Neferet on the deck, and Tamit pushed between us. "Let me tend to the peasant," she said. "It is a woman's job." She bent to Neferet's side.

I watched for a moment, then joined Ahmose and Khufu in the prow, where they watched our progress toward Giza.

The journey was swift in the king's boat. We flew upriver toward the plateau, and it seemed only moments before I could see my pyramid on the horizon.

The sight of it caused me to breathe deeply and to realize that something had changed within me. Something I could not identify.

I looked back to Neferet. She was awake now and talking with Tamit. I saw her smile at the other woman and smiled myself. It would not surprise me if she had claimed Tamit for a friend by the time we reached the harbor.

And then suddenly my legs would not hold me. I turned to the other men, then sank to a bench at the side of the boat and leaned my back against the side. My arms and shoulders felt as though I alone had dragged the weight of a hundred quarry blocks up the pyramid ramps.

I closed my eyes and knew nothing more until we had docked.

I awakened to see a big man pacing the quay, waiting for the boat to be moored. The moment we had been dragged in, Sen was on the boat and at Neferet's side. She patted his hand and nodded. He scooped her up and pushed past me with a look I could not read.

We disembarked and litters awaited us. Axum stood nearby and nodded to me with a trace of a smile on his lips. I pondered that it was a good thing to return with the king.

I crossed the dock to Neferet and Sen. He was placing her carefully onto the chair inside the box. She blinked at me through hazy eyes and smiled.

"Not now, Grand Vizier," Sen said. "She has had enough for one day, I believe. Let her rest." His voice softened. "And rest yourself," he said. "Come tomorrow. And we will speak of the future."

I thought this wise advice and let Pharaoh's slaves carry me home.

Tomorrow. The future.

THIRTY-THREE

I awoke the next morning and felt disoriented in my own bed. It seemed unreal that I should wake here, healthy and whole and free. I bathed quickly and dressed. I then reached to the back of my neck, untied the knotted cord that hung there, and set Merit's gold ankh on the table beside my bed.

Then I set out for the workmen's village.

The half-finished pyramid loomed behind me, already busy with laborers. I would get there eventually. I had other business to attend first.

I entered through the village gate this time, without fear of recognition. I welcomed it, in fact, and greeted each person I passed with a smile and their name if I recalled it. No doubt the laborers passing through on their way to the pyramid thought I had gone mad. Surely they had heard that the Scourge of Anubis was no more.

I reached Sen's house and called through the door. My overseer of constructions was still at home. He greeted me in the passage-way to the courtyard. "What are you doing here?" he asked with a smile.

I laughed. "You promised we would speak of the future today."

Sen's smile faltered. "But I thought you would be with Neferet."

"She is not here?" My heart thudded with disappointment.

"I don't understand," Sen said. "She told me that the king had called you both to the palace."

"Neferet told you that?"

Sen shook his head and looked past me to the open door. "No. That animal woman. Tamit."

"Tamit was here?"

"Yes." Sen studied me like I was a puzzle. "She came at dawn and said that the king had requested Neferet's presence in the palace. Something about the priest and his wanting to show his gratitude. I—I thought she said that you were to be there too."

I frowned. "I heard nothing of it. But perhaps I left before I was summoned. I will find her at the palace then. And later," I smiled at him, "we will have that talk." I left his home, pushing away the now-practiced sense of foreboding that tried to build in my chest.

An hour later, the feeling had only grown.

Neferet was not in the palace. Nor Tamit. Khufu knew nothing about Tamit's message. He was barely arisen from his bed and had summoned no one.

Tamit was not in her home. Nor was her son. "The boy has gone to stay awhile with the prince of the blood," Tamit's head slave told me at the door of her home. A strange expression crossed his face.

"Why?"

The slave opened his mouth, closed it, then opened it again. "So that the two of you could be together."

"Who?"

"You and the princess," he said, with a tone of growing impatience at my stupidity. "After you are married."

"Married?" My own mouth dropped open.

The slave took a deep breath and stared me down. "The princess left in the night, taking many of her favorite belongings with her. I thought she went to your home."

"My home?" I knew that my repetitions of his words seemed foolish, but I seemed barely able to make sense of the words to repeat them. "Why did you think she went to my home?"

"She said that you and she were to be joined forever, that you would live together in a chamber all your own, for eternity."

A strange buzzing began at the base of my neck. "Did she have anyone with her? A girl?"

The slave shook his head. "No, she left in the darkness. Alone."

I left him standing in the doorway, no doubt still puzzled.

A chamber all our own. For all eternity.

By the gods, the woman had gone mad.

I raced from Tamit's house, along the path to the entrance of the royal estate, then up the plateau toward the pyramid.

The structure crawled with laborers, as usual, and around the base hundreds of stonemasons worked to dress the stones that would soon travel upward. Calls of managers to their gangs drifted down toward me. My breath soon came in short gasps as I propelled myself up the hill.

The truth about Amunet, about Rashidi—it must have driven Tamit to this madness. She wished to die now. And she wanted me to join her. Why she had taken Neferet, I could not fathom.

She has always had a certain coldness about her.

I remembered the way she had said that it should have been Merit who drowned in the marsh instead of her sister. Even after Mentu was murdered, she still threw insults at him, calling his unattractive features beastly, as if to draw attention to the way in which he had died in the slaughterhouse.

My steps slowed, then stopped.

And Ebo. She had told me that he was too loyal. Like a pet. An animal. Ebo, who had died from the drug given to animals in the temple.

I looked up to the pyramid, and it was as if missing parts of a whole fell into place with each new memory.

Rashidi in the marsh, telling me I was a fool. That I still did not understand the truth. He was about to say more when he was silenced by Tamit's arrow. The supposedly misplaced arrow of an expert archer.

I ran now, my blood boiling in my veins. Past the stone meeting table where I should have been talking with my overseers. Past the work gang fixing ropes around a new block, preparing to haul it up the ramp.

I fled up the ramp myself, to the entrance of the pyramid on the north side, not far below the topmost course.

A supervisor watched me come, frowned as I passed him, and called after me when I grabbed a small torch and disappeared into the stone.

The corridor I had created to lead to the subterranean burial chamber descended for two hundred cubits at a steep incline of a seqed of two cubits. I used the footholds as best I could, but my anxiety caused me to slip more than climb down. Not far down the corridor, I reached the intersecting ascending corridor, which led upward to the burial chambers Khufu had decided should be built above ground. The descending corridor continued.

Down and down I went, hunched over to barely more than half my height, as though falling into the underworld. Behind and far above me, the sunlight faded until it seemed but a faraway star in a black sky.

The awful oppressiveness of countless tons of stone threatened to drive me to madness, and the heavy air seemed thick with dust.

Finally, deep in the bedrock of the Giza plateau, the corridor leveled to horizontal, to a passageway that forced me forward on my hands and knees. I left the torch in the chamber behind me, led now by another light in the chamber ahead. A light that held both relief and terror for me.

I crawled for twenty cubits, until the tunnel finally opened up and I had breached the underground chamber, which was lit by a small oil lamp set on the floor near the wall. I stood painfully and looked around me.

A horrible sliding sound came from behind. I spun in time to see the blocking stone crash to the floor of the chamber. Beside it, Tamit stood holding the release rope.

Neither of us spoke. We only looked at each other.

And then I pulled my gaze away to scan the chamber. It was a huge room and twice the height of a man. In the center of the chamber was a deep square pit.

"Where is she? Where is Neferet?" Then I saw her on the floor, laid out on the far side of the chamber, her arms crossed on her chest in the repose of death. "What have you done?" I ran to Neferet and dropped at her side. In the darkness I could not see if she was injured. A strange smell hovered about her. It took me only a moment to recognize the drug used to kill Ebo.

"She is only sleeping," Tamit said. "I gave her a small amount."

I stood and turned to face her. "You? All of this was you?"

I noticed now that the chamber was not empty. The walls were lined with household goods, food and wine jugs, small lamps, jewelry and clothes. "Why? How did you get these things in here?" My voice was hollow and dead in the earthbound chamber.

She smiled and approached me. "For us, Hemi. I brought all of it for us." She put her hands on my chest and I pulled away. She frowned. "It was not easy. I had to lower it all down." She pointed to a large basket, with a long rope strung through its handles. "It took most of the night. And getting her down here," she jabbed a finger at Neferet, "was not easy, either."

"Why, Tamit? I don't understand any of this."

Her eyes narrowed and she touched my chest again. I let her alone, hoping she would give me answers.

"Are you still so unaware of your own charms, Hemi? You never notice the trail of women who follow you around, hoping for your attention, do you? The same way you never noticed me."

"You have always flirted with everyone, Tamit."

She rubbed her fingers along my shoulders. "Only when you were present, Hemi. Only for you. All those years ago, when I used to throw myself at your brother. He knew better. He knew I only tried to make you jealous. But then, you would not have me. And I had to marry. Thankfully, my husband did not live long."

Her hands ran up to the back of my head, raising gooseflesh on my skin.

"But Merit? And Mentu? Ebo?"

She sighed and turned away. "Nothing turned out as I planned. I was confused." She crossed to the other side of the chamber and picked up a string of colored stones. The turquoise caught the light and glowed like cats' eyes. "When Rashidi told me that you killed Amunet, I—I am afraid that all the passion I felt for you turned to rage. I found that as much as I had wanted you before, now I only wanted you to pay. For murdering my sister, for rejecting me. I thought at first I would kill you." She ran the stones through her fingers. "But then I wanted you to suffer first. And so I killed the others and arranged to have you blamed."

"You gave money to Ebo and said that it was from me."

She turned and smiled. "Yes. And I told Rashidi that you and Mentu had argued before he died."

"And the masks?"

"I had them specially commissioned."

"The artist—"

She waved a hand. "He could not be left to tell who had hired him."

"But why? Why did you cover their faces?"

Tamit stroked the jewels at her throat. "It has always been about secrets, hasn't it, Hemi. Secrets, deception, lies. Masks seemed . . . appropriate."

"And did you really think I would take my own life, as Khufu ordered?"

She bit her lip. "I was disappointed that he gave you that choice. I thought surely he would execute you since you killed his wife. I underestimated his esteem for you." She came back to stand before me and lifted her chin to look into my eyes. I remained still, watching her painted lips.

"And then you escaped," she said, "and ruined my plan. I knew that if you found Rashidi, he would not remain silent for long. He knew it was I who killed them." She touched my lips with her fingers. "When Khufu told us that it was he who killed my sister, I realized that my feelings for you had not been false, and I knew then that I must have you."

"But Khufu—"

"What can I do to raise my hand against a god?" She stood on her toes and kissed my lips. "And now at last," she said, "you have the truth." She turned brightly to her belongings, stacked against the chamber wall, and began arranging them as though this were her home.

The truth. It pounded against the walls of my heart, screaming at me. I had sought justice. Neferet stirred and moaned, and I wondered if she would now deny that justice and truth existed. But I knew she would not deny it. Nor could I.

In that moment, under the perfect angles of the pyramid, I acknowledged what I had always known: Order exists. It is in the math. It is in the stars. It is even in the music. Order and, therefore, truth and justice are chiseled into the bedrock of the earth.

But with justice, I knew, came condemnation. There could be no other honest conclusion. I had built my life one layer at a time, with precision. Like the pyramid, I had tried to be perfect in order to reach the gods. But I had done too much to violate order and truth to ever achieve perfection. I suspected that even the tools I used to measure my life were faulty. Perhaps I didn't even know what perfection was.

Yet I knew my heart could not be weighed and found innocent. I was nothing more than a pyramid of my own construction, with dark and hidden chambers and full of death. And only the atonement offered by a merciful god could make me righteous.

All of this I realized in the breath of a moment, while Tamit went about arranging her household. She now cut my revelations short by turning back to me, the lamp in her hands. "It is time," she said.

"Time for what?" I inched closer to the side of the chamber where Neferet lay.

"I have brought all we need, Hemi," she extended a hand toward her things. "Everything for the afterlife. Even a peasant to serve us. But you did not think I would leave us here to die slowly, did you?"

For the first time since I entered the chamber, I felt the tickle of panic at the base of my spine. "Tamit, think of your son."

"He will be well cared for," she said. "And someday, perhaps he will be Kawab's grand vizier." She stepped to the edge of the square pit at the center of the chamber and held the burning oil lamp aloft.

"What are you doing?"

"It will not take long," she said. And she dropped the lamp.

I watched it tumble into the dark pit, lighting the sides as it fell. When it hit the bottom, it exploded into a ball of fire.

Tamit had filled the pit with straw and dried grasses. The pile blazed like an altar sacrifice, blinding me. I backed away. The fire would soon devour the air inside the chamber. The smoke would likely kill us before we succumbed to the flames.

"Come to me, Hemi," she said, holding out her hands. "Come and lay beside me. We did not live our lives together. But we can enter the afterlife together."

I glanced at the blocked entrance to the chamber. I could lift the stone momentarily, I thought.

Tamit followed my look. "You could escape, Hemi," she said. "But not with her."

Neferet was now sitting up and looking at me in confusion.

Tamit was right. I could not lift the stone and run under it with Neferet in my arms.

My eyes teared with the smoke. Tamit coughed, and my lungs grew ashy a moment later.

Without another thought, I leaped into the burning pit.

THIRTY-FOUR

The fire fed on the dry grass with a ferocious hunger. I acted quickly. Using my feet, I separated the unburned straw from the fire. When the fire had no more fuel, I began to stamp it out. The flames licked at my feet and ankles, singing the hair from my legs. The reeds of my sandals smoldered then fell apart. I ignored the pain and covered the flames with my feet.

Finally, when there were only dying embers, I backed away and looked up.

Above me, Tamit had already lit another lamp. She must have brought a fire stick along with everything else. She smiled. "What now, Hemi? I have plenty up here to burn. And you are down there."

I stared at her.

Another voice filled the chamber. "You'll have to kill me first," Neferet said.

I saw Tamit turn. She leaned over to set the lamp on the ground and was still bent over when Neferet kicked her in the stomach. I heard the air whoosh from her, but Tamit stood, laughing.

"I think our peasant will serve us well and strongly in the afterlife, Hemi."

I clawed and scraped at the wall of the pit but found no purchase. There was a flash of white above me. I could make out little but heard sounds of a struggle. Then there was a shuffling, sliding sound, and Tamit tipped over the side of the pit and fell at my feet.

Neferet appeared above us, holding the lamp.

"I don't like her, Hemi," she said. "Not at all."

I bent to check on Tamit. She was unconscious, but she still breathed.

Neferet threw a rope down to me. "Hold there a moment, Hemi," she said, her voice muffled. And then the other end of the rope tumbled down, so that two heavy lines reached me.

"You can climb up now," Neferet said, leaning over the pit. "I've anchored it."

With a last glance at Tamit, I reached for the rope. I climbed using only my arms, to avoid placing my burned feet against the side of the pit. I reached the top and fell into Neferet's waiting embrace.

"Now what?" Neferet asked, pulling away.

"Now we find a way to lift the stone."

A few minutes later I had rigged a pulley in the opposite direction of the drop and prepared to open the chamber. I dragged on the ropes and the blocking stone lifted a fraction from its resting place.

Behind me Neferet called down into the pit, "We are leaving, Tamit."

"Is she awake?" I asked.

Neferet nodded. "Climb the rope, Tamit. It will hold."

I marveled at the mercy she could show her tormentor. For all that Tamit had done, and for the others who deserved justice, I could have left her there to pay for her sins.

But even then, I remembered my own need for mercy, the hope Neferet's God offered for a future atonement.

"Climb the rope, Tamit!" I said, hoping she still had some desire to please me.

Neferet stood and held her hands out. "Stop, Tamit!" She turned and stared at me in horror. "She—she is rebuilding the fire!"

I bore down on the pulley again. And then again, the muscles cording in my neck. "Come, Neferet." The stone cleared the entrance. "We must go. Now!"

She hesitated, looked back, then crawled through the door and disappeared into the passageway beyond.

I braced a knee under the stone and bit back a scream of pain at the pressure on my burned foot.

By tiny spans and with great effort, I wedged my shoulders under the stone, holding the stone up with the strength of my back. The smoke built behind me, billowing out of the chamber and up the corridor.

And then I was through and the stone slammed down behind me.

"Hemi?"

In the darkness I found Neferet, perhaps ten cubits ahead of me.

"I am well. Right behind you."

We crawled to the corridor, then half stood and began the two-hundred-cubit climb to the sunlight.

With every painful step, I felt that I was moving toward my true life. And when we emerged at last into the blazing desert sun, I knew that I had been reborn.

Neferet stood beside me as I looked down with new eyes upon the lively harbor, the chaos of the quarry, and the extravagance of the royal estate. But when I looked at Neferet, all else faded to a sandy haze and there were only her eyes and her smile.

I pulled her to me, and in the sight of laborers and overseers alike, I kissed the woman who had led me back to life.

EPILOGUE

When the seventy days were accomplished for Merit's purification, we carried her mummified body to her now-completed tomb and laid her inside. That day I buried another man's wife.

And the next day I took one of my own.

Many years have passed since I climbed out of the half-finished pyramid and began anew. The Horizon of Khufu is complete, gleaming white with a gold pinnacle, and angled in perfection across the western sky. A thing of wonder and beauty in stone.

But not so much like the man who built it. Not anymore. What had begun as dry stone at the edge of a barren desert had been allowed to grow and flourish. I discovered, in the years to come, that ma'at was not quite what I had thought. There is room for what I had believed to be disorder. Creativity, freedom, and beauty—these are gifts from the One. Neferet taught me this. And love is part of that freedom.

Yes, the pyramid is my legacy in stone. But there is another legacy, one I am most proud of. Three sons Neferet has given me. Three strong sons who have grown into men of integrity, men who are ready to take their place among the People of the One.

We still meet behind closed doors. I play my harp often, letting the wild notes carry me away until Neferet laughs and kisses the top of my head.

Beside the pyramid, not far to the east of the completed mortuary temple, a tomb lies waiting for me. Two simple chambers, with sculptures of my precious family carved there, and a life-size statue of myself, sculpted with the right fist of justice and the left hand of mercy. But this tomb is not my final destiny, for there is One Who Comes who will make a way for me.

And so I wait. And watch.

The past is gone. The future is secure.

And I have a life to live.

Author's Note

The list of the Seven Wonders of the Ancient World evolved slowly, from their first mention by the Greek historian Herodotus in 450 BC, to the poet Antipater in the second century BC. Though only the oldest of the seven, the Great Pyramid of Giza, still stands, their mystique has endured, each a wonder of engineering and a testimony to the creativity of ancient peoples.

The Great Pyramid of Giza was probably built around 2500 BC. It was commissioned by Khufu and directed by his grand vizier, Hemiunu. The pyramid reached a height of 480 feet, about the size of a fifty-story building, and stands nearly that tall today. Excavations beside the pyramid have uncovered Hemiunu's mastaba tomb among the many tombs of nobles and officials, and further excavations are continuing nearby, to uncover the quarry and the workmen's village.

It was my great privilege to visit Egypt while writing *City of the Dead*. I was able to explore the Giza Plateau, to crawl around the inside of Khufu's Great Pyramid, and to get a taste of what life was like nearly five thousand years ago!

I invite you to visit my Web site, www.TLHigley.com, to experience the sights and sounds and beauty of this amazing country, and to learn more about what is fact and what is fiction within the book. While you are there, please take a moment to share your heart with me. I love to hear from readers about the adventure of their own lives!

T. L. Higley inside Hemiunu's family tomb in Giza, Egypt

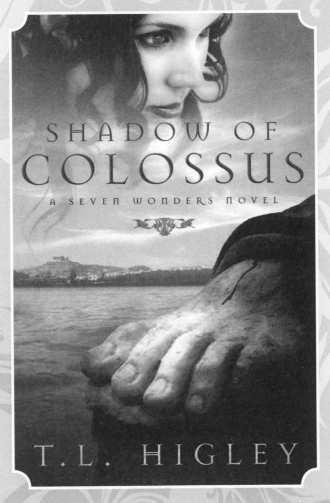